KU-036-722

JAISHREE MISRA

A Scandalous Secret

AVON

AVON

A division of HarperCollins*Publishers*
77–85 Fulham Palace Road,
London W6 8JB

www.harpercollins.co.uk

A Paperback Original 2011
1

Copyright © Jaishree Misra 2011

Jaishree Misra asserts the moral right to
be identified as the author of this work

A catalogue record for this book is
available from the British Library

ISBN-13: 978-1-84756-186-2

Set in Minion by Palimpsest Book Production Limited,
Falkirk, Stirlingshire

Printed and bound in Great Britain by
Clays Ltd, St Ives plc

Mixed Sources

Product group from well-managed
forests and other controlled sources
www.fsc.org Cert no. SW-COC-001806
© 1996 Forest Stewardship Council

FSC is a non-profit international organisation established
to promote the responsible management of the world's forests.
Products carrying the FSC label are independently certified
to assure consumers that they come from forests that are managed
to meet the social, economic and ecological needs
of present and future generations.

Find out more about HarperCollins and the environment at
www.harpercollins.co.uk/green

For AM

Chapter One

Neha stood at the door to her spacious living room in Delhi, surveying the party that was now in full flow. It hadn't yet reached that freewheeling stage when people, mellowed by the fine wines and Scotches on offer, would start drifting around unreservedly, chatting without embarrassment or restraint to relative strangers. At the moment, most of her guests were gathered in small knots around the room, sticking to the people they knew, but loud bursts of laughter indicated that a good time was already being had. Waiters hired for the night were working the room with trays of drinks and canapés, and some kind of nondescript piano music was tinkling through the eight-speaker Bose system, Sharat's proud new acquisition. It would need to be turned off for the Divakar Brothers' live performance that would take place a little later on in the garden, but experience had taught Neha to keep things subtle at the start.

Virtually everyone invited had already come, even the customary stragglers who made it a point to arrive close to midnight, complaining about receiving three party invites for the same night. Whatever they said, Neha knew with quiet confidence that people did not usually turn down invitations to her famously lavish and elegant soirées but, given the status of many of her guests, she was nevertheless touched when she saw such busy and eminent people turn up at her place so unfailingly.

Although smaller, more intimate dinner parties were a regular feature of the Chaturvedi household, Sharat and Neha held two large parties every year; one sometime before Diwali and the other a lunch in the garden at the start of spring. The hundred-odd invitations issued were carefully considered affairs, sent – everyone knew – only to the very influential or very well connected. The very point of them, Sharat sometimes said, was to allow people to relax and meet each other without the fear of journalists or paparazzi lurking around the corner. Yellow journalism had been the bane of many of their famous friends' lives and, horrifyingly, Neha had recently been hearing of parties where – without any warning – the press pack would descend, secretly invited by publicity-hungry hosts who wanted to be mentioned on the party pages of *The Times of India*.

At the Chaturvedis' parties, however, guests came safe in the knowledge that there would be no press presence – if one did not count people like Girish, that is: a golfing buddy of Sharat's who happened to be the head of India's biggest television channel. What the couple generally aimed to do with their list of invitees was ensure that guests were either among their own kind or thrown together with people it would be advantageous for them to meet. Both Neha and Sharat liked to be generous in this matter and, partially due to the understated and tranquil atmosphere of the Chaturvedi home, their guests' guards were often let down in ways that invariably led to the most exciting meeting of minds. Not everyone saw it like this, of course; and once, when a nasty piece appeared in a gossip magazine accusing Sharat of what the journalist

2

referred to as 'control freakery', Neha was tempted to ring up the editor to give him a piece of her mind. Sharat eventually dissuaded her from making that call but Neha had felt terribly hurt on behalf of her gentle husband, knowing as she did that the really gratifying part of the whole exercise for Sharat was when people he had helped called up later to thank him for the part he had played in their good fortune. 'Completely inadvertent and pure chance,' was the modest manner in which Sharat generally responded, although this too wasn't entirely true. He gave away far too often, and in often unsubtle ways, his total delight at having been involved in transactions that were important enough to make it to the national papers. Sharat's pleasure in the parties they threw was really very simple: he genuinely liked putting people together in fortuitous circumstances, hoping that some mutual good would come of their meeting, even if there was no particular or immediate advantage to him. He sometimes joked that he had probably been a marriage broker in his previous life.

Only this morning, Sharat had appeared on the veranda while Neha was overseeing the decoration of the garden shrubs with fairy lights. He had looked with pride at the pair of massive bottle palms that straddled the entrance to the sweeping driveway.

'Remember their names?' he enquired with a laugh.

'Of course,' Neha had replied absently, her attention now on the marigold flower chains that were being looped around the pillars running the length of the veranda. She had earlier tried explaining to the man on the ladder that the two faux Doric columns flanking the front entrance had to be exact mirror images of each other, the flower garland on the left spiralling clockwise

3

while the one on the right went anticlockwise. It was the kind of feature no one would probably notice, but attention paid to such seemingly insignificant detail was what made for a perfect evening, in Neha's opinion. It was also what led Sharat to call her 'OCD' but he would be just as quick to admit how much he relied on her exacting standards.

'Zurich and Americana,' Sharat grinned, still looking at the palms with his arms crossed over his chest and rocking on his heels, obviously continuing to enjoy the memory from five years ago.

The palms had acquired their names because they were a present from Arul Sinha, the head of global investments at Zurich Bank, who had sent them after a lunch party where he had struck a lucrative deal with American Steels. Neha remembered the glee with which Arul – a schoolmate of Sharat's youngest uncle – had greeted the news that Doug Fairbanks III was going to be at their lunch too. ('You know *Doug*? Hey, you guys know everyone, *yaar*,' he had said, only pretending to be jealous given the vast spread of his own network of contacts.)

Neha cast a glance at the elegant palms whose fronds were a lush green in the morning sunshine. 'I'm always astonished that these two giants didn't just survive, but even thrived in the heat of that summer,' she said. 'Do you remember how they arrived in the middle of May, Sharat? Ten feet tall, and with such massive root balls, in the back of a truck? I used to expect every morning to wake up and find them all dead and shrivelled up in the garden. But just look at them now – and they're probably not even fully grown yet!'

Sharat laughed at the memory of that chaotic morning. 'Typical Arul, that kind of attention to detail. Sending not just a pair of palms but a complete team of labourers and gardeners who set to work planting them with some kind of crazy Swiss efficiency. I bet he even ensured that they would grow to identical width and height before shipping them over from China!'

'Well, whatever he did, it worked – our Delhi heat notwithstanding. If anything, they've grown a bit too big now, towering over everything else in the garden,' Neha said, turning her attention back to the flower wallah who was perched on his ladder awaiting his next instructions.

'I've always wanted to ask Arul if his business deal enjoyed as swift a growth as the trees, but that would be prying, I guess,' Sharat continued.

Neha smiled. She had no doubt that the deal would have been hugely successful, not just because of Arul Sinha's business skills but also Sharat's famed Midas touch. But he would be embarrassed if she said that, and now she was distracted by the large roll of black insulation tape that the flower wallah was using to tape the end of the garland to the pillar. '*Ooffo, yeh kya leke aaye ho?*' she asked, her voice exasperated as she turned to call for her own roll of imported extra-strong and, more importantly, colourless sticking tape.

It was Sharat's turn to grin. Neha was a fine one to joke about Arul's attention to detail. She was at least as finicky as the best Swiss bankers, and on the morning of their big parties, Sharat generally made it a point to stay well out of her way. He put an arm around his wife's shoulder and dropped a discreet kiss on her neck. 'Going to go have a shave. Got that meeting with Prasad, remember?' Sharat explained as he turned to go indoors, although Neha was by now too preoccupied to even register his departure.

He was still smiling as he walked down the corridor, thinking of Arul's typically flamboyant present. Generally, the gifts he and Neha received took more veiled forms, people's gratitude for useful introductions coming in subtle ways, via favours and preferential treatment and, quite simply, the kind of magical opening of doors without which life in India could be very difficult. Sharat recognized this and, in his customary pragmatic way, knew that the goodwill caused by his generous networking would do no harm when the time came for return favours to be called upon. Neha did not get this, though, remaining always a little discomfited by what she considered a mild form of nepotism even though she quietly indulged him whenever necessary. In a strange way, that was what Sharat loved most about his wife: she was exactly as she seemed. With Neha, what you saw was what you got. There was no hidden agenda, no gossip, never any secret deal-making, nothing underhand at all.

Neha surveyed the crowded drawing room again and flicked her eyes at a passing waiter, signalling that the Home Minister's wine glass required topping up. She couldn't help noticing as she walked on that the dapper politician was deep in conversation with V. Kaushalya, the rather comely head of the Indian Institute of Arts whom Neha regularly met for lunches at the Museum of Modern Art café and who was beautifully turned out tonight in the most gorgeous cream silk Kancheepuram sari. Now, what interesting transaction could be brewing there, Neha wondered. It could just as easily be personal as professional, given the minister's reputation for enjoying the company of beautiful women and Kaushalya, an ex-Bharatanatyam dancer, still cut a stunning figure, even in her fifties.

Neha continued to weave her way through the room that was now full of the rustle of silk and organza, stopping to enquire after one elderly guest's health before steering someone else across the floor in order to make a mutually useful introduction. She had long grown practised at spotting pairs of guests who looked like they had got 'stuck' and needed to be moved along. Although she had at first resisted Sharat's fondness for parties and gathering dozens of people around himself, Neha had to admit that, over the years, she too had gradually grown to enjoy the business of playing hostess and using her elegant home to its fullest advantage. Why, an art collection like hers was meant to be shared and admired, not stashed away. Not that she wished to draw attention to her wealth at all – God forbid! – but, in recent times, Neha had learnt to derive amusement from seeing herself referred to in the society pages as 'the legendary hostess' or 'famous socialite Neha Chaturvedi'. She, Neha Chaturvedi, who had been the class bluestocking with her nose firmly stuck between the pages of a book all through her school days! She wasn't even much of a cook but, luckily, she had never had to worry a jot about the catering arrangements, seeing that Jasmeet, her old school chum and best friend, was one of Delhi's best known food consultants and took able charge of all arrangements weeks before any party, making numerous trips to INA market to buy spices and condiments and sourcing the best fish that would be brought to Delhi in a huge refrigerator van from the Orissa coast.

Tonight, however – and perhaps for the very first time – Neha was having immense difficulty facing up to her hostessing duties. She had been nursing a headache all afternoon, despite popping two paracetamols with her evening cup of tea, and was now feeling both nauseous and dizzy. As she recalled the reason for her distress, that now familiar cold hand squeezed at her heart again, robbing her of breath. This had been happening at regular intervals all day, sometimes at intervals of ten minutes, only disappearing briefly when the caterers had arrived, their purposeful colonization of her kitchen providing a temporary distraction from her unease. Even the arrival of her guests had not been diversion enough as Neha found herself listening to all the usual social inanities regarding Delhi's traffic and how long it was since they had all seen each other. She had listened and murmured assent and nodded politely but all conversation, even her own, seemed to be coming from a tunnel somewhere far away. Her mind, normally capable of focusing in calm and orderly fashion on the welfare of her guests, had behaved like a trapped bird all day today, flapping and darting frantically about inside her head. Once again, Neha felt her insides go deathly still as she remembered the reason. She could not help coming to an abrupt standstill in the middle of her drawing room, feeling for a milli-second like she might drown in the sea of conversation that was swirling around her. Was this what a panic attack felt like, Neha wondered, wrapping the *pallav* of her mauve Chanderi sari around her shoulders and trying to steady herself. Try as she might, Neha simply could not get on with the job at hand. She was only just about managing to keep the smile plastered on her face because, every so often, something would remind her of the letter and she would feel close to collapsing again.

It was incredible – the kind of thing that happened only in movies – but there, upstairs in her *Godrej almirah*, locked away in the secret compartment that housed her

8

diamond jewellery, was a letter with a British stamp that had arrived in the post that very morning. Luckily the maid had brought it in only after Sharat had left for an early meeting and so he had not been around to see her open it. He would surely have noticed her shock, for – however adept Neha had grown at masking her feelings behind an inscrutable smile, even from such a beloved husband – she simply would not have been able to cover up the sudden paling of her skin and lips, the trembling of her fingers as she read the scribbled lines and the dizziness that had finally caused her to crumple in a heap onto one of the armchairs on the veranda.

'*Dear Neha . . .*' the letter had started, in a scrawly, childish hand that was nothing like her own neat and precise handwriting.

Dear Neha Chaturvedi,

You will no doubt be very surprised to receive this letter. I will not beat about the bush as there is no easy way to say these things. You see, I am the daughter you gave away for adoption in 1993. You may well question my motives, but this is of far less concern to me than the explanation that I believe it is my right to ask you for.

I am planning to make a trip to India because I have a few things to set straight before starting university this autumn. Please let me know when and where we can meet. And please do not ignore this letter, as you have ignored me all these years.

My postal and email addresses are in the letterhead at the top, as is my mobile phone number, so you have several ways to contact me. I hope you do, but as I have your address, you should know that I will not think twice before coming straight to your house in

Delhi unless you offer me an alternative place to meet.
This will, I warn you, be regardless of your own
circumstances, seeing how little you have cared for
mine all these years.

    However, I hope that will be unnecessary and I am
in anticipation of a speedy reply,
    Sonya Shaw.

Chapter Two

Sonya lay under her duvet and looked around the bedroom of her house in Orpington, memorising its every familiar and comforting detail. She tried to assess if this was another lump-in-the-throat moment, the likes of which there had been many since her plans had formed: plans not just for college but the fast-approaching trip to India too.

While there was still no response to the letter she had sent to Delhi, there was nothing that could be employed to dredge up much emotion on a peaceful morning like this. The room was awash with cheery sunshine, Mum was clattering about in the kitchen downstairs and Sonya had to admit, all was well in her world. Nevertheless, as had happened yesterday, and the day before, virtually the very first thought to assail her as she opened her eyes was that frigging letter. It was probably too early to be expecting a reply from Neha Chaturvedi just yet, as Sonya's Indian friend, Priyal, had told her the Indian postal system was nothing like Britain's. But what if her letter had never made it to its destination? It was entirely possible, of course, as getting the address had been no more than a series of stabs in the dark. But how annoying if Sonya would never even know if the lack of response was due to Neha Chaturvedi's indifference or just an abysmal foreign postal system!

Trying to quell a sudden attack of butterflies in her stomach at the thought of India, Sonya decided to get up and abruptly swung her legs out from under the bedclothes. She stretched hard before getting up and padding her way across to her en-suite bathroom. Her eyes were not fully opened yet but she often said she could traverse her room blindfolded, this having been her designated space since she was a baby. It had, of course, been converted over the years from a bright yellow nursery that Sonya still had a fuzzy memory of, to a very pink girl's room that was probably its longest incarnation until it metamorphosed into its present deliberately dark and somewhat gothic teenage space some years ago. Sonya sometimes thought of the room as being almost like a relative because of the way in which it had grown up alongside her. Suddenly, the thought of leaving it was quite unbearable and, yes – there it was – that great big lump forming in her throat yet again as she splashed her face with water in the sink and looked at herself in the mirror. Her skin, typically quick to turn golden-brown in the summer, was glowing with good health but she remembered, with a quick small flash of sadness, how she had scrubbed her face raw one summer many years ago, desperate to be less brown than she was so she could blend in better with her very pale-skinned cousins who were visiting from Canada. Luckily she had soon got over that phase with some help from a school counsellor but – even now – it didn't take much for some small thing to rear its head up like a little devil and remind her of how little she was like the parents who had adopted her. In the way she looked, the way she spoke, even the way she thought about things. Much as she adored her mum and dad, they really were chalk to her cheese. But now she was actually planning on separating from them, the thought of it was unbearable.

Of course, it was right and proper to be sentimental at times like this, even though Estella had always scoffed at her ready propensity for tears. How on earth Sonya had ever become best friends with such a hard nut was inexplicable but Estella's toughness came – by her own admission – from the procession of formidable old Italian matriarchs on her mother's side of the family. Sonya pulled her toothbrush out of the mug. Well, she certainly wasn't going to be apologetic about her current heightened emotional state, she thought as she squeezed toothpaste onto the bristles and started to brush.

The trip to India was nearly upon them now but, strangely, Sonya hadn't got around to doing her packing yet. She, who was usually so OCD her packing was done weeks before a holiday. It was two weeks before their departure for Lanzarote a few summers ago that her dad had discovered Sonya was getting her toothbrush out of her suitcase every morning. She wasn't that bad anymore, but, with only a few days to go now for India, she had not even got her case out of the loft. She wasn't sure she could explain it but a strange kind of malaise had crept over her a few weeks ago. Perhaps she could blame Mum and Dad for being so negative about her going off to India. Or perhaps it was that at some level Sonya was herself terrified of what she would find when she got there. But she really ought to get packed today, given that she and Estella were due to fly next week . . .

Sonya wandered back into her bedroom and sat with a thump on her cushioned window seat instead. She looked out of the bay window and saw a clutch of children wearing uniforms at the bus stop down the road while an empty milk float trundled past her gate. It was obviously much earlier than she'd thought, and so Sonya lay back against the cushions and put her feet up, enjoying the feel of the sun on her toes. Distractions were aplenty as most of the clutter that was visible from Sonya's present perch held – as her mum sometimes said – 'a memory or three'. Half the things in the room were presents from Mum and Dad anyway, all kinds of mementos and photographs that marked birthdays and special events. But that clay cat, grinning from atop the dresser, was a present from Estella given to mark the day they left junior school. And around its neck were two pendants: one a red plastic heart that Tim had given her on Valentine's Day along with a bronze skull pendant that Sonya had bought at a Limp Bizkit heavy metal concert last year. Nestled between the cat's legs was a glass vial filled with various different types of sand, a memento from their family holiday in Lanzarote five years ago. Being a sentimental sort, Sonya found it hard to throw anything away and, among the vast collection of hairbands that hung colourfully from a mug-tree, were a few tiny ones decorated with plastic flowers that dated all the way back to her childhood when she had first heard of art collections and declared herself to be a Hairband Collector instead.

All in all, the style of her room was what Estella – who had herself gone all Scandinavian minimalist in design taste – once tartly described as 'Terence Conran's worst nightmare'. It was true that, every time the look and style of her room was revamped, Sonya had determinedly hung on to some of its previous features – her 'Higgledy-Piggledy House' Mum had called it, but she wasn't going to have it any other way.

Sonya grinned, remembering shooing Dad away when he had got into one of his redecorating fits recently, demanding that her room be kept exactly as it was when she left for uni. It had taken some convincing because there had been six rolls of expensive Farrow & Ball wallpaper left over from the study room – smart stripes in maroon and gold – that Dad was convinced would be a centre piece if used on the eastern wall, while the rest of her bedroom remained its existing plummy purple. But she couldn't get rid of her purple walls – this grown-up look had been carefully chosen as a treat for her sixteenth birthday two years ago. She'd gone with her father to the huge out-of-town B&Q to choose the colour and they had come back with not just brushes and cans of paint, but a set of mirrored black wardrobes that Dad had spent the whole weekend putting together just so that it would be ready for her party. And what a party that had been; with a marquee erected in the back garden to accommodate the sixty-odd guests who had been invited, plus a live band. The planning had gone on for weeks and poor Mum had suffered terribly from varicose veins afterwards – the main reason why Sonya had insisted they didn't go down the same route for her recent eighteenth which had consequently been a much quieter and more intimate affair. She'd spent the morning with Granny Shaw and later taken the train up to London with Mum and Dad to have dinner at their favourite Indian restaurant: Rasa on Charlotte Street, whose fish curries Dad described as 'divine' even as he went red in the face, his brow breaking out into a sweat because of the chillies that, despite all his protestations, he had never really grown accustomed to. Dinner had been followed by the new Alan Bennett play at the National Theatre and later, walking with arms linked, across Waterloo Bridge, all three of them had declared it one of Sonya's best birthday celebrations ever.

Sonya's musings were interrupted by the ring of her mobile phone and the sight of Estella's smiling face flashing on the screen. The customary half a dozen phone calls they exchanged every day had suddenly doubled because of the forthcoming party at Estella's this weekend. It wasn't quite a joint eighteenth birthday party as their birthdays were six months apart; the celebration was more about both of them getting into the colleges of their choice. The downer was that, with Sonya heading off to Oxford and Estella to Bristol, they were going to be physically separated for the first time in thirteen years. The trip around India was a last hurrah to all the years they had spent, if Sonya's mum was to be believed, behaving like twins conjoined at the heart.

Sonya pressed her thumb on the green talk button and put the phone to her ear. 'Wassup?' she queried, sitting up against her cushions and propping her feet up on the window frame.

'I think I'm suffering from party nerves,' Estella said, in a loud hammed-up moan. 'Nothing normally wakes me this early. Must be the nerves.'

'Nerves? What are you blethering on about, you don't own any nerves, Stel! Even your mum says she's never seen you lose your head over anything.'

'Not true! There must be something I agitate over,' Estella replied, not sounding very sure of her capacity to agitate.

'Nope. Not a hint of a nerve. Or heart for that matter. Totally cold-hearted and unfazed, for instance by the fact that you and I are shortly due to be torn asunder for the first time in thirteen years.'

'Oh that! No cause for distress, Sonya darling. Oxford and Bristol are hardly at opposite ends of the earth, are they? And we'll both be back home for Christmas before you know it!'

Sonya briefly considered feeling hurt by Estella's seeming lack of concern but it was typical of her best friend to face life-changing moments without so much as batting an eyelid. But she had to admit, Estella's customary breezy insouciance had been oddly comforting on occasion. It sure was difficult to get too stressed around someone who was so laid-back she was almost horizontal. 'You're right, I guess,' Sonya replied. 'But don't pretend to have nerves just because it's what you think you should be having on the eve of a party. Everything's well under control from what I can see.'

'It's a bit weird, though, that everything's been delegated and there's no more to be done. Now I just want it to go well and for everyone to enjoy themselves.'

'Of course they'll enjoy themselves, silly. I have to admit, though, that the party's hardly topmost in my mind, given the holiday in India coming so soon after. Perhaps we should have spaced them out by a week so we could have planned both things properly. I can't seem to get too excited about India at the moment.'

'You're daft. I'm so excited I can hardly stand still! Don't forget there wasn't the time to space things out. Not with us having to get back to England in time for the start of uni.'

'Yeah, shame really that the visas took so long or we could even have managed an extra week in India. Maybe I'll start getting excited once this party's out of the way.'

'Fuck me sideways with a broomstick, Sonya!' Estella squawked. 'The party's nothing compared to this India holiday. It's once-in-a-lifetime kinda stuff!'

'Well, it sure solved a lot of people's questions about eighteenth birthday presents,' Sonya laughed.

'Personally, I think both our parents have got off rather lightly with buying just the air tickets, especially seeing what troupers the extended families have been,' Estella joked.

'Too right. Your Uncle Gianni insisting we go all the way down south to Kerala was just the best. Imagine insisting on getting my ticket too!'

'My Uncle G's the sweetest. Helps that he's loaded, of course. By the way, I'm off tomorrow to buy the backpack that Auntie Maria's given me money for.'

'Listen, we should make a date soon to investigate that travel shop in Soho too,' Sonya reminded.

'Which? Oh the one Toby told us about that specializes in tropical stuff? But I thought your mum's already kitted us out with tubes of insect repellent and various other forms of goo?'

'No, no, not that kind of thing. This shop does clothing and equipment and stuff.'

'You make it sound like we're headed off into the jungle, ready to hack our way through tropical undergrowth! I hardly think Delhi and Kerala require special clothing, Sonya.'

'Well, we have to get shots down at the GP's surgery so it's not exactly a trip down the road to Bromley, is it?'

Estella laughed. 'It certainly ain't that. I can't wait to be off. Just need to get this damned party out of the way first. Oh fuck, I just remembered, Mum asked me to call Alberto's deli for some salami. Gotta go!'

After her friend had hung up, Sonya continued to lie stretched in her bay window, sunning her propped-up legs. She had fitted perfectly into this space until she was about ten but now, at a lanky five foot eight, she had to fold herself up in all sorts of ingenious ways in order to tuck herself in. She picked up a cushion and clutched it against her chest, trying to quell another flutter of anticipation. This trip – till recently some kind of distant and unlikely endeavour – had suddenly become a lot more real. Before anyone knew it, she would be off, flying into the unknown . . . an unknown past, by any measure, a curious concept. Finding out about a whole new family . . .

Sonya tried to infuse herself with determination and pulled herself back into a sitting position. She plumped up the pillows in the bay window, instructing herself to get on with the task at hand. But instead she stayed where she was, scrolling through the apps on her phone to inspect her calendar. It had been five days since she'd sent that letter and she hadn't mentioned it to either Estella or her parents yet. Only Priyal knew and that was only because Sonya had needed a source of information on all matters related to India. Priyal had suggested that a letter to Delhi could take anything from five days to two weeks to arrive.

What would Neha Chaturvedi's response be when it did finally get to her, Sonya wondered. Not that she *cared*, or anything, but if she *did*, she'd have given an arm and a leg to be a fly on the wall when that letter got opened. She had written three different versions and had eventually gone for the hard-hitting one because no other tone had seemed quite appropriate; certainly not namby-pamby politeness! Besides, pussy-footing about and avoiding tackling important issues just wasn't her style.

Sonya rolled to one side and slipped a sheet of paper out from under the mattress in her bay window. She'd kept a photocopy of the letter she had sent as writing it had been such a momentous task, she felt it important to keep a record of it. However, over subsequent examinings, Sonya had doodled absent-mindedly on the margins which were now covered in pictures of stubby little aeroplanes and, for some odd reason, the repetitive image of a spiralling tornado.

Had she been overly melodramatic, Sonya wondered as she cast her eye over her scrawly writing. Perhaps the tone she'd adopted had turned just a tad too aggressive? It wasn't entirely made up of course, because Sonya did feel genuinely hurt and angry with all that she now knew of her adoption. In her more logical moments, she knew it was crazy to feel so angry, especially given what an ace set of cards life had dealt her since she was adopted by Mum and Dad. But that didn't take away from the fact that life could have been dire, thanks to the actions of the woman who had given birth to her.

To prevent her runaway thoughts from messing up her head again, Sonya got up and turned on the radio. She did a few energetic toe-touches and stretches to Michael Bublé and sang along, trying to lighten her mood. She smiled at her reflection in the mirrored wardrobe. By working herself up into such a tizz over India, perhaps she was merely living up to the name her father had given her when she was six: Drama Diva. He often had a little dig at Mum as well while he was at it, dubbing her Drama Queen and calling them both his Deeply Dramatic Duo. He was a fine one to talk, given how teary he had been of late; almost as bad as Mum. Of course it was all due to the India plan, and poor Dad wasn't as expert at masking his feelings as he seemed to think. With a mere five days to go before Sonya's departure, both her parents had taken to behaving as though they were acting in a Ken Loach weepie, welling up at the silliest of things and quickly blinking away tears that they thought Sonya hadn't seen. Of course, Sonya understood all the reasons for which her darling mum felt threatened by her going off in search of her real mother but it was really so unnecessary, given how poorly Sonya thought of the woman who had given her away.

Sonya danced her way to the photograph that hung above the writing bureau, taken on her sixth birthday. She looked at her six-year-old self, standing before a Smarties-encrusted chocolate cake, flanked by her parents, both of whom were wearing silly paper hats. They looked so happy. As though that smiling threesome, caught in the camera lens, was the only thing of any importance in the whole wide world. Sonya's heart did another guilty flip. She hated the thought of causing her parents distress. She had been quite shocked when she had overheard Mum remark to Dad that what they were going through was about the most painful thing that had happened to her since the string of miscarriages she had endured in her twenties.

It was an instantly sobering thought and Sonya stopped dancing to return to the window seat. After another last glance at the photocopied letter, she slipped it back under the mattress. She had also kept a copy, imagining – perhaps dramatically – the kind of events it could set off; legal proceedings even! If that was the case, she certainly didn't want to be caught out, unable to remember what she had written. Not that she was frightened or anything – after all UK laws did actively encourage people to rediscover the details of their birth. But in the end, the final draft had been secretly photocopied on Dad's scanner in his den before she had stuffed it into an envelope. She had sealed it before she could stop herself and then cycled like the clappers down to the post office on the High Street to make sure she did not change her mind. But, although it had been sent in haste, Sonya knew – hand on heart – that she had thought long and hard about the possible consequences of taking this step of contacting her birth mother. It was quite honestly the most difficult decision she had ever made in her life but Sonya had eventually made it, comforted by the sheer numbers of other adoptees who had done the same thing. All the information on the internet (and there was lots of it) had strengthened her, and left her with a strange sense of entitlement. There were so many blogs and websites that told her it was her right to know what had happened in her past. That past was hers and no one else's but, at the moment, all she had was a great gaping hole in her head and in her heart. When she was small, Mum and Dad had tried to tell her everything they knew about her adoption, but everything they knew was in fact pitifully little. They had, for instance, told her that she had an Indian mother but had no idea why she had given her up, or what had happened to her since. They knew that her father was white, English or Scottish, but there was absolutely no more information on him, not even a name. There were times when Sonya had wanted to scream in frustration and other times when, rather dramatically, she wondered if perhaps Mum and Dad were deliberately covering up her story because it was either really sordid or really exciting. And then, some-time around the age of thirteen, Sonya had simply stopped asking. All her questions had ended at the same old cipher and so there was little point. Especially when there were so many other things to focus her mind on at the time: bodily changes and intense crushes, a whole host of new areas to feel messed up about!

Now that Sonya was eighteen, however, and given more

right by law to investigate her past, everyone else simply had to understand that this trip to India was something she had no choice about. She had to discover the circumstances of her birth and it was now almost as though forces stronger than her had taken over, compelling her to embark on this treacherous path.

Chapter Three

By midnight, Neha was so exhausted by her hostess duties that she could feel her legs begin to buckle under her. Yet, she managed to keep smiling as she bid goodbye to Kitty Singhania, an erstwhile beauty queen who had gone on to found a hugely successful cosmetics empire.

'Sorry I have to leave early, darling. But don't you go forgetting my lunch at the Taj next week!' Kitty instructed, in that admonishing tone that was her trademark.

'Have I *ever* forgetting your birthday, Kitty darling?' Neha purred as she hugged her guest lightly and kissed the air on either side of her face.

Kitty acknowledged her rejoinder with a laugh. 'I must admit, you never do, darling Neha. Always the first to call on the day. Well, thank you again for a fabulous party. You and Sharat really do know how to throw a bash. Oh, and thank you for introducing me to André – it really would be wonderful to break into the French market. I hope it works!'

After Kitty's white Audi had swept out of the gates, Neha nodded at the security guards who were swiftly and diligently closing the large black exit gates that led on to Prithviraj Road. The Chaturvedi household's security normally subsisted on the presence of just one elderly

Gurkha at the entrance but extra guards and police personnel were always drafted in on party nights to ensure the safety of the many VIPs who would attend. It was one of Neha's worst nightmares that something unfortunate would happen when her house was full of celebrities and millionaires and it was not for nothing that the Inspector General of Delhi's police force was always a valued guest at her parties too.

Tonight, however, all that was the last thing on Neha's mind. It was as if the letter hidden in her cupboard upstairs had taken on some kind of ghostly form that had been floating about all night, creeping up on her at unexpected moments to mock and taunt her as she tried to engage with her guests. Neha stopped with one foot on the broad marble step that led up to the veranda, taking in great gulps of the heady scent of the creeper that hung abundantly over the roof. The fragrance of jasmine was meant to have a calming effect, according to her yoga instructor who sometimes held her sessions out here on the veranda, but nothing short of a strong tranquillizer would work today.

Sounds of merrymaking still filtered through the doorways as Neha's raw silk curtains drifted in the breeze: chatter and laughter and the clink of china and cutlery as guests helped themselves at the lavish buffet tables in the dining room. From the pergola at the far end of the eastern garden, the Divakar Brothers' live performance was just audible: thin strains of the sitar playing a melancholy raga over the more robust notes of a harmonium.

'Please, please help me stay strong and calm,' Neha thought in desperation, imagining what all the people who were currently enjoying her hospitality would think if they read that letter right now. Not having any children of their own, the scandal of a secret child would rock Neha and Sharat's world and destroy Sharat's political ambitions and, surely, their marriage too. It was too terrifying to bear thinking about.

Neha looked up at the moon, large and heavy, rising through the gulmohar trees. Such a perfect night. Delhi had seen off the last of the monsoon rains and was now starting to cool in readiness for the winter. But Neha could not derive any of her customary pleasure from the soothing breezes that were carrying in lush smells from her garden. Instead, for the hundredth time since the letter came, she imagined the emergence in her near-flawless world of the secret that she had managed to hold on to for eighteen years. Public knowledge that she'd not only had a child before marrying Sharat, but had gone on to abandon it, would tear their lives apart on so many different levels. Not merely because everyone would discover what a hypocrite she really was, but also because Sharat would no longer be able to present their marriage in the manner he loved: a gracious young couple who were pillars of the establishment and could always be relied on to help all their friends and acquaintances progress with their own hopes and ambitions.

Neha clutched her stomach as it twisted in a painful spasm again. It had been doing that all evening – it could be due either to hunger or anxiety, she couldn't tell. She usually ate a bowl of daal with a chapatti before any of her parties; a bit of useful 'hostessing' advice that Jasmeet had imparted years ago. Today the letter had caused her to forget this useful ritual. She tried to massage the pain away and, with one hand still resting on her flat stomach, Neha considered the painful question of her childless marriage suddenly: a thought she had not dwelt on for

27

some time now. Of course, she remembered it off and on but not with the kind of anguish that was assailing her right now . . .

Standing in the shadows of the flower-bedecked pillars, Neha bent over and let out a long, low moan. She had not felt sadder in a long, long time than she did tonight. Although Sharat seemed to have come to terms with their childlessness in his own way over the past few years, for Neha it had remained the biggest irony of her life. For one, he knew nothing of the child she had already had. But Neha had lived with that anomaly mocking her all these years: how, indeed, could it be anything but fair that Neha should be punished with a childless marriage for having given away the baby that had been born to her all those years ago?

She saw again the untidy handwriting in the letter, the girlish signature that ended in a flamboyantly curling loop. 'Sonya' . . .

Stumbling on the steps leading up to the veranda, Neha gripped the back of one of her wicker chairs, trying to steady herself. Another burst of laughter emerged through the French windows and, for one horrible moment, Neha felt as though everyone at the party was laughing at her. She had to sit down for a moment; clear her head before going back in there with a smile on her face . . .

Sinking onto the chair, Neha tried to contain her runaway thoughts. The baby . . . the baby she had given away had not even had a name.

'It's best you don't go choosing a name, my dear. Because, you see, harsh as it sounds, it's crucial you don't bond with the child. Now that the decision's been made to give her up, you see. Naming her will only create a bond. So will breast-feeding.

*I'll fetch you a pump and you can expel your milk into that.
We'll give it to her in a bottle. Your decision has been made;
it's best to let her go . . .' The room had swum around, causing
the hospital counsellor's face to disappear for a few seconds
into the grey murk . . .*

Was that why Neha had never been able to see her baby
as having any human potential at all? She had followed
all those instructions to the tee, refusing to bond with the
child who would never be hers. And, later, she had quite
deliberately never thought of its welfare, or kept track of
its age and possible circumstances. That was the only way
to survive the experience. Only she knew the reasons for
which she had taken that decision. It was not one she
would make today but, at that tender age, she had been
a different person. Except, who would believe her if she
said that now? Certainly not the child she had given
away . . .

Another burst of laughter made Neha sit up straight
and square her shoulders. She needed to get back to her
guests before her absence was noticed. If someone came
in search of her, what would they think to see her sitting
by herself on the veranda while her party was in full swing?
She needed to ensure everyone had eaten, that the dessert
tables were elegantly laid out. Rose petals! Had they
remembered the rose petals? Neha had this afternoon
asked her chef to ensure that pink rose petals were scattered over the pile of *kesar kulfi* that should by now be
melting to a delicious creaminess. The timing had to be
just right, the *kulfis* removed from their metal moulds
exactly fifteen minutes before they were served in order
to maximize their texture and flavour. But, suddenly, it
all seemed so inconsequential, this ridiculous bid for

perfection. What had been the point of all this? These famed parties, this stunning mansion, the dream life that she and Sharat seemingly had ... perhaps she had been trying to make things look so perfect because she knew that they were not perfect at all ...

Neha looked around herself in a panic, feeling a terrible surging in her stomach, recalling old terrors she had thought were over. For so many years the fear that she would get found out had followed Neha around, infecting everything she had done. It had even caused her to do deliberately badly in the Foreign Service entrance exams, despite her father's continuing ambitions on her behalf. She had never been able to tell him, but the truth was that she was terrified of finding herself in the kind of job that would have propelled her into the public eye, thus exposing her to someone who may know her secret. All she had wanted then was to to burrow herself into a hole and disappear from public view. What if she was recognized? What if everyone found out what she had done? It was too horrible to even contemplate. But, slowly, as the years had moved on and those events had receded into the distant past, Neha had almost begun to feel as though that life had belonged to a different girl. After all, she had never put a foot wrong subsequently. And then she had met Sharat and, in his shining goodness, Neha had finally found a kind of forgetfulness.

'You and I are of the same type, Neha darling. Thank God we both enjoy people and have the same genuine urge to help humanity ... together we should make a beautiful home where our friends and family and, in fact, all kinds of needy people will always find an open door ... I feel so grateful that you have agreed to marry

30

me. Not only do I love you but you are my perfect life companion . . .'

Neha now closed her eyes as Sharat's voice chose that moment to float into the veranda. From inside the room, she heard him say something indistinct and she savoured his loud familiar belly laugh as someone responded with a joke.

Neha got up resolutely and made for the French windows. She would return to her party; pretend that all was well. And all *was* well for now. She ought to hang on to that, cherish every moment of what she might soon lose. It was strange to be so out of control but, in all the planning and secrecy, the one thing Neha had never considered was that the baby she had given up would grow up and become an independent young woman in her own right. One who would have a mind of her own. And, regardless of all the careful control exerted by Neha, all the covering up of her tracks, one who would set out one day in search of her.

Chapter Four

The eighteenth birthday party was to be held in the grounds of an old flour mill on the outskirts of Orpington. There were no houses around for at least a mile and the place had been favoured as a better party venue than both Sonya's and Estella's homes because, being so remote, it was the least likely to lead to neighbourly complaints. The party was going to be big too, with almost all of their classmates from Duke High invited, along with several of their boyfriends and girlfriends who went to other schools. Then, Estella's large brood of cousins from her Italian side had also wanted to come and so, all in all, about fifty teenagers were expected to descend on the mill this weekend. Both sets of parents had been prevailed upon to stay away, a stipulation they had agreed to only on the condition that Bob, the miller who stayed in a cottage on the premises, would be around to ensure that no illegal activities took place. Estella couldn't help feeling some relief at the thought that she wasn't entirely in charge. Curmudgeonly old Bob would ensure no prankster got into the mill to do something stupid like scatter flour everywhere or pee into the water wheel.

Partially to counter the quiet, rustic surroundings, the invitation had specified fancy dress. It was, after all, the last chance to meet before everyone departed for universities all over the country. Estella had decided in her usual pragmatic fashion – and in the interests of her hostessing duties – to be a British Midland air stewardess, having borrowed a uniform from a cousin who was the same size as her. Sonya's boyfriend, Tim, was going to be Julius Caesar, complete with a plastic bag hidden on his person that would squirt fake blood if anyone attempted to assassinate him. As for Sonya, after much deliberation and wavering between 'Indian princess' and 'Bollywood heroine', she had finally decided on the former. Sonya had grown increasingly excited as she had put her costume together, borrowing a beautiful sari from Priyal that was a rich turquoise blue with thousands of tiny sequins sewn on. Priyal's mum had shown her how to wear it, and even helped take the blouse in as Priyal was at least half a stone bigger than Sonya. Quantities of fake gold jewellery had come from a shop in Tooting and, during a practice run with the sari and jewellery, Priyal had looped a gold chain around Sonya's head so that the large pendant hung down the middle of her forehead. Priyal had then stepped back to take in the full effect and the expression on her face had given Sonya goosebumps. It was more complimentary than any words would ever be. Priyal, who almost never used any compliment stronger than a rather desultory 'cool', had shaken her head and let out a low whistle before muttering, 'Awesome!' Then, in more typical fashion, she had added, 'You look like a bloody maharani, mate.'

To complete the royal look, Sonya had forsaken her customary ponytail and had this evening been to a beauty parlour in town. The stylist had blow-dried her hair into a silky black curtain that hung to her bare midriff, and had also shown her how to apply eyeshadow to accentuate her dark, sweeping brows and large eyes. Back in her bedroom and now in her full regalia, Sonya examined herself in the full-length mirror. The heavy smoky grey eye make-up did indeed make her look very sophisticated, regal almost, even if she said so herself! She did a delighted little twirl, looking coquettishly at herself over her shoulder and pouting suggestively. Was the look more Bollywood heroine or Indian princess? Sonya couldn't tell. Then her pleasure wavered momentarily as she felt a sudden clutch of nervousness at what Mum and Dad would say when she appeared downstairs looking as over-the-top 'Indian' as this. She never liked to rub their noses in the fact that she wasn't their biological daughter, and choosing this outfit may well be misunderstood, given how anxious they were feeling about her India trip. It was stupid of her not to have thought of it before.

Her parents were watching *The Weakest Link* when Sonya floated silently into the living room, trying to be subtle and unobtrusive. She caught sight of her father cocking a glance in her direction before raising a quizzical brow at his wife. 'I saw that!' Sonya warned.

Richard Shaw had the grace to look sheepish. He got up and kissed his daughter on her forehead before holding her by the shoulders at arm's length. 'You look beautiful, darling. It's just that we don't usually see you with so much make-up on. It makes you look . . . well . . . older. Isn't that right, Laura darling?' He turned to his wife with a pleading expression on his face. Sonya realized how studiously he'd avoided mentioning the Indian look, even though she had been talking about her planned Bollywood costume for days and it was now staring them in the face. Laura Shaw smiled briefly at Sonya and nodded in appreciation, but she soon returned her gaze to the television screen. Her rather anxious expression made it seem as though far more interesting events were unfolding in the BBC studio than in her own living room.

Sonya threw her eyes upwards. 'C'mon, guys, it's just a fancy dress party, for God's sake!' she cried in exasperation. 'You'd have thought I'd seriously gone native, the way you're behaving!'

'Don't be dramatic, darling,' Richard said, going across to the sideboard in the hall to search for the car keys. 'You must admit, though, that it's quite strange seeing you dressed like that, given everything.'

'Given *what*?' Sonya asked, flouncing after her father into the hall, 'that I'm off to India? For Chrissake, Dad, it's a two-week holiday, not a religious conversion!'

'I know, darling,' Richard said, coming up to Sonya to tap her arm with the back of his hand. He dropped his voice. 'And Mum knows it too. However, you must understand her distress at this sudden decision of yours to go to India, Sonya. It has come out of the blue a bit. Go on, darling, go in there, beg a compliment off her and you'll both feel the better for it.'

Sonya hesitated for a moment before returning to the living room. She stood at the door for a second before walking in. 'I'm off, Mum,' she said in a small voice. 'Wish me luck. Stel's even lined up a prize for best costume, you know.'

Laura roused herself on the sofa and looked up at Sonya again. Taking in her daughter's exotic beauty with nervousness she was eventually unable to prevent herself from melting at Sonya's sheer loveliness. Laura patted the sofa next to her and said, 'Come here, you.' As Sonya approached, she added, 'You really do look lovely, Sonya darling. Dad and I don't mean to be nasty. It's just that you don't look like our little girl when you're dressed up like that, you know . . . and, to be honest, I really can't bear such a harsh reminder. Not at this time anyway. Just before you go off in search of *her* . . . you know what I mean . . .'

'I know, I know, Mum,' Sonya said, kneeling before her mother. 'But it's only a spot of fun, dressing up like this. It certainly doesn't mean I'm trying to become someone else. Or make some kind of bid for acceptance by my birth family. Remember I'm always and only *your* little girl. I don't need to keep telling you that no one else will ever matter to me as much as you and Dad, do I?'

They held hands briefly as Sonya rested her cheek against her mother's knee. Then she got up, fumbling awkwardly with the folds of her sari. 'I'd better go easy with this thing,' she said, 'there's about a million safety pins stuck around me to keep it in place and I must return it to Priyal without tearing it!'

'Yes, I bumped into Priyal's mum at Asda this morning . . . Mrs Guptee?'

'Gupta,' Sonya corrected.

'Yes, Mrs Gupta. And she did go on a bit about how lovely you looked when you first tried these clothes on at her house. She kept saying "Stunning," and that English women generally didn't look right in saris. Well, she's obviously never seen Princess Di and Jemima Khan when they wore them, has she? Why, even Cherie Blair didn't look half bad in Indian costume, despite being a bit ungainly, so I don't know what Mrs Gupta was on about.' Laura hesitated for a moment before asking her daughter, 'By the way, she doesn't *know*, does she?'

Sonya restrained herself from rolling her eyes upwards in exasperation again. She knew exactly what her mum was talking about and it both amused and saddened her to think that her beloved mother was feeling so threatened, even by a passing compliment from someone as harmless as Mrs Gupta. 'No, she doesn't know, Mum,' she lied firmly, 'and nor does Priyal. I've told you, apart from Stel and Tim, no one else knows why I'm going to India.'

Laura looked marginally reassured. 'Best keep it that way,' she said, 'after all we don't know yet what's going to happen once you're there, do we?' Then, taking a deep breath, she put on a bright air that did not convince Sonya at all. 'Well, off with you then,' Laura said. 'Don't forget to take the salads out of the fridge, and the marinated lamb chops. I've added extra Tabasco, just like Estella said. And have a lovely time, won't you.' Laura nodded gratefully at Richard who was standing in the doorway, already carrying the two large plastic boxes full of salad. 'Oh, and let Dad know when you want picking up from the mill?'

In the car, Sonya leaned over to give her father a peck on his cheek as he started the car. 'What's that for, Princess?' he queried, although Sonya could see how pleased he was with the unexpected display of affection.

'For always being such a skilled peacemaker. And for knowing exactly how to make both Mum and me feel instantly soothed.'

'Ah, long years of practice,' Richard said. 'Don't forget I grew up in a house full of women. Three sisters is enough to drive most fellers around the bend but, golly, what an education that was!'

They drove to the outskirts of Orpington in companionable silence, Richard humming along to a Phil Collins track on Radio 2 while Sonya straightened her smudged eye make-up in the car mirror, unused as she was to wearing kohl rather than the customary eye-pencil. 'So, what are you listening to these days, sweetheart? I notice you've put all your old Kurt Cobain CDs in that pile for Oxfam,' Richard said suddenly.

Sonya smiled. Dad tried with such sincerity to be matey and she had never had the heart to tell him that she wouldn't be able to get through naming half the bands she listened to without having him keel right over in shock. She had, in fact, carefully hidden the new Fuck Jesus CD under her bed to minimize the chance of offending her very innocent and strait-laced parents. 'Oh, nothing special, just this and that,' she replied vaguely, looking out at the streetlights on the Sevenoaks Road. 'The mill comes up somewhere here, Dad,' she added. 'We'd better slow down.'

Richard peered through the dusk. A few stray raindrops were falling on the windscreen. 'Oh dear,' he said, 'it's been spitting and spotting like this all evening. I do hope it doesn't start to pour and ruin your party! Now, if I remember, there's a sharp bend in the road just before you see the sign for Wentworth Mill.'

'Good memory!' Sonya said. 'It was at least six years ago that we all came here for that bread-making course.'

'Well, I was here more recently with the Council on one of our team-building days so I should know where it is, really. Ah, and bingo, there we go!' Richard swung the car onto a small dirt track that wound its way through an open field in which a few sodden sheep were grazing. They drove past a pond that sat next to the water mill and pulled up in a small yard where Estella's Polo was already parked. Sonya disembarked, holding up the edges of her sari to prevent it from getting muddy.

'Hey Bollywood princess, don't you look just gorgeous!' came a cry from the door where Estella was emerging in her stewardess cap and uniform.

'Actually not such a great idea on a wet evening,' Sonya replied, ruefully looking down at her shimmering clothes. She cast an envious look at Estella's short skirt and flat-heeled pumps, 'Look at you – not just smart but sensible too!'

'Ah, but then that's me all over: smart and sensible! Oh, and surely you merely forgot to say "sexy" too,' Estella replied, twirling a plump leg in what she imagined was a coquettish manner before yelling a cheery greeting to Richard who was getting out of the far side of his car. Richard blew a kiss at her and then turned to get the salad and lamb chops out of the back seat. Someone – possibly one of the Wentworth cousins – came running out of the mill to help. He was dressed as a bishop but, as he heaved the boxes over his shoulder and carried them into the building, a pair of stout and very unbishoplike Doc Martens was revealed under his robes.

Richard turned when another car pulled into the yard. Its four occupants – Spiderman, Wonder Woman, a vicar and a tart – emerged amidst a hail of raunchy greetings. It was definitely time to go. Richard waved to Sonya and Estella before climbing with haste back into his car, grinning widely as he reversed. 'Have fun, girls, and be good!' he said, rolling his window back up before driving off.

Sonya followed the others into the bakery part of the mill, which is where the food and drink were to be laid out in the event of rain. Estella's mother ran a small artisan bread business from the premises, supplying local restaurants and delis with her popular sourdough bread. Mrs Wentworth had obviously been baking furiously for the party as Sonya could see piles and piles of crusty rolls and her famous giant white bloomer loaves at one end of the table.

Unable to sustain the demure Indian look for very long, Sonya was swigging her second can of Corona when Timothy arrived. His face brightened as it always did when he saw her but, because his Roman toga was too long, he stumbled on the top step of the mill while stepping over the threshold in a pair of outsized gladiator sandals. What would have been a nasty tumble was fortuitously stopped by his colliding with Wonder Woman, which led to both of them falling in a giggling heap onto a few bags of wholemeal flour. It was a funny sight that had all the observers bursting into affectionate laughter, but Sonya looked away from her boyfriend making a spectacle of himself, mortified. Tim was unfazed, however, and Sonya guessed that he was probably already a little drunk. Being a naturally shy sort, he often downed a bottle of beer before leaving for a party. 'A pint of Dutch courage,' he had once said while waving a lager glass of Stella Artois in a pub, and Sonya was sure he had meant it. She watched the burly Benedict pull Tim up now and stick him back on his sandaled feet. Benedict, who had gone by the name of Big Ben since Year Seven, twinkled across at Sonya. 'I know I just said you were a fabulous eyeful tonight, Ms Shaw, but I failed to realize this was the effect you would have on poor old Tim!'

'Mind you don't distract him when he's stood next to the water wheel,' someone else warned.

'Too right. Can't have Julius Caesar die in a *drowning* accident, for fuck's sake,' came another quip.

Cheerfully ignoring them all, Tim wandered across to Sonya for a kiss but received only a perfunctory peck on the cheek. 'What's that about?' he asked; charged up, Sonya was sure, by the beer. He was never aggressive normally. She shrugged and turned away. If she was to be honest, it wasn't merely the drink. She had been feeling distinctly cooler towards him for days anyway, the only problem being that good old bumbling Tim had completely failed to take the hint so far! Typically, Estella noticed her discomfiture, however, and Sonya saw her shoot a sympathetic look in her direction as Tim leaned in proprietorally to insist on sticking his tongue into her mouth.

Sonya shrugged away from his grasp, cheering up slightly when she saw Chelsea Brigham-Smith walking into the mill, her face almost unrecognisable under layers of luminous green paint and a witch's hat. She was exactly the person Sonya needed to talk to on the eve of her departure for India, because it was Chelsea who had told her about the Adoption Register at another party a few months ago. She had just been through the procedure of searching for her own birth family at the time, a story that had provided Sonya with the impetus she had perhaps been subconsciously seeking.

'Hey, Chels,' Sonya said, waving to catch her attention.

'Hi, Sonya,' Chelsea replied, walking over, 'don't you look super in your Indian clothes! Sure suits you, all this drapey, shimmery stuff.'

'Oh thanks. Don't suppose you want me to return the compliment, given your witch's garb! This is Tim, by the way,' Sonya added, mumbling, 'my boyfriend,' as an afterthought under her breath. She turned to Tim. 'Chelsea was my classmate back in primary school before she went off to Cheltenham Ladies' College,' she said, waiting while Tim and Chelsea shook hands and exchanged pleasantries. Then she grabbed Chelsea's arm, unable to contain her news any more. 'You'll never believe this, Chels. I've been meaning to call and say – I did eventually follow up your advice and contact the Registrar General, you know.'

'You did!? And?'

Sonya took a deep breath, aware that the more people she told, the more she was breaking her promise to Laura. 'And . . .' she paused, unable to resist a bit of drama, 'And I've traced my birth mother too. All the way to India, as it happens.'

'Cor! I remember you said you were half Indian but, bloody hell, that's a long way away. Not quite like my little trip around to that council block in Merton I told you about, eh?'

Conscious of Tim standing by, Sonya said, 'You don't mind if I put Tim in the picture, do you, Chels?' She waited until Chelsea nodded before explaining, 'Chelsea's an adopted child too, Tim, and, when she turned eighteen recently, she went off in search of her birth parents. I more or less got the idea from her when we met at Tabitha Stott's birthday party recently.'

'Was it difficult, your search?' Tim asked Chelsea.

'Took all of two weeks,' Chelsea laughed, 'and eventually I found the couple who gave birth to me living not more than a mile away from where I grew up in Wimbledon Village!'

'Wow!' Tim responded, 'What was that like?'

'Terrifying, I can tell you now,' Chelsea said, her blackened witch's teeth gleaming as she laughed. 'I took to waking up in a cold sweat for days after, imagining them trying to break into my parents' house to get me. And anything else they could find while they were there!'

'But you're still glad you did it, yes?' Sonya asked.

Chelsea nodded. 'I think I needed to plug a few gaps in my head. Luckily, I had the full support of my parents who helped me every inch of the way. My dad especially. But he was an adopted child himself, you see, so I think

43

he really understood. Are your parents okay about your search?'

Sonya hesitated for a moment, reluctant to say anything disloyal about her parents. 'Poor Mum and Dad,' she said. 'They're just a bit confused right now. But they'll come around in the end, I know. They love me far too much.'

'Well, what have you found out so far?' Chelsea persisted.

'Not a great deal. Just that the woman who gave birth to me lives in India. Apparently, she refused to divulge the name of the man who'd fathered me so there's nothing on him in the records. But, as I'm going to India next week, I may have more to tell you after that.'

'Going to *India*? Hey, what an adventure – my trip to Merton does rather pale by comparison! Are you going too?' Chelsea asked Tim.

'No,' Sonya responded swiftly, 'I'm going with Estella, actually.'

'Cool,' Chelsea repeated, although Sonya knew that was not how Tim felt at all.

A couple of hours later, Sonya told herself mournfully that the party wasn't quite working. Only for her, that is, going by the general whoops of merriment that were audible from the yard outside and the growing mountain of empty beer cans she could see just outside the door. She cast a glance around the mill from her uncomfortable perch on a wooden stool. She was sitting as close as she possibly could to the ovens without singeing her eyebrows because she had found herself freezing to death in her skimpy sari. It was also preventing her from helping Estella, who was at this moment laying out great platters of food on the trestle tables at the far end of the kitchen. This was supposed to have been a joint party, Sonia thought with an annoyed humph. But here she was, stupidly forced into being a guest because she was sure she would trip and snag Priyal's mum's beautiful sari if she ventured to undertake domestic chores while wearing it. How on earth did Indian women go to parties and do their household chores wearing these things, she wondered.

Chapter Five

Sharat walked towards the breakfast room, humming a jaunty tune. Last night's party had been an unqualified success and the icing on the cake had been the Home Minister's promise as he'd left. 'Don't worry, I'll have a word with the PM,' Vir-ji had said, leaning out of the window of his liveried car. 'Leave it with me for a few days, Sharat. And keep your fingers crossed – there are many vying for the same seat, you know!'

It had been less than a year ago that Sharat had first voiced his ambition of becoming an MP to a few friends with political connections and, even though he knew what an asset he would be to any party, the haste with which Congress party had opened its doors had been astonishing. Now, from his very energising conversation with the Home Minister last night, it was clearly only a matter of time before the offer of a safe seat came. One of the South Delhi constituencies would be best, Sharat thought, areas where the educated newly rich were desperate to see the face of politics change for the better. And better he would make it, that he was sure of. It was a natural calling, to be mindful of the welfare of other, less fortunate people. He had insisted on egalitarianism even as a child: persuading his mother to give away his clothes to the cook's son before he had

47

even outgrown them and preferring to play cricket with the children of their factory workers rather than Scrabble and caroms with Shashi, his sickly and rather snobbish cousin who was Sharat's only companion in the family home. Most of all, he was fortunate to have money from the cloth mills started by his grandfather and didn't see the need to waste his time building up more wealth, especially when there were no children to pass it on to. Even his cousin, Shashi, was childless.

'Morning, sweetheart,' Sharat said, his voice cheery as he saw Neha's figure already seated in her customary swing chair that overlooked the blooming flower beds in the garden. He noticed in a glance that she looked exhausted. 'Still recovering from last night, eh?' he enquired, unfurling a yellow gingham napkin over his lap. When Neha only muttered a response, Sharat looked at her more carefully. She really didn't look very well. At thirty-seven, she was still a very attractive woman, with creamy smooth skin and a trim figure, but this morning her skin was sallow and there were grey shadows under her eyes. It was also unusual to see her still in her dressing gown, rather than in the exercise gear she usually wore for her walk around Lodhi Gardens. 'It was a fabulous party, thanks in no small measure to you,' Sharat said, leaning over to plant a big wet kiss on Neha's cheek. Helping himself to a cinnamon bagel from the toast rack, he proceeded to spread a generous smear of butter on it, grinning as he saw Neha wince visibly. Neha did enough exercise for both of them, Sharat sometimes said jocularly, content in the knowledge that he was blessed with a naturally thin frame. Of late, however, Neha had been at him to stay off the fatty foods because of the slightly high cholesterol count that had been revealed in his last six-monthly checkup. But Sharat really did love the raisin and cinnamon bagels that Neha bought for him from the Hyatt bakery, and a bagel without butter was worse than poories without aloo. 'Carbs and fat, a marriage made in heaven, just like ours,' he sometimes teased.

'You're unusually quiet, Neh. Are you okay?' Sharat asked, turning in his chair to face his wife as he took a sip of coffee and chewed on his bagel. 'Didn't you think it all went wonderfully well yesterday?'

Neha finally roused herself, sitting up from her slouching position. She swallowed a mouthful of coffee and put her cup down before speaking. 'It did go very well. No, I'm fine, Sharat, just a bit tired.'

'Well, you won't have to do this for another six months,' Sharat said, unscrewing the pot of marmalade. 'By the way, I'm thinking of going off to Lucknow for a couple of days.'

'Oh, when?'

'Well, if I can get on the evening flight, I may even go today. It's important for me to go see the old boy and get his blessing, given what the Home Minister said last night. I may even ask him to contribute to the campaign. Which I think he'll readily do. Want to come?'

Neha thought for a minute before shaking her head. 'No thanks, Sharat. But I may get away for a couple of days myself.'

'Anywhere special? You were talking about Damascus and Samarkand the other day, weren't you?' Sharat enquired.

'Not right now, that'll take some planning. No, I was thinking of a week in Ananda up in the Himalayas, actually. Or any other decent spa within easy reach. I've been longing for some R&R for a while but it's been one thing after another, as you know,' Neha replied.

'Ananda's a great idea, sweetheart,' Sharat said. 'You love it there, don't you? I must say I was worried at the thought of you wandering around Samarkand on your own. Let's do that together some other time, yes?'

'Well, Sandhya went on her own to Samarkand and Tashkent, and said it was fine. But, yes, I'd rather go there with you. There's no hurry . . .'

'For now, Ananda will be the best break and do you some good before the winter sets in too. And I'm happy for you to indulge, seeing how little I care for all that alternative yoga-shoga stuff myself! Get Chacko to book it for you today.'

Sharat left the house in a flurry of phone calls, still talking into his BlackBerry as he got into the back seat of his Mercedes. As was customary, Neha stood on the step watching his car leave the gates to be swallowed into the morning traffic on Prithviraj Road. If she could only tell Sharat about the letter . . . Over the years, she had grown used to telling him everything, even the tiniest details collected over the day. But this was different. This was a revelation that would shatter his world . . . rob him of every last ounce of love and trust he had for her . . .

Neha turned and returned indoors, her steps lethargic and heavy as she climbed the sweeping stairs up to her bedroom on the first floor. She locked the big teak door behind her and then, almost as though pulled by a magnetic force, made for the cupboard where the letter lay. She had not been able to reread it since it had arrived yesterday but she had thought of virtually nothing else. Her sleep had been broken by strange dreams in which she was wandering through a paediatrics ward full of screaming babies.

Using the big bunch of keys that was almost always tucked into the waistband of her trousers or sari, Neha unlocked the outer doors before opening the safe that housed her jewellery when it was taken out of the bank vault. She had tucked the letter behind a stack of cheque books and could see a corner of the white envelope sticking out from under the large blue velvet case of her antique pearl choker. Holding the letter to her chest, Neha climbed back into bed and pulled the silk *razai* over herself. She read and reread the words, running the tip of her forefinger over the childish writing and the name 'Sonya', before starting to cry. At first, she cried quietly, sobbing softly into balled fists, the letter lying now in her lap. Then, helplessly, as the tears grew more copious, Neha tried desperately to muffle her moaning and hiccupping by holding a pillow over her face. It was the kind of weeping fit she had not indulged in since she was a child. The floodgates had opened up and Neha – strong and controlled and always in charge – was back to being a frightened and confused teenager all over again.

The thin blue line on the home pregnancy kit was unmistakable. Could it be faulty? Please, please, let it be faulty! It had to be wrong! This was not how pregnancies happened, surely. But someone was outside the toilet now, awaiting their turn. Must hurry, get rid of the evidence, stuff it into the bin, cover it up with lots of tissue, pull the flush and get out before anyone realizes something's wrong!

I emerged from the toilet, and my life was changed. I was a child no more because I now had a dark secret. Nothing like the kind of secret children keep. A big and terrible secret that would need to be covered up, like that pregnancy kit in the bin, hastily shoved under soiled tissues and detritus.

Chapter Six

Waking up the day after her party, Sonya studiously avoided looking at herself as she went past the mirrored wardrobes to her bathroom. Day-old mascara was terrible – more panda than princess on the morning after!

She slipped off her nightshirt and examined the top half of her body critically. Tim had told her again last night that she had the perfect figure, trying to be romantic by snogging her under the stars and struggling to stick his clammy palm under her sari blouse, telling her how much he was going to miss her. But, in reality, there had been nothing romantic at all about that fumbling grope in the middle of a wet field stinking of manure. Sonya had finally shoved Tim away, put out by his sour beery breath and worried he would tread on the edge of her sari and get mud all over it. His eagerness to please was truly starting to irritate rather than endear. He had made such an ass of himself at the party too – he'd never been able to handle too much drink. When on a sudden impulse a few of the girls had piled into a car to go into Orpington town centre for ice creams, he had insisted on coming along. And then, instead of going into the ice-cream parlour, he'd stood outside, still dressed in his Roman toga and squirting startled passers-by with his plastic sword that doubled as a water pistol. One elderly pensioner had been so enraged by the unexpected attack that he had chased Tim down the road, waving his brolly and shouting profanities until Tim had been rescued by an escape car full of giggling girls.

Sonya counted in her head while brushing her teeth. Tim had been her boyfriend for eight months now and, at first, Sonya had thought they were made for each other, both of them being clever and bookish and ardent followers of Man U. But lately (and she should admit that perhaps her unexpected four As and subsequent admission to Oxford had something to do with it), Sonya had started to find Timothy's adoration clingy and suffocating. She would probably upset Mum something terrible if she dumped him, however, as Laura had taken an early shine to Timothy's shambling diffident manner. She had always been a bit of a sucker for middle-class manners and speech too, all that mumbling and swallowing of consonants. 'An accent snob, that's what you are, Mum,' Sonya was given to joke. 'Oh, and a sucker for the starving millions! You don't need to feed him every day, you know. He's perfectly well-fed at his own house.' But the mere sight of Tim's thin, gangling frame entering their home seemed to set Laura off on a reforming mission into the kitchen, where Timothy had of late become a habitual visitor, treated to the Shaw household's typically robust and nutritious meals. 'You may not think so now but this lad will make something of his life,' Laura Shaw often said soon after Tim had gone, sometimes adding darkly, as though reading her daughter's mind, 'Do hang onto him, love – good boyfriends are like gold dust, you'll soon discover.'

Sonya towelled herself dry before she wandered back into her room and opened her wardrobe to find something suitable for what promised to be a warm day. Was there a dress code for a dump-your-boyfriend-day, Sonya wondered, only half joking with herself. It was best not to look too scrummy, lest the dumpee's pain was thus intensified. And not too plain so as to cause no pain at all! Sonya shook her head. Perhaps she did not need to agonize so much over splitting up with Tim. It was very likely that his imminent departure for Durham University would finish things off between them anyway, the distance between Oxford and Durham being not inconsiderable for a pair of penurious students. But Sonya had always liked clear lines and stated intentions and the last thing she wanted was to skulk around avoiding Tim when it was so much easier to just tell him the truth.

Would she miss him at some point, Sonya wondered, hooking together her bra while staring at herself hard in the mirror, trying to induce some guilt. Then she shrugged her shoulders. Given the way Tim had whinged on about her going off to Asia with Estella, she thought not. And it wasn't even as if *he* presented a viable option! His delicate stomach had made him nervous of travelling abroad (a take-away from the Shalimar down the road invariably brought on the runs, from what he'd once let slip) and so Tim had never been seriously considered as a travelling companion for the two girls, despite both their parents suggesting it at some point. Besides, in a crisis, Sonya was sure that she and Estella would keep their heads a lot better than Tim ever would.

Twirling a pair of knickers on her forefinger, Sonya turned to examine her smooth, bare bum in the full-length mirror. *Hmmm . . . not bad at all*, she thought, finally recognizing – this recognition having come only well into her teens – how lucky she was to have her unusual golden skin tone that never required the hours on sunbeds and pots of tanning cream that so many of her friends were slaves to. There were some advantages to being of mixed race. Someone at school had, in fact, recently told her that the blend of Indian and European was one of the best because Indian genes, being not as strong as African or Chinese, provided just the right element of exotica to balance out the normal pallor of Caucasian skin without taking over. Her hair was darker than the usual mousy English colouring for one, and her skin came out in what she now knew was a lovely light coffee by June. Dad, being Welsh, had darker aspects to him and it was only when they saw him that people who knew nothing of Sonya's adoption looked reassured. You could see their puzzlement at Sonya's long dark tresses and tanned skin, so starkly different from her mother's pale and rather washed-out blonde looks.

Sonya pulled on her knickers and a tee-shirt and looked more closely at her face again, searching – as she had been doing more and more of late – for traces of Indianness in her bone structure. Virtually everyone had complimented her on how beautiful she looked at last night's party and Sonya had even caught herself the other day leafing through one of those glossy Indian bridal magazines in WH Smith, looking at the models wearing heavy clothes and make up and searching for some kind of commonality. There was certainly something about her oval-shaped face and high cheekbones that set her apart from the average English look but, on the other hand, not a single model in the Indian magazines had eyes like hers: their startling shade of blue was far from exotic.

Sonya had always known about her Indian blood, of course: Meg Hawkins, her first social worker, told her in as much detail as she was allowed at the time that her biological mother was of Indian origin and her biological father Anglo-Saxon. Although she knew very little further detail, Sonya had always imagined that her biological mother was the sort who lived somewhere like Southall or Tooting, a woman suppressed and cowed-down and forced into giving up her illegitimate but adored love child by a cruelly conservative family who hated the idea of a cross-cultural and mixed-race union. While she had briefly thrived on the drama of this storyline, that world seemed so alien to the cosy suburban English one in which Sonya had grown up that her curiosity (or, indeed, any desire at all to explore her roots) had been quelled many years ago.

And then she had met Chelsea. Or rather, met her again, since Chelsea had gone away to board after primary school. Sonya had always known that, like her, Chelsea had been adopted as a child, but they had never talked about this in any detail until they had bumped into each other at another old schoolmate's birthday party, just a couple of months ago. In the course of their conversation, Chelsea mentioned having traced her birth parents to a council estate in Merton, describing the sense of relief that had swept over her at knowing how lucky she had been to be adopted. For reasons she could not explain, the story had intrigued Sonya and led to her contacting the Registrar General after her own eighteenth birthday in order to have a look at her birth records. It had been a mere lark at first, some far-off niggling curiosity about her antecedents. She had even told Mum (and the adoption social worker who had provided the initial counselling) that, like Chelsea, it was only her medical history that she was interested in. But the information from the agency that had arranged her adoption had taken Sonya completely by surprise, rattling her very foundations. Who would've imagined that her biological mother was a woman who lived in India, rather than Southall or Tooting, and – here was the really astonishing bit – that she had been a student at Oxford too, the very same university to which Sonya was due to go this autumn! It was not just the coincidence of this fact, but the idea that an educated woman had chosen to give her up that had been the really shocking thing to Sonya. Her birth mother was obviously one who'd had choices, not a suffering voiceless woman at all. Sonya could still recall the acrid taste in her mouth at that discovery, the shock and sudden hurt at the knowledge that she had not been prised away from her poor and defenceless mother's care by over-zealous social workers, as she had always imagined, but had, in fact, coolly been given away. That was the really galling bit: that the woman who was her natural mother had made such a cold and deliberate choice, never turning around once to look back at the baby she had abandoned in England.

It was anger that was propelling Sonya on in this search, nothing else. Pure unadulterated anger. She had tried to reassure Mum and Dad of that fact but it seemed to bring them little comfort.

'Sonya darling!' Sonya heard her mother's high-pitched voice float up the stairs.

Sonya opened her bedroom door to shout back. 'Up here Mum. What's up?'

'Dad's on the phone. He's in town and wants to know if you need one of those multi-plug thingies for your laptop.'

'Okay, coming!' Sonya said, hastily pulling on a pair of

shorts before running down the stairs in long loping strides. It was best not to leave Mum with instructions on anything technical, Sonya thought as she took the handset off her mother. 'Hey, Dad,' she said, clicking the speaker phone on.

'Darling, you will need an adaptor to be able to use your laptop and hair dryer while you're abroad,' Richard Shaw's voice floated into the room. 'I'm in Boots and can see some in the travel section. The one I'm looking at here – a multi-way plug – says "Thailand", "Singapore" and . . . oh here, "India" among the list of countries so it should be all right. Apparently they use round-pin plugs in India.'

'I hadn't thought of all that,' Sonya said, adding, 'Thanks Dad.'

'No trouble, darling,' Richard responded lightly. 'Clever-looking thing, this, like a Rubik's cube except with buttons and pop-out pins on all the sides.'

'Hope it's not expensive,' Sonya said, conscious of the fact that her parents had already had to lay out vast amounts on her holiday.

But her father's response was typically dismissive, 'Naaaah, just a couple of quid.'

'Aw, thanks. You home for lunch, Dad?'

'Yes. Ask Mum if she wants me to pick up anything?'

Sonya looked enquiringly at her mother who was emptying the dishwasher, stacking plates in the cupboard above. Laura shook her head. 'I went to the shops yesterday, we're all stocked up,' she said.

'Think we're okay, Dad,' Sonya said into the phone. 'Mum stocked up yesterday, which must mean we have supplies to last us till Christmas.'

Richard laughed before hanging up but Sonya saw that

her mother's face was unsmiling. She had been sulking on and off like this for days. It really wasn't like her to be so consistently down in the dumps. Realizing suddenly that it was uncharitable to describe Laura's distress as 'sulks', Sonya walked across the kitchen, leaned over the open dishwasher and kissed her cheek loudly. 'Cheer up, Mum,' she said, 'I'm not going for good, am I?' To her horror, Laura's eyes filled with tears and, before Sonya knew it, her mother had turned away, shoulders shaking as she suddenly broke down. 'Oh, Mum,' Sonya said, suddenly close to tears herself, 'Don't cry, please. You've got to understand why I'm doing this. Please?'

'But I can't, darling,' Laura sobbed, tearing off a strip of kitchen paper to wipe her eyes. 'It may be stupid of me but I just can't understand why you would want to go on such a punishing quest. As it is, Dad and I would have been beside ourselves worrying about you being so far away. But somewhere like India! All that poverty and disease. And trying to find your natural mother? Why, Sonya? Have you lacked for anything at all in your life with us?'

'Of course not, Mum!' Sonya cried. 'Why would you even ask that?'

'Then *why*?' her mother asked again, her tone anguished.

'Mum, Mum,' Sonya responded, dodging around the dishwasher to take her mother's plump frame in her arms and squeeze her tightly. 'It's so hard to explain but this has nothing at all to do with Dad and you. It's just something I need to do. For me. When Chelsea told me about her search, it made utter sense, you know. Even though what she found at the end of it was a squalid council flat and a smelly old couple. It was just something she needed to know – don't you understand?'

'I'm trying,' Laura said, now looking mutinous through

her tears. 'Chelsea may have made light of it but the whole experience must have been terribly traumatic at the time. And so unnecessary, especially given what a lovely family she has. I met them at least twice back in your primary school days and, really, they couldn't have been a nicer family. Anyway, how can this search for your birth mother be nothing to do with us? I feel as if we must have failed you in some way.'

'Of course you haven't!' Sonya responded crossly. 'But let me do this, please – Chelsea's parents did. You hear all the time of people going off in search of themselves, don't you? Well, it's something like that, Mum. It's been like a missing piece in a jigsaw puzzle. Or a gap in my teeth that's annoyed and irritated me for years.'

'But you always seemed so happy, so . . . so contented,' Laura cut in, 'And we've told you everything we possibly could, everything we knew, Sonya.'

'That's exactly the point, Mum. "Everything we knew" isn't really very much. I read somewhere once that when children who've been adopted or are in foster care don't know about their biological parents, it's as if they're carrying great big holes in their heads. And what do you think they do? They allow their imaginations to rush in and fill those holes with the most impossible fantasies. At least I haven't done that. But I do need to know the truth now, Mum. And there's no one who can tell me but *her*.' By now, Sonya had released Laura and they stood looking at each other by the dishwasher, both their eyes full of angry tears.

After a pause, Laura bent to collect the dishes. 'The truth can sometimes hurt terribly,' she muttered softly. 'And that's what we're scared of. Dad and I simply couldn't bear to see you get rejected a second time over, darling.

And by the same woman. I mean, you were such a darling little baby. Only someone truly cold and heartless could have picked you up and given you away. And then walked away from you without once turning back to enquire after your welfare.'

Sonya looked down at the floor tiles. Then she picked up the tea towel and wiped the casserole dish, before kneeling to put it in its usual place. After a few minutes, she looked up at her mother and said softly, 'I know, Mum. I know you and Dad have only ever wanted to shield me from painful stuff. And you always have. But I'm eighteen now. About to leave for uni. You won't be able to protect me from everything, y'know.'

'Well, you can't blame me for trying. I might not be your biological mother but I doubt anyone will love you as much as I do,' Laura replied defiantly.

Deciding to lighten the mood, Sonya turned her expression impish. 'Perhaps I should smuggle you into Balliol and have you set up home under my bed? With a little hob and a little kettle so you can be ready with one of your famous cuppas at a moment's notice? Bet you'd like that, wouldn'tcha?' Sonya got to her feet and stuck her forefinger into Laura's soft belly, trying to make her laugh.

'Go on, you,' Laura said gruffly, pushing Sonya's hand away, but Sonya could see her mother was now smiling, albeit reluctantly. She sighed under her breath, glad that the present crisis had blown over. Growing up with a rather over-emotional mother, Sonya had grown adept at spotting a tantrum brewing from miles away and she knew it wouldn't be long before another bout of maternal tears emerged from somewhere. And who knew what her impending chat with Tim would do to Mum and to her? One bout of tears in a day was more than any girl ought to deal with, for Chrissake. Perhaps she ought to disappear into her room and do something really innocuous like read a book! Oh yeah, or do her packing . . . Dumping Tim could wait for another day or two, really.

Chapter Seven

On the evening after her dinner party, Neha mustered the energy to visit her parents. She had not seen much of them in the past week, busy as she had been, calling and reminding all her guests of their party invitations and getting the house and garden spruced up. Besides, she needed to tell her parents she was leaving for Ananda the following day. Neha hoped her mother would not ask to come along, seeing what short notice it was and how little she had enjoyed it on the one occasion Neha had taken her along. This time she really did need some space to sort out the mess in her head.

As the car pulled into the porch of her parents' small and neat Kailash Colony home – the house in which Neha had grown up – her mother's trim figure emerged from indoors, followed as usual by the family's two boxer dogs whose stubby tails started wriggling furiously at the sight of Neha's car. Neha made her habitual fuss over the dogs, both of whom adored her, before she briefly hugged her mother.

'You look tired. Too much partygoing, huh?' her mother said.

Neha shot her a glance to assess whether she was being sarcastic or disapproving but her mother's handsome face was impassive. 'Where's Papa?'

'Gone to the golf club,' came her reply. 'But he said I was to hold on to you till he got back.'

'Oh, I can't if he's going to get too late, Mama. Sharat's leaving for Lucknow and I should see him off. And I have to send some things his mother's asked for too.'

'She's always asking for "some things", isn't she?' Mrs Chaturvedi said drily. There was no mistaking the sarcasm now. Neha's mother and mother-in-law had never seen eye-to-eye, a situation caused partially by the disparity in their social standing. Neha's mother had always considered herself far more sophisticated than Sharat's, despite the fact that the latter had a great deal more money and lived in a Lucknow mansion that was five times the size of her home. Luckily such tensions had never affected Neha's own relationship with Sharat's parents which, except for the odd hiccup, had remained close and warm. 'What is it that she wants this time?' her mother pressed.

'Oh, just a couple of sets of jewellery that she left with Tribhovandas for polishing last time she was here,' Neha replied.

'Hmmm,' her mother said with a distant expression on her face, and Neha knew she was now thinking of all the jewellery that Sharat's mother still hadn't passed on to her. It was her mother's oft-expressed belief that Sharat's mother had grown too old to wear heavy jewellery. 'Women above a certain age should stick to a nice pair of solitaires and a delicate pearl string for the neck,' she sometimes said, shuddering at the massive old *ranihaars* and pendants that Sharat's mother often wore to family weddings. Furthermore, it was her firm opinion that the keys to the locker that housed the famed antique collection of the Lucknow Chaturvedis should now be rightfully handed to the family's only daughter-in-law, which of course was Neha. For her part, Neha had always resisted this notion, not merely because she had plenty of jewellery already – both her own as well as pieces bought for her by Sharat over the years – but also because she considered it extremely unbecoming to squabble over things as inconsequential as keys to bank lockers. Neha, who was far more interested in contemporary art, preferred to spend her money on paintings and artefacts to furnish her elegant home with, rather than squandering it away on jewellery she hardly ever wore. She decided to change the subject quickly before her mother embarked on the habitual harangue.

'Our party went off very well,' Neha remarked, realizing that her mother had forgotten all about it, even though she had mentioned it a few times in the past few weeks.

'Oh yes. You had your party. Who came?'

'Well, the usual crowd mostly. One starts running out of different people to call in a place like Delhi! But the Home Minister was there this time. And spoke very positively to Sharat about his chances of getting a seat in the next election.'

'Achcha? Where will it be, his seat?' her mother exclaimed, her face finally losing its dissatisfied expression. Neha smiled. Perhaps Sharat's political prospects would finally provide common ground between her parents and in-laws! She tried to imagine all of them together in a campaigning vehicle before hastily dismissing the thought.

'Well, Sharat's hoping for one of the South Delhi constituencies, naturally. But everyone wants those and they don't usually get given to political novices. At this stage, he'll take what he gets.'

'That is very wise,' her mother said, adding grudgingly, 'Luckily, however unsophisticated his mother may be, she has somehow brought up a most sensible boy.'

Neha did not have to think up a response to that as the tea service made a timely arrival, brought out by Bahadur, who had worked with her parents since she was a child. Neha enquired after the old cook's family back in Nepal before turning her attention back to the dogs who had perked up at the sight of food. The trolley was elaborately laid out with bone china quarter plates and lace-edged linen serviettes, as was customary in her mother's house, and, with the fuss of pouring and serving, the conversation turned to more general matters.

Neha, thinking again about the arrival of the letter from England, realized suddenly why she had never got around to confiding in her mother, even as a nineteen-year-old. She looked at her mother's prim figure and pursed lips as she poured the tea and realized, with a suddenly very heavy feeling, how little her mother had changed over the years. Neha knew there was little point in looking for help and sympathy now, all these years down the line and with so much more to lose. It would be counterproductive and, besides, given her parents' age, Neha could not discount what the shock of discovering they had a secret grand-daughter could do to them. No, she would have to face this by herself. And face it as bravely as she could. Blinking back a sudden rush of tears, Neha bent over to feed two very excited boxers an unexpected bounty of chocolate cake.

Swiftly gathering herself together, Neha took the cup of tea her mother was holding out. 'Shall I call Papa and see where he's got to?' she asked.

Her mother glanced at her wristwatch. 'Hmm, by now he should have left the greens. Yes, call him if you're short of time.'

Neha flipped her phone open and clicked on her father's

name. '*Haanji*, Papa, where are you? I'm at Kailash Colony, having tea with Mama. Okay, good, I'll wait.' She slid the phone back into its case and picked up her tea cup again. 'He's not far, just at the Moolchand flyover,' she said.

Neha talked to her mother about the usual things, her mother filling her in on the family gossip regarding a cousin's acrimonious divorce before moving on to the difficulty she was having in finding a good driver and her own health problems. Their subjects of conversation never changed very much, Neha having long trained herself to keep things innocuous. When her father arrived, she got up to give him a relieved hug. Her relationship with her genial father had always been much warmer but, with retirement, he too had developed a general complaining air that left little room for genuine communication.

'How was the golf, Papa?'

'Good, *beta*, good,' he responded, sinking into a chair with a groan and taking the cup of tea his wife was offering him. 'And how are things with you and Sharat? Did your party go well?' he enquired.

'Sharat's going to get a South Delhi seat,' Neha's mother cut in.

'He hopes he'll get it, Mama,' Neha clarified. 'The Minister was only promising to talk to the PM. Nothing *pukka* yet.'

'That's what this country needs,' her father said, 'more educated and upstanding people like Sharat coming into politics. That's the only way we can get all the *goonda* elements out. Look at the way they behave in Parliament – did you see those scenes on TV yesterday? Throwing chappals and chairs at the Speaker – ruddy shameful! Can you imagine any other Parliament in the world allowing such a thing? The whole lot of them should be sacked, I say.'

The conversation stayed in that vein and, an hour later, returning home from her parents' house, Neha felt exhausted. Increasingly, her communication with her parents was ceasing to be meaningful, their conversations skimming only the surfaces of their real feelings. But how could she blame them? It was she who had first introduced lies into their relationship.

'The course was too tough for me, Mama, I just could not cope' . . . 'I was homesick and . . . and there was a gang of girls that was bullying me . . . yes, bullying me . . . no, I don't want to go into all that . . . leave me alone, please!'

Tears, recriminations, it went on for weeks, all through the summer holidays, Mama and Papa obviously hoping that I would change my mind by the time term was due to start again. But I held out – I had no choice – and, gradually, the nagging stopped. Mama had scoffed at all my excuses, even as I wept in her arms. What had really hurt, though, was that even if there were moments when Mama perhaps doubted the veracity of my story, she never once stopped to ask the actual reason for my hasty return home. She had never really been able to cope with strong emotion. Everything in her world needed to be neat and immaculate: not just inanimate things like her home and its furnishings but her marriage, her daughter's prospects, her very emotions. But, they had to relent finally . . .

The literature department at Lady Shri Ram College was good, taking me into their second year on the basis of my having spent a year at Oxford. They were impressed, clearly, and mystified at my having chosen to come back. But they too bought my story about having been bullied. 'Great Britain is very racist, I am told,' the Head of Department said, looking sympathetic. 'It was in fact so bad, she actually fell sick,' my father said, waving his arm in my direction, where I sat huddled on a metal chair. The weight I had lost, both during and after my pregnancy, bore that out. I was all skin and bones then and the principal needed no more persuasion. I could finally say goodbye to my Oxford dream.

Neha looked out of the window of her car, not seeing the Delhi traffic or the crowds or the late September sunshine falling on the windscreen. She was far away, back in her college days, remembering how she had kept her head down and completed both her BA and MA, topping Delhi University in her final year. It had been no effort, immersed as she had been in her books at that time. Getting the gold medal had led to an offer to teach in the faculty but Neha turned it down, having by then met Sharat through Ramu Uncle, a family friend. Sharat and she had met only a couple of times before the formal marriage proposal came – it was all very handy, given that they were both Chaturvedis with all kinds of family ties that went back generations. Neha's parents were over-joyed and there was no reason to let them down again. It was, after all, what Ramu Uncle described as 'a most advantageous match'.

She now looked down at her beringed fingers, the stones in the gold bands catching the sun and sending little pinpricks of light dancing around the plush leather interior of the car. Despite generally shying away from jewellery, Neha was sentimental about these three rings and almost never took them off; her wedding and engagement rings and the cluster of diamonds that Sharat had given her on their tenth wedding anniversary. He was a perfect husband – mild mannered and courteous and generous with his wealth – and Neha was well aware of how many friends and cousins envied her her good fortune. Neha herself felt fortunate that, after all her problems at university, she had finally found someone like Sharat – her rock.

And so it was that, with all the charmed events that had gradually come after her return from England, Neha had eventually given her parents little cause for complaint. They now probably barely even remembered that Oxford dream they had all once shared. The topic hardly ever came up. It would be ridiculous indeed to harp on about that, given how Neha's life had eventually turned out. Oh yes, today, seeing Neha return to her Prithviraj Road home in a gleaming Mercedes car, even Mama would be forced to admit that – apart from not having borne a child so far – her daughter's life was pretty immaculate too.

Chapter Eight

In the kitchen of the Shaw household, Laura gave her special chicken broth a final stir before taking out a stack of soup bowls from the cupboard. Richard wandered in, inhaling appreciatively. 'Tim's upstairs, I take it,' he said, cocking a brow at the fourth place setting on the kitchen table.

'They've been up there all afternoon,' Laura responded, starting to ladle the broth into bowls. 'Probably getting Sonya's suitcase packed. Y'know, I'd have been so much happier if Tim had been going along too. The thought of two girls wandering around on their own in India worries me terribly . . .'

'Wonder why he didn't offer,' Richard said, nibbling on a breadstick.

'Tim? Oh, I don't think he was even given a chance. Sonya's reaction to that suggestion was even stronger than when I asked if you could go along. Remember how indignant she was then?'

'Well, I could see why she didn't want me trailing after her and Stel, cramping their style. But Tim would have been a nice halfway compromise. Most girls *want* to go off on holiday with their boyfriends, don't they?' Richard's face wore a genuinely baffled expression.

Laura sighed, 'I think we both know that our Sonya just isn't like "most girls". Poor ol' Tim . . . from what I can tell, she's been giving him quite the brush-off lately.'

'Oh?'

Laura smiled as she brought the tray to the table. Despite being one of the most sensitive souls she knew, Richard tended not to notice things until they were right under his nose or carefully pointed out to him. 'It's a shame really,' she explained. 'Tim's such a nice lad. But Sonya was saying the other day that she thinks she's outgrown him. *Outgrown* him – I ask you!'

Richard shook his head and took a steaming bowl off the tray that Laura was holding. 'What is it with these kids? We never even imagined we had the option of outgrowing each other, did we, darling?'

Laura put the tray down and ruffled her husband's thinning hair, reaching out to pat the swell of his belly with her other hand. 'Hmmm, maybe you outgrew me just a little bit around here, chuck,' she joked. Before he could think of a retort, she left the kitchen to call up the stairs. 'Sonya, supper!'

Sonya's distant 'Coming!' floated down as Laura returned to the table. 'They're not like we were, today's kids,' Laura continued, sitting down. 'So much more hard-nosed about everything.'

Richard, who always tended to be more forgiving in his opinions, responded in his usual mild fashion. 'I don't know if I'd call it hard-nosed or being pragmatic. And that may not necessarily be a bad thing . . .'

They stopped talking as footsteps came thumping down the stairs and the subject of their conversation flounced in, boyfriend in tow. 'Ah, come on in, you two, soup's going cold,' Richard welcomed them cheerily.

'Tim's not staying,' Sonya said, sitting down and pulling a bowl towards herself.

'Oh dear, whyever not? I've made plenty,' Laura cried.

Tim opened his mouth to respond but Sonya spoke first. 'His mum wants him home for supper because she's going out and Chloe needs babysitting.' Tim nodded dolefully by way of confirmation while Sonya sprinkled garlic croutons from a packet into her soup.

'Quick bowl of soup before you go, old chap?' Richard asked, ignoring the glare Sonya threw at him.

Tim shot a look at Sonya and then shuffled his feet around before responding hesitantly. 'It's awfully kind of you, Mr Shaw. Oh, and Mrs Shaw, of course. I really do so enjoy your food. But I really have to be off. My mother will be waiting . . . she has aerobics classes on Thursday nights, you see . . .'

'Ah, one can't be late for one's aerobics,' Richard said, getting up to fetch himself a second helping of soup from the tureen.

'It's sweet of you, Tim, to be taking care of your baby sister,' Laura said, adding, 'if I'd known you had to be home, I'd have served supper earlier. It would have been no effort . . .'

'Well, he's already late and you'll make him even later if you don't let him go now,' Sonya said, blowing at the liquid in her soup spoon.

'Yes, better be off,' Tim said, straightening up. He bowed in one direction and then the other as though in royal company while mumbling, 'Good night, Mr Shaw, good night, Mrs Shaw . . . See ya, Sonya . . .' He threw a last pleading look at Sonya who waved vaguely in his direction before he ambled reluctantly out of the room.

Laura cocked her head at the door, frowning at Sonya. 'Do go and see him off, darling,' she hissed.

Richard nodded in agreement. 'Yes, it's the least you can do, sweetheart.'

Sonya rolled her eyes upwards and slurped her soup before yelling loudly, 'Bye Tim, mind how you go!' But the sound of the front door closing indicated that Tim had already left without hearing her.

Laura sighed deeply. Sonya had been a lovely child and they had sailed through her adolescent years without any of the tantrums and rebellion Laura had heard terrifying tales of from various exhausted friends with teenage children. But something had got into Sonya lately and Laura couldn't help blaming the whole Adoption Register thing, and especially that Chelsea who had first told Sonya about it. It was too late to wish it away now, as Richard constantly reminded her, but Laura would have done anything to turn the hands of the clock back to before that horrid day on which Sonya had come back from a party talking about wanting to look for her birth mother.

Laura glanced now at her beautiful adopted daughter who was slurping down her soup apparently without a care in the world. What did she know of the pain that Laura and Richard had gone through, first with all the miscarriages they had suffered, and then at the hands of Social Services while they were being screened as potential adopters? Each step in that tortuous process had felt like a gargantuan hurdle, all that tedious form-filling and those interviews, people wandering about their home, sticking their noses into everything and asking awkward questions. From what Laura could remember, virtually every single social worker they had come in contact with had been insensitive to the point of rudeness during the years it had taken them to be assessed. There had even been one who had suggested that Laura wanted to adopt a child only to satisfy her own emotional neediness! 'Your need to be needed,' the smug cow had said, smirking! But everything – yes, *all* of that – had seemed worthwhile when they had finally got their dream child.

Laura still carried that first sight of Sonya close to her heart, like a precious faded photograph. She had been less than a month old when the Shaws were first told about her. Social Services had not considered them ideal at first, the child being of mixed race. But, as the right ethnic mix had not been on offer amongst the many waiting couples on the agency's adoption lists, Laura and Richard had eventually been offered Sonya, though only on a conditional basis at first. There were still many post-placement assessments to be conducted, they were warned. But, the minute Laura had been handed the tiny swaddled bundle, she had known without a doubt that this child had been meant all along to be hers. Laura had looked down at the most beautiful baby she had ever seen; blue eyes like enormous cornflowers in her tiny face and a shock of the blackest hair Laura had ever seen on a baby. The foster mother had handed her a small bottle of milk and Sonya, eagerly taking the teat into her rosebud mouth, had drunk deeply and trustingly, her little peachy cheeks working in and out as she sucked. Holding baby and bottle, Laura had felt a wellspring of emotion so deep it was as though her entire inner self was washed through with it, reviving her spirits and reorganizing her whole life in that one moment. And Sonya, as though sensing that love, had finished all the milk and then snuggled into the crook of her adoptive mother's arm with a little sigh before falling into a sound sleep.

Oh, how she and Richard had poured all they had into bringing Sonya up! Laura had swiftly given up her job as a classroom assistant ('It never was going to be a proper career, was it?' she explained to anyone who asked) and Richard took to working twice as hard to climb the ladder in the Planning Department of Bromley Council so that their child would want for nothing. And that was exactly what they had done: given Sonya everything that was within their reach, stretching themselves to achieve ballet lessons and school trips and even horse riding when Sonya had read *Sea Biscuit* and briefly wanted to become an equestrienne. And now, that adored child was embarking on a search for the woman who had so heartlessly abandoned her. Going as far as India to seek her out! It was madness, in Laura's view; nothing less. Sonya's birth mother had even refused to breast-feed the child, from what the social worker had told them at the time. Given all that they knew, Sonya's decision to seek the woman out was confusing and hurtful and Laura, looking at Sonya and Richard josh around the soup tureen in her kitchen pretending to fight over the last dregs of soup, felt a sudden clutch of terror at what might lie ahead.

Chapter Nine

It was only when she was two hundred kilometres outside Delhi that Neha started to feel a bit calmer about her situation. Ananda never failed to dispel the worst case of the blues. Neha generally preferred going to the spa by train, but no tickets had been available at such short notice and so she had asked her chauffeur to take the new Fortuner which would not be required while Sharat was in Lucknow. The road up to Meerut had been fraught, as always, with manic drivers who seemed to have fingers glued to their horns. But after crossing into forest land, the drive turned all winding and leafy, and in the distance the foothills of the Himalayas were rising in soft green folds. Neha tried to relax, leaning back on the capacious seat and watching the last rays of sunshine dipping in and out between the trees.

Dusk was falling by the time they got to Ananda. As the tall metal gates were opened up by a set of guards, Neha looked up at the old palace that was glowing orange in the light of the setting sun. It looked like the family who lived in the palace was not in residence; the windows were all shut and barred and only a couple of rooms on the ground floor were gleaming dimly with light. Neha was grateful as she would have been expected to make her routine social call, had the Thakurs been around. Not that she normally minded – her parents had been friendly with the family for years and she was particularly fond of Urmila Rani, the ninety-year-old matriarch who had been her grandmother's classmate at Loreto Convent in Calcutta – but today Neha had come to Ananda with the specific purpose of shutting out the noise and confusion of everything around her. She really could not have coped with a social call.

'Running away?' Jasmeet had enquired when Neha called her fifty kilometers outside Delhi, on suddenly remembering that she had forgotten to return Jasmeet's serving dishes before leaving in the morning.

'Of course not! Why would I be running away? Sharat's in Lucknow,' Neha had responded hotly, lapsing into embarrassed silence when Jasmeet clarified what she had meant.

'Running away from the heat, I meant, stupid. It's still thirty-eight degrees. And we are nearly into October, imagine! But, bloody hell – Ananda! You could have told me, I might have also wanted to come along, Neha!'

'You mentioned this was a busy time for you . . .' Neha muttered before trailing off. Much as she adored her old schoolmate, the company of someone as boisterous as Jasmeet would have been unbearable at this time.

'Busy is too right, *yaar*,' Jasmeet said. 'God I'm so fucking busy it's not funny. Dinner party at the Swedish Embassy tonight, that bloody two *crore* Walia wedding next week. I think I'm going mad. And now you've got my best serving dishes, dammit!'

'Oh, sorry, Jas!' Neha said. 'Listen, I'll call Ram Singh straight away and ask him to have them sent with Sharat's driver. He should be free, seeing that Sharat's in Lucknow.'

'Humph!' Jasmeet grumbled, adding, 'What's gotten into you anyway? It's not at all like you to be forgetful.'

'I know, I know. I'm so sorry. What can I say . . . it was just so inconsiderate of me, Jasmeet darling. Forgive me? Please?'

'Oh okay, then. You are one of my best clients after all,' Jasmeet responded cheekily and before Neha could think of a retort, she hung up in typically abrupt fashion, with a grunt.

Neha's car was soon pulling into the vast colonnaded porch at the reception building. After she had disembarked, a pair of girls stepped forward with flower garlands and trays of sandalwood and vermilion. The *aarti* ceremony done, Neha walked into the hush of the dark cool building and sank into a sofa with a sigh. There was never a better place in which to get away from it all than Ananda, in her opinion. The very air up here, suffused with the fragrance of pine needles and herbs, was restorative. Merely breathing it in was part of the healing process, she believed. Over the years Neha had recommended the mountain spa to many friends who had turned to her in moments of crisis, but this was perhaps the first time she herself had needed to come here for reasons more compelling than the mere lure of massages. She counted on her fingers. This was probably her tenth visit, the first time being many years ago when Sharat and she had driven up from Delhi with a small group of friends. Neha smiled, remembering one conversation.

'It's the bloody Gulag over here! Uniforms and set meal times and prison walls!'

'Come on, Sharat, don't exaggerate!'

'I'm not! It's incredible that people pay to be tortured in this way! And the yoga, that's the other thing – setting alarms

for five in the morning so that you can shiver on a mountain top while some torturer twists your body into impossible positions. I'm in agony everywhere today. Look, see here, even my shoulder blades are all tensed up!'

Sharat had roundly declared the experience not one he would ever want to repeat. But, for Neha on that occasion, it was as if she had reached paradise. Now a veteran of ten visits, she knew the routine well. She smiled at the girl who was bringing her the welcome drink of cold herb tea and downed it in one gulp.

'Oh god, already seven pm!' she said, glancing at her watch as she got up. 'I think I should have something light to eat and then get to bed early. Can't miss morning yoga! There's something so fabulous about watching the sun rise from behind the mountains while doing pranayama. How we Delhi wallahs ever try to practise yoga inside air-conditioned closed rooms, I don't know.'

The girl smiled. 'Did you wish to see the schedule of treatments that have been lined up for your week, Mrs Chaturvedi? You may want to change something?'

'No, I'll do all that tomorrow at the spa reception,' Neha replied, nodding at the two staff members before she left the building.

Neha took the familiar path down to the block that housed the rooms, going past the marble pergola where her yoga lessons were sometimes conducted, and cocked her head to listen out for the pretty sound of the running rill of water that lay behind it. The sun had long faded from the peaks of the surrounding mountains, which were now shrouded in a hazy purple mist. The spa too had shut down for the night, as had the swimming pool, which was now gently rippling, black and pristine. But the cluster of buildings that housed Ananda's accommodation was well lit and Neha made for it, knowing that her suitcase would by now be unpacked, her things already neatly laid out in the cupboards.

She entered the room she was always given – twenty-seven – and caught her breath in the way she could never help whenever she saw the huge uncurtained window of the luxurious bathroom. All the windows on this side of the building overlooked the Rishikesh valley beneath, which, as evening fell, became a sparse sprinkling of lights. Without even going into the bedroom, Neha ran herself a warm bath using some of Ananda's famed bath salts. She would lie in it for an hour at least and admire the way the stars melded seamlessly into the lights scattering the valley below. She would try not to remember Sonya's letter. Or let it worry her, despite the veiled threat. For threat it certainly was, much as Neha wanted to imagine otherwise. The tone of the letter was unmistakably cold and purposeful. And who could blame the child, given what she had done to her? There had been no point even contemplating a reply . . . what could she possibly say that would not upset the girl even more?

Neha undressed, leaving a scattering of clothes on the floor as she climbed with relief into the fragrant bath water. What Sonya had not mentioned, Neha realized as she sank into the tub, was when exactly she was coming to India. The envelope had an English stamp and postmark but it was always possible that the sender had overtaken it on its journey and, in that case, perhaps she was already here in the country! Surely Sonya wouldn't have wanted to give her too much prior notice, Neha considered, for that would only allow her to escape. Exactly as she had done, in fact. It was with some relief that Neha realized that Sonya would not find her here in the mountains.

That was for sure. Ananda's privacy rules were stringent and, apart from Sharat, their parents and Jasmeet, no one else knew where she was this week. But what if . . . an awful thought suddenly came to Neha, making her shoot up into a sitting position in the bathtub . . . what if Sonya turned up at the Delhi house while she was here at Ananda! Sharat would be back from Lucknow by Tuesday and might well be at home if Sonya turned up there. That was the address the girl had used, after all. Neha sank back into the bath and allowed the soapy water to close over her head. How utterly devastating if Sharat were to find out everything by actually meeting Sonya. Neha simply could not bear the thought of his hurt. How betrayed he would feel to know that his adored wife had been lying consistently to him all throughout their marriage! Why, she had even refused to see an obstetrician to investigate their childlessness, for fear that medical tests would reveal a previous pregnancy.

'We don't need to know what the reasons are, it will just cause tensions between us, Sharat.'

'Why should it . . . perhaps one of these tests will reveal a problem that can be solved or treated, Neha . . .'

'And, if it's something untreatable, won't it just lie there between us, forming silences and barriers? We just need to relax and enjoy each other and someday I'm sure I'll get pregnant, just like that.'

'You could be right, darling, Raju Chacha and Asha Chachi were married years before Shashi was born. Even my parents had been married five years before I emerged. Maybe we're just a bit slow in my family!' Sharat had laughed.

'And, you know, now that we've been married seven years,

there's a part of me that feels we're so happy we don't need children, Sharat. I'm contented merely to be married to you . . . please tell me it's the same for you?'

All those lies . . . how much lower could one fall? Neha came up from the water again, gasping for breath, as all those distant conversations ran furiously through her head. Tears pushed at the back of her eyes as she thought of how she would willingly drown herself right here in this bathtub if she only had the courage. That would solve her problem of facing Sharat, and facing the daughter she had given away. She wanted to retch, the thoughts racing through her head, churning her stomach. Perhaps she could slit her wrists. She had seen it in a movie recently . . . an American film about troubled teenagers, from what she could recall . . . *The Rules of Attraction*, that was it. Like that poor young girl in it, all she had to do was slice a blade over her wrists, lean back in the bathtub and allow the water to slowly bleed the life out of her. It was such a tempting thought . . . if only she could find a blade in her toilet kit . . . If she searched hard enough, perhaps she would find one belonging to Sharat . . .

Neha scrambled out of the bath and lunged for her toilet kit. Its contents scattered all over the floor and she fell to her knees, searching frantically among the bottles and brushes for a blade . . . something, anything, even a pair of nail scissors might do it . . .

Chapter Ten

Sonya glowered at Tim from her cross-legged perch on the rusty old merry-go-round. 'You don't understand at all, Tim,' she said. She knew she ought to stop herself from saying any more for she would only be sharp-tongued and hurtful, given her current frame of mind. But Tim's negativity about her Indian trip was now really starting to annoy. First he had moaned about how she was going to be away during their last couple of weeks together before departing for uni, and now he had just said it was plain silly to go off in search of an identity when she ought to be proud of the one she already had! Perhaps he had not meant it to sound the way it did but Sonya thought it sheer cheek on Tim's part to be so presumptuous. She could not stop herself from snapping back. 'Well, it's all very well for you, isn't it?' By now she was so cross, there was no curbing her sharp tongue. 'You, with your perfect 2.4 family and identity.'

Tim stopped swinging himself as he went instantly pink around the collar of his sweatshirt. He looked at Sonya with that kicked-puppy expression she loathed. It was uncharitable of her perhaps but she also couldn't help noticing the gaucheness with which his long legs were bent to accommodate his lanky frame on the child-sized swing. 'I don't know what you mean, Sonya,' he said, mounting a feeble defence. My parents are divorced, remember?'

'Yeah, right,' Sonya said, determined to be one up on the suffering scale. 'Like that comes anywhere near finding out that you were given away at birth.'

'Well, I was thirteen when they divorced . . . hardly the best time for a lad to have to cope with warring parents.'

Sonya took a deep breath and shifted to a swing next to the one Tim was sitting on. It was easier not to be facing him while having such an awkward and – she had to admit – ludicrous conversation. She looked across the playing fields and tried to make her voice kinder. 'Look, Tim, I'm not going to start drawing up a list of who-suffered-what. I don't doubt it was hard for you when your parents split up but you've had five years to get over it. However, what I'm going through is here and now. And, no, I'm not happy about making my poor parents miserable. And, yes, I am very scared of what I'll find at the other end. But it's something I've just got to do.'

'I've never suggested you shouldn't, Sonya. But don't shut me out like this. For days now you've treated me like I'm a stranger.'

'Don't exaggerate.'

'I'm not! Stranger at best, enemy most other times.'

'Fucking hell, now you *are* exaggerating!'

Tim looked down at his shoes while Sonya scowled at the football nets in the distance. She had anticipated a fractious dialogue, which was partially why she had asked to meet Tim at the children's park that lay at the edge of the old school playground, halfway between both their houses. Her house would have been about the worst place in which to have a row. It was best not to further vex her mum with knowledge of an untimely split; who knew what she would read into that when she was already so convinced her daughter was upping and leaving forever? And Sonya really, *really* did not need her parents trying to patch things up between Tim and her on the eve of her departure for India.

The silence between them hung heavy. Not much happened in Orpington on a Sunday evening and this playground was generally a favourite haunt of what Richard called 'the town's yoof'. However, no one else was around today on this September afternoon and Sonya guessed they were either thronging the town's pubs, given the warm evening it had become, or lining up outside the cinema as Estella was doing tonight. Cigarette butts and empty cans of drink littered the ground beneath their feet and the smell of barbecuing meat was blowing in from some nearby back garden. Sonya kicked at a crisp packet that was stubbornly blowing around her ankles, everything irritated her these days.

Sonya got up suddenly, causing the wooden swing to bang the backs of her knees. Blinking back the pain, she stopped herself from crying out. The last thing she wanted was fake, solicitous concern from Tim! What she wanted was a swift exit because another few minutes of Tim's company was doubtless going to make her scream. This was the moment to say it and Sonya forced the words out of her mouth, the sentences coming rushing out in a sudden torrent running one into another. 'I'm sorry, Tim. It's been brewing for days but I just haven't had the chance to tell you . . . I don't think I want to be your girlfriend any more. Please don't think I haven't thought about it a lot. After all, we're such old mates. But it's just not working, is it? And I thought it fairer to tell you before I go to India. Rather than have you waiting for me and maybe even running up a huge phone bill while I'm there. Anyway, we're off to far-apart unis so the chances of us being able to make this work are pretty remote anyway, aren't they?' Sonya finally looked at Tim, scared of what she would find. She really, *really* did not want to have to deal with another bout of tears. Not after Mum's histrionics and even Dad being unnaturally grouchy these days. But Tim wasn't crying, as she'd half anticipated. Instead, he was sitting silently, still swinging himself gently, almost as though he had not heard her at all.

'Tim?' Sonya said tentatively. But, no, he was still silent. Well, what could be more exasperating than that – a dumbass boyfriend who didn't even know he was being dumped when it was slapping him right in the face? There was no point hanging around waiting for Tim to come up with some kind of sensible rejoinder. He could always call her when he did think of something to say!

Without another word and with the backs of her legs still stinging, Sonya turned and walked out of the playground. From across the road, she could see a number two bus approaching and so she started to run. Waving her arms desperately, she got it to halt and raced towards it, hoping desperately that Tim wasn't following her. Once she had clambered aboard and the electric doors had creaked shut, Sonya looked back at the playground and saw that, far from following her, Tim was still sitting where she'd left him, his shoulders slumped as he moved his legs listlessly back and forth like an automaton. Suddenly she felt oddly annoyed that he *hadn't* followed her; which was, of course, being what Mum called 'plain cussed'.

Spotting an empty window seat, Sonya sat down with

a thump and looked back at the playground. Weirdly, she couldn't help feeling a bit sorry for Tim too, but as the bus started to move he did not as much as look up in her direction. Even from this distance and through the grimy bus window, she could see that he wore a defeated air. Had she really been that mean to him? Sonya forced herself not to melt and call Tim to apologize. It was all so complicated and her head felt so very messed up. All she knew was that she was off tomorrow to the kind of places and experiences that Tim would not in a million years be able to comprehend, and she was damned if she was going to have her relationship with him complicate her life any more than it already had.

Chapter Eleven

When the floor was icy cold, and Neha's body had started to ache with stiffness, she finally dragged herself up. She was still naked, the water from her untowelled body having long dried, but she found a thick white bathrobe hanging behind the bathroom door and pulled it on. Hardly aware that she was stepping all over the strewn contents of her toilet kit, she slowly made her way to the bed. She collapsed onto the mattress, unaware of how long she had lain on the bathroom floor, weeping uncontrollably at not being able to find a blade. The storm over, she now felt spent, her body numb and her tears all dried up.

She lay silently on top of the blanket, looking at nothing and feeling nothing. Maybe she did not need to return to Delhi at all. Neha wondered blankly if she could just head off from Ananda – into the distant mountains perhaps, where nobody would know her, where she could start all over again . . . Or maybe she could just stay forever in this room, cocooned in the silent dark. Here she would not need to pretend happiness or contentment, those qualities everyone was convinced she fully possessed. Here she could cry if she wanted, or lie silently, or even rant and rave at the injustices of life. No one would hear her at all, as the rooms were built to ensure complete quiet and privacy. She need never turn that doorknob that led to the world ever again . . .

The lights in the room had not been turned on since she had arrived and, down in the valley below, the lights of Rishikesh too had dimmed to virtual darkness. Neha did not know what time it was. She was all by herself in this dark void.

How foolish it had been to imagine that her past would not catch up on her. Or that there could be no punishment for a mother who had given up her child. Neha saw, for the hundredth time since receiving the letter, the moment she had done it . . . picked up the small mewling bundle that had lain on her lap to hand her over to the waiting social worker.

'She'll go first to a foster home,' the social worker with the kindly face said. 'The foster mum is a very experienced carer – a woman now in her sixties – and she will look after her until she's old enough to be handed over to the adoptive parents. Don't cry, my dear child, what you're doing is brave and unselfish. And just think of those desperate couples waiting for years to get a baby like her. How overjoyed one of them will soon be. And it'll all be due to you. Yes, you. Your baby will have a lovely life where you're sending her, believe me.'

Neha had believed her because she had no option. She had hung on to that assurance, examining it every which way in years to come, never sure whether it was genuinely true or said merely to comfort her. Now, soon, that question would be answered. When her grown daughter stood before her and told her directly whether she had done the right thing by her or not. Except that Neha did not think she had the strength to bear the accusations that she knew would come.

Chapter Twelve

Laura watched Sonya throw a handful of cotton bras into her suitcase. 'It will be bloody warm,' Sonya smiled, adding cheekily, 'I can see us being braless most of the time. Commando style even, if it gets too bad.'

Laura knew her daughter was only teasing and so she ignored her, even though the thought of Sonya wandering around India without any underwear on was deeply distressing. Laura herself had only travelled as far as the Canary Islands – visiting Tenerife with Richard after one of their miscarriages and Lanzarote more recently, when Sonya was about thirteen. Laura had noticed the topless sunbathers on Lanzarote's beaches but, of course, it would never have even crossed her mind to follow suit. She was far too conservative for that kind of exhibitionist nonsense. 'Why on earth people want to behave in public as though they're in their own bathrooms beats me,' she had said to Richard.

On that holiday, fed up with eating burgers and fries for three days on the trot, Sonya had scornfully accused her mother of behaving like a 'pleb', but Laura had not even understood what that meant and suspected that Sonya didn't either. It was one of those rare occasions on which Richard had got very cross with Sonya, grounding her inside their holiday apartment for a whole day and refusing to speak to her until she had apologized to her mother. That, Laura remembered, was the first time she had openly stated her fears to Richard about Sonya having perhaps inherited traits that they had absolutely no control over. They had been sharing a bottle of Rioja on the balcony of their apartment while Sonya was sulking behind the closed door to her room. 'Who knows, darling,' Richard had replied in his usual calm fashion, 'after all, no one's ever come up with conclusive evidence in the whole nature versus nurture debate, have they? We'll just have to wait and see. And you have to admit that, by and large, she's a lovely lass . . .'

But it was a thought that had come to Laura more and more often as Sonya had grown. There were things about the child . . . curious little quirks and habits . . . the haughty way in which she held her head sometimes, or the sharp caustic cleverness with which she spoke, that had clearly come from somewhere else. There had been Christmases when, with both families gathered around, Laura had looked at Sonya and observed with sudden shock how unlike all of them she was. And this despite the fact that she had been a mere babe-in-arms when they had got her.

Sitting now in Sonya's bay window and folding the day's laundry, Laura watched Sonya unwind her long legs to get up off the floor and stride across to the wardrobe at the other end of the room. Wearing quantities of grey-blue kohl around her eyes and a whole collection of silver bracelets jangling on her arms, Sonya looked like some exotic creature who belonged in the pages of a glamour magazine and not this twee little suburban semi-detached in which she had grown up.

Laura shook out a pair of leggings before folding them on her lap. She added them to the neat pile growing next to her and sighed. There was only so much moulding and shaping one could do given a headstrong creature like Sonya, she thought, her heart awash with despondency. Then, glancing at the laden bookshelves above Sonya's desk, Laura forced herself to feel more cheerful. Not all the differences between them were bad. After all, Sonya's admission to Oxford was a first in both their families and a cause for immense pride. Laura could count her relatives that had gone to university on the fingers of one hand, let alone any of them getting somewhere as grand as Oxford! What was worrying, however, was that what Laura had come to think of as Sonya's 'otherness' was growing more marked as she got older and now, with this trip to India, Laura genuinely feared she might lose her altogether.

She got up from the bay window and picked up the stack of clothes. 'Which of these tee-shirts did you want to take with you, darling?' she asked the top of her daughter's head.

Sonya looked up from where she was kneeling on the floor and said, 'Oh ta, Mum. Hmm, think I'll take just the plain white and perhaps that grey Quicksilver one. Gotta stay cool, but white will be such a bother to keep clean while travelling.'

'Well, I've thrown a small tube of Vanish in among your toiletries,' Laura said, 'you could always do a bit of hand-washing in your hotel room.'

'You think of everything, Mummy,' Sonya replied, leaping

up to throw her arms dramatically around her mother and swing her off her feet. 'What on earth am I going to do without you, huh?'

Laura struggled, smiling. That was the other thing about Sonya, her exuberant brand of love that was so . . . so *un-English*, if Laura was to be honest with herself. There was no other way to describe it. It was nothing like Richard's quiet steadiness or her own brand of rather uncertain and diffident love. Sonya – beautiful and wilful and charming – was like a Bollywood diva. And this Laura knew without having seen a single Bollywood film in her life!

The following morning, Laura stood next to Richard at the bottom of their drive, watching Sonya load her suitcase into the boot of Clive Wentworth's battered old four-wheel drive. Both girls were chattering excitedly and Laura tried to keep the smile fixed on her face so as not to spoil their big moment. It was, after all, the very first time away from home for both of them, if one didn't count the handful of short school trips they had been on, none further away than Europe. 'A practice run for uni and then the great wide world,' Sonya had said of this trip and she was right. In just over a month's time, she would be off anyway, leaving home with more than just a holiday suitcase and quite probably for good. Despite all the mental steeling, it was a heartbreaking thought to Laura.

Sonya was giving Richard one of her big bear hugs now and Laura braced her shoulders, instructing herself sternly not to cry. When Sonya leaned over to give her a hug and kiss, Laura amazed herself with her capacity to stay calm and cheerful. She now used her most upbeat voice to say,

'You go have a blast, hon. But call us whenever you can, okay? We'll miss you . . .' Oddly enough, it was Sonya who had tears glistening in her eyes as she pulled away from her mother's hug and leapt into the back seat of the Wentworths' car to be driven away.

Chapter Thirteen

Neha sat up, unsure of how many hours had passed since she had stumbled from the bathroom and onto the bed. Her mouth was parched and the darkness felt suffocating, as though it was reaching into her throat trying to choke her. She reached out for the switches beside the headboard and blinked her smarting eyes as the room flooded with light. She needed to distract herself otherwise her thoughts were going to drive her crazy. Perhaps she ought to call room service and get something to eat as her stomach was rumbling terribly. But, despite her hunger, the thought of food made her feel sick. Neha looked around her for something, anything that she could read. She had not bothered to bring along her laptop this time, having learnt from previous visits that there was patchy internet access at Ananda, and, in her state of distraction, she had even forgotten to bring her usual tranche of books. But she spotted a newspaper rack in the corner and got up to look for some lightweight magazine section that would tell her about diets and skincare, or how to tell if your partner was cheating on you.

Neha riffled through the usual collection of Indian newspapers and pulled out the *International Herald Tribune*. She took the paper to the sofa and spread it out on the table in front of her as she sat down. For a few seconds, the newsprint was a complete blur, letters and symbols all merging into one another before her swollen eyes. The picture on the front page was in full colour, however, showing the British Prime Minister and his wife holding their newborn baby outside Downing Street. David Cameron was beaming into the camera but his wife was smiling softly as she looked down at her lace-wrapped child. Her hands were a mother's hands, gentle and strong, held in the shape of a cradle.

Neha had observed all such details in new mothers before; the glowing skin and secret smile, that serene Madonna-like look . . . as though it was in this precise moment that women achieved the acme of their existence. Even Jasmeet, usually brisk and bordering on belligerent, even she had turned all soft and maternal when her girls were newborn. Neha had tried to assist with their care when the girls were small, Jasmeet never being able to hang on to good *ayahs* for very long, and the two children called her *Maasi*: mother's sister. They weren't the only ones. Over the years, most of Neha's female friends and relatives had given birth and Neha had unerringly run the same routine – buying bootees and blankets as gifts, or miniature gold chains and pendants embossed with baby Krishna's image for those more closely related. She would carry those gifts beautifully wrapped and often add a little something for the new mother or any older children too. She would then enter bedrooms that smelt sweetly of milk and talcum powder and bend over cradles before steeling herself to ask permission to pick up and hold the child. How appealing and yet how heartbreaking, those tiny angelic beings. Neha would stroke peach-like cheeks with longing and feel minuscule fingers wrap themselves around her own, mistakenly assuming ownership. Yes, she had done all that without cracking and always, always successfully masking her pain.

It was time now to do that all over again. For Sharat's sake this time. Neha sat very still, looking out at the night and trying to gather her thoughts. She knew she ought not to be cowardly and abandon Sharat until *he* told her he did not want her any more. Which he was very likely to do when he found out about Sonya. But that would have to be his decision, not hers. After all, he had been so unfailingly gentle and kind in the face of their not having children. And if she could survive giving up her baby when she was no more than a child herself, surely there was nothing she was not strong enough to face now.

Chapter Fourteen

Sonya looked down at the massive city that her plane was circling over, almost unable to believe she was finally arriving in India. The earth looked dry and dusty, despite the inflight magazine's information about monsoons in August and September. Her heart was beating like a tin drum, both from excitement and anxiety. It was crazy to think she was finally here, the land she had thought of so much these past few months, trying to figure out her links to it. More frighteningly, she was on the brink of confronting the woman who had given birth to her, and then heartlessly given her away. It should be a relief to finally solve the biggest questions to have dogged her life so far but, at this point in time, Sonya could only feel a kind of numbness.

The stewardess was announcing something about landing in Delhi's new international airport and finally, with a screeching of engines and wheels, they had arrived. The airport terminal was surprisingly smart and looked much larger than Heathrow. The man at the immigration desk was polite and efficient and the baggage came through on the carousel without too much delay. Sonya's first impressions of India were very favourable indeed.

However, all resemblances to cosy, first-world Britain came to an abrupt end when the girls had gone past customs and looked outside the immense glass windows that lined the arrivals area. Sonya felt overwhelmed by the surging crowd she could see, dark-faced people wearing desperate expressions as though they had been standing in the searing sun all morning holding a placard bearing the name of someone who was refusing to arrive. She clutched at Estella's hand, seeing a similar look of alarm on her friend's face as the two of them prepared for this first episode of their Indian adventure.

The heat hit them like a blast as they left the air-conditioned airport building and made for the prepaid taxi queue that their *Lonely Planet* guide had helpfully told them about. They had so far impressed themselves, dealing confidently with the Delhi police who handled the taxi service and, before that, an Indian version of the Bureau de Change. But, now that they were actually on foreign soil, both girls felt a frisson of fear and uncertainty pass through them. Neither of them had travelled without at least one parent or teacher before, and never as far as this. And Delhi was only their first stop in a brief but complicated itinerary. They were to spend a week here, possibly squeezing in a couple of days to Agra and the Taj, followed by Goa and a beach resort near Cochin before they flew back to London.

Having paid what sounded like a vast amount of rupees to receive a taxi token, the girls looked around for the vehicle whose number they had been given. Everywhere was a sea of curious brown faces. There was no hostility but Sonya was struck by how frankly some men stared at them, their eyes boring into their faces and sometimes even wandering across their chests and legs. Finally, what looked like a rusty old Morris Minor, half black and half yellow, rattled up towards them. The number was matched up with a lot of shouting and gesticulating on the part of the driver and the girls clambered in with their suitcases and back-packs.

'Bloody hell, it's a furnace,' Estella said, with a giggle.

'The guide book said late September can sometimes be very hot and muggy. So weird, given that September generally spells the start to our winter. After all, we're in the same hemisphere.' Sonya fanned her face furiously with the *Easy Hindi Translation* book Mum had found for her in Bromley library. The book had been no use at all at the airport but she wouldn't tell her mother that. Sonya had attempted a couple of sentences of what sounded like total gobbledegook at the airport, and received blank looks for all her pains so, as far as she could see, the book was going to be returned to the library unread.

'Well, Indian winters are hardly likely to be anything like the winters we know!' Estella said, clipping her short hair up to keep it away from her neck. Sonya saw that she was already quite red from the heat.

'I dunno. It does get quite cold up here in the northern part of the country, I believe. I've been *studying*, unlike some others I could mention,' Sonya said, referring to Estella's typical insouciance which had been in marked contrast to her own assiduous research on all aspects of India. 'It'll be all right on the night' had always been one of Estella's favourite sayings but, for Sonya, this was not a mere holiday but a mission. She had to be sure she was getting everything right because so much rested on the success of her trip.

'Hey, have we told this Johnny where to go?' Estella

asked, looking out of the window in sudden concern. They had left the airport way behind and were now whizzing down a busy road. Sonya noticed with alarm the intensity with which the taxi driver was hitting the accelerator, leaning forward in his seat as though he could get his car to go faster by the force of sheer willpower. Luckily it was only an old rattletrap of a vehicle, but the man was nevertheless managing to weave through Delhi's traffic like a demented racing car driver.

'Don't think we need to. The address is on that bit of paper we gave him,' Sonya gasped, clinging to a tattered leather loop that was hanging from the roof to prevent being flung about. There were no seat belts in the back seat although the driver had a makeshift one loosely wound around himself.

'You sure we were meant to give that counterfoil to him? I thought the man in the booth said we were to hold on to it till we got to our hotel.'

'I think you could be right. Shitty-poos!' Sonya shot a worried look at the tiny scrap of yellow paper that sat on the dashboard, well out of her reach. 'I can't very well ask him for it now, can I?'

'No, fuck, that'd be making it too obvious that we don't trust him.' Estella looked horrified at the thought of upsetting one of the first Indians she had met by making such racist assumptions.

'Hmm, he doesn't seem too happy a chappie anyway, the way he's driving this thing. Like he got out of bed intent on killing someone today. I just don't want that someone to be us!'

'If he can't kill by car, he may even decide to do it the easy way,' Estella giggled again, adding cheerfully, 'Well, there's two of us and just one of him if he does attack.'

'And he's only a weedy little specimen,' Sonya added, trying to sound more confident than she felt.

Not that she would ever admit it to Mum and Dad, or even Estella for that matter, but – while dear old Estella had snored her way across the skies above Europe and the Middle East – Sonya, finding it impossible to sleep, had found herself getting more and more nervous at the thought of what lay ahead in India. Perhaps she was even developing some form of paranoia – evidenced by her panicky reaction to a fellow passenger who had got out of his seat just before the plane was due to land. The man had pulled a guitar case out of the overhead locker and made for the front of the aircraft and Sonya's instinctive terrified response had been: '*Hijacker!*' Seconds later, she had been forced to confront her knee-jerk reaction to the brown-skinned man sporting facial hair. Her shame and embarrassment had been so great that she had not even mentioned the incident to Estella when she had surfaced from her slumber a few minutes after.

Equally stupidly, Sonya could not now help questioning herself of the wisdom of her endeavour here in Delhi. It was still not too late to put brakes on the whole thing. The letter had been sent and could not be retracted, of course. It had probably already succeeded in alarming the pants off Neha Chaturvedi. But, having achieved that, it was perfectly possible for Sonya to now do nothing more. It would serve the woman right to live in uncertainty for the rest of her days, wondering whether her abandoned daughter was going to turn up someday or not. Sonya could even have saved the bother of travelling all the way out to India and spared both Estella and herself the near-death experience they were going through now! She felt extremely vulnerable, clinging to her seat as the taxi careened down the road, overtaking cars and trucks recklessly and in every which way. Besides, it was so hot and sticky, even her chest and tummy were sweating. She should have listened to Mum and gone with them to the Canaries again, as had been mooted before this trip came to be. But her doubt didn't quite cancel out her determination – she needed to have some answers before she embarked on the next chapter of her life. For some reason, she felt it imperative to know where she had come from before she set off for university to seek out her own identity.

'Hey look, it says "Defence Services Enclave" on that blue board there,' Estella said, twenty minutes later when they stopped at a traffic light. She pointed out of the window to the far side of the road. 'Wasn't that what we were asked to look out for?'

'Sure is, well spotted!' Sonya said, relief flooding through her at the confirmation that they were not being kidnapped. Her friend Priyal had regaled her back in Orpington with tales of cousins to whom horrific things had happened in India but Sonya had taken the precaution of corresponding with the Indian family who ran the B&B they were due to stay in and their teenaged son had emailed a very useful set of directions to get to the place.

She jumped at a tapping on the window pane next to her and looked straight out at a beggar woman who was standing inches away, clutching a scrawny baby in one arm and stretching out her other hand beseechingly. A pair of flies was buzzing around the child's face, occasionally settling on an open sore next to its mouth. Sonya suppressed a shudder and threw a confused look at

Estella, who had also gone a little pale at the sight of such abject poverty. 'Should we give her something, Stel?' Sonya asked. 'I really want to give her some food or money, you know.'

'I'm not sure, Son. I think I remember one of the guide-books saying that giving money to beggars was illegal. And we've got no food on us, except for chewing gum and mints.'

'But who would know if we did give her some money? There's no one checking, is there?'

'I guess . . . what should we give her? I haven't got my head around the currency here yet . . .'

Sonya scrabbled around in her backpack, looking for her purse but, before she could find it, the driver had started up the taxi again and was doing a crazy U-turn at the traffic lights in order to head back for the sign-posted gate. Sonya looked back at the beggar woman, feeling wretched at having failed to give her anything, but she saw through the manic traffic that she appeared not even to have noticed, now tapping on the window of another car standing at the lights. Even though Sonya had fully anticipated seeing beggars here in India, her first encounter had made her feel rather crummy and, with a sudden sharp consciousness of how fortunate she was, Sonya felt terrible at having joked so lightly that the taxi driver might have been trying to kidnap them. This was, all said and done, a poor country and she had no right to be making fun of people so much more unfortunate than her.

'Our B&B should be no more than ten minutes from this gate,' she said, peering out at the dusty trees that lined the road they had taken. Dust was swirling around in the hot air, sticking to everything, especially the windows of the car.

'Homestay was the term used on the website, wasn't it? So perhaps that's what they call B&Bs here,' Estella replied, looking at the numbers on the gates they were passing. The taxi man had finally slowed down, allowing them to search for the house.

'Ah, here it is – stop, stop!' Sonya said to the driver, tapping his shoulder as she spotted the name 'Mahajan' in big brass letters on the gatepost. The car screeched to a halt in a cloud of dust and the two girls disembarked with some relief.

'I think he's expecting a tip,' Sonya said as the taxi driver gave them their prepaid receipt and muttered something in Hindi.

'Don't think we're meant to give him any more,' Estella replied. 'Aren't those the rules of these prepaid thingies?'

'There may be some kind of tipping system. Shit, I was planning to ask back at the airport but this damned *Easy Hindi Translation* thing was distracting me. I'm sure I read something in *Lonely Planet* about tips. Should I check?'

'Oh, let's just give him something. No skin off our noses,' the ever-pragmatic Estella said swiftly.

Sonya, who had all their Indian money, started to fish around in her backpack again. 'I don't mind giving him a tip, except that my wallet's bulging a bit with all those rupees we bought at the Bureau de Change and I'm not sure it'd be wise to wave thousands of rupees around while giving him just ten rupees or whatever,' she said, keeping her hand within the safety of the backpack.

'Perhaps we should have sorted it out at the airport,' Estella said, looking nervously as Sonya's small purse emerged. It was fat with notes.

'How much do you think?'

'Golly, I haven't a clue!'

'What's it say on here . . . have a look . . .'

'Hmmm, let's see now, that's a hundred rupee note, right?'

'Lemme see . . . yes, I think it is. Unless they write things in pence here, or – what is it again? – paisa, right? But, assuming this is a hundred rupees, this is . . . what . . . divide that by seventy . . . about one pound fifty, isn't it?'

'That should do, shouldn't it?'

'I guess,' Sonya said doubtfully, handing the note with some trepidation across to the driver while looking searchingly at his face. Both girls were startled by the brilliance of the smile they received in return as the man took the money and slipped it into his shirt pocket. He bowed before getting back into his car.

'So now we know a hundred rupees is a generous tip!' Sonya laughed as the taxi sped off with no further ado.

They opened the gate to the house and walked up a drive that was flanked by bright orange flowerpots. Soon, a figure appeared at the door and a large sari-clad woman of about fifty came hurtling down the path. 'Welcome, welcome to my humble house! I am Kusum Mahajan,' the woman said, oozing warmth with a huge smile on her face. 'Can I help you with carrying anything? Rajoooo!! *Idhar aa!*'

'No, no, it's fine really, we can manage these,' Sonya said in embarrassment as a small boy who looked no more than ten ran up to carry their bags.

'Let him take them. They look heavy and have to be taken upstairs. Don't worry, Rajoo is stronger than he looks.'

There seemed no choice but to let the boy take both

their backpacks, although Sonya looked on in concern as the lad staggered off on skinny legs in the direction of a spiral stairway. She watched him lug his twin burden to a room above the garage. She ought to go after him and retrieve it but Mrs Mahajan was still talking, now pressing tea and coffee on them.

'Actually, tea would be lovely,' Estella said.

'Okay,' Mrs Mahajan looked satisfied finally and beamed happily at the two girls. 'So pretty you are, both of you,' she said, looking more closely at Sonya to add, 'You could even be Indian with your long black-black hair and tanned skin. Only your big blue eyes make you look like a foreigner but, here in India, we have people with light eyes too. Like my nephew whose mother is Kashmiri. He has got blue eyes too, just like yours . . .'

Before she could say any more, Estella cut in quickly. 'D'you mind if we use the loo before tea, Mrs Mahajan?'

'Nooo problem. Make yourselves comfortable first. You girls just go up to that room. Where Rajoo went. He will show you the bathroom and everything. I will get tea made and have it sent up with Ramod.'

It sounded as though Mrs Mahajan employed a whole army of domestic help, Sonya thought: one to make the tea, one to carry it, quite probably one to drink it for you too, like royals of yore. She followed Estella up the spiral stairs. Their room was charming, twin beds covered in colourful Indian prints and a massive ceiling fan, bigger than anything Sonya had ever seen before. Bright yellow curtains hung at the windows. The bathroom was basic compared to what she was accustomed to back in England, with a limestone floor and a plastic pail that had a matching mug hooked onto its edge. Sonya saw no evidence of a shower unit. However, there was a loo and a washbasin and fresh supplies of soap and shampoo and even an outsized bottle of talcum powder. Everything looked and smelt sparkly clean.

'Can't complain!' Estella said, looking around in delight.

'I think we've done all right with the accommodation at least,' Sonya replied after the boy had departed the room.

'All right? I think you've hit the jackpot with this one, girl,' Estella said in her typical jolly-voiced hyperbolic style, before throwing herself onto the bed with a loud groan.

Sonya smiled with pride, continuing to potter around the room, lifting up interesting knick-knacks to examine and looking at the pictures on the wall, all of which seemed to be old lithographs of Indian temples and monuments. Finding this place had taken days of research until one of her teachers had suggested googling 'Homestays in India'. As soon as Sonya had done so, she had realized that she and Estella would be a lot better off staying with an Indian family, rather than in some seedy backpackers' hotel in the old part of the city. Much more reassuring for both sets of parents too. Which reminded her, she ought to call or text them to say they had reached their B&B in Delhi with no trouble.

Sonya sat down on the edge of the bed, pleased with Estella's reaction to the room. 'Too right, Stel. I think I can now safely pat myself on the back for finding this place. And there I was so unnecessarily worrying my head off back in England. That lady – Mrs Mahajan – she seems nice too, I guess, despite the garrulousness.'

'Yeah, I wondered if you were uncomfortable with all that "You look like an Indian" stuff. But she meant well

117

and seems nice and mumsy. Just what we need so far from home, I guess,' Estella replied. She stretched and turned onto her side to face her friend. 'So what's the agenda then?' she asked. 'I'll bet you have it all chalked out and printed off and filed away somewhere safe! When did you want to get going with your plans? We only have five days in Delhi before we travel on, remember? Be nice to try to get a bit of extra time in Agra, if we can manage it, and take a good old gander at the old Taj Mahal. It does seem beautiful in the pictures. What a testament of love; can you imagine if someone built a palace in your honour . . .'

Sonya was suddenly silent, not hearing any of Estella's prattle. Yes, she had started off with a plan, and a mission. But, now that she was on the threshold of making the biggest discovery of her life, she felt unnerved and not keen at all to upset her neat little applecart. Perhaps she ought to postpone things a bit. At least until they had got used to Delhi itself. 'Hmmm, yes. Let's get rested first and then check with the Mahajans about local transport and all that,' she said rather vaguely, remembering too that she hadn't yet told Estella about the letter she had shot off to Neha Chaturvedi.

'Are we thinking of going up to the Chaturvedi house to sort of lurk around a bit?' Estella asked. 'We can't get arrested for *lurking*, can we?'

Sonya laughed. 'Think we're okay on that score,' she said. 'But it may be wise to wait till it's a bit cooler in the evening to . . . er, lurk comfortably, I guess.'

'I hope it's not miles away. Have you any idea?' Estella asked, turning her head to look out of the window at the blazing sunshine.

'I looked up the street on Google Earth. It's in central

Delhi apparently, rather a prosperous leafy area from what I could tell.'

'I know I sound like my mum, but isn't technology amazing?' Estella said as she got up to open her suitcase and start unpacking her things into a small wooden chest of drawers by her bedside. 'On the subject of addresses, I've been meaning to ask how you managed to trace it in the first place?'

'Cloak and dagger to be honest,' Sonya replied, looking a little shamefaced. Estella was looking enquiringly at her and so she ploughed on. 'Well, the Delhi address I got from the adoption report was one that I guessed was Neha Chaturvedi's parents' home. So I wrote a letter to that address, pretending to be an old Oxford classmate of hers looking to surprise her with a Christmas card. I'd created a new email address especially and – what do you know – a week later, her father emailed back with her current postal address. A pleasant one-liner, saying how glad he was that someone who knew Neha back at Oxford was trying to make contact. He was quite happy to maintain the secrecy so she would get a nice surprise. So, you see, it's all as easy as pie when you put your mind to a bit of machinating.'

'Cool,' Estella said, admiringly.

'Well, it was a bit sneaky, I guess. And you know me. I hate beating about the bush when there's a job to be done. But I didn't think the direct approach was appropriate in this instance.'

'Sure,' Estella nodded in agreement, returning to stacking her clothes in the chest of drawers.

Having unpacked, the girls went downstairs in search of Mrs Mahajan. They found her in the kitchen, supervising two boys in the preparation of what looked like a chicken curry.

'I have to help them. They are not good at European-style cooking, you see,' she said, beaming.

The aromas emanating from the pot did not smell particularly European to either of the two girls. 'Oh don't bother if it's for us,' Estella said. 'We both adore Indian food, don't we, Sonya?'

Sonya nodded obediently, even though very spicy Indian food sometimes upset her stomach. Mum had asked her not to overdo it on the first day but she had to take the plunge at some point.

Mrs Mahajan looked pleased. 'If you like Indian food, I will make Indian food, no problem. Today I am already making chicken roast and pasta bake but tomorrow I will do butter chicken, okay?'

Estella peered into the pot, examining with doubt Mrs Mahajan's version of roast chicken which was bubbling away in a creamy brown gravy but Sonya – aware that food was one of Estella's favourite subjects – hastily put paid to any further culinary discourse by saying, 'Mrs Mahajan, we need your advice, please. What's the public transport like to get around Delhi? Buses?'

Mrs Mahajan handed the ladle to one of her many minions with instructions in Hindi before turning to Sonya. 'There is no such thing as good public transport in Delhi,' she said, shaking her head gloomily. 'There is a metro now in most parts of Delhi but there is no stop that is very close to this side yet. And the buses are not good for girls like you. Too crowded and with too many dirty men. But I can do something for you . . .' The two girls looked at Mrs Mahajan expectantly as she glanced at her watch. '*Oho*, he will still be in his classes now.' She looked up. 'I am talking about Keshav. I will ask Keshav who never says no to me. He is the son of my driver and

I have looked after him like my own son. We paid for his schooling and now he is studying history in Sri Ram College. Very bright boy. He can drive also so we will ask him to take you around for your sightseeing and shopping. He is a good boy, always calls me *Didi* – you know, "sister". Today he may be busy but the weekend is coming and he will definitely be free then.'

Sonya and Estella smiled at each other in delight. This was a major problem solved. 'We're getting good at this adventure lark, ain't we, girl?' Estella said before turning to their landlady to say, 'Oh yes please, Mrs Mahajan. Keshav sounds just the perfect escort, thank you!'

'When do you want to go out? Now?' Mrs Mahajan asked.

Estella looked at Sonya and nodded. 'Yeah, I guess,' Sonya said doubtfully.

'Well, Keshav will be in college now but, depending on where you are going, I could arrange a taxi or an auto-rickshaw just for this afternoon. Where would you like to go? If it is for sightseeing, I suggest you wait till tomorrow when Keshav does not have classes,' Mrs Mahajan said.

'Sightseeing can wait till tomorrow for sure. This is just a visit,' Estella said. She turned to Sonya, 'Do you remember the address of the place we need to get to?'

Sonya knew it well. 'Prithviraj Road,' she replied, stumbling a bit on the pronunciation.

'Oh very nice area – friends of yours?' Mrs Mahajan asked, looking impressed and a bit curious. Sonya nodded, careful not to give anything away with her expression. Luckily, Mrs Mahajan took the hint. 'Prithviraj Road is in central Delhi,' she continued, 'No problem getting there at all. Leave it with me until you freshen up. Would you like some lunch before going? Maybe have some lunch first, rest a little bit and then, when the sun has cooled down, you can go, yes?'

'Oh yes please, lunch sounds fab,' Estella said brightly, although Sonya's stomach was roiling with nervousness, not helped by the smell of Mrs Mahajan's gravy.

Sonya made an excuse and escaped to their room while Estella stayed helping Mrs Mahajan to lay the table. She ran up the stairs, feeling breathless. It was incredible to think that the moment had come upon her so soon. All those weeks of planning what she would say to her birth mother when she saw her were finally culminating in the visit they would make this evening. In just a couple of hours' time. Would she have the courage? Would she lose her tongue? Sonya stumbled into the room and stood near her bed, trying to calm her breathing. But her head was spinning so fast she had to sit down. She had wanted to take things slowly but events had sort of run away with her back there in the kitchen. Dear Estella meant well and had probably assumed that she was in a hurry to get going with the real reason for which they had come to Delhi but Sonya was suddenly very unsure of the wisdom of this move. She was now so close – the moment she had dreamt of for days now – she almost couldn't bear the thought. It was too late to turn around. Not after having dragged Estella all this way out to India anyway. And she still hadn't told her about the letter she had sent! Sonya took a few deep breaths, sternly instructing herself to remain composed, before returning to the main house for lunch.

Lunch done, the girls retired to their room, suddenly exhausted by the strange and slightly greasy 'roast' and

Mrs Mahajan's endless chatter. But, at five o'clock, the Mahajans' gardener interrupted the girls' afternoon slumber by appearing at their door to tell them that he had summoned an auto-rickshaw for them as requested. 'It is waiting. Waiting charge one hour hundred rupee,' he said.

'Better get our skates on,' Estella said blearily, getting out of bed. She had worked off her flight fatigue by falling into a deep slumber while Sonya had lain awake, listening to the unfamiliar sound of the air conditioner hum at their window. It effectively blanked out all the sounds that Sonya generally associated with warm afternoons back home: bird-song and lawnmowers and the screams of children playing in the park across the road. Here there was only this low throbbing hum which should have soothed her to sleep as it had done Estella. Instead the sound had permeated Sonya's head, going around and around in her brain, setting her already chaotic thoughts off on a crazy merry-go-round.

They got ready hastily, Sonya changing her shorts and tee-shirt for a pair of jeans and a cotton shirt which she felt made her look older, more in charge. She certainly didn't want to turn up looking like a ditzy teenager, she thought, looking soberly at herself in the bathroom mirror as she brushed her hair and fastened it back with a white butterfly clip.

At the gates, they clambered into the waiting auto-rickshaw with Mrs Mahajan looking on in concern. 'Hold tight, don't fall out, sometimes the bumps can be quite bad,' she instructed, adding, 'I thought it would be fun for you girls to try travelling in one of our auto-rickshaws but now suddenly I am not so sure!' She was still talking as the driver started up his engine noisily and took off down the road.

They weaved their way through what was presumably Delhi's commuter traffic, making slow progress down choked and potholed streets. The noise around them was at an incredible level: car horns and cycle bells and the blare of buses. And no windows that could be rolled up to cocoon them as, except for a thin canvas roof, the auto-rickshaw was completely open to the elements. The stench too was unbearable; Sonya had never 'smelt' traffic before – a most unpalatable mix of diesel and petrol and smoke and rubber. Mrs Mahajan had been right about the bumps as well but Estella seemed to be enjoying herself, looking out at all the unfamiliar sights with shining eyes. Sonya, however, felt sicker and sicker as they went along, clutching in her hand the slip of paper on which she had scribbled the name and address: *Neha Chaturvedi. 54 Prithviraj Road, New Delhi 110001.*

What would it be like meeting her after all this antici-pation? And how would *she* react?

The auto-rickshaw slowed down as it turned onto a wide and leafy road. 'Prithviraj Road,' the driver said, half turning in his seat to look at the two girls. It looked like another world around here – so very different to the Delhi they had just driven through. Suddenly the traffic had thinned out and the noisy chaos had abated to a distant hum.

'What's the number again, Sonya?' Estella asked, reaching out for the bit of paper in Sonya's hand.

'Fifty-four,' Sonya croaked, by now barely able to speak for her nerves. They coasted along for another couple of minutes before the driver pulled up outside a set of tall metal gates. A wall covered with profusely flowering bougainvillea revealed only glimpses of the house beyond, but they could see enough and it was Estella who summed up what they were both thinking when she clutched Sonya's arm and breathed in awe, 'Bloody hell, Sonya, it's a fucking palace!'

Chapter Fifteen

At Delhi's domestic terminal, Sharat walked past baggage collection and hurried towards the exit doors. He had no suitcases to collect and his phone call to Ram Singh had confirmed that a driver would be waiting for him as he emerged from the airport building. He almost never travelled with luggage when he went to Lucknow, not merely because his mother maintained a whole wardrobe of expensive clothes for him back in his childhood bedroom, but also because of the time he saved by not having to wait for the baggage carousel to start moving.

Spotting Nek Chand, his tall and turbaned driver, Sharat walked swiftly in his direction. Nek Chand bowed before taking his valise and Sharat followed him through the car park. He sank into the back seat of his roomy Mercedes and slipped out his phone from his pocket. Neha's number persisted in being out of reach. It was most annoying. The signals at Ananda were usually bad but this time they really did take the biscuit! Perhaps it was something to do with all the rains they'd been having this monsoon, unusually heavy for North India.

With a click of irritation, Sharat replaced his mobile phone in his pocket. He had not been able to speak to Neha once since she had left Delhi two days ago, which was not how he liked it at all. He never minded admitting how much he had come to depend on his wonderful wife over the years – it was a well-known fact that he was a devoted husband – but then Neha gave him good reason to be so devoted, as he didn't mind admitting sometimes! In particular, it was the manner in which she had handled the growing sorrow of their childlessness that Sharat admired. Many other women would have been filled with self-pity but – apart from the very rare occasions on which Neha seemed to retreat into a kind of silent shell – she had always maintained an air of calm and dignified acceptance, focusing on her charity work, specifically fundraising for Nirmalya orphanages and the street theatre group she had founded for slum children a few years ago. She was indeed the most perfect wife that a man could ask for. And when pushing his political ambitions, Neha was a publicist's dream.

'*Memsahib ka koi khabar hai*?' he asked Nek Chand. But, as he should have guessed, the driver knew nothing of Neha's whereabouts and shook his head apologetically. Perhaps Ram Singh back at the house would have a better idea.

Sharat's silver car traversed the evening traffic smoothly, arriving at the Prithviraj Road house while there was still plenty of light in the sky. Time enough for a relaxing sundowner on the lawn as the sun set over the garden. Perhaps that would bring some uplift, even though Sharat would have chosen Neha's company to a stiff whisky any day! The guard swung the gates open and Sharat noted with pleasure how green and immaculate everything was, thanks to the recent rainfall. The flowerbeds were forming neat colourful borders to the lawn that was now covered in lengthening shadows cast by the surrounding trees.

He got out of the car and looked up in surprise as he walked up the stairs to the veranda. A pair of foreigners – two young girls wearing jeans and tee-shirts – were sitting on the wicker sofas. Ram Singh was hovering nearby with an anxious look on his face. He rushed forward on spotting Sharat, blaming the guard for having let the girls in without permission. 'What could I do, sahib, but make them sit here on the veranda?' he said in Hindi, his expression contrite.

Sharat waved him away. They were only a pair of girls, obviously not conmen or burglars come to steal something away! 'Hello? Can I help you?' he asked them.

'Ah, well . . .' the dark-haired one spoke up. 'We're here to meet Neha Chaturvedi actually . . .' she trailed off.

English accent, Sharat noted. She had mangled his and Neha's surname to incomprehensibility, but that was forgivable.

'I'm afraid Neha isn't here,' Sharat said. 'Can I help? I'm her husband . . .'

'When will she be back?' It was the same girl speaking again. She was very pretty, large eyes startlingly blue against dark hair and golden skin. Her manner, however, was a bit rude and abrupt, Sharat thought.

'Sorry, I'm not at liberty to say when Neha will be back,' he replied. Realizing that this time it was he who sounded discourteous, Sharat added with a smile, 'Not for any other reason than that I never know myself when my wife comes and goes!' He laughed but noticed that neither girl smiled. This was getting curiouser by the minute. Who was this humourless pair in search of Neha? He persisted. 'Do you need assistance with anything? Perhaps I . . .'

But the dark-haired girl, who was obviously chief spokesperson for them, got up suddenly. 'Best we go, Stel,' she said, 'No point hanging around.' With this, the plumper blonde girl got up too and picked up their bags. The blonde shot Sharat a semi-apologetic look but the dark-haired girl continued to wear a tough expression on her face, not making eye contact with Sharat as they swiftly exited the veranda down the front stairs. Sharat watched them walk down the drive to the gates. It was very odd. The dark-haired girl looked vaguely familiar but Sharat was sure he would have remembered if he had met her before. They might merely be part of Neha's theatre group that sometimes invited young volunteers from abroad. Occasionally Sharat was dragged along to performances but the faces ended up looking the same to him under all that make-up.

He shrugged, walking indoors. Without feeling too positive, he tried Neha's number again but the message remained the same: 'The Airtel number you are trying to reach is currently not available.' Sharat cursed under his breath. Things had a strange way of falling apart in Neha's absence; either it was the cook demanding to go to his village or the phone lines going down or, like last time, the desktop computer breaking down completely. Perhaps all these things happened while Neha was around too, but then she ensured he never got to hear of them. Not that this was a domestic crisis, of course, but something about the visit of the two foreigners had left Sharat feeling a bit uneasy. He wasn't normally given to weird hunches but it was as though a distant storm was brewing and about to break over their heads. He desperately wanted to talk to Neha. Hearing her low-pitched soft voice always had a calming effect on him. Sharat pulled out his phone and clicked on Neha's name for the umpteenth time. Amazingly, this time he was rewarded with a ringing tone. Distant and shaky but a ringing tone all right! He held his breath, hoping Neha wasn't in the middle of one of those lengthy Ananda massages. He never understood why she so enjoyed all that alternative stuff; it was completely alien to him. Suddenly the ringing stopped and Neha's voice came on the line.

'Hello, Sharat?'

'Yes, yes, it's me,' Sharat breathed in relief, 'God, I've been trying endlessly since yesterday!'

'I know, I've been trying since yesterday too but, because of the rains, the landlines here are down.'

'Are you okay, Neha? Enjoying yourself?'

'Of course, I always enjoy Ananda. It's very quiet too, hardly any other guests as it's off-season. Just a group from South Africa who are en route to a Vedanta conference in Pune and the usual sprinkling of Americans. But how are things there? Your parents in Lucknow? Are they okay?'

'They're fine, just the usual health grumbles.'

'Pita-ji's arthritis?'

'Bad. Poor guy can hardly walk. You should've come along, it would have made him even happier to see you.'

'Oh, sorry, Sharat, but I wasn't thinking straight after our party. I'll go see them soon, I promise. And anything further from Vir Saksena?'

While Sharat was telling Neha of his plans to meet the Home Minister the following day, the line went dead. Sharat clicked the phone off in frustration and it was only much later that he remembered he had not had the chance to tell Neha about the mysterious visit by the two foreign girls.

Chapter Sixteen

Sonya managed to hold on until they had exited the Chaturvedi gates but, the minute they were outside on the pavement, she burst into tears. Estella put her arm around her friend's shoulders, trying to comfort her while also very conscious that the staring from all around was getting embarrassing. A pair of men at a nearby cab rank were looking curiously at Sonya sobbing on Estella's shoulder and people in passing cars were swivelling their heads around to see better – the sight of a delirious sobbing foreigner was a sight to behold. But Sonya was completely oblivious to the unwanted attention.

Estella patted her back. 'Never mind, Sonya, stop crying,' she pleaded. 'We'll try again after a couple of days. Besides, you got her mobile number from the butler guy, didn't you, so we could attempt calling that later, yes? That was a clever way to get her phone number, pretending you were a friend's daughter passing through Delhi . . .'

But Sonya was barely listening and Estella trailed off. She patted her friend's back again as she tried to quell her tears. After a while, Sonya finally spoke, her words emerging through heaving sobs. 'Bitch . . . bitch . . .' she said, her face red and streaming.

'C'mon . . .' Estella said, trying to be fair. 'She didn't know we were going to drop in today, did she? So she wasn't really avoiding us by not being there, I guess . . .'

'But she did know, Stel!' Sonya exploded.

'What do you mean?'

'I'd written to say I was coming . . .'

'You what!? But you never said . . .' Estella asked, confused.

'I know, I know, I've been meaning to tell you but just hadn't got around to it, Stel.'

'Fuck me, what did you *say* to her? And did you say we would be going today? I mean, you're not suggesting she's deliberately avoided our visit, are you?'

Sonya shook her head, relieved that Estella at least wasn't cross with her for writing to Neha. 'No, I hadn't mentioned any specific date. But, when I sent the letter, I didn't even know for sure if she'd get it, you know, if the address was correct. But now that I know it's the right address, I bet she got the letter. And simply didn't reply. Bitch.' Sonya suppressed an angry shiver.

'Which means that she may indeed be avoiding meeting you,' Estella said, trying to work her way through the muddle of information. 'That would be a bummer, having come so far.'

'Besides, she's so fucking wealthy! They're bloody *loaded*!'

'Certainly would seem so,' Estella said, even though she wasn't very sure why that fact should upset Sonya so greatly. It was, to Estella's mind, all a little exciting if she were to be honest. For one, the trip out to central Delhi in an auto-rickshaw had been great fun, a mode of transport that was quirky and quick and cost no more than a couple of pounds. Then, on discovering the Chaturvedi house, it had turned out to be a beautiful sprawling white mansion behind forbidding metal gates, manned by the obligatory servants (they had seen at least four: a guard, a valet, two gardeners and a pair of chauffeurs wearing white peaked caps). Having inveigled their way in, they had found an empty but amazingly elegant home that made Estella think instantly of *The Great Gatsby*; deep verandas lined with cushioned white wicker chairs that overlooked trim flowerbeds and manicured lawns that were hissing softly with sprinklers. A pair of gardeners was toiling at one end of the garden, weeding and trimming the edges of a creeper hanging over a shed, while someone else was stacking vast quantities of garden furniture inside it. It was a scene that was redolent with good taste and bucketloads of money. And, just as they were taking all this in open-mouthed, that suave Indian businessman wearing a smart suit and with just the right amount of silver sprinkled in his dark hair had turned up in his shiny sleek Mercedes, as though aware that he was the last prop required to complete a nearly perfect picture. Not that Estella had seen many Bollywood films but, as far as she knew, the kind of wealth evident at the Chaturvedi place was the stuff of Bollywood's most overblown escapist fantasies. Without a hint of kitsch, though, seeing how muted and elegant everything was. It had all been so stylish, in fact, that Estella had promptly lost her tongue when Mr Debonair had turned up in his Mercedes, leaving poor Sonya to do all the talking.

But this wasn't the moment to discuss all that with Sonya, who was still very upset. 'I just don't get it, Stel,' Sonya continued tearfully, 'Neha Chaturvedi is educated, she's clearly rich. From what I can see, the woman lacks nothing and yet . . . yet she gave me up?

Okay, let's say she had some compelling reason to do it then but, in all these years, she's never once bothered to try and make sure I was okay? Nor even replied to my letter! I mean, what possible justification can there be for any of that? All kinds of terrible events could have befallen me when I was a baby! I might have never been adopted and been in and out of foster homes. Or in a children's home and been the victim of the worst abuse all through my childhood for all she knew. But, did she care? Did she heck!'

Estella patted her hand, 'Well, thankfully none of that happened, hon,' she said, 'and you ended up with your lovely parents in Orps. Oh, and got little old moi for a best mate!' Estella paused, hoping Sonya would smile but she was still distraught and so she tried changing course. 'Maybe Neha wasn't rich then. When she had you, I mean,' Estella offered. 'Maybe she was just a penniless student and couldn't afford to keep you and later *became* rich by marrying that man in the Mercedes . . .' she trailed off again as Sonya shot her an anguished look. Another thought occurred to Estella, who had now stopped in the middle of the pavement. 'That could be it, Sonya. She had an arranged marriage to a rich guy, who was told nothing about your birth, and she's never been able to tell him because she would end up losing everything.' Estella now had Sonya's full attention and so she warmed to her theme. 'I mean, it's a pretty conservative society here in India, isn't it? A baby before marriage would destroy a woman's prospects, I'd have thought.'

Sonya's tears had dried up. She gestured to a nearby cement bench and they walked across and sat down. Traffic was hurtling past them on the road but Sonya seemed oblivious to it as she spoke, her voice now low-pitched and sombre. 'I think you've got it, Stel.'

'Got it?'

'The rich guy . . . the husband. He's the reason she's never searched for me. She's scared she'll lose him. They probably have their own children and she must be terrified of losing their love too . . .'

'Yessss . . .' Estella said doubtfully, feeling a little shiver of apprehension pass through her at the hard expression on her friend's face.

'So that's what I need to do,' Sonya continued. 'I need to tell *him*.' She got up abruptly, intending to start retracing her steps in the direction from which they had walked. 'Come along,' she said, turning to find that Estella wasn't following her – she was still seated on the park bench with an aghast expression on her face. 'Aren't you coming with me?' she asked.

Estella paused for a minute and then slowly shook her head. She had never disagreed with her best friend before, except in the most minor things. In fact she had set out on this trip with Sonya, determined to help and support her through what was sure to be a painful process of self-discovery. But what Sonya was proposing now was cruel and heartless. It wasn't what Estella had come to India for at all. She stayed sitting on the bench, her face mutinous as Sonya looked at her incredulously.

'I can't believe you're chickening out now, at the last minute, having come so far!' Sonya cried.

Estella took a deep breath, steeling herself to speak calmly to her already upset friend. 'I'm not chickening out, Sonya.

Maybe I misunderstood, but we didn't come here to ruin anyone's life, did we?'

Sonya looked confused for a moment but soon gathered her thoughts. She raised her head and stood tall, a determined expression on her face. 'You know what, Stel?' she said slowly. 'If these people's lives are ruined by this, I don't particularly care. After all, *she* didn't seem to care about what would happen to me after I was born, did she?'

'How do you know that, Sonya? Maybe she did grieve terribly . . . And what about that man – the one back at the house – he hasn't done anything to harm you. You don't even know him! And yet you want to ruin their lives. And your begrudging her her life and wealth? I don't get that at all.'

'I am not,' Sonya muttered darkly, but without looking at Estella's face.

'Yes, you are, from what I can see,' Estella countered. 'I mean what if – just what *if* – we'd got here and found that your birth mother was a really poor woman, like Chelsea's birth parents. Someone like that beggar woman we saw at the traffic lights. Would you have been so angry then? No, obviously not! You'd have forgiven her instantly. What's got into you, Sonya? You were never like this!'

'Like what?' Sonya's voice was still sharp.

'This . . . this vindictive sort of person, Sonya. Look at you! The whole expression on your face has changed. You don't even *look* like yourself any more.'

'I don't know what the fuck you mean,' Sonya looked defensive but Estella could see that her words were finally having some kind of effect. Sonya was now looking down, grinding the heel of her sandal into a clump of mud by the side of the pavement, as if she could take out all her anger on it. Then she looked up and spoke in a small voice. 'Please tell me what I should do, Stel, I'm so confused . . .' she said as tears started to flow down her stained cheeks again.

Chapter Seventeen

The therapist indicated that the massage had ended by gently chiming a minuscule pair of brass cymbals. Neha, lying face down on the massage bed, savoured the feeling of a body revitalized by the hot stone therapy she had just undergone, even though her mind still refused to be soothed. After she had heard the door click behind the departing masseuse, Neha turned over in order to breathe more freely. The cluster of green bamboo outside the bare window was rustling in the breeze and throwing shadows across the ceiling. Neha gazed at their shadow-play for a few minutes, seeing not the immaculate high ceiling of Ananda's therapy room but another one from a long time ago.

Someone had painted the ceiling of the delivery room in Oxford's John Radcliffe Hospital with a plethora of cartoon characters. It was an image that had not returned to Neha for a while but she saw it now with surprising clarity – those larger-than-life cartoon characters that someone had reckoned would be the best way to welcome Oxford's newborns to the world. There was Winnie the Pooh holding a pot of honey, Goofy and Donald dancing a jig and little Minnie Mouse smiling from under an enormous parasol.

I tried to find some amusement in the idea of the painter lying on his back in Da Vinci style while painting these Disney characters. They all looked so cheery and happy, dancing on that ceiling, their jollity gut-wrenching when set against my anguish.

There were bloodcurdling screams coming from the woman who was struggling to have her baby on the next bed. I listened to her, terrified of what lay ahead for me. But I managed to remain tight-lipped and trembling when my turn came and the pain started to tear through my body. I would not give in to such unseemly shouting. What was to come later would be so much worse anyway.

And it was. How did one compare one kind of pain with another? Was physical suffering more bearable than emotional anguish? All I know, thinking of the clawing, tearing of childbirth the following day, was that it was far more painful to be holding my baby in my arms with the certain knowledge that I would soon be giving her away.

The sweet-faced massage therapist came back into the room and, surprised to see Neha still lying down, approached her with a look of concern. 'Ma'am, are you okay? You are not feeling giddy?'

'No, no, I'm fine, thanks,' Neha reassured her as she sat up. She pulled the towel around her body, feeling a sudden chill.

'Did you like the hot stone massage?'

'It was very good, thank you,' Neha said, trying to smile.

'Would you like to book another session before you go?'

'Yes, I might . . .'

'If you wish, you can see if I am free when you schedule it, ma'am. My name is Amminikutty,' the girl said in a soft south Indian accent. She was kneeling on the floor before a cupboard as she prepared a bath tray for Neha. Getting to her feet, she pointing to its various constituents. 'Ma'am, this is the body scrub, a mix of shikakai and powdered lentils. And in this ceramic pot is the herbal shampoo. I will leave you to have your shower but, if you need any help, I am right outside. Be careful when you stand up, there is oil on your feet.'

Neha nodded but waited until the girl had left the room before she got off the bed and unwound her towel. She stood before the tall mirrors in the dressing area, massaging the remaining oil into her skin, stopping as her fingers reached her abdomen. She ran her fingers lightly over her flat stomach. She had not acquired any stretch marks after her childbirth. Perhaps it was due to the elasticity her skin had had when she was in her teens, although she could not discount the concerned efforts of Nicki and Clare, both of whom had older sisters with children and knew, therefore, all about cocoa butter and StriVectin cream.

'My sister's tum is as flat as a washboard and totally blemish-free — she swears by this.' Nicki held out a tube of cream.

'And, next time I'm home, I'll root through me mum's wardrobe to find tops and jogging bottoms that'll mask your little bump nicely. Not that it shows anyway. You're quite small, aren't you?' They both looked down at my stomach and Clare continued speaking, 'I reckon it's because you're quite tall — sort of stretches you upwards, doesn't it?'

'No one will be able to tell you're pregnant, Neha, not in those loose tee-shirts you wear anyway. Don't you go worrying about that. In fact, don't you go worrying about anything but looking after yourself . . .'

Every so often Neha remembered their love and kindness . . . before she quickly shoved away the thought that those friends too had had to be forsaken, along with so much else from that distant time.

Once showered and dressed, Neha wandered across to Ananda's dining hall, remembering as her tummy growled that she had had a very early breakfast in order to attend the morning's Vedanta lecture on anger management. There was only a small handful of people still lunching at this late hour. A couple were sitting out on the balcony, braving the occasional forays made by hungry monkeys, while a few stray loners like her were scattered around the large hall. From her many trips to Ananda, Neha had figured out how many people there were in the world who needed to escape to the solitude that was on offer here.

She took a table near a large plate-glass window overlooking the valley and ordered a lime juice with mint and crushed ice before examining the day's menu. Despite her hungry stomach, her mind was still refusing to connect with any of the excellent choices that were on offer. She was staring blankly at the description of vegetable pulao with raita, written for the benefit of Ananda's many foreign visitors, when her thoughts were interrupted by a figure materializing before her.

'Are you lunching alone?' a male voice with an American accent asked.

Neha looked up, unable to conceal a small frown. 'Yes,' she said, looking up at an oldish man with silver hair and an open, pleasant countenance.

'Mind if I join you?' the man persisted gently, glancing at the empty chair opposite her.

Neha hesitated momentarily, wondering if she ought

to show her irritation at the intrusion. But the man's expression was non-threatening and friendly and suddenly she felt like company; company that would be completely free of the kind of expectations that usually accompanied interactions with friends and relations. And company that would distract her from her tormented train of thought too. Ananda was about the safest place to befriend strangers. Everyone who came here seemed to share a certain mindset that was all to do with healing and support. Neha smiled and waved at the chair across the table. 'Please join me,' she said.

'Hi, I'm Arif,' the man said as they shook hands over the table.

'Hello, I'm Neha.'

'Hello, Neha, very pleased to have met you and thank you for letting me join you in your lunch,' Arif said with mock formality as he shook out his napkin over his knees. Neha saw that his eyes – kindly eyes – were twinkling. She could not tell how old the man was but she guessed he was probably around her father's age.

Neha, adopting the same faux-pompous tone, replied, 'I am very pleased to be joined at lunch, for lunching was not an activity ever meant to be conducted with either seriousness or solitude.'

Arif smiled. 'Do you mind if I ask where that accent's from. It's either British or posh Indian. Can I guess – the latter?'

'That depends on what "posh Indian" means,' Neha replied lightly. 'If you mean royalty, then, no. But if you mean to ask if I was brought up properly and taught to mind my manners, you'll find a lot of Indians fit that description, actually.'

'No, I meant to ask if a British education played a part somewhere,' Arif replied.

Despite the American-style directness, Neha liked the good-natured curiosity with which her dining companion was conducting his inquisition. 'Well, yes and no,' she replied, 'because I'm not sure a year at Oxford can qualify as a "British education". It's very unlikely to have left a lasting impression anyway!'

'Just a year? I didn't think Oxford University had any one-year courses, unless you did a post-grad diploma?'

It was another rather inquisitive question and this time Neha ignored it. Luckily, they were interrupted at that moment by the waiter arriving to take their lunch orders. They returned to their conversation after the waiter had departed but Arif appeared to have forgotten his earlier query.

Over a leisurely lunch, Neha discovered that Arif was a recently retired lawyer from Los Angeles, on his way back home from visiting his parents in Iran, and passing through India for the first time. He had specialized in 'Californian Lemon Law' he said, clarifying, 'You know, when people are sold a lemon. In this case, cars. But I'm glad to have left that particular rat-race. My epiphany came in the shape of a Vedanta lecture that someone once dragged me to in Beverley Hills. And it's been more fun than I'd have ever thought, this pursuit of the meaningful. Especially when it brings me to beautiful places like your country . . . I just love what I've seen of it so far.'

Neha found herself enjoying the elderly American's peculiar brand of warm curiosity which seemed to apply to everything he had seen and done in India. She was also surprised at how easily she fell into the kind of banter she associated with her long-gone days at Oxford. Certainly, her social life in Delhi, which was invariably a much more formal affair, was not conducive to this sort of instantly laid-back conversation at all and, by the time their plates were being cleared, she and Arif were chatting like old friends.

'Hey, Neha, I've been meaning to ask someone what exactly the standard greeting here is. I thought *namaste* was how Indians greeted each other but, here at Ananda, I keep hearing the word *namashka*. Everyone you pass in this place kinda bobs their head and says *namashka* – I hope I'm saying it properly? – I just wanted to be sure I was getting it right before returning the compliment!'

Neha smiled. 'It's just another way of saying *namaste*, a bit more formal, I guess. You're nearly there, actually. It's *namashkar* – n-a-m-a-s-h-k-a-r – but you're right, the "r" is mostly silent.' Then she laughed. 'Did you see that film *The Love Guru*?' Arif looked questioningly at Neha and so she explained, 'You know, the Mike Myers spoof on Indian ashrams? I saw a DVD of it recently.'

Arif shook his head. 'Never seen it. Any good?' he enquired.

'Patchily funny,' Neha replied. 'Funnier in retrospect, actually, now that I'm here. A lot of things here at Ananda are suddenly reminding me of the ashram in the film. Including your question about the endless *namashkar*s. The Americans in the film don't have a clue what *namashkar* is, of course, and so they go around greeting everyone with the word 'Mariska!'

'Mariska?' Arif responded, puzzled, before he got the joke and burst into a loud guffaw. 'Mariska Hargitay, the actress! Is she in it?'

Neha nodded, quite forgetting her troubles now as she too sat back, enjoying Arif's mirth. 'In fact, the yoga teacher who took my session this morning reminded me of the character in the film who's played by Ben Kingsley – a teacher going by the irresistible name of 'Guru Tuggin-my-phuddha!' She giggled at the memory. 'Sorry that pun won't mean anything to a non-Hindi speaker, I just realized.'

'Teach me, teach me! I'm willing to learn,' Arif replied, 'Especially if it means expanding my lexicon of rude words.'

'Oh, I couldn't,' Neha protested, reddening, 'It's really rude!'

'All the more reason,' Arif insisted. 'If you won't tell me, I'm going to ask that guy over there.' He turned in his chair to call out to a waiter, 'Excuse me, but could you tell me the meaning of a Hindi expression please – I believe it goes "tuggin' my . . ."'

Neha stopped Arif by grabbing his forearm with a small anguished cry. She was still laughing but was by now quite flushed from embarrassment, 'You can't just ask someone that, Arif, it's really, really, *really* rude!'

'Can't be ruder than "dick", can it?' he asked innocently.

'Oh well, okay,' Neha said, wiping her eyes with her napkin. 'That's what it means then.'

'Dick? Is that it?'

'Yes, if you insist, "dick". Although it is a ruder version, I have to say.'

'Pooda? Have I said it right?'

Neha flapped her hands in distress again and dropped her voice to a near whisper in order to correct Arif's pronounciation, 'Shhh . . . shhh . . . not pooda but *phuddha*. Oh, I can't believe I'm saying this. But, please, the waiter's coming back to our table now. Believe me, this is *not* the time!'

'Oh, okay, I'll behave,' Arif said, straightening the expression on his face to one of extreme solemnity. He took the dessert menu off the waiter and scanned it before looking up at the waiter. 'I'll have the sorbet, please,' he said with an exaggerated serious air.

'And I'll have the kheer,' Neha said.

This time it was Arif who burst into loud laughter, puzzling both Neha and the waiter as he doubled over and rocked in his chair. 'I can't believe you just said that!' he accused Neha as the waiter walked away, shaking his head.

'What did I just say?' Neha asked, confused.

'That word!'

'What word? I just asked for kheer.'

'Shhh . . . shhh . . . don't!' Arif implored, looking over his shoulder as though terrified someone would hear them. 'It's very, very rude!'

Neha laughed nervously. 'You're pulling my leg, aren't you?'

'No, no, I promise I'm not,' Arif replied, pressing his napkin over his watering eyes.

Neha, suddenly uncertain, dropped her voice as she repeated. 'Kheer? *Kheer* is a rude word?' She saw Arif nodding. 'In what language? For heaven's sake it's just a kind of rice pudding!'

'I know,' Arif said, his eyes creased with laughter. 'I discovered it on my first day in India, in fact. That the name for India's favourite dessert is one of the rudest words in the Persian language!'

Chapter Eighteen

By the time Sonya and Estella had made their way back to the Mahajans' B&B from their aborted visit to the Chaturvedi residence, they were wiped out, both from the heat and their earlier roadside argument. The sight of Mrs Mahajan standing in her darkening garden with her sari hitched up while she hosed down her hydrangea bushes was like a tonic and both girls melted at the warmth with which they were greeted by their landlady and offered all manner of food and drink.

'Oh, yes please, we'd love some tea, Mrs Mahajan,' Estella said.

'Don't be all British, calling me Mrs Mahajan and all. Just call me Aunty, okay? Kusum Aunty. While you are here in Delhi, you are in my care, just as if you are my own nieces. Or daughters even.' Mrs Mahajan stopped scolding for a minute and peered at the pair of tired and dusty faces before her. 'Are you girls all right?' Without waiting for an answer, she carried on, 'Delhi can be a very bad place, very aggressive. The men especially are very bad, always staring at young girls, especially young foreigners like you. You must be careful. And, if you have any bad experiences, you just come and tell me. I will sort it out. Now you go upstairs and get freshened up and I will send tea upstairs for you. Then we will have an early dinner, okay? Maybe at about seven thirty or eight? After Mr Mahajan comes back from the office?'

Promising meekly to do all that was being demanded of them, the two girls proceeded to their room above the garage. The sun had sunk behind the treetops in a blaze of orange and gold but both girls were too exhausted and dispirited to notice the beautiful Delhi dusk. When a pot of tea was brought upstairs, along with a platter of strange round biscuits and a bowl of fudge-like milk sweets, Estella fussed over the tray, stirring sugar into Sonya's tea and carrying it across to where she was sitting, leaning her back on the headboard of the bed.

'Thanks, Stel,' Sonya said, sitting up and taking the mug off her. In the mirror across the room, even she could see what a wan expression she wore on her face.

Estella sat at the edge of her bed and said, 'I'm sorry I made you cry, Sonya; you know I didn't mean any of what I said earlier.'

Sonya was silent for a moment before she spoke. 'No, I'm glad you stopped me when you did, Stel. It would have been totally counterproductive to go back to the Chaturvedi house and talk to the husband. I wasn't thinking straight. The adoption social worker back in England warned me my feelings would be on a rollercoaster when I tried to search for my birth parents.'

'Didn't she ever try discouraging you from embarking on this search?' Estella asked.

Sonya shook her head. 'No, not at all, actually. I think people now understand how important it is for adopted children to be able to find out about their pasts, so there are now all sorts of laws to help them discover the circumstances of their birth and history.'

152

'I've never asked you how traumatic it was, trying to piece the information together. I knew you were doing it these past few weeks but it all seemed a little exciting, to be honest, and you never seemed too fazed by anything. It's different being here, I guess.'

Sonya sighed before answering. 'That's the funny bit, Stel. It was so bloody easy back in England, almost as if the information was lying there just waiting for me to walk in and look for it. All I had to do was go to the British Adoption and Fostering website and from then on it was a cakewalk. The folks at the Births Register helped me locate the adoption agency that had handled my case. I was allowed to read the reports they had written up at the time and there it was: the name Neha Chaturvedi and quite a lot of detail about her time in Oxford as a student.'

'Nothing about your birth father?'

Sonya shook her head, 'No. Because he didn't want any involvement apparently. And Neha didn't offer any information on him at the time. As a matter of fact, she signed papers expressing her wish not to be contacted by me. But the rules have changed since, you see.'

Estella raised her eyebrows. 'God, that does make her sound callous, I've got to say. What were the reasons she gave you up? Did the report say?'

Sonya shook her head again, her voice starting to wobble precariously once more. 'It just said something vague about her knowing there was no future to be had with my birth father and her needing to get on with her own life. I suspect she had some kind of student fling at Oxford and then wanted out. Easy-peasy, eh?'

'Poor Sonya,' Estella said softly, putting her arm around her friend as she started to weep again. 'You've been through the wringer with this, haven't you? Listen, you'll tell me, won't you, if you want to give this quest up and go home?'

At that Sonya shook her head vigorously. 'I'll be damned if I'm going without resolving a few things first. I'm not after revenge, Stel, but people shouldn't be allowed to get away with this kind of an irresponsible attitude, y'know.'

'I dunno . . . I'm still terrified you may have the wrong person, Sonya.'

Sonya blew her nose before replying. 'I can't be surer of the information I have, Stel. Perhaps I just got lucky because Neha doesn't seem to have changed her surname. Either that or it's some kind of caste name: Chaturvedi. All I did was Google the name I saw on the birth certificate and suddenly there was all this information. Apparently they're a bit of a power couple and there's loads of stuff about them online, mostly magazine articles. I even found a couple of pictures.'

'You don't say! Fuck, was she anything like you expected?'

'I don't know what I expected,' Sonya replied. 'The pictures were a bit fuzzy anyway. All I could see was a couple arm-in-arm and smiling. One taken at an art gallery and another at some kind of Bollywood event.'

'But how do you know you have the right person, Sonya? There could be millions of people with the same name here in India.'

'Too many of the details matched. It had to be her. The name, age, the year she spent in Oxford that exactly matches my birth date. One magazine article even mentioned that she returned from England to continue her undergrad studies here in India because she was homesick for her parents. Yes, I know, fucking ironic, isn't it? No pregnancy was ever mentioned in that article, so it looks like she managed to keep her little secret very well.'

'Bloody Nora,' Estella muttered, sipping contemplatively on her tea. Sonya was silent and so she asked tentatively, 'So what do we do now, Son?'

Sonya took a few minutes before replying, her voice pensive. 'I just have to wait until she gets back from wherever she's gone.'

'And the phone number we've got? Did you not want to try calling her?'

Sonya shook her head vigorously. 'The more I think of it, no. Simply because I think she's gone into hiding having received my letter and, if I let her know that I'm actually here in Delhi, chances are she'll never surface. Quite likely she has swish pads and hideyholes all over the country, going by the affluence that we saw today.' Sonya's blue eyes turned icy again as they narrowed, making her normally pretty face harden into a mask Estella could not read. 'I really do need to meet her face to face to ask her a few things,' Sonya said, adding more to herself than to her friend, 'and I'm running out of time.'

Half an hour later, when Estella went for a shower, Sonya lay back on her bed, willing herself to rest and recharge before going down for dinner with the Mahajans. But her mind kept darting back to the mansion she had seen earlier on Prithviraj Road; sweeping and graceful and enormous, and so different from the yellow-brick semi in which she had grown up in back in Orpington. They had not seen the entire house, of course, but it was not difficult to imagine what the rest of it would be like from the glimpses of wealth that had been so obviously on view, even if they were unintended.

After an initial bit of hesitation and a tetchy exchange in Hindi to the guard who had escorted them in, a butlerish sort in crisp Indian clothes had eventually seated them on a pair of wicker hammock chairs generously filled with blue and green silk cushions. He had then gone indoors before reappearing with two tall glasses of iced water. Both she and Estella had accepted the drink gratefully, as the evening was hot and still, and butler-man had stood over them as they drained their glasses. When he had gone back indoors, they had sat silently, even Estella's normal chatter seemingly quelled by the hush of their luxurious surroundings. From that deep, cool veranda fringed with heavily budding rose creepers, they had looked out over an expanse of emerald lawn that was being painstakingly weeded by one gardener on his knees while the other expertly wielded a pair of shears, clipping away like an attentive hairdresser. A couple of cars were visible at the bottom of the drive and a man in a peaked cap was polishing them to glittering perfection. Someone else was stacking white garden chairs and putting them away in a shed. Then the butler, whose reserve appeared to be gradually thawing, emerged again, this time with two small silver bowls filled with cashew nuts and raisins . . . Sonya smiled, thinking of how even Estella had turned down this offering, open-mouthed and clearly reduced to awed silence by the general air of sumptuousness at the Chaturvedi house. Rather reassuring to know that it wasn't just Sonya who had felt dwarfed by the experience.

As the sound of running water was stilled in the bathroom and Estella broke out into a sudden warbling rendition of Lady Gaga, Sonya got up to gather her own toiletries together and choose a set of fresh clothes, mulling over her response to the evening's events. What was most galling to Sonya was that, from all her reading on the subject, she knew that most adoptees who set off to discover their natural parents had quite the opposite experience to her own. Most people shared Chelsea Brigham-Smith's experience – finding her birth parents living in a squalid council flat, with open food cans littering every surface and cats slinking all over the place. However ghastly, surely that was easier to deal with – the knowledge of having been given up by people who clearly could not cope with parenthood, socially or financially. Chelsea had described her experience as a swift dawning of realization, a genuine understanding and a final closing of that door. But Sonya did not feel like that at all. Far from understanding and forgiving, it felt like a cruel insult to imagine that her birth mother lived in surroundings so much more lavish than the ones in which she herself had grown up. Her birth mother was certainly no voiceless and downtrodden woman who had been forced to give her up. No, the woman was a bloody memsahib, living in the lap of luxury, and Sonya could only think that she had been discarded as an inconvenience that didn't fit in with that scheme. Briefly, she couldn't help imagining what life would have been like for her had she not been given up: the wealth and the luxury, the servants waiting hand and foot on her, the cavalcade of fancy cars . . . and then she hastily put the thought out of her head. That was not only stupid and fanciful but also terribly disloyal to poor old Mum and Dad back at home.

Chapter Nineteen

By her third day in Ananda, Neha felt as though Arif was an old friend, although this she knew was born of sheer relief at being able to talk to someone who knew nothing at all about either her present problems or her background. She had briefly mentioned a husband with political ambitions to Arif, who was himself a widower with grown children, but he had not quizzed her further, perhaps because he knew little about the Indian political scene. He had also not asked the standard questions about where she lived which, in Delhi, was usually an immediate giveaway of one's financial and social standing.

'Hey, did you want to come on this trek tomorrow?' Arif asked as they were drinking jasmine tea on the terrace one evening. He was leafing through the resort's brochure as Neha, resting between treatments, sipped contentedly.

'The one to the hilltop temple?' Neha asked. 'I've heard people talk about it but have never been. I tend to come here to Ananda and just flop.'

'Five kilometres . . . gentle uphill climb . . . Jeep pickup to return to the resort,' Arif read out loud.

'I can manage five kilometres easily,' Neha said, adding, 'and I like the sound of the Jeep pickup! Although I'm not that keen on uphill, I have to say.'

'I doubt it will be too bad. That just wouldn't be Ananda, would it?'

'Too right. Even the adventure trails have to be sort of *uber*-luxury, air-conditioned and padded with cushions.'

'Sounds like my kind of trek,' Arif grinned. 'Shall we try it then? Tomorrow morning?'

'I'm certainly game,' Neha smiled.

'Right, then. I'll book us on. Think we may need to be accompanied by a guide.'

'And it's a crack of dawn start,' Neha warned, getting up with a look at her watch. 'Well, I'm off for my second treatment of the day. *Shirodhara*. This is the life, eh? Just floating from treatment to treatment . . .'

'Enjoy!' Arif grinned before returning to his reading.

Neha walked towards the spa building, surprised at how a bit of normal conversation and laughter had revived her spirits. The human mind was indeed a wonderful thing, able to expand and take on quantities of emotion without cracking. And in Arif she had found a particularly entertaining companion, one who was as capable of fun as serious philosophical discourse, as she had discovered at the Vedanta lecture this morning. Just chatting with him about life in general, she found she was feeling altogether stronger about the situation with Sonya, and ready to face whatever awaited her in Delhi when she returned. Off and on she had toyed with the idea of calling the number in Sonya's letter but a terrible fear assailed her every time she thought of the events that might be sparked off. Besides, what reasonable explanation could she ever have for abandoning her child?

The following morning, Neha discarded the regulation Ananda uniform of cotton kurta-pyjama for jeans and a tee-shirt in preparation for her trek. Luckily she had packed a pair of trainers and so she wore these before pulling a light jumper on as the pre-dawn air was light and cold. Making her way out of the darkened corridors, she headed for the meeting point in the spa building. Arif was already waiting, seated on the silk sofas with a couple of other guests and the guide who had been organized by the resort. The hotel had provided a small picnic of fruit and drink and the small group soon set off, leaving Ananda's wrought-iron gates to start walking towards the foothills. The distant mountains were edged with a pale silvery light as the time for sunrise approached and soon the skies were turning a buttery yellow.

In an hour, the group was climbing and, when they reached a grassy flat stretch, the guide suggested they stop for a snack. Sitting on a rocky outcrop, Neha was munching on an apple when she felt the phone in her satchel buzz. After that short aborted call from Sharat a night ago, she had lost her phone signal again and so she hastily fished the instrument out of her purse, answering it in a hurry as she saw Sharat's name flash on the screen.

'Darling!' she heard her husband say, with relief in his voice at finally having managed to get her.

'Oh, Sharat, I can't believe I finally have a signal. Could be because I'm outside the spa right now, actually, on a trek. It's the only thing about Ananda I don't like, the lousy phone signals!'

'Well, part of the reason people go there is to get away from it all,' Sharat laughed.

'I didn't need to get away from you, for heaven's sake! Tell me, are you okay?'

'Yes, I'm fine. It's been a bit busy so perhaps it's just as well you're not here.'

'Things okay at home? Ram Singh does tend to take things easy if I'm not around to supervise.'

'Naah, he's managing all right. Even made "Eenglees" cuisine for my dinner last night.'

'English cuisine?' Neha laughed. 'What did he turn out? Don't tell me roast beef and Yorkshire pudding?'

'Oh, nothing as elaborate as that. Just some potato cutlets, boiled vegetables and coleslaw actually. Oh "Eenglees" reminds me. I forgot to say the last time I called – a pair of girls were here asking for you a couple of days ago. Foreigners. English, I'd guess from their accents.'

Neha's blood suddenly ran cold. She felt faint as her surroundings swam around her. It took her a few seconds to regain her composure and she had to swallow hard before she could speak. 'English girls? Looking for me? Did they say why?' she asked finally, her voice sounding strangulated to her ears.

'No, they seemed strangely reticent, in fact,' Sharat replied. 'I asked them to return in a few days but Ram Singh later said that he gave them your mobile number. Not that they'd have been able to get through to you at Ananda! But it was a reminder that we must instruct Ram Singh not to give out our numbers to all and sundry. Maybe he was just rattled by them being foreigners. I'm sure they won't call and pester you while you're there but I thought I should warn you. Probably something to do with your drama troupe, I'd say. Were you expecting a pair of English volunteers?'

'Did they not give you their names?' Neha asked, her heart still beating rapidly.

'Nope. Nothing. They were in a great hurry to get out of here when they found you weren't around. Wouldn't accept anything to eat or drink except for a glass of water,' Ram Singh said. 'Very peculiar.'

Neha heard little of the rest of Sharat's conversation as he told her about his meeting with the Home Minister. When he had finally hung up, she sat holding her phone in her limp hand, staring unseeingly at the distant mountains. Then she jumped as a hand tapped her shoulder.

'Jeez, I didn't mean to frighten you,' Arif said. He stopped smiling as he saw the expression on Neha's face. 'Hey, are you okay?' he asked.

Neha nodded, getting to her feet. She dusted the grass off her jeans, avoiding eye contact, certain that her face would give everything away. She had plainly not succeeded, for Arif was looking at her now with concern in his eyes.

'Not bad news, I hope?' he enquired, glancing at the phone that Neha was tucking into her bag.

'No, thanks for asking,' Neha replied, aware that her voice was still shaking. Luckily the crackly phone signals would have prevented Sharat from hearing her shock.

Neha and Arif joined the rest of the group who were already assembled at the gravel path and followed them as the hike resumed. Neha's mind was in utter turmoil and she could barely hear the banter among the rest of the group, let alone join in. Arif was, however, his usual cheerful self, joining in the general chatter with all sorts of wisecracks. Every so often, he darted a glance in Neha's direction, conscious, she knew, of her sudden change of mood. Partially to mollify him, she made a couple of attempts at conversation but it was no use. Her mind was darting all over the place. Sharat's news of the foreigners' visit was simply devastating. Of course, one of those girls was Sonya. It could be no one else. Which meant she had kept her word. Sonya was, as her letter had threatened, now in India and in search of her. How long would she be able to hide, Neha wondered? How long before she would have to face the inevitable and let everything come out? What did Sonya want from her? And what would it do to Sharat and their world? It was just too frightening to contemplate.

When the group finally reached its destination two hours later, there were loud groans as realization dawned that they would need to climb a tall flight of stairs to get to the temple. Neha silently joined those who had already started tramping up. Even though she was tired and her legs ached, she barely noticed her fatigue. When she arrived at the temple, she lined up alongside the others, awaiting the blessings of the priest. An old man with a lined and kindly face tied a red thread around her wrist and marked her forehead with vermilion while chanting something under his breath. Neha looked into the darkened interior of the minuscule temple and prayed for forgiveness. What she had done to her baby was among the worst things a woman could do. And, while she had always thought that she had already been punished by being robbed of more children, clearly her trial was only just about to start.

Chapter Twenty

Later that evening, back in her room at Ananda, Neha stood looking out at the dusk falling on the valley as the phone behind her rang and rang. She knew it was Arif, calling to check on her welfare after the trek, but she simply did not have the heart to respond. It had been partially to avoid his questions that Neha had climbed into the front seat of the vehicle that had come to pick them up from the hilltop temple and she had spent most of the rest of the day in her room, pleading illness. She cancelled both the body scrub and the yoga session that had been booked earlier and, when the light headache she had nursed all day started to worsen, she ordered a salad lunch in her room. Off and on, the phone had rung and Neha guessed it was poor Arif, worrying about her. While Neha longed to talk to someone about her dilemma, she didn't think an American tourist, in India for the very first time, would either understand or be able to help in any way. Nevertheless, it would be sweet relief to be able to unload some of her burden. And so much easier to talk to someone she was very unlikely to ever meet again. Arif was, after all, a Vedanta enthusiast and in possession of a wise and philosophical bent of mind . . .

Neha finally lunged at the telephone to stop its incessant ringing. 'Hello,' she said softly.

'Heyyyy, are you okay? I've been worrying about you!' Arif's voice was friendly and cheerful.

Neha sank on the edge of her bed, wondering how to respond to such an innocent question. And one to which the answer was so very complicated. After a pause, she said, 'It's really sweet of you to be enquiring, Arif, and I'm sorry I've been so aloof.'

'That doesn't answer my question,' Arif insisted in his inimitable style.

Neha took a deep breath before replying, 'Well, the honest answer is no, I'm not okay, Arif. But I'm not telling you what the problem is simply because there's nothing you – or anyone else for that matter – can do.'

'Try me,' Arif said. When Neha remained silent, he added, 'It was that phone call while we were on the trek, wasn't it?'

Tears started coursing down Neha's face and she tried stemming them by balling up a face towel to press over her eyes. She was sure Arif could hear her crying and she made another attempt to gather herself together. Finally she spoke, her voice shaking. 'No, . . . it wasn't the phone call, Arif. That was from my husband, who also knows nothing about this problem of mine . . .' she trailed off and took a deep breath. 'It's something that goes back much further . . . it's . . . what shall I say . . . it's a secret . . . a scandalous secret from my past . . .'

'Neha, I'm coming to your room,' Arif said in a firm voice. 'Whatever it is, you must know that I'm not going to judge you. But you need to talk. Something is eating you up and it's not right that you should be carrying this burden on your own. Can I come?' he asked.

Neha accepted his request, feeling immeasurable relief suddenly course through her body. She thought of the foolishness of unburdening her eighteen-year-old secret on someone she had barely met, but suddenly she knew that she had no other option if she wanted to keep from going mad.

In a few minutes, Arif was knocking at her door. Neha opened it and stood aside to let him in. He took the armchair in the corner of the room while Neha seated herself on the sofa opposite him. Outside, the valley had darkened to complete blackness and the lights of the village were starting to come on, one by one. Neha glanced hesitantly at Arif's face and saw nothing but his usual open and curious expression. Unusually, however, he was silent, giving her the opportunity to speak.

'You won't judge me?' she asked.

Arif's eyes were sympathetic. 'You know I won't,' he promised firmly.

Neha looked down at her hands, suddenly unable to meet such a clear and direct gaze. Playing with the rings Sharat had given her, she started to tell her story.

Chapter Twenty-One

It was 1992, my eighteenth birthday party – the last time I was happy in a totally, absolutely unqualified way. We had a double celebration that night, marking not just my birthday but the admission offer from Oxford University too. The whole Chaturvedi clan had gathered – thirty-six of us – in the Blue Room of the Delhi Gymkhana and we ate and drank far too much, even Mama – normally so collected, so much in control – was tipsy on two glasses of wine, openly telling Satish Mama of how proud she was of me, much to my surprise. And the very next day, with my stomach still full of reshmi kebabs and chilli fish, I was taken to IGI airport to board my flight for England.

All twenty aunties and uncles didn't come to the airport, of course – it was a Saturday and businesses and offices had to be attended. But my gang of twelve cousins and a whole lot of friends and classmates turned up, overwhelmed with excitement as I was the first amongst us all to be going abroad to study. There was such a celebratory atmosphere at the airport but, as the time for my flight approached, Papa's excitement seemed to deflate a bit. Compared to the bright, blown-up exhilaration of the previous evening, he looked all shrivelled up and old and very, very anxious about letting me go. Mama kept him in check, even though she too was not in best form. As for me, whatever anxiety I had felt throughout the process of preparing and packing for Oxford was quite suddenly gone, vanished into thin air. Maybe it was because Papa and Mama were doing all the worrying, but suddenly I was on top of the world. I felt so lucky, so blessed. Oxford University only happened to the luckiest of people, and I was one of them. I thought nothing or nobody could touch me.

Despite her distracted state, Mama still managed to corner me at the airport for some last-minute advice before I checked in: 'Boys,' she said, 'boys will chase you for one thing and one thing alone. So be careful, okay Neha?' I nodded. That was easy. Boys had never interested me that much anyway.

I made a friend on the flight. An Englishwoman who had been to a naturopathy centre in Gurgaon and was going back to start up something similar in Surrey. She gave me her address and said I was to visit if I was in the area, which was so sweet. It felt like a good omen that the first English person I had met was so nice. I was never really the chatty type but, so excited was I at the thought of flying to England, I talked to dozens of people on that flight, all the flight attendants, the people queuing up outside the toilet, everyone. And then, there we were, nine hours later, about to arrive in England! The place I had been reading about since I was five! Truly Blake's green and pleasant land, I thought as we circled Heathrow and I saw squares of green patched together in a soft swelling blanket.

A distant relative had been pressed into picking me up from Heathrow. Mummy and Papa had insisted, even though I had begged to be allowed to take a taxi or a coach, as instructed by the university literature sent to overseas students. Mahinder Tau-ji, Papa's elderly cousin, was standing at arrivals with a placard that had my name on it, and my *photograph that Papa had sent earlier to be quite sure he would not miss me. As Tau-ji and his son took me to their car with my suitcase, I could tell soon enough that they were a bit put out by having had to accommodate my arrival and, typically, Papa had not bothered to check that it was in fact quite a long journey they'd had to undertake to pick me up. So I insisted that they take me only as far as the gates of Wadham College and this seemed to please everyone.*

'You're sure you don't need us to come in and help sort your paperwork and rooms and all those things out?' Tinnu, the son, asked half-heartedly when we pulled into Oxford. He had already slipped into the conversation the fact that he was missing a local cricket match, so I shook my head vehemently.

'No, no, it's fine, really. Mama and Papa were just worrying about me needlessly when they asked you to come. The university people have been great, they've already sent me all the information I need. And my suitcase has wheels so even that's not a problem. I'll be fine, really.'

It suited me fine. I really did want to be by myself when I walked into that quadrangle for the first time anyway. Who in their right mind would want to be accompanied by a dour old man and his surly son while stepping into the most golden moment of their life?

For me, it was like reliving scenes from all the many old films I'd pored over – like the race scene in Chariots of Fire. *I'd watched that sequence so many times over, savouring not the excitement of the race so much, but the setting: the rectangular clipped green lawns, the college quad, the ancient ivy-clad walls, the students – all floppy-haired and fresh-faced, wearing stripey blazers and boaters – as they stood around the contestants, cheering. Back in India, while preparing for the UCAS application, I'd taken to watching* films set in Oxford and Cambridge and seeing myself in them, at first with a kind of pained uncertainty and then, since the arrival of the confirmation letter, with over-whelming excitement at the idea that I was finally on my way to being there myself. Of course, the scene in that film depicted Trinity College in Cambridge and I was going to Oxford but that was immaterial. I'd known all along that I would get to either Oxford or Cambridge and, beyond that, nothing else mattered at all. It went all the way back, in fact, to when I was six and my father first showed me a black-and-white picture of Oxford to ask if I'd like to study there someday. The picture of spires rising through dense tree cover made it seem like some heavenly paradise. But it was only as I grew that I realized its true significance. 'Neha Chaturvedi, MA Oxon': I saw the words embossed in gold on the visiting card I would one day have. Letters that, my father said, would open up all kinds of doors in India when I returned with my degree.

I stood that day in the quadrangle of Wadham College, feeling ready to faint. I was finally there. There was a churning feeling in my stomach because I'd fantasized about that moment for so long, it was almost as though I was still dreaming. And then, in the middle of that strange and magical moment, I met Simon.

His voice came from behind me, a hesitant hello. I turned to see one of those floppy-haired boys from the movies, only without a boater and a blazer. Like me, he was in jeans, carried a suitcase in one hand and wore a lost expression on his face. 'I'm looking for the college office,' he said.

'I think this is it,' I replied, waving one hand at the building before us, even though I suspected that his opening line was only an excuse to talk to me as, unlike me, most other new pupils would have been to the college at least once before.

'Oh, is it? What luck,' he replied, breaking into a suddenly impish expression and looking, I was sure, more closely at me than at the college building. 'You're new here too?' he asked.

I had a sudden thought: I'd been solemnly promising my mother at the airport that I'd steer clear of English boys and, here I was, my very first afternoon in Oxford, allowing a boy to openly lie to me and run blue-green eyes up and down my person in a clearly appreciative manner. He seemed nice, though, and I decided to follow my hunch that he wasn't about to leap on me as Mummy seemed to fear would be the intention of all the boys I was going to meet in England. Completely ignoring her terse last-minute airport advice, I fell into step next to Simon as he pointed to a temporary sign around the quadrangle that was marked 'Porter's Lodge'.

He told me his name was Simon Atkinson and that he was a fresher too, reading Chemistry. We walked together, the wheels of our suitcases clattering on the uneven paving as we went towards the office to enquire about our halls. That was the other thing Mummy had been anxious about: mixed halls, or what at Wadham appeared to be called 'staircases', which is where the students lived. ('What, girls and boys are not separated?' my mother had enquired when the college brochure first came, her forehead creased with worry.) Papa had been more blasé, his delight at my getting admission to Oxford University overwhelming all other concerns.

We got chatting, Simon and I, while awaiting our turn in the queue.

'Delhi!? What brought an Indian lass all the way out here? Not Wadham's liberal credentials, surely?' he asked.

I wasn't sure what he meant but I told him about the Big

Oxford Dream my father had passed on to me. 'It was always going to be either Oxford or Cambridge,' I explained to Simon, 'my father's plan being to propel me towards the Indian Foreign Service, to become a diplomat, you see.'

I didn't go on to elaborate that my father was in the Indian Administrative Service and always considered it a lowlier profession, especially as two of his wealthier schoolmates who went on to Oxford had made it to the Indian Foreign Service. Somewhere along the way, Papa's dreams for himself simply became his dreams for me. If I hadn't been an only child, perhaps that expectation would have lain on a brother but my mother had suffered from secondary infertility and, as their only child, I became the repository of all the hopes and dreams that my father might have reserved for a son.

'Gosh, that's pretty focused,' Simon said. 'I'm not at all sure of what I'll do after graduating. I certainly have no career plan right now!'

'Really?' I asked him, not quite believing his nonchalant attitude. He must have been pretty clever to make it to Oxford so his casual statement surprised me.

'Yeah,' he replied, however, with apparent sincerity, 'all I know at the moment is that I'm at uni to have a bloody good time. Which is why I didn't want to do something like Economics. It would only make me sensible about money and prevent me being able to fully enjoy my college days. This is a once-in-a-lifetime chance to acquire a degree in BGT.'

'BGT?' I asked, puzzled.

'I told you: Bloody Good Time.'

I found his lackadaisical attitude startling but also rather refreshing. My own preparation for Oxford had taken all my life! Not just all my life but much of my parents' lives *too. We'd been lucky that the UCAS information, the essays and exams and even the final telephone interview had all been conducted under the careful guidance of Papa's two school friends who had been to Oxford. I couldn't have asked for finer mentors – Tippy Uncle called me every week from South Africa, where he was in the Indian mission, and Suri Uncle was in the Ministry of External Affairs in Delhi, always available at the end of a phone line. My coaching could not have been more personalized and intensive and, by the time I'd had the letter requesting a telephone interview with the tutors, both Tippy Uncle and Suri Uncle were already patting me on the back and congratulating what they called 'The Team'. My family's combined three-way ambition was going to be achieved, finally.*

I told Simon about some of that while we were queuing and, by the time we'd both been assigned our rooms, we were friends. He said he would 'swing by' my staircase later on in the evening so we could explore 'Oxford's watering holes'. Again, I only had a vague idea of what he meant but it felt really good to have someone I could consider a friend so early on in my college life.

Despite a bit of home-sickness (especially for the food), that first week at Wadham was actually great fun. Classes weren't going to start for a week and all everyone seemed interested in was what was called the 'Freshers' Bop' which I realised as we went along was what we in India would have called a dance party. Music and food and drink and what the English seemed to love doing: fancy dress. I was a naturally shy person but Oxford life was bringing out new qualities and confidence in me. I also befriended a really lovely pair of girls called Clare and Nicki, who shared the room next door to mine. The college had given me a tiny single room but placed them together – they thought probably because they were both from Suffolk, Nicki saying, 'To most of these Oxford dons, that's a foreign land'. They were very sweet and protective about me, taking me under their wing because I knew so little about life in England. We became a threesome on our staircase and Simon kind of tagged along. His digs were in the Bowra Building, at the back of the college, but he turned up on our staircase at what Nicki (who was the funny one) called 'the drop of a boater'. We didn't mind. Simon was the gregarious type and through him we met all sorts of wild and interesting people. But, even though Simon had so many friends, I was a bit flattered that he spent all evening at the Freshers' Bop attached to my side and supplying Clare, Nicki and me with drinks throughout the night.

Once classes began, it started to get quite busy. I enrolled in all kinds of societies and clubs but never lost sight of how important it was to do well academically. So much effort had gone into my being at Oxford, I couldn't mess around. Simon, on the other hand, was clearly applying himself to the business he had come to Oxford for, his degree in BGT. He started asking me out on dates – innocent enough, movies and picnics – but I resisted, telling him quite honestly about how it would upset and worry my family back home in India if they thought I was neglecting my studies in order to go steady with someone. He seemed to understand, apparently contented enough to hang around me whenever he could. Nicki and Clare joined the water-polo team. I didn't because I'd never been the sporty type and Simon was clearly delighted because it left us together as a twosome a lot of the time. I had my first kiss at this time, six weeks into term; Simon and I had spent the afternoon reading in my room and, quite suddenly, he reached out and kissed me on the lips. I wasn't especially shocked or anything. I mean, it had definitely been brewing for some time so I half expected it. But, when he started to wriggle his tongue into my mouth and run his hand over my breasts, I pulled away and told him I wasn't enjoying it. He was hurt, I think, but took it with good grace and, after less than an hour's awkwardness, we were friends again and off on a long cycle ride around Oxford. He was like that, Simon, so puppy-like in his adoration and so eager to please. Looking back, I ask myself why I wasn't more tempted by the idea of him as a boyfriend, but then he wasn't the only distraction. In fact, it was amazing how much diversion was on offer all the time; a fancy dress party or ball almost every weekend, crazy drinking sessions in the bars and pubs around the college (I stuck to the OJ, with an occasional glass of wine) but most of the students were bright enough and focused enough to carry on with their research and their studies alongside all the socialising. Certainly Simon kept getting decent enough grades despite hanging around our staircase so much, don't ask me how. It might sound arrogant but I suppose we were the crème de la crème, those of us who'd got into Oxford. Even now I remember that feeling – so blind and so very foolish – of being young and smart and clever and so on top of the world that no one and nothing could ever topple us . . .

Yes . . . and it was in the middle of that heady carefree time – getting on for winter – that I met Alastair . . .

Alastair Henderson was a tutor in the department but one we generally had little to do with. Simon used the term 'foxy academic' to describe him once, you know, the kind of academic that gets sought after by the media for being both eloquent and good-looking. The students referred to him as 'Hottie Henders' and joked sometimes that we saw more of him on TV than in college. The BBC was using him as an anchor for a poetry series that summer and so he had a good excuse to never be around. But, one winter afternoon, when I'd gone for a one-on-one tutorial with Mr Waddell, who should be awaiting me in Waddie's study but the great Alastair Henderson himself? I was startled when he opened the door – not just because he wasn't the grey-haired and avuncular old tutor I normally saw on a Tuesday afternoon, but because he had a glass of whisky in one hand and looked more ready for casual social interaction than a tutorial.

'Kurt's had to go up to London this morning so I'm afraid it's me you've got,' he said in that kind of uninterested, drawly manner that girls tend to find so sexy. 'I'm Alastair Henderson. You can call me anything you like, Alastair, Al, or that strange moniker I'm told the students have so kindly bestowed on me; can't tell why.' He turned to me and asked, his blue gaze suddenly piercing, 'And who, may I ask, are you?'

'I'm Neha,' I said, adding – although I wasn't sure why – 'I'm an overseas student. From India.'

'Ah, Neha from India,' he said, as though I was the very person he had been waiting to meet all these years. He was smiling but his eyes were inscrutable and it felt as though he was poking fun at me, rather than being genuinely friendly. 'Well, Neha-from-India,' he continued, 'I'm here to answer any questions you may have on incest in the Greek myths or religion and the metaphysical poets or,' he waved an arm in the air, 'just life and love, if you like. Oh, and I may use this opportunity to fill in the gaps of my knowledge on the Indian poets whenever we meet, if that's acceptable. Do you read Tagore? Or is it the Balzacs of Bollywood that you follow?'

I was completely tongue-tied by him. Everything about Alastair was aimed at doing that to a girl: the taciturn good looks, the intense gaze, the drawling questions, half-amused

178

and half-serious. He was everything sweet, uncomplicated that Simon wasn't and, by the end of that afternoon, I was madly and deeply in love.

Of course, I'd had crushes before – film stars and pop singers. But this was different. It was an ache that grabbed me somewhere deep inside my stomach, leaving me shaky and weak and unable to concentrate on anything else. For days after that first tutorial, I went over every word we'd spoken, thinking of the many things I should have said to impress Alastair with my wit and erudition. I took to attending all future tutorials with my heart in my mouth, always hoping desperately that it would be him opening the door again. But it never was.

Sightings of him around the college were also rare. Once I ran all the way across the quad when I thought I'd spotted him, hoping to pretend to have bumped into him, but by the time I got to the other side, he'd disappeared.

And then that evening in December. It was the 2nd. I remember the date so well. College hadn't closed for Christmas yet. My parents were insisting I go and stay with Mahinder Tau-ji and his family in Leicester for the hols but I had an assignment to hand in first. After class that day, I found a note in my pigeonhole. '7pm in the library,' it said, and it was signed simply 'Alastair'.

I had two hours to go before seven and I got myself in a real state about it, unable to eat anything or hear a word of what Clare and Nicki were chattering about over dinner in the refectory. For some reason I can't explain, I didn't tell them about my note from Alastair and so, after dinner, when there was talk about going down to the Oxford Union bar, I excused myself with talk of a deadline on my assignment.

'Need any help?' Simon asked. 'I'm happy to skip going

179

if you need a reader/writer/transcriber/coffee-maker/general dogsbody?' He was looking at me so hopefully, I felt mean and devious when I shook my head and made some excuse to get rid of him along with the others.

I was frantic when Clare delayed their departure by disappearing to the toilet, and I watched the hands of the clock in the junior common room inch painfully towards seven o'clock. But finally they had all gone and, after the sound of their laughter had faded down the stairs, I hastily dabbed on some lip gloss, brushed my hair and took the route through the back quad to the library. It was freezing cold, of course, and both the Great Hall and the chapel were pitch dark. Only parts of the garden were illuminated intermittently by the light from students' rooms. I nearly twisted my ankle as I ran up the steep stairs to get to the library quicker, managing to get there a few minutes before seven, to find a scattering of students at work but no Alastair. I hung around, pretending to be reading, but keeping an eye on the main entrance all the while. For a moment, I thought the note might have been some kind of hoax, a prank played by one of my classmates. But eventually – it must have been around a quarter past seven – Alastair strolled in, hands in his pockets and ducking his head under the door out of habit like a lot of tall men do. He seemed in no hurry to keep our appointment but glanced around, looking for me I hoped. I raised my hand to wave at him and hastily shoved the book I'd been pretending to read back on the shelf.

I knew I must have sounded breathless as I ran up to him. 'I thought you weren't coming,' I said, trying not to sound complaining.

There was no apology from him at all. Instead, he gave me one of those enigmatic looks of his and beckoned before turning. I wondered where we were going as he loped along in his customary long strides past the bookshelves and I trotted along behind him, trying to keep up. We left the library through another door and made our way down some stairs before disappearing through the labyrinthine corridors of the back quad. Alastair pulled out a brass key tied onto a greying piece of ribbon from his pocket as we approached a scuffed wooden door. I wondered for one crazy moment if this was the famed room I'd heard of where old Bibles were stored, imagining Alastair might be keen to show me some of Wadham's history, but I was ushered into a kind of anteroom, something like a private study, also book-lined but with a couple of armchairs around a small round table that was heaped with dusty leather hardbacks. Along one wall was a sideboard with a decanter of whisky and some glasses and nearby was a leather couch with some faded tapestry cushions thrown on. There was a musty air to the place, mixed in with the smell of spirits and pipe smoke. Very alpha male. Very Alastair Henderson.

Of course, despite my naivety, I wasn't such a fool and I did wonder if this was where Alastair brought pretty female students to seduce them but, curiously, I wasn't anxious at the thought at all. There was something exciting about the uncertainty and mystery surrounding our unexpected meeting and – if I'm to be honest – I wouldn't have minded in the slightest if Alastair had attempted to flirt or even seduce me. But he couldn't have been more proper, decorous almost, and the summons turned out to be for no more than a tutorial, a lecture of sorts on Gerard Manley Hopkins. I'd written a paper recently on the subject and assumed that Alastair was either impressed enough by it to spare this extra time, or perhaps spurred on by disgust and disappointment into giving me this unexpected tutorial. However, he made no mention of my essay at all and I didn't dare ask.

We sat on the armchairs at first but, as the books on the table between us were piled high, Alastair suggested we move to the couch where he draped himself so languidly, his knee was virtually touching mine. But, despite my being all keyed up in anticipation of something significant about to happen, Alastair remained his rather remote self, hardly deviating from the topic of Hopkins and regarding me with a cool and slightly amused gaze above steepled fingers whenever I spoke.

I returned to my room an hour later, feeling a strange emptiness I could not understand. I'd never been in love before and decided that that could be the only explanation for the strange ennui and disappointment I felt after leaving Alastair in that room. All through my schooldays, boys had never really figured; the ones I knew in Delhi were all pretty stupid anyway. My focus had been only on getting to Oxford, but now that that had been achieved a horrible feeling of discontent assailed me. I sat alone in my room for a while, contemplating going in search of the others down at the Union. Of course, that's what I should have done. But the thought of their inane chatter was suddenly revolting and so I did the unthinkable. I took the back stairs again and returned to the library, running all the way down the path and across the frozen garden. The library never shut but, typically, there was hardly anyone around – most of the students had either gone out or were back in their rooms and only a couple of people were busy around the photocopier. I stole past and walked hurriedly to the little room where Alastair had taken our tutorial. My heart was thumping so hard, I was sure it was audible all around the silent corridors. I knocked, softly at first and, when there was no reply, more insistently, feeling sure by now that Alastair would have left for the night. But the door opened abruptly and there he was. He had taken his tweed jacket off and was in rolled-up shirtsleeves and trousers, holding an open book under one arm, the obligatory glass of whisky in the other. His drowsy expression vanished when he saw me and was replaced by a look of genuine surprise.

'Is something wrong?' he asked. 'Leave your scarf behind?'

I did not reply but stepped in and leaned against the door to close it behind me. Realization dawned as Alastair spotted the expression on my face and he took a step back.

'I had to see you again,' I said swiftly. 'I had to talk to you properly, you know, and not about the Metaphysicals or the Romantics . . .'

He tried to make light of my intentions and adopted a jokey patronising tone. 'Now, now, young woman. Neha-from-India. I'm not sure I know what you mean but . . .'

I stopped him by reaching out and placing my arms around his neck. For one terrible moment I thought that he was going to shove me away, turn me around and marshal me out of his room. Again, I now know that's what should have happened. It would've been much the better thing for him to have rebuffed me then, however much it would have hurt my ego. But, instead, as I tightened my hold and pressed my lips on his as I'd seen in movies, I felt him physically melt. His body, stiff and unyielding one minute, was suddenly pliant and then semi-aggressive as he leaned his frame against mine, squashing me against the door. Before I knew it, he had fished out the key from his pocket again and locked the door behind me . . .

We made love. I was a novice but my passion overrode my lack of experience, I thought. Alastair seemed surprised at my being a virgin and was gentle enough but, after it was all over, he got off the couch and pulled his clothes on without saying another word. The expression on his face was suddenly sort of angry and irritated.

I watched him walk across the room, my heart sinking, wondering if I'd failed to satisfy him and wondering whether I should entice him back to the couch to start all over again. But I saw him pick my clothes off the floor and, from where he stood, he flung them over my body. 'Okay, get dressed Neha-from-India,' he drawled. 'Go home and forget all about this. I think we'd both agree it's been a dreadful mistake.'

I sat up and tried pleading with him, telling him I loved him. But Alastair had reverted to being his old remote self. 'Look, this should never have happened,' he said finally. 'I have a girlfriend in London whom I plan to marry in the summer. I simply lost my head when you came in and accosted me like that. You're a beautiful woman and . . .'

'You're making it up about a girlfriend, aren't you? Just to get rid of me now, I know . . .'

He looked exasperated. 'Of course I'm not making it up . . .'

'Who is she? How come no one's ever mentioned a girlfriend? The students here know everything. I think you're making it up but, even if she exists, you could leave her for me. I'll show you what true love is. Alastair, please, I love you. I think about you all the time . . .'

He threw his head backwards at this, closing his eyes. 'Of course you don't love me, you silly girl. It's nothing more than the overheated imagination of an aspiring poet . . . Love, for Chrissake! Well, whatever love means, you'll soon go on to have that with some young plonker who's probably currently in second year.'

I tried pleading again but, at this point, his tone changed and I felt he was starting to get seriously angry. 'Look, I'll get the sack if this comes out. You wouldn't want that, would you? Why don't I ensure I never take tutorials for you again

*and, for your part, I'd appreciate it if you promise to keep
away from me around the college. And never tell a soul.
Okay? That's a good girl. Now, get up, get your clothes on
and scoot out of here. Run along now, chop chop.'*

Chapter Twenty-Two

Neha's voice hung in the air as she finally looked across the room at Arif. He sat unmoving on the chair, his expression sympathetic. Finally he spoke. 'You're not going to say that it was Alastair Henderson who called while we were trekking, are you?'

Neha shook her head. 'No, it wasn't him. There's more to the story, Arif. I just didn't know how much to burden you with.'

'I've already said, you can tell me anything. I may look old and crusty but I'm quite unshockable,' he laughed. 'And, so far, what you've recounted is a pretty universal story . . . happens to girls all over the world.'

Neha got up to turn on the bedside table lamps to dispel the gloom. She sat down again and looked at the darkened windows, seeing her own reflection looking back. She started to talk again, her voice low. 'You're right; up to this point, it's probably a fairly unremarkable story. There must be many girls who nurse their first crushes on someone older than themselves, someone unreachable. But I wonder how many go on to throw themselves relentlessly at the object of their affections and behave so very stupidly . . .'

'Well, despite the way you narrate the story, Neha, it

certainly sounds as though your Mr Henderson wasn't an entirely innocent party.'

'You're very sweet to sympathize with me but I really did throw myself at him,' Neha protested gently.

'Come, Neha. All that stuff about him playing the uninterested professorial type and keeping you guessing with his erratic behaviour. Imagine inviting you to his lair and then holding an innocent tutorial instead – he was building up the anticipation, can't you see? Deliberately manipulating you into doing exactly what he wanted. There are hundreds of men like that, Neha. Men too clever to be accused of actively seducing a young woman but, all the while, getting girls exactly where they want them to be. I bet, if you'd asked around, you'd have found his tactics had succeeded with many others girls around the college too. It's about power, for some men. Power and the thrill of deceit – two elements that cause men who have everything to forget that they have everything. It's strange, and not so strange perhaps, that when people possess all they could possibly want, they simply want more. As for Alastair Henderson, young women must have been very easy to come by, given his position. Did you ever ask what his reputation in college was with the female students?'

Neha shook her head. 'No, I couldn't. It wouldn't have taken much for people to realize why I was asking. At the end of that evening, I promised Alastair I wouldn't come near him again but I thought my heart was quite broken.'

'Oh, you poor thing. You were how old? Nineteen?'

'Eighteen.'

Arif shook his head. 'And I can imagine how hard it would have been for you, as a young foreign student, to take it up with the authorities too.'

'It wasn't just that, Arif. I genuinely thought I loved Alastair. And that was why . . . when I found I was pregnant . . . I kept it secret at first. I actually thought I'd got lucky to be pregnant with his child . . .'

'Pregnant?! Good grief!' Arif's expression was suddenly astounded.

Neha put her hands over her face and started to weep quietly. After a few seconds, Arif got up to sit next to her on the sofa. He put his arm around her shoulder. 'You poor, poor thing,' he said softly, 'What a lot to deal with at eighteen.'

'I was such an idiot,' Neha said, her voice muffled through her fingers. 'There were so many things I could have done to help myself. But I thought that, if I carried the pregnancy through, I could bring Alastair around. Make him love me, y'know. So I didn't even tell anyone at first, worried that someone would make me get rid of it. I wanted the chance it gave me of persuading Alastair that we could have a relationship.'

'That's such a classic error, Neha. And so many girls do exactly that. Don't be hard on yourself,' Arif comforted. Then he asked cautiously, 'So did you have the baby?'

Neha nodded, wiping the tears off her face with the palms of her hands. 'I did, Arif. And I can hardly believe it myself now. No one in college found out for a long time because, being tall, my pregnancy was quite well concealed. I told Alastair about it when I was three months gone and begged and pleaded with him once more to take some interest in me. And in our baby. But he didn't want to know. In fact, by the time we returned after the Easter break, he'd vanished from campus without leaving a forwarding address. Someone said he'd gone to an American university on sabbatical . . . another rumour was that he was shooting

189

a new BBC series in Tuscany. No one knew where he was; the college office was quite tight-lipped. Perhaps they were used to silly young female students trying to get hold of his address or phone number. I had to confide in someone, I needed help, and so, I finally told Clare and Nicki.

'Please don't think badly of me . . .'

'Of you? Don't be daft! It's him, Henders, I feel infuriated with. He should be hung, drawn and quartered, taking advantage of you like that!'

'He didn't really . . .'

'For Chrissake, Neha, don't be defending him. He's an opportunistic bastard and clearly knew what he was doing.'

'But what do we do now, Nick?' Clare said, 'Neha needs to discuss this with someone urgently.'

'Do you want to report him to the Dean?'

'No!' My response was vehement. Perhaps I still held a candle for him, who knows. But I didn't want trouble of any sort.

'Neha could be right, Nicki. Things will get very messy if Henderson is named. Especially if he denies it. There could be all sorts of repercussions, an enquiry and stuff. Certainly there'll be no keeping it quiet after that.'

'I don't want that. Please.'

'Poor Neha. Well, if you go somewhere like the student surgery, they'll never insist on knowing who the father is if you don't want to tell.'

'The college counsellor, I think, as a first port of call. She seems really nice. I had to go see her about my stolen bike, remember? Something tells me she'll be no-nonsense and helpful.'

'We kept it to ourselves at first, and the college counsellor was, as Nicki said, just lovely. Not asking too many questions and not judgemental at all. Eventually I told Simon too. Only because it was difficult to keep it quiet from him because he was around so much . . . I've never seen so much hurt on a person's face. For one crazy moment, I thought he might do something dramatic – like hunt down Alastair – but he didn't. In fact, after a couple of days, he suddenly went all cool on me and began avoiding me himself, which was surprisingly hurtful. Nicki said it was just that he was too distressed to cope but I think he actually thought the less of me after that and so started avoiding me. I missed him and his friendship, oddly much more than I missed seeing Alastair. But my situation was now getting urgent as the GP said it was too late for an abortion. I had to go through with it and have the baby. And so, when it was very definite that Alastair was never coming back and there were three months left before I was due, I decided to give the child up for adoption.'

'Oh my word,' Arif breathed.

Neha looked directly at him, a pleading expression on her face. 'Please don't think badly of me. I can hardly forgive myself now. But, at the time, with Alastair refusing to have anything to do with it, and the thought of how anguished my parents would be if they found out, I thought I had no choice.'

'Of course, I won't judge you. I understand completely. It must have been so terribly confusing and so traumatic,' Arif said. 'Forgive me, but how did you cope with what was left of the pregnancy once you'd made that decision?'

Neha shook her head, hugging a cushion to her stomach. 'Very badly. I was a wreck all through the summer. Nicki took me to her mum's house for the holidays. Her mum was a residential social worker for people with disabilities

191

in Stowmarket – a quiet little place in rural Suffolk where nobody knew me. But, as the pregnancy progressed, I decided I couldn't go back to uni after having the baby . . .'

'Neha, my dear, you're not the first girl to fall pregnant like this. Why, there was a girl back in Nicki's school who got pregnant when she was fifteen and she was helped by Social Services to keep the baby. She returned to school too.'

'Keep the baby? I couldn't, Mrs Perkins. How would I continue with the course?'

'Perhaps someone could come out from India to help? Your mother?'

'My mother? . . . My mother would kill me if she found out about this!'

'Oh dear, Neha . . . an abortion's completely out of the question now, as you know. It's a huge decision to make when you're in this state but would you consider giving up the baby for adoption? You don't have to answer that question now, my dear, just think about it as one of the possibilities ahead of you. You're not alone, don't forget, not when you've got us . . .'

'I want to go home, Mrs Perkins,' I said, breaking down. She gathered me in her arms. 'I'm so grateful to all of you,' I sobbed, 'but I want to be back where I was, back home and with my parents. I don't want this baby. I won't know how to deal with it. I just want to go home . . .'

'. . . That was how it happened. More than anything else, I wanted to be far away from everything to do with Alastair, from that one stupid act of mine that had overturned my life. I needed to start afresh to hold on to my sanity, to remind me of who I was. So I spent the summer holidays at Nikki's house in Stowmarket, which felt like a sanctuary after Oxford. My parents thought that I was pursuing a research assistantship in Scotland, which is how I escaped having to see Mahinder Tau-ji and his family throughout that time. And then, in September – the baby was due just before term started – I returned to Oxford to deliver it. As had been agreed, the baby was taken off me soon after her birth and, four days later, I was on a flight back to India.' Neha's voice was so quiet at this point that Arif could barely hear her.

There was a long silence before Arif spoke. 'Did you eventually tell your parents?' he asked in a tentative voice.

Neha shook her head. 'Never. No one in India ever found out. Not my parents, not even my best friend. I was too scared. And too ashamed. And, after the initial few letters to Nicki and Clare, I stopped writing to them as well. It was just too painful to carry on pretending this thing hadn't happened.'

'I can understand that,' Arif said. 'They were still living the life you'd lost.'

Neha nodded and looked down. 'So, having left my terrible secret back in England there was no one in my world who knew what I had done,' she said in a wan voice.

'What did you do? Did you continue your education after you got back?' Arif asked.

'Eventually,' Neha said. 'For a while I was a total disaster, weeping and breaking down at the slightest excuse. My parents thought it was because I had been unable to deal with Oxford. I gave them a story about having been bullied. Whether they believed it or not, they had no choice and had to accept that I wasn't going back. They could not have forced me to return, given the state I was in . . . At first my father was enraged. He wanted to write to Wadham, to the UK government, to everyone. But I persuaded him to let it go. I needed to move on, I told him, and I asked to be enrolled at Delhi University.'

'And that was what you did . . .'

Neha nodded. 'I finally completed my degree at Lady Shri Ram College in New Delhi, followed by a master's.' She paused before speaking again. 'Towards the end of my final year, a marriage proposal came from a family who were distantly related to us. I was twenty-three when I married Sharat, the most wonderful husband one could ask for . . .' At this point, Neha trailed off, her voice wobbling again.

'I don't suppose you could ever tell him about the baby . . .' It was more a statement than a question.

Neha looked at Arif, her eyes dark and glistening. 'If Sharat ever found out, it would kill him,' she said quietly. 'You see, we never had children of our own, despite being desperately keen at first . . .'

Arif was lost for words. After a pause, he said, 'Jeez. What horrible irony, Neha. I'm so sorry . . .'

Neha started to cry again and Arif got up to fetch a box of tissues from the toilet. Handing them to Neha, he sat down again. 'Thank you for trusting me enough to tell me everything. It can't have been easy.' He waited a few minutes for Neha to compose herself before speaking again. 'I can certainly understand the trauma you've been through but I gather your life settled into relative peace after that. Has something happened since? Who called while we were on the trek?'

There was a long silence before Neha could bring herself to speak again. 'I've had a letter, Arif. From my daughter . . . well, the baby I gave birth to. She's now eighteen and she wants to meet me. I don't know what for but I can tell she's angry. I don't blame her for that – I would have been too in those circumstances – but she's here in India and has already been to my house in Delhi. I gathered that from my husband, who didn't realize who she was . . . I'm very, very frightened, Arif.'

Chapter Twenty-Three

Sonya looked up at the towering Qutb Minar, the tip of which was glowing angry red in the sun. Keshav, the driver and guide that Mrs Mahajan had arranged for them, had just said that the minaret had been built in the twelfth century, which made it as old as the Tower of London. Sonya had to admit that the stonework was in pristine condition and very well maintained, without all the scaffolding and plastic sheeting that invariably surrounded the Tower. So not everything in India was a total mess, apparently.

Estella crouched down and pointed her camera upwards to try and fit the tall structure into her viewfinder. 'I think I've got the whole thing,' she said excitedly as she caught up with Sonya. 'Look,' she said, showing them the digital image on her screen. Sonya caught a whiff of Keshav's perfumed hair gel as he came a bit too close and hastily stepped back. She had struggled much more than Estella had with the male gaze in India and, like Mrs Mahajan, Keshav too seemed curious about where Sonya was from, asking whether she was Italian or Turkish, insisting that she was not as English as Estella. This could have been funny, given that it was Estella who was half Italian, but Sonya had felt strangely insulted. She had also caught

Keshav looking at her intently on a few occasions with a touch of insolence, a sort of open sizing-up, even though he was curiously subservient around the Mahajans, folding his hands in greeting and slipping off his trainers before entering the house. She noticed too that Mr Mahajan had ordered him rather peremptorily to fetch his slippers from indoors and, although he had swiftly complied, his face had flushed slightly at being made to perform such a menial task in front of the foreign visitors.

He wasn't a typical guide, of course. As Mrs Mahajan had repeated again at breakfast, Keshav was the son of their driver and, having had his schooling paid for by the Mahajans, he was now studying history at Delhi University. 'Keshav will be much better at showing you the sights properly than all these guide types who pretend to be history experts but are talking nonsense half the time. He can drive and his English is very good also,' Mrs Mahajan had declared with an air of deep satisfaction at being able to offer such a rare and wonderful resource to her guests. Keshav had looked on as she said this, a remote stand-off expression on his face.

Mrs Mahajan's intentions were no doubt noble but, as far as Sonya could see, both Keshav's skills of driving and English left much to be desired. He drove as maniacally as everyone else in Delhi and used peculiar words like 'prepone'. Only a timely glare from Estella had prevented Sonya from dissolving into giggles when Keshav had given his email address as Keshav-at-the-rate-of-gmail.com. Estella was, typically, managing some friendly banter, toning her English expressions down to accommodate him, but Sonya was damned if she was going to take such trouble over one of the million Indian guys who thought nothing of staring at her as though he were mentally undressing her. She had already decided that this was going to be her one and only trip to India. The men stared even more than Italian men did. It was too hot, too crowded and, worst of all, as predicted, the food had given her the runs on their very first day here. Her stomach still hurt slightly but she had recovered enough to make this tentative trip out at Mrs Mahajan's insistence.

Worse than all else, Neha appeared to have given her the slip very effectively, there being no response at all from the mobile number they had collected at the house yesterday. So now, despite the importance of the mission she had set out with, Sonya had been reduced to becoming a gawping tourist! What a laughing stock she would be to people like Chelsea back at home to whom she'd so excitedly announced her intentions of tracing her birth mother in India. Perhaps she should have listened to Mum and been more discreet.

'If you come this way, I will show you the world-famous Ashoka pillar,' Keshav said to the two girls.

Sonya wondered why she had never heard of it if it was world-famous and reluctantly followed Keshav and Estella into a second courtyard. Keshav pointed proudly to a squat metal structure around which tourists were milling and taking photographs. Estella was quick to join them, clicking picture after picture, turning her digital camera this way and that as though she were on assignment with the *National Geographic*. Sonya was sure Estella would end up deleting most of the pictures at the rate at which she was going, but who was she to throw a dampener on her friend's enthusiasm?

When she had finally tired of playing ace photographer, Estella returned to Sonya's side to exclaim once again at how wonderful everything was. Partially to bring some reality to the situation, Sonya found herself saying, 'For Chrissake, it's only a tichy little pillar, Stel. I expected a second minaret when Keshav said "famous"'. She was aware of how peevish her voice sounded but both Estella and Keshav ignored her which only made her feel worse. She didn't mean to be tetchy, it was just that this whole trip was turning out to be nothing like she had imagined, and she couldn't contain her frustration any more.

'The belief is that you can make a wish if your arms can stretch all the way around the pillar,' Keshav said, looping his arms in a circle and interlocking his fingers to illustrate his point. 'But they have now blocked it off because it was getting . . . how do you say . . . eroded?'

'Yes, that's right, "eroded"', Estella smiled. 'Hey, I think I want to see if I can wriggle through the cordon to make a wish. I *like* hugging pillars.'

'Whatever,' Sonya responded sourly. 'As long as you don't go and get yourself arrested. I'm happy to admire from afar.'

'You can wait here and I'll go with Estella, no issues,' Keshav responded, using another strange Indian turn of phrase.

Sonya seated herself wearily on a stone parapet as Estella followed Keshav across the paved quadrangle that was thronging with mostly Indian tourists. She knew she was being unnecessarily prickly but she hadn't exactly been in the most positive frame of mind ever since coming to Delhi and finding that Neha Chaturvedi had gone underground. Despite telling Estella that she wasn't going to, Sonya had been sneaking calls off and on on the mobile number they had been given. She had no intention of *speaking*, of course – she merely wanted to hear what Neha sounded like. But it was as if the phone had been disabled completely. All Sonya got, every time she called, was an automated message about being out of range. It was frustrating and annoying and, even though she had solemnly promised Estella yesterday that she would not storm into the Chaturvedi house to reveal all, there were moments when she felt tempted to take matters into her own hands again. It would be interesting to see how the suave businessman, smug in his silver Mercedes, responded to suddenly acquiring a stepdaughter!

From a distance, Sonya watched Keshav point to the top of the pillar while Estella obligingly raised her camera and took a few shots. She grinned and said something that made Keshav laugh. Sonya envied Estella's easy ability to fit in and get on with whoever she was thrown together with but, as the pair walked back in her direction and Sonya saw Keshav give her another one of his piercing looks, she turned her face away again. She didn't know what it was but there was something ominous about him, her gut feeling was telling her he wasn't to be trusted.

Or maybe she had imagined his look, because surprisingly, Keshav and Estella walked right past her, still talking animatedly. Sonya quelled the impulse to call after Estella and remind her whose friend she was – that would be churlish. After a short pause, she got up and trailed reluctantly after the pair. Listening with barely suppressed annoyance to Estella, Sonya noted how intently her friend was taking in everything Keshav said, even asking earnest questions like, 'So Hindu temples were razed to build this?' Fucking hell, such excessive eagerness, the man would think Estella was panting for him. They seemed to be headed back to the car park and Sonya felt another flash of irritation that they were not even consulting her in their plans.

Why, *she* might have wanted to hang around the Qutb Minar for a bit, for all they cared!

When Keshav left them at the gates to fetch the car, Sonya questioned Estella in a voice that was dry and sarcastic. 'So, am I imagining it or are you starting to fancy Keshav a bit?'

Estella giggled. 'You've got to admit he's quite a dish!'

'Dish!? This guy? You've gotta be kidding, Stel! I don't trust him one bit.'

'Oh come on, Sonya. He's like a younger version of Robert Pattinson!'

'Chalk and cheese! This guy's all moony eyes and over-grown eyelashes. Wimpy looks – yuck,' Sonya dismissed.

'Come now, there's nothing wimpy about Keshav and I'm sure you can see that. He may have the longest lashes but, cor, he's definitely something of a hunk.'

Sonya saved her retort for later as 'the hunk' had arrived in Mrs Mahajan's Ambassador car, taking the corner as though he were a Formula One driver and pulling up before them in an impressive cloud of dust. The girls got in, Sonya content to let Estella have the front seat as Keshav was obviously trying to impress.

'You can also sit here, if you want,' Keshav said, pointing to the bench seat in front. 'There's space for three people very easily.'

'Keshav's right. You'll be able to hear him better from here too,' Estella said, losing no time in moving right up against Keshav. Sonya wanted to puke at the sight of Estella virtually sitting in Keshav's lap, but she pursed her lips and shook her head.

'It's all right. I don't need to hear everything,' she said primly as she deliberately climbed into the back seat. She saw Keshav give her one of his dark intense looks in the rear-view mirror and, so that she wouldn't keep catching his stares, she pulled out the *Lonely Planet* guide and pretended to be reading it. Perhaps that would help him concentrate on the road, else it was very likely they would plough straight into the back of a bus.

They made their way down Delhi's crowded roads to the old city. Mrs Mahajan had suggested a few places for them to explore, giving instructions to Keshav in the morning to take them for lunch to a street that specialized in stuffed parathas. Sonya already knew what parathas were as Mr Mahajan, who worked long hours in an advertising agency, took two to work every morning wrapped in tin foil with a bit of pickle. She hoped her stomach was not going to revolt again at the fried food.

Old Delhi was a sea of humanity and the crowds had what Sonya could only describe as a 'crowd-smell', a whiff of musty clothes and unwashed bodies that was masked only by the reek of the open drains that were running along the edges of the road, giving off an overwhelming stench. She felt quite faint as she reluctantly got out of the car and felt the crowd jostle her straightaway. 'You must be careful about your bags here. Many thieves and pickpockets,' Keshav said, pointing at Sonya's small rucksack. 'Do you want me to carry it for you?' he asked but Sonya shook her head, hitching it onto her front and clutching at it with both hands. She followed Keshav, with Estella bringing up the rear, as they pushed their way past thousands of people who all seemed to be going in the opposite direction to them. They made slow progress towards a huge sandstone structure at the end of the street.

'This is the famous Red Fort,' Keshav said with pride as they reached the forecourt. He made it sound almost as though he had constructed the fort himself, brick by brick, Sonya thought ungraciously. At least they had come away from the crowds and so she breathed easier as they walked down to the ticket office. Keshav kept looking at Sonya with an odd expression that she didn't know how to read. The sun was beating fiercely down on their heads and Sonya was grateful she had remembered to pack a floppy hat. She suddenly felt faintly weepy and nostalgic as the image of her quaint little girlie-goth room back in Orpington popped unbidden into her head, followed by the thought of the large jug of home-made lemonade Mum always had in the fridge on hot summer days.

'When the Indians rose against the British in 1857, this is where they camped out,' Keshav was saying to Estella, waving one hand at the fort.

'Really? I had no idea that the Indians wanted to get rid of the Brits,' Estella said, adding hastily, 'Well, until Gandhi and all that . . . that was in the forties or fifties, wasn't it?'

Sonya stifled a smile. History had never been dear old Estella's best subject, but Sonya had to admit that even she knew nothing about the Indians rising against the British in the nineteenth century.

'It was not all Indians, some actually fought beside the British in 1857. But nobody really likes foreign rule, so the feeling of wanting to get rid of it grew over the years,' Keshav explained.

'But we were always taught that Indians were really happy with the Brits bringing in the railways and the legal system? Isn't that right, Son?' Estella turned to Sonya for affirmation, adding by way of explanation to Keshav, 'Sonya was the history whizzo at school, not me!'

Sonya tried to look modest as Keshav turned the full

glare of his attention on her again. 'I must say I don't know much about this war against the British. Wasn't it more like a mutiny within the army?' she asked.

Keshav looked indignant. 'It was major,' he asserted. 'We call it our First War of Independence. Many people on both sides died. They say that, when the British finally broke into the Red Fort, their anger was so major, these streets were like rivers of blood. Even innocent shopkeepers, like these you see here today, were put to death.'

Sonya suppressed a shudder as she looked around her. By now they had reached a small bazaar area inside the fort where traders were selling kitschy gift items like miniature marble Taj Mahals and caparisoned wooden elephants and horses. A couple of little girls in grubby Indian clothes had run up to wave a clutch of painted wooden flutes. 'Buy, buy! Cheap, cheap!' they said like a pair of sparrows. She felt suddenly terribly and inexplicably saddened by the thought of those poor shopkeepers and children being murdered so ruthlessly by their British rulers. Despite being half Indian, Sonya had always felt relatively untouched by such stories from India. Even Richard Attenborough's *Gandhi*, which she had gone to see with her parents in the Bromley Odeon, had not moved her to feel any kinship with the country and its people. So it was curious how big a difference was made by being physically present in India. Quite unexpectedly, Sonya felt very close to the soil she was standing on and touched to tears by the suffering of its people. Perhaps it was just the heat doing strange things to her head!

She quickened her steps to catch up with Estella and Keshav. The latter was leading the way to the hall of public audience, explaining how the Mughal emperors met their subjects here to take their petitions. Sonya breathed a sigh of relief to be finally in a cool and airy place and, tuning out Keshav's authoritative, overbearing voice – at times his knowledge came out with so much arrogance – she wandered across to explore the anterooms that led off the great hall. Pigeons were cooing in the rafters and, through the windows, she could see tourists and picnickers on the lawns. She leaned against a windowsill, feeling the breeze on her face and watching a large family group playing with a Frisbee, before sitting down to unpack vast quantities of food. On hearing footsteps, she turned and was startled to see Keshav appear at the arched entrance. His expression was unfriendly and there was no sign of Estella behind him.

'Look, I want to ask you – have I done anything to upset you?' he asked abruptly. His voice was loud and echoed in the tiny room.

Taken aback, Sonya tried to gather her thoughts. 'What do you mean?' she asked, frowning, her face going rapidly hot again.

'What I mean is that you have been rude and nasty to me all day. And I don't know why,' Keshav replied in a sharp voice. 'Please understand, I don't have to be taking you out like this on a college holiday. It's only because Didi asked that I agreed to be your guide today. My father has worked for many years with Didi's family, they paid for my education and so there was no way I would say no, okay? But you have behaved all morning as though I am forcing my company on you. You're no better than me, okay. Just because you were born in England that doesn't make you more important. If your friend was not so nice to me, I would leave you here to take a taxi back to the house. Is that what you want me to do? Just say and

I will do it!' Keshav stuck his chin out belligerently, his dark eyes fixed on Sonya's face.

Sonya was shocked into sudden silence by his outburst. She felt confused and, if truth be told, also a little frightened by the aggressive expression on Keshav's face. And where the hell was Estella? Keshav was blocking the door and so she couldn't even run outside in search of her friend. Suddenly she was terribly overwhelmed by it all. She was tired and befuddled and homesick and it didn't help at all that Keshav was staring in such a hostile fashion at her, as though egging her on to fight. Without further ado, Sonya promptly burst into tears.

The expression on Keshav's face changed instantly. After a moment's confusion, he walked up to Sonya and tried to peer into her face but it was covered by her hands, tears flowing copiously between her fingers. He then held her by the shoulders, his voice now suddenly gentle. 'Hey, c'mon, stop crying. Didi will be so angry with me too'. But Sonya continued to bawl, wiping her eyes and nose with the palms of her hands as she could find no tissues in her pocket. 'I won't leave you here to take a taxi, okay?' Keshav said, trying to compensate for his earlier outburst as Sonya now collapsed against him completely, burying her face in his chest. He looked frantically around for Estella.

'It's not . . . it's not you . . .' Sonya finally managed to mumble against his shirt.

'Not, me? Thank God! I thought you were being snobbish because I was just a driver. You just were so angry with me all the time!'

'No, you haven't upset me at all, and I'm not angry with you . . .' Sonya hiccupped.

'Then what is it? Why are you crying so badly?'

207

'I don't know . . .' she wailed, drawing away even though it was nice to have someone hold her. All her gut instinct about Keshav was melting away as she was enjoying the feel of his arms around her shoulders.

Keshav tried again, looking intently at her face. 'Has someone done something to upset you? Some eve-teasing or something?'

Sonya did not know what eve-teasing was but she guessed from Keshav's gesture that he thought the gaggle of boys in the next room might have been rude in some way. She shook her head. 'No, no, please don't go fighting with them! It's just . . . just . . .' She trailed off, falling back against Keshav's chest again.

At that moment, Estella walked in. She nearly dropped her camera in astonishment at seeing Sonya, all red in the face and weeping in Keshav's arms. 'Hey, hon, what is it? Why are you crying? What have you . . .' She shot an accusing look at Keshav as though it had to be his fault.

Keshav dropped his hands from Sonya's shoulders and tried to push her away. But Sonya continued to cling to him while explaining to Estella, 'No, it wasn't anything he did, Stel! It's just . . . it just became all too much for me. I think it's the heat . . . or maybe just everything else . . .'

'What has become too much? What is everything else?' Keshav asked, still terribly confused.

Estella decided to take charge. 'It's a long story, Keshav, and I'm not sure we can tell you the whole thing just yet. Sonya's just overwhelmed by some stuff going on in her life, that's all.' She gave Sonya a questioning look, seeming unwilling to divulge all to Keshav.

But Sonya, warm and comforted in Keshav's arms, said,

'Let's go sit under a tree somewhere and we'll tell you all about it. I think that's the least we can do now . . .'

An hour later, stretched out flat on their backs side-by-side under the shade of a large mango tree, Estella and Sonya recounted the story of what had brought them to India. Keshav, who had been largely silent through their narration, keen to hear all the details, reached a hand out to Sonya. 'I'm sorry I shouted at you earlier,' he said. 'You have a major decision ahead of you and I can really understand the tension you must be going through.'

Sonya squeezed Keshav's hand and continued to hold it loosely as she looked up through the branches of the tree at the bright blue sky. She felt suddenly awash with pleasure at having bridged the horrible gulf that had formed so unnecessarily between them. It was suddenly so heartwarming to think that she might have made a friend here in India, someone who could really help in whatever way he could. Sonya turned her head towards him and said impulsively, 'And I'm so sorry I was so crabby with you, Keshav. It was childish of me to take out my personal problems on you like that. Will you ever forgive me?'

His dark eyes looked back at her as he gave her a slow smile. Sonya's heart did a little squeezy turnover. Estella was right, Keshav did look a bit like Robert Pattinson! Something around the chin and jaw, perhaps. Estella looked on, seeming suddenly a little wary.

'I don't know about "crabby" but I do know what "hungry" means,' Keshav said, patting his abdomen. 'Shall we go to Paratheywali Gali and fill up our stomachs first? Mine is growling,' he replied.

Estella sat up. 'I've been trying all day to say that name . . . Praataa . . . but I'm afraid I'm totally stumped by it.'

'Stumped?' Keshav asked. 'To me that's a cricket word.'

'Yes, it's meant to come from cricket, I think. Means the same thing: knocked out,' Sonya laughed.

Keshav shook his head as he got up and dusted the grass off his clothes. 'You people do speak English really stupidly sometimes, same words with many different meanings,' he complained.

Sonya and Estella dissolved into laughter and Estella clarified. 'No, it's you who speaks English funny sometimes.'

'Me? But everyone here praises my English! We in India are taught to speak English properly in our schools, with grammar lessons and all that. Maybe only the *way* we say things is different. You know like accent and all,' Keshav protested.

Sonya took his hand again as they started to walk back towards the car park. 'Your English is just beautiful, Keshav,' she said. 'And don't let anyone tell you otherwise. Especially not Estella who's really just a jumped-up chav.' She dodged behind Keshav as Estella raised her camera bag to whack her.

Laughing, Keshav said, 'No fighting, girls. Don't behave like chavs. But tell me, what does "chav" mean?'

Suddenly conscious of her hand in his, Sonya sneaked a glance at Keshav and, possibly because he did not want her to withdraw it, he squeezed her palm tightly. They walked along, and Sonya felt suddenly shy at this unexpected turn their relationship had taken. No words had been exchanged to signify such a momentous change but the shift was palpable and, during the rest of the afternoon, Sonya found herself reaching for Keshav's arm whenever the opportunity arose. Using silly excuses such as needing his help to cross lanes and parking lots, enjoying having someone in this alien environent to rely on. Keshav too seemed conscious of the unexpected transformation in his status and, at a craft bazaar called Dilli Haat, he bought a conch-shell necklace and clipped it around Sonya's neck in an extravagant gesture of new-found friendship.

On seeing this, Estella's expression – which had been mildly perturbed on first spotting Sonya and Keshav walking hand in hand – now turned seriously anxious. When Keshav went to buy a round of tea, she used the opportunity to whisper a kindly warning but Sonya shrugged it off. 'I don't think I want to "go easy", Stel, even though that's undoubtedly sound advice. Keshav's lovely, so sweet and kind. I really do need something like this to help distract me from everything that brought me to India.' Estella did not look much reassured and so Sonya added a tad sheepishly, 'And . . . um . . . with regard to me flirting a bit with Keshav, I'd broken up with Tim before leaving anyway . . . been meaning to tell you . . .'

'No, I wasn't thinking of old Tim. No, it's *this* that worries me. All this . . . Keshav . . . India . . . it's all so alien, really . . .' Estella waved her hand around her as she trailed off, unable to express her concern fully. Then she spoke swiftly, suddenly conscious that Keshav would be back before too long. 'I meant to say it earlier today too but just didn't get the chance. I think he's completely potty about you, Sonya.'

'No way,' Sonya said, outwardly embarrassed but secretly pleased.

'Oh yes he is. I spotted it first thing this morning. He seems to secretly examine your every movement, it's a bit eerie. Which is probably why he was so upset by your giving him the brush-off at first. I say "go easy" more for his sake, actually. You won't break his heart, will you? Don't go forgetting that we only have a few days here in Delhi.'

Sonya shook her head. 'I don't intend hurting him at all, Stel,' she said vehemently. 'And I'm not rushing into anything anyway. It's just that I feel a bit ridiculous about all that I said earlier. In a way, I feel I kinda need to make up for having been such a cow earlier, y'know . . .'

'I know. But it's worth remembering that we barely know him, hon. And he does live in a completely different world to ours too.'

They stopped talking as Keshav arrived, carrying sweet tea in three earthen cups. He passed the cups around before sitting down and turning to the girls, his eyes shining with a strange excitement. 'Listen, I want to help you with this problem that has brought you to my country,' he said. 'You need someone like me to help you to track down Sonya's mother and I think together we can come up with a really good plan.'

Chapter Twenty-Four

Neha watched the landscape change as the car she was travelling in descended the mountains. She had bid goodbye to Arif at Ananda but not before exchanging telephone numbers and email addresses, and a solemn promise that he would contact her when he passed through Delhi to catch his flight back to LA next week.

'I want you to meet Sharat too,' Neha had said before ordering, 'Come and have dinner!'

Arif had nodded, although he too would have been aware of how precarious Neha's position was when she got back home. No mention was made of the problem awaiting her as both of them were conscious of the Ananda staff who had also lined up to bid Neha goodbye. Arif and she had discussed Sonya's letter in detail and the only solution they had managed to come up with was that Neha should explain matters to Sonya if she did make contact, and appeal to her better nature to remain discreet about it for everyone's sake.

'Surely she'll understand what you had gone through then. And at such a young age,' Arif had insisted.

But Neha had been less optimistic. 'She's exactly that age now, Arif. And may have a very different sense of right and wrong to the one I did then. Also, who knows

213

what she's been through in her own life? She may be a very angry young woman. And not without good reason, you must admit.'

Neha felt that familiar prickle of fear pass through her body as she thought again of the consequences of her secret being revealed. Thanks to Arif's company, there had been moments during these past few days in Ananda when she had not thought about it at all but now, on the road back to Delhi and her beloved husband, the aching fear with which she had departed her home was slowly overcoming her again. What would it be like to lose Sharat, she wondered? From friends who had been through terrible crises in their marriages, Neha knew how lucky she had been to have never had to seriously consider that question before. But now, here it was, staring her right in the face. It would be the equivalent of taking a knife and carving a hole in Sharat's chest, when he found out about her lies. Despite his apparent urbanity, he was at heart a small-town Lucknow lad with a deeply conservative streak, and what she had done would seem the ultimate betrayal to him. She had no doubt about that.

'What I love most about you is your honesty, Neha. Yes, that's what I fell in love with when we first met three years ago.'

'Honesty!? For heaven's sake, there must be other qualities a man would mention – sexy, doe-eyed, "home-maker", that's a big one in India – and you go for honesty! Only someone like you, Sharat Chaturvedi!'

They had been celebrating their third wedding anniversary at their favourite Chinese restaurant just down the road from their new house. It had been a high point in their lives: they had recently moved into the Prithviraj Road bungalow that Sharat had inherited from his grandparents in the summer. Neha was happily occupied with refurbishing the place and visiting art fairs around the world in search of the best paintings and artefacts for the house. And their childlessness was a sorrow that had not revealed itself yet.

Neha tried to distract herself by looking out of the car window for the road signs to Haridwar. She had asked to be taken there for the religious ritual of Ganga Aarti before catching the night train back to Delhi. There was something faintly comforting about the belief that the holy river absolved everyone who bathed in it of all their sins, but even Neha knew she was now clutching at straws.

The car pulled up at the jetty from where Neha was to take a boat to the opposite bank. Parmarth Ashram lay across the river that flowed briskly past, brown and choppy, and Neha trailed her hand in the water as the boat chugged its way across. She joined the crowds that were thronging the ashram for evening worship and took her place on the steps overlooking the river. Dozens of small boys clad in orange and red robes – trainee priests at the ashram – were already chanting bhajans as the sun started to sink towards the river. The chanting grew louder as the sun disappeared in a blaze of orange, and oil lamps were passed from hand to hand. The sensory experience was so intense that, for a moment, Neha forgot everything, giving herself up to the river and to the gods. She closed her eyes and prayed for forgiveness, taking an impulsive vow that, rather than live with the pain and shame of hurting Sharat, she would return to the River Ganges and allow it to take her life.

'D'you know, if anything were to happen to you, Neha, I'd take my life and join you wherever you had gone.' He had

been depressed that day by the news of a tragic accident that had killed a young cousin.

'Shush, don't talk like that, Sharat. Nothing's going to happen to me.'

'No, really, Neha,' he insisted, 'we don't even have to worry about children and what will happen to them. In that sense we are lucky. We should make a pact that neither of us will even attempt to live without the other . . .'

She barely slept on the train and, when it pulled into New Delhi railway station, an hour late, she found a text message from Sharat, saying that the car and driver would be waiting for her in the VIP car park near the Ajmeri Gate entrance. A porter carried her suitcase to the car park and she picked her way past sleeping beggars and ragged bundles of clothes. On spotting her, the driver ran to get her suitcase and she climbed into the car, weary and exhausted. Delhi had finally gone to sleep at that late hour. She didn't usually get to see the city like this, calm and traffic-free, eerily beautiful through the smoked glass windows of the car. But she could not truly relish any of it. All she wanted at this point was to be in her home and near Sharat, both of which she was soon about to lose.

The house was quiet as she walked in. Ram Singh hurried down the corridor to get her suitcase out of the car. Neha's whispered enquiry about Sharat revealed that he had gone to sleep. It was, after all, just past midnight and Sharat was an early riser. Neha let herself into their bedroom. The curtains were drawn and although she couldn't see Sharat in the dark, she could hear his soft snores from the direction of the bed. Slipping off her shoes, Neha crawled under the *razai* and wrapped her arm around the sleeping body of her husband. She felt him stir slightly before he settled back against the familiarity of her curves with a deep sigh. Neha could feel the steady beat of Sharat's heart under her palm and she tenderly kissed one shoulder blade. Her entire being melted with love for her husband. He was worth fighting tooth and nail for and she was damned if she was going to give up her marriage without doing her best to save it first.

Chapter Twenty-Five

After Keshav had deposited Sonya and Estella back at the Mahajan household in time for dinner, they spent a little time with the family in their TV lounge before turning in for their baths and bed. Typically, Estella was out for the count as soon as her head had touched the pillow but Sonya spent a sleepless night, listening to the sounds of all sorts of unfamiliar creatures coming to life outside the window. She tried to count a persistent frog's croaks in a bid to fall asleep but got to two thousand before finally giving up. Her eyes were wide open, her nerves on edge. Then, getting up to splash water over her face for the umpteenth time, she told herself that it was the heat that was preventing her from falling asleep. Or perhaps it was her stomach that was still a little dicky from all the unfamiliar foods she had introduced to it since arriving in India. She eyed herself dubiously in the bathroom mirror and grimaced. Of course, it was none of those things. It wasn't even the annoying disappearance of Neha Chaturvedi, to be honest. Without a doubt, her current restless state was all due to what Estella had referred to as 'The Keshav Effect'. She'd be kidding herself if she tried blaming the heat or food or anything else. It was all very well trying to convince Estella of this earlier but what was the point in pulling the wool over her own eyes?

Sonya glared at herself. In her white cotton nightshirt, face scrubbed free of make-up and hair pulled back off her face in a pink scrunchie, she looked like a bewildered and frightened little girl. And that's exactly how she felt. No boy had ever made her feel like this before: not just confused but also oddly insecure. Here she was in this exotic land in these incredible circumstances and now she'd met a boy like no other in the UK. Perhaps it wasn't Keshav inveigling his way under her skin but India playing tricks on her mind. Many who had visited the country had written about its propensity to baffle and confound, like Forster in *Passage to India*, a book that had gripped Sonya when she had read it at school. She had subsequently got the film version of it from Blockbuster and watched it all by herself, knowing that it wasn't really Mum and Dad's scene. Sonya now piled her hair up on top of her head and twisted her neck around, wondering if she even looked a bit like Judy Davis who had played Adela Quested.

Sonya returned from the bathroom a few minutes later, retying her hair in exasperation in order to keep it off her sweaty neck. She cast an annoyed glance at Estella, supine and snoring peacefully. Despite being a terrible flirt some-times, dear old Estella wasn't half the romantic she was, invariably stepping back at exactly the right moment, almost never making an ass of herself. As for Sonya, despite having started off on such a bad note with Keshav only this morning, she had managed a bizarre three-hundred-and-sixty-degree turnaround in her feelings for him. What was it with her? Was it *because* she had been instantly attracted to Keshav that she had initially put up such fierce defences? And – even if the attraction was now mutual (and surely it was, given all the hand-holding and necklace-buying) – what was she to do about their total and complete incompatibility? And the fact that they only had a few days in Delhi? Estella was quite correct in warning her of it too. After all, she wasn't really the type to indulge in a one-night stand.

Sonya wandered across to the window. The night was warm and the air hung sticky and heavy over the garden, although a pair of fireflies were zipping and dancing around under a street light. After watching them for a while, Sonya returned to her bed and lay down again with a thump. She had to force herself to sleep if she wanted to go out again with Keshav tomorrow, as planned. But the anticipation of seeing him again in a few hours was making her feel dizzy.

It was such a strange thing, her attraction for Keshav. The man had a certain swagger about him that, in another context, Sonya would have considered most maddening: arrogant at times and so forthright with his opinions. There was, in fact, little about him that she would, under normal circumstances, have found appealing. But, lying sleepless in the dark somewhere in the heart of India and so far away from home, all Sonya knew was that she had found Keshav more and more personable – charismatic even – as the day had progressed. She had been especially touched by the caring manner in which he had escorted her and Estella to the crowded street on which they had lunched, treating them as though they were the two most precious charges he had ever been responsible for. He had also proven to be possessed of superhuman tolerance when they had later gone to the craft bazaar for their shopping. While she and Estella had gone a bit wild buying junk jewellery and gifts for family and friends back at home,

Keshav had waited patiently, smiling with amusement as he leant on various shop counters watching them haggle, stepping in to help only when necessary. And then doing so in a fabulously manful way, switching fluently between Hindi and English. When she had felt his fingers brush her neck as he had clasped the necklace around it, Sonya had felt an electric surge hit her heart, the kind of high-voltage moment that she had almost never experienced with Tim back at home.

Poor old Tim . . . Sonya had a sudden guilty flash of the last time she had seen him, sitting on the swings in Orpington Park while she had made good her escape on a bus. She hadn't been very nice to him. He was, after all, not merely a schoolmate but had been one of her best friends too, their friendship going as far back as middle school. But Sonya knew without a doubt that she would never in a million years be able to feel for Tim the way she already did for Keshav. Despite all their differences, it was with Keshav that she was more likely to experience that *thing* – that magical quality which had eluded her so far. It must exist. Surely she was not immune to that thrilling explosion of feelings that Emily back at school had once described as 'a lightning flash through the body, reaching the very tips of your fingers and toes'. Sonya had never once felt anything remotely resembling that in all her time with Tim. Was it right to spurn the opportunity for such an experience now, when it was staring her right in the face?

It was close on midnight when Sonya's eyes finally closed themselves in a restless, fitful sleep.

Keshav turned up at the Mahajan household early the next morning, as promised. It was Sunday and so the whole family was sitting in the garden, enjoying breakfast outdoors under the generous shade of a mulberry tree. Mr Mahajan was teaching calculus to his fifteen-year-old son, Rishi, who seemed a distinctly reluctant student from what Sonya could see. Despite Mrs Mahajan's efforts, both Sonya and Estella had cried off helping Rishi, stating a common aversion for any subject even remotely mathematical. Instead, they read the newspapers and made further travel plans with the help of their guide book while helping themselves to the generous bowl of cut papaya that had been laid out on the garden table.

Sonya's heart lurched slightly as the gates opened and she saw Keshav come striding down the garden path. He was wearing a clean white shirt today, matched with blue jeans, and seemed to have taken particular care over his appearance with a shave so close it had left his face shiny smooth. Sonya personally preferred the unshaven careless-ness he had displayed the previous day – the 'Banderas look' that most of the young fellows in Delhi seemed to sport – but he still looked rather scrummy. She fingered a strand of her hair nervously, hoping she was looking nice too, given that she had woken at the crack of dawn in order to wash her hair and iron her lacy blue Topshop shift dress. She had even run her new smoke-grey eye-kohl around her eyes in an effort to make herself look more Indian.

Keshav received an ecstatic welcome from Rishi but Sonya could not tell if this was genuine fondness on the part of the boy or merely a means to escape the rigours of his calculus lesson. 'Keshav *bhaiyya*, can we watch the Australia-India test match together tonight? On the high definition LCD?' the boy said in a wheedling voice, doing his best to tempt the older lad.

Keshav tousled Rishi's hair and replied, 'Maybe not tonight, Rishi. I have some other plans . . . but the next one is with you definitely, *theekh hai*?' He smiled at Sonya and Estella, and Sonya hoped desperately that his evening plans included her for, like Rishi, she too was extremely keen on Keshav's company tonight.

Sonya watched Keshav now as he talked to Mrs Mahajan in Hindi, feeling a strange ache in the pit of her stomach. Estella flashed her a warning look and moved her head sideways to signal that they should leave the breakfast table. They had made plans with Keshav to go into central Delhi and try once more to track Neha Chaturvedi down so there was serious work at hand. Both girls mumbled excuses and got up from their chairs.

'I hope you don't mind if we use the car again today, Mrs Mahajan,' Estella asked. 'We'll keep tabs, of course, on the mileage so we can settle up before we leave.'

'Of course, it is no problem at all,' Mrs Mahajan replied, stacking the cereal bowls, 'We have the other car if we need to go out anywhere. Anyway Sundays are usually quiet days at home for us. Mr Mahajan likes to sleep after breakfast, you see! So tired is he from his working week.'

Mr Mahajan, who tended not to say very much when his more garrulous wife was around, nodded and beamed beatifically at the mention of his forthcoming morning nap.

Mrs Mahajan carried on speaking as the plates were cleared. 'You girls go and enjoy yourselves. Keshav tells me you are going to Lodhi Gardens and Humayun's Tomb. Oh, and that lunch you will be having along with your shopping at Khan Market, so I won't expect you back before evening, yes?'

Sonya and Estella looked at Keshav for confirmation as

neither had made any contribution to the itinerary. He nodded and so Estella said, 'That's right, Mrs Mahajan. Keshav's very generous to spare us a precious Sunday. He's what would be called a "diamond geezer" in Britain.'

Mr Mahajan seemed very pleased with this description for Keshav and the girls could hear him laughing and repeating the words 'diamond geezer' a couple of times as they went upstairs to gather their belongings from their room above the garage.

Fifteen minutes later, they were piling their bags, cameras and water bottles into the back seat of Mrs Mahajan's spacious Ambassador. This time they decided to sit together on the front seat and Estella heroically stepped aside to allow Sonya to get in next to Keshav. Sonya wondered if her friend had suddenly grown a little distrustful of Keshav as she seemed to be a little on-guard. But she rewarded Estella with a grateful smile as she climbed into the car and moved up so close to Keshav she could feel her bare leg brush against the material of his jeans. She managed to curb herself from laying a proprietorial hand on Keshav's thigh. Perhaps if Estella hadn't been around, she'd have felt less inhibited and thrown all caution to the winds . . .

Keshav drove them quickly into central Delhi, heading for Prithviraj Road. The plan was simple. They were going to make one more direct attempt at meeting Neha Chaturvedi at her house but, if she continued to evade Sonya, they would follow her around the city, exerting pressure on her by tailing her car until she agreed to meet Sonya and explain herself. Sonya, relieved at finally getting some action, was enthused by the idea; although the more cautious Estella had to be assured by Keshav that following someone around at a safe distance wasn't illegal in India.

When they arrived at Prithviraj Road, Sonya pointed out the large black gates and the discreet brass nameplate that said 'Chaturvedi'. Keshav let out a low whistle. 'I knew they would be rich people when you said Prithviraj Road,' he said. 'But this! These people are majorly rich, man,' he said excitedly.

'So what do we do now?' Estella asked, her voice wobbling with nervousness.

'Let's go and ask the chowkidar if madam is in,' Keshav suggested.

'You go – you can speak Hindi,' Sonya urged.

Keshav thought for a second before saying, 'No, I think it would be better for one of you to go. You see, the chowkidar will be much happier to talk to a girl than a boy. He may even let you into the house.'

'He did last time,' Estella recalled. 'Well, I think it's the same guy. Can you tell, Son?'

Sonya peered through the dusty windshield. 'Can't tell . . . I think it's the same guy but that might not be good news for us – he might be wiser after last time and have strict orders not to let us in again!'

'Foreigners are welcomed everywhere in India,' Keshav reassured them, adding gruffly, 'They're like VIPs wherever they go.'

'Okay, bull-by-the-horns and all that,' Estella said suddenly, opening the door of the car.

She got out and Sonya scrambled after her in haste. Together they walked up to the guard's hut. An old Nepalese face peered out at them from over the wall. 'Excuse me, we're looking for Neha Chaturvedi,' Estella said.

The guard looked uncertain.

'Is madam in the house?' Sonya asked, trying not to betray her anxiety.

This time the guard nodded almost imperceptibly. Sonya clutched so hard at Estella's arm, she made her friend yelp. 'Did you see that, Stel? He nodded. She's in!' Sonya hissed.

Perhaps their behaviour seemed suspicious, or the guard had been given stern instructions not to let them through after their last visit. Whatever the case, the man remained implacable, refusing point blank to open the gates for them on this occasion. Just when Sonya was contemplating calling Keshav for help, the guard compromised by allowing them to make a phone call to the house from a small telephone instrument that was wired up to his cabin. He dialled the number for them and held the mouthpiece a few centimetres away from his face as he bellowed, 'Ram Singh, madam *ke liye koi* visitor *hain.*'

Sonya and Estella could hear a voice crackle down the line in response before things went silent. They waited, shifting from foot to foot as the guard held firmly onto the telephone and eyed them with increasing suspicion. It was all taking so much time that, before long, Keshav too emerged from the car and stood next to the girls. Finally, after what seemed like aeons, the telephone line crackled again and this time, the guard stood to attention as he answered with a brisk, '*Ji*, memsahib.' Then he handed the phone to Estella. With a look of complete alarm on her face, Estella hastily passed the instrument on to Sonya, behaving almost as though it would burn her. Face now pale and eyes wide, Sonya took the telephone between trembling hands and held it to her ear.

'Hello?' she said, her voice low.

An equally muted voice responded. 'Yes?'

'Is that . . . is that Neha? Neha Chaturvedi?' Sonya asked.

227

'Yes,' came the hesitant response.

Sonya paused to take a breath before speaking again. She could feel both Estella's and Keshav's hands on her shoulders, offering silent support. 'I wrote you a letter recently,' she said. 'I'm Sonya Shaw.'

There was a long silence before the voice spoke, its tenor remaining unchanged, low and grave, as though this phone call had been expected all along. 'Hello, Sonya. Yes, I received your letter. I was going to respond but needed some time to think.' Sonya remained silent as she did not know what to say next and, after a pause, Neha spoke again, her voice dropping now to a whisper. 'You are outside my gate?'

'Yes,' Sonya responded.

'Look . . .' Neha said, her voice still barely a whisper. Sonya thought she discerned a tremble in her voice too as she continued, 'We need to talk properly. Not like this. Can you . . . can you meet me in Lodhi Gardens in half an hour?'

'Lodhi Gardens?' Sonya repeated for Keshav's benefit and he nodded vigorously.

'Do you know where it is?' Neha asked. 'It's just around the corner from here.'

'I can find it,' Sonya said.

'I'll be there in half an hour – eleven thirty – near the duck pond. Ask someone for directions,' Neha said before abruptly hanging up.

Sonya returned the phone instrument to the guard and managed to make it back to the car before she burst into tears. Both Estella and Keshav wrapped their arms tightly around her while she wept as though a storm were raging through her. Then she sat up abruptly and wiped her face with her hands, saying as firmly as she could, 'I mustn't cave in now. Gotta keep my head. She wants to meet me.'

'Bloody Nora. When?' Estella asked.

'Eleven thirty. How far is Lodhi Gardens from here, Keshav?'

'Two minutes,' was his response. 'Ten minutes max, including parking etcetera. Do you want to head off there now?'

Sonya nodded. 'Yes, please. We'll need to find the duck pond too.'

'Are you okay, hon?' Estella enquired as Keshav started up the car. Sonya nodded. She felt suddenly drained of all emotion, the anger and rage with which she had first embarked on this journey having worn her out at the most crucial moment. Estella persisted. 'Do you want me to be with you when you meet her, Son? Or do you want to do this on your own?'

Sonya considered her options. After a while, she said, 'I should meet her on my own, Stel. But would you and Keshav be somewhere nearby, please? Within calling distance?'

Estella nodded soberly. 'Of course. We'll be right there for you, don't you worry.'

In a few minutes they were at Lodhi Gardens and Keshav pulled the Ambassador into a small car park. They entered lush green gardens through a small metal gate. It was a beautiful park, full of old trees and even older tombs and monuments that were so much a part of the Delhi landscape. But Sonya had no appetite for the lovely surroundings. Her insides felt so tightly wound up, she was scared she might puke. Her Dad's pet name of 'Drama Diva' notwithstanding, this was truly the most momentous encounter Sonya knew she would ever face in her life.

Chapter Twenty-Six

Neha replaced the phone receiver with trembling hands. Her heart was thumping so hard, she felt faint and had to grip the edge of the marble counter for a few seconds in order to regain her balance. She looked surreptitiously over her shoulder even though she had taken the call in the kitchen, a part of the house that Sharat never visited. Only Ram Singh was pottering at the stove, and he clearly had not thought anything of the memsahib taking a call in the kitchen. Neha's thoughts were racing. She had left Sharat in the breakfast room on the far side of the house, absorbed in the Sunday papers. Surely he would not notice her absence for an hour or so. She had to go to Lodhi Gardens – there was no way she could avoid this meeting any more . . .

Neha slipped upstairs to wear something more sober than the pink tracksuit she had worn for her yoga session that morning. The terrible irony of doing something as mundane as choosing what to wear when she met her grown daughter for the first time struck Neha as she stood before her walk-in wardrobe and stared blankly at rack after rack of elegant clothes. She tried to suppress her panic by reminding herself that Sonya could be a very angry young woman or even a hard-nosed trickster with an agenda of her own. Neha recognized that she was employing cynicism as a defence. In truth, she couldn't help hoping that she was wrong to be pessimistic about this meeting with Sonya.

Neha hastily pulled on a pair of white trousers and a mauve cotton top and slipped her feet into a pair of plimsolls. Then, quite deliberately, she took her phone and shoved it into the back of her dressing-table drawer. She neither wanted anyone to know where she was nor to receive any phone calls for the next hour or so.

Suddenly oddly calm, Neha returned downstairs and did a quick check on Sharat. He was still sunk in his favourite cane armchair that overlooked the back garden, engrossed in a newspaper article, his favourite Homer Simpson mug bought on a trip to New York full of steaming fresh coffee at his elbow.

Heart thudding, she turned and walked swiftly to the side door next to the dining room and silently exited into the garden. The gardeners were unperturbed to see the memsahib walking down the jasmine path, accustomed as they were to her using the back route into Lodhi Gardens for her morning and evening walks. Neha greeted them but carried on walking quickly, glancing at her watch as she left the compound through the side gate and crossed the service road. She had ten minutes to reach the duck pond, a distance that usually took no more than five minutes, and so she slowed her pace as she entered the park, trying to harness the maelstrom of feelings raging within her.

What would she say to Sonya? How would she greet her? Would Sonya be able to cope with her grief and anger . . . for surely those were the emotions the poor girl would feel for a mother who had abandoned her? Or were her intentions altogether more sinister?

These were Neha's muddled thoughts as she walked around the corner and saw a young girl standing by herself under a jacaranda tree, facing the duck pond. She stopped in her tracks and took in a sharp breath, because from this distance the girl could have been her, and time could have magically spiralled backwards to when she herself was eighteen. Sonya was tall and slim and her hair, like Neha's, was tied back in a thick, dark ponytail that hung down her back to her waist. The girl turned to lean her back on the cement railings and Neha saw an English countenance, a higher forehead, a nose much sharper than hers and eyes that were a blazing blue. Alastair's eyes.

'Please, Alastair, I'm going to have a baby – our baby . . .'

'You can't be serious. Our baby, indeed. Such sentimental tosh! There is no "our"; we don't have a relationship. Do you understand that, Neha? So there can be no baby, don't you see? What you need is a good gynaecologist, woman. Go straight to the Brooke Centre on Mead Street; they'll help you to get rid of it over there. It's a free service too. Don't delay things till it's too late, for God's sake.'

'I don't want to get rid of it. Whether you like it or not, this is our baby, Alastair. Please, we can have a good life together if we try.'

'Together? There is no together! Why don't you get it? It was a mistake – a one-night stand! You threw yourself at me and I succumbed, as simple as that; the oldest story in the world. Whoever said anything about marriage and – for God's sake – babies! You must be deluded if you think you can threaten me like this . . .'

Neha started to walk again, more slowly than before, as the girl spotted her and looked questioningly in her direction.

'Sonya?' Neha asked, coming to a halt two feet in front of her daughter.

Neha could barely hear the girl's reply as she nodded and said in a low voice, 'Yes, I'm Sonya.'

Neha wanted to reach out and touch her, some primal instinct propelling her forward, but she forced herself to stay where she was. Sonya was English, after all, and probably quite unused to tactile contact from someone she was not familiar with . . . from someone she hated?

'Please tell me what I can do for you, Sonya?' Neha asked, her fingers clutched into tight fists inside her pockets. She was trying to keep her voice gentle but she was aware of how harshly the words seemed to be escaping her lips.

The girl's eyes widened slightly before she deliberately narrowed them, making her face far less attractive than before. Her voice too was now sharper. 'You owe me an explanation, I believe,' she said in a suddenly clipped cut-glass accent that made her sound so much like Alastair.

It was best to be direct, Neha thought. 'What is it you want? Do you want me to explain about the decision to give you up for adoption?' Sonya nodded in response. 'First of all, how much do you know?' Neha asked.

An expression of irritation passed over Sonya's face at being faced with a question. But she took a deep breath and replied. 'My parents told me all along that I was adopted. They said it made me more special than everyone else and that's certainly how they made me feel – very special and very loved. Apart from knowing that I was mixed race, born to an Indian woman and an Englishman, they knew little else so that's all they could tell me.'

Neha felt as though little knives had stabbed into her with Sonya's use of words like 'my parents', 'very special' and 'very loved'. She couldn't help wondering if it was deliberate on Sonya's part to make her feel that way.

'Well?' Sonya's voice was brusque.

'Well what Sonya?' Neha's voice continued to stay calm and low-pitched.

'Well, are you going to tell me anything more?' Sonya demanded.

'What more do you want to know?'

Sonya paused. 'Mostly why you did it, I suppose.' Her tone was still unsympathetic.

'Why did I give you up?' Neha asked, her mind going strangely blank for a few seconds as the most traumatic event of her life rose to the surface again, dislodging every single good thing that had happened since. Suddenly, with her long-lost daughter standing before her, the sadness overwhelming Neha was so powerful she thought she might faint. Then she steadied herself and repeated. 'Why did I give you up?' After a pause – 'Because . . . because I had no choice, Sonya.'

Sonya cut in angrily. 'That's what I thought. That's how I comforted myself all these years. Until I saw the social worker's report recently.'

'Report?' Neha asked.

'Yes, the adoption social worker wrote a report at the time. Have you not seen it?'

Neha shook her head. 'What was in the report, Sonya?' she whispered.

Now Sonya was distraught, her face twisted as her emotions took over. 'That you were an educated woman, studying in Oxford, that you were articulate and smart and intelligent and well off. Which can only mean one

235

thing . . . that you had *choices*! They *asked* you what your choice was. They offered you support to look after me. You *had* the choice not to give me up, but you *did*. And . . . and . . . far worse, having given me up, you never once turned around to enquire if I was all right. If life had treated *me* kindly. While you . . . *you* went on to a superbly comfortable life in a bloody mansion here in Delhi – I've seen it for myself even though you're trying to lock me out! Tall gates and guards and cooks and servants. You live like a fucking princess and have the fucking cheek to tell me that you had no *choice*?!'

Neha reached out a hand as though trying to physically fend off Sonya's angry words. She opened her mouth to plead with Sonya but the girl was backing away from her now, her face all red and blotchy, tears spouting uncontrollably from her eyes. And, before Neha could utter another word, a pair of youngsters – an English girl and an Indian lad – had appeared from behind a tree and dragged Sonya away. Sonya was so distraught that she was unable to resist and allowed herself to be pulled away.

Neha stood watching helplessly as the twosome led Sonya in the direction of the gates, each holding an arm of hers. Sonya did not turn back but the boy, putting an arm protectively around Sonya's shoulder, turned and cast a glance back at Neha. Even though they were already at some distance, and her vision was blurred by tears, Neha could see how full of hate that look was.

Chapter Twenty-Seven

There were no more tears from Sonya that afternoon, but she was silent and taciturn as Keshav insisted on carrying on with their sightseeing trip around Delhi. 'It will make you feel better,' he said, 'I promise.'

But Sonya only got gradually more depressed as the day progressed, her mind darting heedlessly back to the meeting with Neha. She had to admit that Neha looked like a nice enough woman, not quite the snotty bitch she had expected. It also did not help that she looked so young, and sort of vulnerable as she had shouted at her; she was way younger than Mum and Dad. Doing the sums in her head, Sonya realized that Neha was probably only in her mid-thirties: fifteen years younger than her mother back in Orpington. Shockingly (and even though Sonya had prepared herself for this possibility) Neha also resembled her rather more than anticipated. It wasn't so much their face or features but a general air and manner that they seemed to share. That impact of seeing herself mirrored in someone else – a stranger, and a stranger she reviled – had been more of a shock than Sonya had imagined, almost akin to a physical blow to the stomach.

While Estella had offered mostly silent sympathy, Keshav had been quite relentlessly playing the buffoon all afternoon, trying to cheer Sonya up with a series of inane and not very funny jokes. Finally, exhausted, they ended up in Khan Market where Keshav took them into a roughly cobbled back lane and up a narrow flight of stairs to a colourful little café that advertised a range of sandwiches, cakes and fresh fruit juices. Sonya could not face eating anything so she sipped on a glass of orange juice as Estella and Keshav ordered grilled sandwiches.

'Hey, let me take you both to a disco tonight,' Keshav said, biting into a giant club sandwich.

'No, not a disco please,' Sonya protested. 'Or go with Stel. I'm just not up to it, Keshav.'

'Well, I'm certainly not going without you,' Estella declared.

'C'mon, Sonya, it will be fine. It is just what you need to pep you up when you're feeling down, no?' Keshav pleaded.

'We're not dressed for it. And it's too far to go home and back again in this traffic, isn't it?' Estella said.

But Keshav was prepared for all objections. 'Your clothes are fine. Or you can always buy something from the shops here if you really want. My friend Gopal lives near here so we can go there to get washed and changed. I'll ring up Didi and tell her we'll be late so that she's not worried and also so that she doesn't make dinner for you.'

Sonya hesitated for only a moment before she nodded. She had been a total killjoy all day, robbing both Estella and Keshav of the fun they ought to be having. Besides, it would be good to do something – anything! – that would help distract her from the dark and twisted direction her thoughts were insisting on taking. 'Okay, let's do this disco thing then,' she said, trying to smile.

'Are you sure, Sonya?' Estella enquired. 'If it's all been

too much for you, we can go back and have a quiet night in, just the two of us? Would you like that?'

'Ah, come on, girls, take a break from all this drama and emotion,' was Keshav's firm reply while Sonya hesitated. And so she gave in, oddly relieved to have someone stronger than her step in and take the decision.

After buying a pair of cheap spangly halternecks from a shop in the market, Sonya and Estella accompanied Keshav to a sprawling bungalow not too far from Khan Market. 'A junior minister in the Civil Aviation Department lives here,' Keshav informed them as they drove in. But, instead of going up the main drive to the big house, Keshav swung the car into a side road that led to the servants' quarters. Sonya remembered suddenly that Keshav was the son of the Mahajans' driver and realized that his friend was far more likely to be living in servants' quarters than in a rich man's bungalow. It suited her fine, of course. At the moment, she hated the smug hypocrisy of all those people who lived in Delhi's giant, sprawling bungalows; big shots who led supremely cosseted lives, waited on hand and foot by dozens of servants to whom they probably paid a pittance!

'Gopal's mother works in the minister's house as a cook,' Keshav explained as he pulled up outside a pair of tiny cottages. She was immensely grateful that Keshav did not consider them – with all their Western ways and talk – to be merely a pair of spoilt rich girls completely alien to his own world, even though he did seem fascinated by their lives in England. His college education and subsequent ease with English had made it easy for Sonya to forget the disparity that would otherwise have existed between them. Even in the few days she had been here, Sonya had observed the bubbles in which the wealthy in India lived, even kindly people like the Mahajans maintaining an us-and-them air with their employees that seemed quite the natural order of things. Even though Keshav had graduated to some kind of halfway world with the assistance of the Mahajans, it hadn't been difficult to notice that he too continued to maintain a discreet formality with them.

The girls got out of the car and shook hands with Keshav's friend, Gopal. He wasn't as polished as Keshav, and his English not as good. But he seemed delighted to be unexpectedly presented with the company of two English girls, falling over himself to make them comfortable in his home as he ushered them in and offered them all manner of food and drink.

'Pepsi? Tea? Coffee?' he offered eagerly.

'Just water, please,' Estella smiled before entering a living room that was minuscule in comparison with the Mahajans', no more than six feet square, with peeling walls that had green damp patches across one side. The furniture comprised a low table and two deckchairs with aluminium frames on which both girls had been seated at Gopal's insistence. Keshav had settled himself on a cotton carpet at Sonya's feet and was fiddling with an ancient radio that sat in one corner of the room. Sonya swigged back her glass of water and was about to put the glass down on the table when Gopal whisked out a tray with a huge smile. He seemed as nice as Keshav and Sonya thought it a pity that she could not speak a word of Hindi to put him at his ease. In the meantime, Keshav appeared to have had some success with the radio which was now issuing forth a tinny strain of Bollywood music. Estella was surprisingly quiet, sitting in the corner defensively with her hands on her lap.

'Is there a toilet I can use?' Sonya asked, and Keshav promptly sprang up to show her where it was.

He ushered her through a doorway covered with a faded curtain and Sonya found herself in a small bedroom with one bed pushed up against the far wall. Keshav held out his hand to help her step over a mattress that had been spread out on the floor. 'I'm sorry about this, it is not what you are used to,' he said. 'Gopal shares this house with his mother, you see. She is a widow and they don't have much money.'

'Oh, don't worry about it, I've lived in all sorts of places on my travels,' Sonya lied. She continued to hold Keshav's hand as he took her through a small blackened kitchen area and out into a small yard. A thin ragged dog sunning himself in the yard looked up with faint curiosity, tapping his tail in the dust as Sonya and Keshav picked their way across the uneven flagstones to an outside toilet.

'I will wait here for you,' Keshav said chivalrously, as Sonya ducked her head and entered a small space that was so dark it took a few moments for her eyes to adjust themselves from the sunshine outside. A naked light bulb hanging from the ceiling suddenly came on and Sonya guessed that Keshav had turned on the switch from outside. She blinked in confusion, stepping back as she saw that she was standing at the edge of a cracked ceramic bowl embedded in the floor, surrounding a hole in the ground. Sonya had never seen this sort of a toilet before but was damned if she was going to ask Keshav for instructions. Instead, using her instincts, she gamely hitched up her short dress, pulled her knickers down and squatted.

By the time she emerged, Keshav had organized a metal bucket full of water and used a plastic mug to scoop water out and pour some over Sonya's hands. She washed her hands using a small piece of soap that was red in colour and had a medicated smell. Then she splashed some water over her hot face and looked up at Keshav, laughing as she suddenly saw the funnier side of this strange new experience. Keshav seemed to get the joke too and, as they laughed together, he lobbed the mug back into the bucket so he could reach out and hold her wet face between his hands. With a tender expression on his face, Keshav laid his lips gently on Sonya's. She froze for a minute and then melted against Keshav as they kissed more passionately, Keshav's arms winding tightly around Sonya's waist, his hands lacing her hair.

They finally pulled apart and Keshav, trapping Sonya's gaze with his mesmeric dark eyes, whispered in a gruff voice, 'Later, yes? Now we better go back inside . . .' Sonya nodded and, still holding Keshav's hand, allowed herself to be led back through the courtyard, past the dog who was now eyeing them with a bored expression on its face. Her lips were still faintly wet from Keshav's kiss and Sonya felt a little frisson at the thought of what might come later. Whatever Keshav had in mind when he said 'later' was something Sonya knew she would find difficult to resist. In a strange way, she already felt totally protected by Keshav, her earlier bruised feelings over the encounter with Neha somehow assuaged by his strong, comforting presence.

Indoors, Gopal and Estella appeared to have overcome their communication problem by cranking up the radio as loud as it would get in order to prance around to a boppy Bollywood song. Sonya was glad to see Estella looking more relaxed. They must have been at it for some time as Sonya saw that the table and chairs had been folded back and leant against the wall to create a dance floor, while poor Estella was already red in the face and quite out of puff.

'Come, join in,' Gopal said, executing what looked like a very complicated twist technique that nearly brought him to the floor.

'Why bother with a disco, eh?' Sonya said, squealing as Keshav grabbed her hands and twirled her around so fast, she nearly careened into Gopal. They danced, all four of them, until the song was finished and then they collapsed onto the floor, laughing and out of breath.

'Omigod, you're quite a dancer, aren't you, Gopal? Twinkle-toes . . .' Estella huffed, lying flat on her back, fanning her face with a magazine.

'I learnt in school how to dance,' Gopal said.

'Yes, the other boys used to tease him because only girls used to go for dance classes in school,' Keshav said.

'*Billy Elliot*!' Estella said, explaining quickly: 'That's an English movie about a boy who has to fight everyone – even his dad – because he wants to become a dancer.'

'Is that what you want to become?' Sonya asked Gopal, 'A professional dancer?'

Gopal appeared not to know how to answer and so Keshav cut in. 'He tried to become a backing dancer in Bollywood but it's not possible without pull.'

'Pull, what?' asked Sonya, puzzled.

'You know, without knowing big people over there . . .' Keshav elaborated hesitantly.

'He means influence, Sonya,' Estella said, always better at working out Keshav's brand of English. 'I guess, like anywhere else, a newbie needs a godfather to get ahead in Bollywood.'

'Yes, a godfather, a "*dada*" we say here in India,' Keshav said, nodding.

'Also, there is not much money in dancing,' Gopal said.

'So Gopal has recently taken a job in an office in Connaught Place,' Keshav added.

'Really, what sort of job?' Sonya asked.

'Peon,' Gopal said.

'Helping to make tea and doing post and photocopying, and all such things,' Keshav explained.

'Oh, that's tragic,' Sonya cried. 'Imagine a dancer being stuck in an office job! I wish we could help . . .'

Gopal shrugged, apparently not wanting to discuss his stalled dancing career any more. Keshav piped up, changing the subject, 'So are we all going to a disco? There's one very near here which is very good called "Ego".'

'Oh, must we? Can't we just hang around here for a bit?' Sonya asked.

Keshav looked at Gopal who nodded. He said something in Hindi and afer a quick look had passed between the two of them, Keshav translated for the benefit of the girls, 'He says his Amma will only come back after twelve o'clock as the minister is having a dinner in his house.'

'Oh, goodie, so we have this bijou little private disco all to ourselves?' Sonya cried. 'We could phone for some food later, couldn't we?'

'Or go to Kake di Hatti on Outer Circle – that's a *dhaba*, you know, where the truck drivers go to eat.'

Sonya's eyes shone with glee. 'Oh, Keshav, I'm *so* glad we met you. Our holiday has been so much more fun. It feels like we're *really* experiencing India, doesn't it, Stel?'

Estella looked at Keshav and smiled somewhat warily. Sonya guessed that Keshav must have had words with Gopal regarding creating some private time for them because, half an hour later, Gopal suggested that he take Estella for a walk. 'I will show you India Gate and buy you ice cream over there,' he said, looking pointedly at Estella.

Estella turned to Sonya, obviously concerned at the pairing off. 'What do you say, hon?' she asked. 'You okay with that?'

'I'll be fine,' Sonya said firmly. By now she too was quite keen to get a bit of time alone with Keshav. Their tacit mutual longing was exciting to say the least and she knew she had what it took to resist any unwanted advances. Just some cuddling and kissing: 'No harm in that', as her mum had nervously pronounced the first time Sonya had asked if she could take Tim up to her room back in Orpington.

Estella still looked faintly worried but she silently pulled her sturdy Timberland trainers back on before leaving the house with Gopal. Sonya watched them walk down the drive before Keshav grabbed her by the waist and drew her back indoors. With one hand holding her firmly as though frightened she would fly away, Keshav pulled the door shut and latched it. Then, wrapping both arms around her body, he kissed Sonya properly, slipping one hand under her blouse to search for the clasp of her bra. Sonya felt his fingers fumble and stopped him by whispering, 'Not now, Keshav. Let's give it time, please . . .'

Keshav drew in his breath shakily but acquiesced, running his palms in a brief frustrated gesture over Sonya's clothed breasts before he firmly pulled her into the bedroom and tumbled with her onto the bedding.

They lay together, kissing some more and Sonya, feeling her whole being set alight, wondered how she had ever considered what she had with Timothy to be the pangs of first love. Surely *this* is the real thing, Sonya thought, feeling herself tingle all over with suppressed longing as she lay with her head on Keshav's arm. She looked up at him in a brief reprieve between his kisses and saw him smile down at her.

'Thank you,' she whispered.

'What are you thanking *me* for, Sonya?'

'For being so wonderful to me through this emotional mess I've got myself into. For making me forget my problems. For being the most gentle, and generous friend . . .'

'For you I will do anything, my Sonya.' Keshav grinned, 'Do you know, in Punjabi "Sonya" means "golden girl". That's what you are: a beautiful, golden girl who has landed in my life like a *pari*.'

'What's a "pari"?' Sonya asked.

'How do you say it . . .' Keshav screwed his forehead up, searching for the word. 'You know, like an angel or a fairy sent by God?' Keshav's voice was now thick with emotion as he lowered his head to kiss her again.

Chapter Twenty-Eight

After her ghastly meeting with Sonya in Lodhi Gardens, Neha stumbled back to her house, barely aware of the people she passed on the way. She was in a state of such distress that she stepped out into Amrita Shergill Marg without looking and nearly walked into the path of a speeding car that swerved and blared its horn angrily at her. Somehow she managed to keep from crying, aware that Sharat would notice in a jiffy if she returned home with her face all blotchy and tear-stained.

Reaching the house, she slipped indoors – Sharat was still in the breakfast room, blissfully unaware of her temporary absence – and so she ran upstairs to the safety of her bathroom. Locking herself in, Neha sat on the small armchair she used for her pedicures, wrapped her arms around her middle and bent over double, the most severe pain assailing her stomach. She desperately wanted to cry . . . for herself and for the girl in the park who had shouted at her with such anguish in her voice. Neha found it shocking that she had caused all that pain to another human being. Her *daughter*. For all these years she had determinedly refrained from thinking about the child she had given away. Even if some stray memory materialized in her head, it was usually ephemeral and unreal. But the girl with the bright blue eyes had been real, and apparently very damaged by what Neha had done. So much anger raging in her heart it was frightening. How far-reaching that decision which, at the time, had been made so swiftly, so thoughtlessly . . .

The scenes were replaying like a television set gone haywire. Neha saw, as clearly as though it was yesterday, the face of the midwife who had given her the baby to hold for a few minutes.

'Children need this initial physical contact with their biological mothers, my dear.'

'Are you sure it's okay? Marge the social worker had sort of warned me against bonding with the baby.'

'Did she now? Well, that Marge has always been a cold fish. No children of her own, I'm told. Honestly, the people they hire to help others with their problems – you'd think the Social would know better sometimes! No, really, take her for just a few minutes. All babies deserve a cuddle first thing, for heaven's sake. It's their first experience of the world after all . . .'

And so I took her in my arms. Tiny and fragile and making strange little clucking noises in her throat while she kept her eyes tightly closed. She was covered in white stuff, and was slippery to hold, but, suddenly, her eyes opened and she looked around, although I couldn't tell if she could see me. They were blue, not like my eyes at all. But her hair was black and thick, like mine, slicked down to her head. So strange to think that she had emerged from me . . . so . . . so strange and yet so moving . . .

Then one of the nurses came along to take her away. I wasn't sure if she was taking her away for a bit, just to clean her up, or if it was for good. Later, I thought I should have looked at her face more closely before she was carried away. Later, it was so hard to remember what she looked like. For a while, she was imprinted on my mind like an instant Polaroid, indelible even when I wanted to forget. But then, slowly, over the years, that picture started to fade and, much as I may have wanted to remember, I could not . . .

After she was taken away, I turned my face into the hospital pillow and wept but, if I were to be honest, I would have recognised that, at that point in time, I was weeping for myself and the mess I had got myself into; my heartbreak over Alastair and the end of not just my Oxford dream, but of youth and hope itself.

Weeping for my baby came much, much later . . . selfishly, oh so selfishly, only when I knew there would not be any more . . .

Neha jumped as someone rattled the doorknob. 'Neha, darling, are you in there?' Sharat's voice called.

Neha gathered her thoughts and replied, her voice sounding thin and unreal to her own ears. 'Yes, it's me.'

'Oh, okay, just wondered where you were . . . hope you haven't forgotten, we have Jasmeet's lunch at the Crowne Plaza . . .'

Neha's heart sank even lower than before. She had forgotten that they had been invited to Jasmeet and Kul's wedding anniversary party. She ought to cry off, make some excuse. She was in no state at all to sit around making frivolous social chit-chat. Neha pulled herself together – she had to, for her husband's sake. Then she flicked the flush and emerged into the bedroom to find Sharat already pulling out clothes from his wardrobe in the dressing area.

'Shall I wear this?' he asked, turning to Neha with a white silk kurta held against his chest. 'Or will it be too much?'

Neha looked at the boyish confusion on Sharat's face, her heart twisting with guilt and pain. He tended to ask her advice on the tiniest of matters, so great was his reliance on her good sense.

'It'll look great, Sharat,' she said. 'Wear it with jeans, rather than a churidar, then it won't look too formal.'

'What are you wearing?' he asked.

Neha hesitated for a moment, wondering whether to plead a headache and stay at home. Then, looking at Sharat's face frowning in concentration as he rummaged around for a pair of jeans, she said, 'I think I'll wear something Indian too, seeing that it's still so hot – a salwaar kameez maybe.'

They got ready, Neha helping Sharat with the buttons on his kurta and then turning to him for help with the clasp on her necklace. Little habits developed over the years that poor Sharat did not know would soon come to an end.

After they were dressed, Neha called for the car. The journey to Gurgaon through the South Delhi traffic was always a bit arduous, but the sight of Jasmeet's cheerful face as they walked into the restaurant of the Crowne Plaza was reassuring. She had, after all, been Neha's classmate and friend since the age of six. They exchanged hugs and Neha gave Jasmeet the small jewellery box that contained a modest pearl and diamond pendant that she had bought as an anniversary gift. Twenty-odd people, most of them familiar to Neha and Sharat, had already formed a noisy group at one end of the dining hall. They now greeted the new arrivals raucously, making room for them to join in.

'Hey, look at you, *yaar*, bloody *thinner* every time I see you!' Reena Singhal complained, looking enviously at Neha's slim figure.

'Not true,' Neha mumbled shyly in response, slipping into a seat next to Reena's. Across the table, Sharat had already struck up an animated conversation with Reena's husband Jimmy, a golfing buddy who had been pursuing him to invest in an Australian gold-mining company for weeks and was now clearly delighted with the opportunity he had been presented to revive his efforts. On the far side of the table were a pair of old classmates of Neha's and Jasmeet's from their schooldays and Neha waved at them by way of greeting, before returning her attention to Reena Singhal's inane chatter which fortunately required very little by way of concentration.

As the conversation flowed around her, Neha considered how little she actually knew all these friends. Jasmeet had stayed in touch far better with their old classmates, unlike Neha who, despite the parties she threw, had developed a reputation for being a somewhat reticent type. Perhaps that had been one of the coping tactics she had employed over the years – keeping everyone, even someone as warm and obliging as Jasmeet, at arm's length. It had always seemed safer not to let anyone come too close, lest they should find out her terrible secret. Left to herself, in fact, Neha would quite probably have never thrown a party in her life; but Sharat loved entertaining so much and now his plans to enter politics had made it *de rigueur*.

Neha looked around the table. Everyone was drinking and picking at the enormous platters of meze snacks as though none of them had a care in the world. Did any of these people have secrets of their own? And how would they react when her past became known? Even

251

Jasmeet . . . Jasmeet, who adored her two pretty teenage daughters more than anything else in the world . . . what would she think of how Neha had walked away from hers?

With the food in her mouth turning to wood, Neha thought again about Sonya. Where would she have gone after they had met? And who were the two youngsters who had come and pulled her away? The girl looked English so had probably come with Sonya from England. But the boy was Indian. Could he too have come with the girls from Britain? Or was he a local friend? Perhaps Sonya was staying with him while she was in Delhi . . .

Neha tried to hold on to her runaway thoughts as the woman sitting across from her asked about her latest art purchase, which had been prominently featured in a society magazine.

'Yes, it's a new Anjolie Ela Menon,' Neha replied politely. 'No, no, not a large canvas at all. Of course, you must come and see it yourself . . .'

Neha caught Sharat's eye from across the far end of the table and returned his smile. Her heart squeezed itself in sudden fear again at the thought of what Sonya's appearance in Delhi would do to him. Such a betrayal by an adored wife would surely finish him off. Perhaps, in a horribly ironic way, it was fortunate there were no children who would be affected by the inevitable destruction of their marriage. Neha cringed now, remembering how she and Sharat had in the past joked wryly that they might have cared less for each other had they *had* children, having observed friends with offspring focus so much emotional energy on the children that there was little left for the spouse.

To calm herself, Neha turned to Jasmeet on her left

who was narrating a story from her last catering assignment. Jasmeet's work led her to meet the most curious characters and she was consequently a treasure house of funny stories. Everyone laughed as she now hammed up her impression of a nouveau riche Delhi businessman trying to pronounce French words like 'canapés' and 'vol-au-vents' and Neha tried to join in the merriment, hoping no one would notice how forced her smile was.

She jumped as her phone rang in her handbag. A quick check revealed an unfamiliar number. Neha wondered if she ought to ignore it but, after a few minutes, it rang again and Neha got up from her chair to take the call. Unable to hear in the din, she walked towards the lobby, hearing a man's voice say, 'Hello? Mrs Neha Chaturvedi?'

'Yes?' she replied, arriving in the airy lobby where the muzak was soft enough for her to hear better.

'Mrs Chaturvedi. I am calling about your daughter, Sonya . . .'

Neha froze. She stopped walking and remained silent as her throat clogged up with fear. The voice said, 'Hello?' again a couple of times and, after an eternity, Neha finally whispered, 'Who is it please?'

The caller seemed to derive confidence from Neha's diffident tone and started speaking again, now using a loud and rapidly escalating voice. 'You do not have to know who I am, okay. It is not for you to ask me any questions. Can you hear me, Mrs Chaturvedi?' he asked roughly.

'Yes, yes I can,' Neha replied, her heart thudding painfully in her chest.

'Mrs Chaturvedi, let me say only this. You have kept your daughter away from your life and you have not told anyone about her? You should be so shamed. All the people are respecting you because of your money and your position.

But they don't know about your secrets. Especially a secret daughter called Sonya who you have never cared for. But I know. And I am wanting to tell everyone about it because people like you always gets away with everything . . . only poor people gets caught. It is not right. Everyone should know about you and what you have done. If you don't tell them, I will.'

And, with that, the caller hung up.

Neha stood stock-still in the lobby, phone still in hand, feeling everything around her reeling and spinning out of control. Only when she sensed that the hotel staff standing behind the reception desk were looking at her curiously did she gather herself together and slowly walk back to the coffee shop to where her friends were still talking and celebrating raucously.

Chapter Twenty-Nine

Sonya was starting to get uncomfortable lying on the lumpy mattress that was occupying the floor of Gopal's room, but she dared not move for fear she would wake Keshav up. He had been very keen to make love to her, reassuring her that Gopal and Estella would not be back for a while from India Gate. But, despite being terribly tempted by his ardent pleas, Sonya had held him off and, thankfully, he had been decent enough not to force himself on her. While she adored him being so close to her, something inside her head talked her out of going all the way so quickly. Instead, they had lain entwined together on the mattress, kissing intermittently and chatting about all manner of things, Keshav seeming fascinated by Sonya's stories of England. Then, abruptly, he had fallen asleep with his head pillowed on her upper arm and was now snoring gently. Delhi's evening sun had swiftly disappeared and it was now the light from a nearby streetlamp that was shining through the faded curtain hanging crookedly across the window.

Sonya wondered how Estella and Gopal were getting on – they had left over an hour ago and would surely be back before too long. Suddenly Sonya was very conscious of needing to get up and make herself decent.

How embarrassing if Gopal and Estella walked in right now and found her languishing in Keshav's arms like a right old slut! Hopefully Estella had understood from their earlier conversation how desperately Sonya had needed to distract herself from the awfulness of her meeting with Neha Chaturvedi. Add to that the intense attentions of a handsome guy like Keshav and it had all been too irresistible. It was without a doubt the warmth of his attention that had melted away the tautness of her earlier nerves and Sonya was grateful to him that she hadn't thought of Neha all evening. Now, of course, it was all seeping back, the horrible queasiness in the pit of her stomach when she thought of the angry exchange they had had back at the park. Sonya wanted to look at her watch to calculate the time difference and plan a call to her parents back home as well. She ought to tell them that she had made contact with Neha and was okay. She'd leave out all the horrible details, and she'd *certainly* leave out any mention of Keshav! But her watch hand was trapped under Keshav's head at the moment . . .

Sonya shifted her arm gently, flexing her numb fingers to stop them tingling. She needed to get to the toilet too and looked down again at the man sleeping with his head laid so trustingly on her arm. He looked like an innocent little boy with eyelashes sweeping down over his cheeks – he really did have the longest lashes! Despite that, he was very macho, Sonya thought, pleasantly muscular and with fine downy chest hair visible through his shirt, which was unbuttoned to the navel.

Her reverie was broken by the sound of Keshav's phone bursting out into a jaunty ringtone. Keshav had told her that it was the title song from the most recent Bollywood hit, but he was unable to understand the reference when

Sonya said that parts of it had been lifted from a Black-Eyed Peas number. The cacophony woke Keshav up. He looked up at Sonya blearily before lunging for the phone with a muttered curse.

'*Haanh*,' he barked, sitting up with the phone held to his ear. '*Arrey, abhi nahin, yaar* . . .' With another muttered curse, he got up and started doing up his buttons. 'Shit, they are coming back,' he said to Sonya before explaining, 'Gopal and Estella. We should get up . . .' Having got to his feet, he held his hands out to Sonya to pull her up. Briefly, Keshav held her, kissing her on the neck before releasing her so she could straighten her clothes and hair too.

They scrambled around, pulling on their shoes and straightening the sheets and Sonya dashed out to the toilet in the nick of time, hearing the sounds of Gopal's and Estella's voices entering the house just as she nipped across the courtyard, clutching her bag to her chest.

When she returned, clothes straightened and hair neatly brushed, the others were sitting in the minuscule living room. Gopal was carrying a paper bag covered in oil stains and Keshav was wolfing down something that looked like a pasty.

'Have one samosa,' Gopal said, holding the bag out to Sonya.

She shook her head. 'Thanks, Gopal, but I think I'll skip it. Feeling a little queasy . . .'

'You alright, hon?' Estella asked, looking concerned.

Sonya waved her away without quite meeting her eyes. Of course, Estella must have been wondering if she and Keshav had just had sex and looked as though she was mentally preparing a lecture about something deadly dull but 'really, really important', like safe sex. Sonya wondered if she should put her out of her misery by telling her of how tame the evening had in fact been, but that wouldn't be possible until they were alone.

Finishing his samosa, Keshav wiped his hands on the back of his jeans and said, 'We should go and get something proper to eat. You know, proper food. I told Didi you were not reaching back home for dinner and she made me promise I would take you for a good dinner.'

'Ooo, fabby!' Estella said. 'Those ice creams have long disappeared, seeing how far we walked. Where should we go?'

'Kake di hatti?' Keshav consulted Gopal with his eyebrows raised. Sonya watched him as the pair discussed the matter briefly in Hindi. Despite the hasty neatening up, Keshav's hair was still all tousled and mussed up. Sonya felt strangely tender looking at him and, in order to distract herself, she turned to Estella. 'Did you have a good time?' she asked.

Estella nodded, 'India Gate was terrific,' she said. 'Something like the Arc de Triomphe, a massive arch with lots of radial roads leading off it. Proper boulevards, just like you see in Paris, but nicer, because there's lots of green lawns and people strolling about buying balloons and stuff from dozens of quaintsy little ice-cream carts. I've never seen such minuscule ice lollies – I had two of course! You should have come,' she said pointedly.

Before Sonya could answer the boys appeared to have made a decision about where to eat – they were getting up and Keshav was going in search of the car keys.

'Spend a penny,' Estella said, making for the toilet.

'Turn the light on before you go in,' Sonya warned, adding, 'and be prepared to squat!'

Sonya picked up her bag and wandered out of the house,

searching for her phone. A call to the UK would probably cost a bomb, but she couldn't put off calling her parents any more. She and Estella had made brief calls to their respective parents from the Mahajan household, using an international calling card that Mr Mahajan had produced. But, knowing her parents, Sonya was sure they would already be worried sick for not having heard from her for over twenty-four hours now.

Outside the night was cool and there was the distant thump of music coming from the main house. Through the hedge, Sonya could discern a few party guests milling about on a lawn. It looked like the party was only just starting but turbaned waiters were already working the small crowd with trays of colourful drinks. The smell of barbecuing meat wafted across to where she stood in the dark, phone held to her ear as it rang distantly.

'Dad!' Sonya said, melting at the sound of her father's dear, familiar 'Hallo'; so comforting in this alien setting.

'Darling!' she heard him exclaim before he went off the phone to yell, 'Laura! Laura, it's Sonya!' Then back to the phone, 'How are you, darling? And where are you now?'

'Still in Delhi,' Sonya laughed, imagining her parents jostling each other to hear her speak, 'And, yes, I'm absolutely fine.'

She heard her mother's voice now. 'Oh, darling, it's *wonderful* to hear your voice. You can't imagine what it's like here without you.'

'Lovely and peaceful, I'd have thought!' Sonya tried to joke before saying, 'Oh, I miss you terribly too, Mum. Especially 'cos I met the Bitch here today.'

'Who? Sorry, darling, your voice isn't very clear . . .'

Sonya decided not to repeat the epithet as, much as her

mother had not wanted her to go in search of Neha, she would probably disapprove even more of Sonya using bad language. 'You know – Neha Chaturvedi. The woman who gave me away,' she said instead.

There was a moment's silence on the line before Sonya heard her father's voice. She could tell how hard he was working at keeping his tone calm. 'Face to face? Goodness . . . what was it like? What's *she* like?' he asked.

'Young!' Sonya said, trying to keep it light. Then she added, 'I don't think she was too keen to meet me but I insisted.'

'Did you talk for long?' Richard asked.

'Oh, all of five minutes,' Sonya said with a wry laugh.

'Five minutes! Was that it? Will you be seeing her again?' Laura asked.

'I guess,' Sonya said noncommitally. She didn't know the answer to that question herself at this point in time, so she wasn't being untruthful. Then, to change the subject, she said. 'On the plus side, Stel and I have made some really terrific friends here. The family we're staying with is just lovely and they're showing us a great time.'

'Oh, that's good,' Richard said before asking, 'Is this call costing you a lot, honey?'

'Typical, Dad!' Sonya laughed. 'Yeah, it's probably costing me a bomb but do we really want to rack up a bigger bill talking about it?' She spotted Keshav emerge from the house in search of her. 'Having said that, though, I think I gotta go. There's a bunch of people waiting to take us out to dinner so I'm off now. Hey Mum, Dad, would you call Estella's folks and tell them too that we're fine and chipper and having a great time? Thanks a mill, love you both, give each other a big hug from me, byeeeee . . .' and, with that, Sonya hung up.

'My parents,' she explained to Keshav but he didn't seem that interested, coming up to her for another kiss. Sonya relented willingly, moulding her body against his and feeling his groin harden instantly. They drew apart as the other two emerged from the house and walked towards them.

'Right, where are we off to then?' Estella asked looking ominously at Sonya.

'The best eating joint in Delhi!' Keshav announced grandly, leading the way to the car. Sonya walked ahead with Keshav, reluctant to discuss her relationship with Keshav right here and now with Estella.

The music from the party was louder now and Sonya could see people in glittering clothes emerge from a procession of cars that was pulling up at the main gate. They were walking down the illuminated drive in pairs and groups and their laughter rose in the air to waft towards them.

'It looks like quite some party,' Sonya observed, getting into the front seat next to Keshav.

'When people have too much black money, they have to spend it so they have parties for their other friends who also have too much money. It goes on like that over here,' he said. His voice was rough as he struggled to start up the ignition, so Sonya couldn't tell if he was joking. The car soon coughed to life and Keshav started to reverse it. He turned it round and drove, not down the main drive, which was now busy with the party guests, instead taking a small pathway down the back of the house towards a wooden gate that led into a service lane.

They made their way through Connaught Place, which Sonya now recognized, and parked near a restaurant on its outer edges. A pink neon sign was advertising an unpronounceable name above a doorway that was half covered by construction debris and rubble. It was clearly a down-at-heel greasy spoon café but a blast of noise and fragrance greeted them as they walked into a space that was heaving with people and food. It was, as Keshav had warned, a truckers' stop, peopled mostly by men with unshaven chins and eyes reddened by either alcohol or lack of sleep. Large steel vessels containing curries bubbled away at the front of the shop while, from within, enormous soft naans and rotis were emerging in large cane baskets. Sonya looked at Estella, whose eyes were also shining with the excitement of being somewhere so authentic and gritty. It was truly thrilling to be experiencing a Delhi they were very unlikely to have seen as tourists on the normal boring trail of forts and monuments.

Keshav was apparently a regular patron of this place, seeing the familiar back-slapping manner with which he was greeted by the waiters, as they eyed-up both Sonya and Estella appreciatively. They were ushered like VIPs to a table at the back of the restaurant and Keshav rattled off a series of Hindi names without even glancing at the menu that was written on a notice board in plastic letters. Even Gopal appeared content to let his friend handle the order and, in minutes, all manner of exotic dishes that would never have been seen on the menu of the Shalimar Tandoori back in Orpington started arriving at their table: brain curry and lamb's trotters and even bull's testicles! They fell upon the food, Sonya suddenly realizing how ravenous she was. Keshav insisted on serving them all and, at one point, even fed Sonya with his fingers, scooping up some curry with a wedge of naan to put it into her mouth with utmost tenderness. Sonya thought she was ready to burst with love for him.

It was close-on midnight when the meal finished and they piled back into the car, Gopal and Estella taking the back seat again while Sonya sat up close to Keshav as he drove, her hand resting on his thigh. Keshav dropped Gopal back at the bottom of his road before driving both girls back to the Mahajans' South Delhi household. It was a half-hour drive and Estella had fallen asleep shortly after getting into the car. Sonya though was watching Delhi's streets slowly go to sleep, wishing the night would never end. She could happily drive on through this starlit, magical city, sitting like this next to Keshav, her stomach humming happily with the most delicious meal she had ever had. But, alas, before she knew it, their car was pulling up outside the Mahajan gate. Tempted as she was to ask Keshav to take her right back – to his house, or Gopal's, anywhere that they could be alone together for another little while – Sonya reluctantly got out of the car. Keshav disembarked with them. He kissed Estella on the cheek and then took Sonya in his arms for another lingering kiss while Estella tactfully disappeared down the garden path in the direction of their room.

'Come to Select City Mall tomorrow morning to meet me,' Keshav said gruffly, pulling away and cupping his hands over Sonya's face. 'Ask Didi where it is and she will arrange transport. Come alone, okay? I want to spend time with you alone, not like this in a group,' he whispered. Sonya nodded before kissing Keshav tenderly on his lower lip. He held her close and she felt her nascent love for him bubbling up from the very bottom of her stomach. Then, reluctantly, he pulled away. 'Go inside,' he said, 'I will wait here until you are inside and I can see that you have closed your door.'

Walking on clouds Sonya ran towards the small spiral

stairway before turning to wave goodbye to Keshav one last time. She was taken aback when Estella suddenly materialised at the top of the stairs. 'God, you scared me there, Stel. All okay? You were out like a light in the car.'

'I'm fine, thanks. More to the point, are *you* okay?' Estella paused briefly before setting off again, 'Look Sonya, I don't mean to be a damp squib but are you sure you know what you're doing? You know I like Keshav, and he's been great showing us round, but we haven't known him that long. I mean, did you actually sleep with him when Gopal and I went off?'

'No, of course I didn't! What do you take me for?' Sonya said defensively.

Estella looked dubious. 'I'm just worried, is all. Please just promise me you'll be careful.' Estella seemed to be holding back saying any more and for that Sonya was thankful.

'Of course I will, darling. Come on, let's hit the sack, I'm exhausted,' Sonya replied before rushing past her friend into the room.

Chapter Thirty

Sharat shot a look at Neha sitting next to him in the car. Jasmeet's birthday celebration had segued from lunch into tea and all that food and conversation had quite exhausted both of them. Neha was sunk in silence, looking out of the window at the remnants of the whole-sale flower market at Andheria Mor as the car languished at a light. The driver had expertly negotiated the evening traffic from Gurgaon and they were over halfway home. Though never an overly chatty person, Neha had been unusually quiet on the journey back from Jasmeet's party. Sharat knew her well enough to realize that something was bothering her. Something, in fact, had been bothering her since their own party ten days ago, which is why he had encouraged her to go off to Ananda. The place was usually very effective in dispelling Neha's occasional dark moods but this time it did not seem to have worked. She had come back from the spa apparently as tightly wound up as she had been on her departure, although she, of course, would have been astonished had Sharat mentioned it. Neha made every effort to do what she thought was a good job at concealing her feelings. It might work with other people, Sharat thought, but not with him. One did not stay married to the same person for fifteen years without getting to recognize their every change of mood.

He reached out over the car seat to pick up Neha's hand that was lying limp on the seat between them. Startled, she looked at him, her eyes large in her face. 'What's up?' he asked gently. 'You're miles away.'

She smiled and shook her head. 'Just been suffering a headache all day.'

'Oh dear, bad one? Migraine?'

'Maybe . . . I would have cancelled going for lunch if it had not been Jasmeet's anniversary.'

Sharat grinned, 'No one ever says no to old Jasmeet if they are in their right mind.'

Neha smiled in agreement. 'Even back in school, she was such a bossy little thing we were all really petrified of her.'

'On the other hand, you've stayed in touch with her since you were both six. So she can't be too unbearable. Unless you *like* being bossed around!'

'Hmm, that must make you a bossy husband, seeing how long I've stayed with you,' Neha remarked, laughing at the very idea because she knew, like everyone else, what a genial person Sharat always was.

Neha's phone rang and, quite suddenly, the smile was wiped off her face. She stared at Sharat with a stricken expression on her face as the ringing went on before she hastily scrambled to pick up her handbag which was lying at her feet. She pulled the phone out of its case and, with barely a glance at its screen, she turned it off.

'What did you do that for?' Sharat asked, surprised at Neha's irrational act.

'Oh nothing . . . I've been getting some crank calls lately.'

'*Crank* calls?'

'No, I don't mean crank calls exactly but, you know, those annoying sales calls. They are like stalkers, those telesales people. I've told them to take my number off their list but they just keep calling and calling. I have a good mind to report the company to someone.'

'What company is it?'

Neha gave Sharat a blank look and said, 'Oh, I don't know, some stupid company. Something to do with telephones . . . Telstar, I think. No, that's an air-conditioning company, isn't it. Maybe Telcom?'

Neha stopped her frantic gabbling and Sharat, rather than continuing to stare at her open-mouthed, turned his head to look out of the window. He ought not to get suspicious without good reason. But how could one help wondering? Neha was behaving very strangely and, although Sharat felt very uneasy, he did not want to ask her the reason right away. He suddenly recalled that story he had heard recently of his old classmate, Anup, whose wife had apparently run off with her physical trainer. The classmates he had been gossiping with at their school reunion had all laughed at the utter triteness of the story but Sharat had not been able to help feeling sorry for the chap he remembered as being a bumbling, well-meaning sort . . .

They travelled on through the Delhi traffic, sitting in the back seat of their elegant Mercedes, but now Sharat too was silent, his earlier good mood suddenly dispelled.

When they reached home, Neha said she was going to have a nap. Sharat watched her going upstairs before walking down the corridor to the study. Suddenly, he was anxious all over again, experiencing a strange deep thudding in his chest that he had not encountered in years. Certainly not since the time he and Neha were trying for children and kept failing, month after month . . .

Sharat sat on an armchair in the study and tried leafing through the papers. But he had read the whole sheaf cover-to-cover this morning and was quickly bored by them. He ran his eye along the vast collection of books that lined the walls but knew he lacked the concentration to read a book right now. Instead, he stretched out on the sofa and, perhaps due to the cheese-laden lasagna he had eaten at lunch, he soon drifted off.

In less than fifteen minutes, Sharat came awake again with a jolt. He lay looking blearily at the ceiling, trying to find his bearings and wondering whether he had perhaps had a bad dream. Then he slowly recalled the reason for which he was feeling a little sick in the stomach . . . It was so uncharacteristic of Neha to lie to him. And, clearly, she had been lying to him, babbling on about crank calls as a reason for not answering the telephone. Perhaps he ought to ask her directly if there was some problem. Crank calls. A likely story!

Sharat took the stairs to the first floor, his bare feet soundless on the marble tiles. The bedroom door was ajar and he walked straight in. Neha was fast asleep on their bed, her forehead creased into an anxious frown, possibly due to the headache she had mentioned earlier. She must have fallen straight into bed as she was still in the same clothes she had worn to Jasmeet's lunch. Even the handbag she had carried was lying next to her on the bed. Sharat saw Neha's phone peeping out from the rim of the bag and, giving in to sudden impulse, he picked it up and took it out of the room. He flicked it open and, in the bright sunshine of the bathroom, he swiftly scrolled through the list of calls she had recently received. Almost all the numbers came up with familiar names against them – 'Mummy', 'Ma', 'Papa', 'Jasmeet' and, of course, 'Sharat' many times over. But she had been called twice from a landline at two-thirty pm, while they had been at lunch in the hotel, and then by an unfamiliar mobile number at four-twelve, which was probably the call she had received while they were in the car. Still being uncharacteristically nosy, Sharat hit the callback button on the landline but, even after twenty rings, there was no reply. Then he dialled the mobile number that had called when they were in the car. He held his breath again as the phone started to ring. This time, after a few seconds, it was answered by a male voice. 'Hello? Hello?' the voice said, adding, 'Hello, is that you, Neha?'

Sharat hung up hastily without replying. He was quite certain he did not recognize the voice. The man who had called Neha had a broad American accent that Sharat would surely recognize if he had heard it before. Who could this person be whom Neha was so reluctant to speak to in front of him? Sharat looked at the phone again, pained and puzzled by what he thought he was piecing together. For the first time since he had married Neha, Sharat suddenly felt very shaken and very uncertain of his marriage.

Chapter Thirty-One

The Coffee Bean Café at the entrance to Select City Mall was buzzing with mostly young people. Sonya took one of the few available two-seater tables, choosing the chair facing the entrance so she could see Keshav when he came in. She rubbed her hands over cold arms. It wasn't merely the powerful air conditioning in the mall that was causing her to break out into goosebumps, but the memory of the evening she had spent with Keshav in Gopal's house. Sonya wondered how on earth she had managed to resist Keshav's passionate advances, knowing that it would be very difficult to continue fending him off. She felt a warm flush overcome her, imagining how wonderful it would be to make love to someone as confident and attentive as Keshav. Comparisons may be odious but clearly poor Tim was not a patch on Keshav when it came to pursuing her. Except for when he was fired up by beer, Tim was hesitant and nervous, as though she were a china doll he might break. Keshav, on the other hand, had been bold and unashamed as he had kissed and caressed her, and was probably as willing to take pleasure as give it. Sonya wondered what she should say if Keshav insisted on taking her somewhere where they could be alone today. Should she resist? Would she have the determination to do so?

Somehow it felt unnecessary to put poor Keshav through such a test again . . . Worrying that Estella would mind her coming out to meet Keshav solo had been quite unnecessary. While she had reiterated the need for Sonya to be careful, Estella was happy to stay at home. 'Clichéd as it may sound, I need to wash my hair, darlin'.' Getting to the mall had been a cinch too as Sonya had merely taken a lift from Mr Mahajan.

She now sipped on her glass of water, looking around the café and through its plate-glass panes, quite astonished by all the affluence she could see around her. The names of the surrounding shops were exactly those of any mall back in England. From where she was seated, Sonya could see 'Clinique' and 'Mango' and 'Nine West'. Although both she and Estella had been trying very hard not to judge India by their Western sensibilities, she couldn't help wondering what India's millions of poor people felt being surrounded by such wealth. Those beggars at the traffic lights, for instance, who tapped piteously on the windows of gleaming air-conditioned foreign cars. The disparity was sometimes staggering. Why, even Keshav had admitted to being quite overwhelmed by India's economic progress, stating quite angrily as they had been eating last night that only two per cent of the population was benefiting from globalisation. 'Only these rich bastards in their massive bungalows and imported cars are getting any advantage out of it,' he said and, later, 'The government also is only there for the business people and together they are both juicing the workers. This place is only meant for the rich.'

Sonya's thoughts were now interrupted when she spotted Keshav come striding in through the glass doors. Once again, she felt physically jolted by how handsome he looked with those dark, brooding looks of his. She raised her arm but Keshav had already seen her and was walking confidently, in his usual assured manner, towards where she was seated.

He bent down and brushed his mouth against hers discreetly and Sonya guessed that kissing in public was not the done thing, even in newly globalized India. 'You have not ordered anything?' he asked.

'Thought I'd wait for you,' Sonya said, adding quickly, 'I'll get it,' when Keshav made as if to go to the counter. Even without the conversation about India's rich and poor, it hadn't been difficult to work out that Keshav didn't have much money to his name. Except for last night's dinner at the *dhaba* (where he appeared to have some kind of credit system and refused to take money from the girls), she and Estella had made sure to pick up all their food and drink costs so far. It was only fair, given that Keshav was taking them around Delhi gratis. His father was chauffeur to the Mahajans and his mother a seamstress in a garment export establishment. Keshav had also mentioned that he often drove taxis at weekends in order to help make ends meet. Sonya had no doubt that he led a rather tough life, but it only made him all the more romantic in her eyes.

Having ordered an Americano for herself and a cold coffee with ice cream for Keshav, Sonya navigated her way back to their table. 'They'll serve it here at our table, apparently,' she remarked, joining Keshav and sitting down next to him on the red leatherette seat. She slipped her wallet back into her bag and smiled. 'I'm getting spoilt. In England, you have to wait ages at the counter and then carry everything back to your table yourself.'

'Really? Here, even in movie theatres, they will bring food and drinks to where you're sitting,' Keshav said.

'You don't say! Waiter service in the cinema – how terrific!

273

I can't wait to drop that in the suggestion box of the cinema back home.'

Keshav was silent for a moment before he spoke. 'So you'll soon be going back to your home. And leaving India,' he said abruptly, his voice suddenly flat and unhappy.

'Well, we don't go straight home after this but on to Agra and Fatehpur Sikri, then Kerala in the south before we return from there straight to England. But, you're right, there's not many days left in Delhi . . . perhaps you could come along to Agra with us? What do you think?' Sonya said, surprised at how deflated she too felt at the thought of leaving Delhi, and leaving Keshav. Only two days ago, she had been depressed and railing against how awful the city was.

But Keshav seemed not to have heard her invitation. 'Don't go, Sonya. Don't leave Delhi. Postpone your ticket back to England,' he said. He sounded so sad, it made Sonya's heart ache. No one had ever made her feel this way before and, suddenly, she wanted to weep.

She reached out for Keshav's hands. They were cold from his iced drink and so she rubbed his fingers to warm them again. 'Oh, Keshav,' she said softly, unable now to look him straight in the eyes because of her own confused feelings. 'It's all been booked weeks in advance and Delhi was only ever going to be for a few days because that was what the travel company back in England had advised. They weren't to know that we would meet in this rather unexpected way, did they?' Keshav did not reflect her smile and so Sonya continued speaking. 'Stel would be ever so disappointed if we didn't go to Agra. And Kerala. I consider myself lucky to have met you and got to know you. So we'll certainly stay in touch, won't we? Until we can be together again, that is . . .'

'But when will that be, Sonya? It could be forever before you come back again to Delhi.'

'It doesn't have to be, my darling. It's just that I have to get back to England now. Stel and I have to get ready for college which will start when we get back, you see. Oh, how it breaks my heart to leave you, Keshav. Having only just met you . . .' Sonya trailed off, close to tears. Then she tried to brighten her voice, looking up at Keshav with an earnest expression. 'But I'll begin making plans to visit again, very soon. I could stay again with the Mahajans, couldn't I, and hang out with you?'

Keshav looked partially mollified but was clearly not completely convinced by Sonya's sincerity. 'You'll come back to India just to see me?' he asked.

Sonya nodded, 'I most certainly will. And *only* to see you – I won't need to do any more sightseeing, will I? As for Neha Chaturvedi, I've done what I set out to achieve in Delhi. Nothing more to be done there. Really, meeting you has been the unexpected bonus in all this, Keshav.'

But Keshav did not appear to have registered the compliment. Instead, he blurted, 'You don't need to see Neha Chaturvedi again? Ask her for anything?'

Sonya thought for a minute before saying firmly, 'No, I don't think I want to see her again. I think I've got it out of my system now, and want to leave it there. I discussed it with Stel too and she feels the same way.'

Keshav's expression turned indignant. 'But this Neha Chaturvedi, she left you when you were a baby, Sonya! How can you just forgive her? I don't know about what happens in England but here, in India, a mother is like a *devi*, you know, a goddess! Sacrificing her last morsel of food for her children!'

His voice was so aggrieved and angry that it startled

Sonya. She was touched by how strongly Keshav felt on her behalf and tried to explain. 'It's usually not that different in England too, Keshav. Mothers generally love their kids to death. I was just one of the unlucky ones – until my parents adopted me, that is. They're really lovely and would love you too if only they could meet you . . .' Sonya trailed off, trying to imagine what her parents back in cosy little Orpington would quite likely say if they did meet Keshav. It was too complicated a scenario to consider right now and so Sonya returned to her original point. 'Look, the whole thing with Neha Chaturvedi was far more upsetting than I'd bargained for, Keshav, especially meeting her like that in the park. For one, I hadn't quite expected someone as young and vulnerable looking as her and . . .'

'Bullshit,' Keshav cut in loudly, 'These people are rich and powerful. Not vul . . . vulner-able . . .' he stumbled on the word and stopped.

Sonya stroked Keshav's forearm gently, trying to soothe his sudden agitated feelings. 'No, really, Keshav, it's okay. I have the most loving Mum and Dad back in England and now I really just want to go home to them. Neha Chaturvedi has never been anything to me, and never will be. Briefly, I was curious about her. And angry with what she had done. But, suddenly I don't feel so strongly any more. Maybe it was meeting you and getting to see India's many complexities through your eyes that changed me, you know!'

But Keshav looked unconvinced. He sipped his coffee through a straw, focusing his attention on the milky liquid in his glass. After a pause, he looked up and straight into Sonya's eyes and said firmly. 'Okay, forget Neha Chaturvedi. But I want to come with you, Sonya. I want to leave this

276

hell that's good only for people like those Chaturvedis, and come with you to England.'

Taken aback, Sonya wondered whether she should laugh off the rather wild suggestion but the expression on Keshav's face was deadly serious. He really did think it was possible to leave India and go with her to England!

'Oh Keshav, darling, I wish it was as easy as that! I know it's unfair but I keep hearing of what a nightmare it is for anyone who isn't a British citizen to get past UK immigration. How on earth would we get you there?'

'I'll get a job, I'll do something. Your mother and father will take care of us until we can get jobs and get married.'

'Married!? Cripes, I hadn't realized we'd got as far as that,' Sonya laughed.

But Keshav seemed to take offence at her laughter. 'You are laughing at me now . . .' he said, his demeanour suddenly surly.

'Of course I'm not laughing at you, Keshav, it just seems to be jumping the gun a bit to be talking about marriage so early on in our relationship . . .' Sonya trailed off, aware of how defensive she must sound. She thought for a second and then opened up again, trying to lighten Keshav's mood. 'What we had yesterday was so beautiful, Keshav, we both know that. But what we need to do is get to know each other better over time . . .'

'How? I am here and you will be there.'

'Communication's so easy now – we can email and message and call and Skype . . . distances matter so little these days . . .'

But Keshav's face was dark and frowning. 'If I can't come with you, then I don't want you to go, Sonya. Stay here with me. I will marry you. Then we can both go to England someday.'

Sonya could not help laughing again as Keshav's suggestions got wilder and wilder. 'Oh, Keshav, you're being a silly goose now. I have a place at Oxford waiting for me and . . .'

But Keshav was now seriously angry, his voice rising over the din of the coffee shop as he pulled his hands out of Sonya's and sat back in his chair. 'You can laugh, all you rich girls,' he said, his voice shaking with emotion. 'You come along to countries like mine and think you can buy anything, even guys like me. And then you go back to your own rich countries. Forgetting all the people you leave behind who tried to make you happy. But you can't do that, you know. There is a price to pay. There *should* be a price to pay. And, if you won't pay it, I will get your mother – that Neha Chaturvedi who lives in her palace on Prithviraj Road – to pay up for you.'

'Keshav, don't . . .' Sonya pleaded, her eyes brimming with sudden shocked tears. 'Please don't be like this. What's happened to you . . . what we had yesterday was so . . .'

'So? So what? I know what you are going to say . . .' At this point Keshav's voice went mocking and high-pitched as he put on a psuedo English accent, 'So byootiful, so laaavely, you kiss so well, I love you Keshav . . .' Then, reverting to a hard tone of voice, he continued, 'They all escape like that. But I won't let you get away too.'

'Who's they?' Sonya asked, suddenly weak and trembling.

'Girls like you,' came Keshav's harsh reply.

'Keshav, I thought. . . .' Sonya trailed off, picking up her bag and clutching it against her chest, her face blanched white. Then she asked, her voice trembling, 'What are you going to do?

Keshav regarded her through narrowed eyes. 'Don't

forget I know where Neha Chaturvedi lives. You also gave me her number that day. I have called her once and will call her again. She will now have to pay the price for what *you* have done to me, teasing me and leading me on like that, only to drop me once you have had your fun. Yes, I know *firangi* girls like you. You're all the same.'

Frightened by Keshav's mean expression and threatening tone of voice, Sonya got up from her chair with a cry and ran towards the door of the coffee shop. She darted out, not daring to look back and, weaving her way past surprised shoppers, she ran and ran until she saw an exit and stumbled out into the bright morning sunshine. Finally looking over her shoulder, she saw that Keshav had thankfully not followed her. She spotted an auto-rickshaw and waved her arm furiously, tumbling into the back seat in a terrible panic.

Back in their room, Sonya and Estella sat cross-legged, facing each other on the bed. Sonya was still flushed and breathless from her earlier encounter with Keshav, the heat emanating from her face and body refusing to subside despite the ceiling fan whirling above their heads at full speed. She had recounted the conversation to Estella in as much detail as she could, going over in her mind precisely what she might have said to upset Keshav so badly.

'Don't torment yourself, hon,' Estella said. 'It wasn't anything you said. He just turned out to be an opportunistic shit, that's all. An old story, alas.'

Sonya started to sniffle. Wiping her nose, she said wretchedly, 'Oh Stel, I'm so, so sorry. It would seem I've spent a whole lot of time on this holiday in floods of tears, haven't I?'

Estella, thankfully, was her usual stoic self. 'Hon, I don't think either of us assumed it was going to be a cakewalk when we set off from Heathrow, did we? It was going to be dramatic, one way or the other, so let's not beat ourselves up about it.'

Sonya blew her nose. 'Well, okay that whole thing with Neha Chaturvedi was bound to be traumatic, yes. But Keshav . . . such an unnecessary complication . . . God, I've been so fucking stupid!'

'Well, let's just try and take stock calmly. Did you think he was being serious about calling Neha Chaturvedi? Or was he just agitated about you leaving him? Without carving an easy passage to the UK for him, that is?'

Sonya winced at the sarcasm. For Estella to take that tone, she must be seriously angry too and Sonya hoped it was with Keshav and not her. She now tried to remember Keshav's exact words and expression when they had rowed back at the mall. 'I think he may make good his threat, Stel,' she said finally, her heart going cold at the thought. 'He even said he had already called her. I just remembered that.'

'He called her *before* his argument with you?'

Sonya nodded. 'So he said.'

'Bloody Nora, he means business then . . .' Estella said slowly.

'But it's blackmail, isn't it, if he uses the information I've given him? That must be illegal here in India too. Do you think we should tell Mrs Mahajan?' Sonya asked. 'She might be able to stop Keshav.'

Estella considered the suggestion before saying, 'Hmmm . . . let's keep that as a last resort. Because we'd then have to tell Mrs Mahajan the full story and that might be more damaging all round. That Neha is obviously very well known here in Delhi, going by her pictures in all those society rags, Mrs Mahajan might not be able to resist such a juicy titbit of goss on her. Besides, she adores Keshav, and may not take our word against his. Oh, cripes, what a mess. I don't know who to trust!'

Sonya, now weeping in earnest, spoke through a wad of tissues, 'But who'd have thought that Keshav . . . he even mentioned other girls, saying I was no better than them. Oh Stel, am I just a trollop? And *such* a bad judge of character?'

'Come on, hon, don't be hard on yourself, I thought he was a right dish when I first got a sight of him . . . I might even have ended up getting my knickers off for him, for heaven's sake. At least you stopped short of that!'

But Estella's clumsy attempt at both kindness and lightening the mood had no effect as Sonya continued to agonize. 'You didn't see the expression on his face, Stel. He was suddenly so nasty, so unlike the friendly and genial guy he'd been so far . . . I mean he seemed so gentle earlier and so . . . so . . . *protective* . . .'

'Well, he was obviously better at dissembling than we thought. Actually, if he does mean business, I can't help feeling a little sorry for Neha, suddenly,' Estella said.

Sonya looked at her friend. 'You know, I've been thinking the exact same thing,' she said slowly. It was a difficult admission to make and Sonya hoped Estella would understand. 'I know I started off wanting Neha to suffer, but I don't feel that way now, having got it all off my chest. If Keshav does take matters into his hands, then she's a sitting duck, isn't she? And the fact that he has all this information on her is . . . well, it's purely my fault, isn't it?'

Estella held Sonya's gaze. 'He won't get away with it. Blackmail's a crime and I'll be damned if I'm going to sit around and let him wreck someone else's life.'

'What do we do?' Sonya asked.

'I think we need to call Neha again,' Estella replied. Her voice was firm. 'Call her again and ask her to meet you so you can explain what's happened. I'll come with you, if you like. It's gotta be done before we leave Delhi.'

Chapter Thirty-Two

In the dentist's waiting room, Neha sat surrounded by dwarf palms, awaiting her monthly appointment as she had been suffering with her fillings of late. Her nerves had been taut as stretched wires since receiving the blackmailer's phone call at Jasmeet's lunch the previous day. She already thought of him as a blackmailer because it seemed sensible to assume that some kind of extortion was the man's intention, even though he had not specified any demands, nor made any further contact yet. Neha was also fairly certain that the blackmailer had called with Sonya's express permission. How else would he have known about Neha's circumstances, or got her number? Her own investigations had come to nothing as, when she had made a tentative attempt to call back, someone had answered the phone and said it was a public telephone booth near Khan Market. Nevertheless, Neha had taken the precaution of making her mobile phone a constant companion ever since, even taking it with her to the bathroom for fear that Sharat would answer it if she left it lying around. She had astonished herself at the calm manner in which she was dealing with this new crisis. Perhaps it was because she now had something definite to deal with, rather than coping with some obscure idea of what might or might not emerge from Sonya's arrival in India. She could legitimately stop feeling guilty about not having rushed to make contact with her on first receiving her letter, although her sadness felt amplified in all sorts of inexplicable ways.

Neha took a deep breath, trying to calm the fluttering in her chest. She was only kidding herself by imagining that the phone call hadn't made the situation worse. At first nothing had seemed more worrying than telling Sharat about the baby she had given away but, with this new development, she would now have to tell him that her daughter had grown into a blackmailer too! Even though Neha knew she had no right to expect good treatment, somehow it pained her terribly to think of what Sonya had done. In the end, she had only been interested in money . . .

Neha jumped as she felt her mobile phone start to buzz. She looked at the number that was flashing silently and saw that it was different from the landline that had been used by Sonya's blackmailer friend. This was the second call she had received from an unfamiliar mobile number and she supposed that that was what blackmailers did: use different phones all the time so that they could not be traced. After a moment's hesitation, Neha decided to answer the call. At least she was by herself, as there was no one else in Dr Kothari's plush waiting room today.

'Hello?' she said, her heart beating loudly in her ears.

'Hello.' It was Sonya's voice. Neha recognized it with no trouble at all.

'What do you want now?' Neha asked after a short pause, her voice cold.

There was a moment's hesitation before Sonya replied. 'Look, I'm sorry I shouted at you in the park,' she said in a voice much softer than before. 'But something . . . something urgent has come up.'

'Why don't you just tell me how much you want?' Neha asked abruptly, aware of how rough and jagged her voice sounded.

'Pardon?'

'You heard me,' Neha spoke more slowly, enunciating every word, 'How much are you and your friend after?'

'I . . . I don't understand,' Sonya stuttered. 'What do you mean "after"? I'm . . . we're not after anything.' Now, pricked, her voice turned sharp in response. 'Are you saying *you* wish to buy my silence?'

'Correct me if I'm wrong but that's your wish, not mine, isn't it? Going by that phone call yesterday . . .'

Neha heard Sonya take a deep breath. 'That wasn't me. I haven't made any phone calls to you since meeting you in the park yesterday. Look, I think there's been a terrible mix-up and perhaps we need to talk. Face to face. There's something important you need to know.'

Neha hesitated for a split second. Could she believe Sonya when she said she had nothing to do with the call she had received yesterday afternoon? And, if that was true, then who was the man on the phone who knew all about their relationship? And why did she want to meet her again? Despite her confused thoughts, Neha instinctively felt that Sonya was telling her the truth – but how could one be sure of anything? Whatever the case, she ought to meet Sonya as soon as possible to get to the bottom of this. Perhaps it could all be sorted out without Sharat needing to know. 'Come to the house this evening,' Neha said, adding as she sensed Sonya's hesitation, 'it's fine. My husband's gone this morning to Mumbai for a couple of days so it's just me.'

'Okay. I'll bring Estella, my friend, if you don't mind.'

'Yes, that's fine. I'll tell the guard to expect the two of you at six o'clock this evening.'

Neha shot a look at Dr Kothari's receptionist but the girl was busy behind her steel and glass counter and did not seem to have heard the exchange at all.

At six, Neha stood on the veranda of her house, watching the evening shadows lengthen slowly in the garden. It was hard to explain but, in spite of the added complications, Neha felt far more serene than the last time she had met Sonya. Ready to face whatever was going to come at her on this occasion. Absently, she plucked at the button rose creeper that hung low on one side of the veranda, removing a few dead heads that had formed. Except for a few stray flowers, the creeper was profuse with unopened buds that were readying themselves for the winter. It was coming up to the time of year that Neha usually loved: the three months between Diwali and Christmas, when her garden gradually unfurled and bloomed, and much more time was spent outdoors than the summer months allowed. She gazed at the vast expanse of clean green lawn, remembering how she used to look at it longingly in the early years of her marriage to Sharat, imagining it littered with tricycles and trampolines . . .

Hearing voices at the gate, she looked out and saw Sonya with the girl who had dragged her away in the park. Satisfied with how calm she felt, Neha walked to the top of the steps where she awaited the two girls as they came down the drive. Neither girl was smiling but Neha sensed there was no hostility this time. Once again, Neha experienced a sharp feeling of *déjà vu* as she watched Sonya's tall figure walk gracefully towards her. It was like watching herself walk through time.

'Hello,' Neha said, coming down the stairs and reaching out a hand first to the bigger girl who took it and shook it firmly.

'I'm Estella. Thanks for allowing me to come with Sonya,' the girl said. Her direct manner and plummy voice reminded Neha faintly of her old classmate Clare, back at Oxford, and perhaps that was cause enough to instantly warm to her.

Then Neha turned to Sonya and stretched a hand in her direction, experiencing that same mix of feelings as when she had first laid eyes on her. Sonya took her hand and their fingers brushed briefly together before they were withdrawn. Quelling her turmoil, Neha turned away. 'Come, let's go in,' she said.

She led the way indoors through the main hallway. As they entered her vast living room, Neha saw both girls cast awestruck looks around. She wished instantly that she had taken them down the hall to the breakfast room instead, which was much smaller and cosier. Her living room had once been described in an interiors magazine as 'an immense art gallery, every wall and corner graced with expensive paintings and *objets d'art*' – the room was a commanding one, with its three separate seating areas and an enormous grand piano set to one side that no one ever used except for when musicians were hired at their parties. Neha hoped the room would not make the girls uneasy. She had only thought to come in here because it offered the most privacy. It was so important that they should feel able to talk freely.

'Can I get you some tea?' she asked. Both girls nodded and so Neha pressed a button on the intercom to call Ram

Singh in the kitchen. Then she turned to the pair, both of whom wore timid expressions on their faces today, quite unlike the girls she had met in the park. It was best to take charge and be as direct as was permissible. She tried to keep her voice subdued and gentle. 'Do you want to start by telling me about the misunderstanding that you referred to earlier on the phone, Sonya?'

Sonya shot a look at Estella who nodded. Then Sonya spoke, her voice low-pitched, nervous. She made only occasional eye contact with Neha, keeping her gaze mostly on the silver rings that she was continually twisting around on her fingers. 'Soon after coming here, to India, I . . . we met a boy called Keshav who was helping us with our travels and sightseeing around Delhi. He seemed awfully nice and I'm afraid I got close enough to him to tell him why I was in India . . .'

'He was the boy who was in the park with you on Sunday?' Neha queried.

Sonya nodded. 'We had come here earlier with him too, to the gates of the house, that is . . .'

'Which is how he knows where you live,' Estella cut in.

'So?' Neha asked, still faintly puzzled by the piecemeal information.

'Well, unfortunately he now knows a lot about you . . .' Estella said.

'And he's subsequently fallen out with me,' Sonya said swiftly, reddening as she looked down at her trainers.

'Why has he fallen out with you? Neha asked.

Sonya looked up and met her gaze, 'Because he thinks I led him up the garden path and he's now disillusioned and angry . . .'

'That's nonsense. Sonya isn't expressing this very well, I'm afraid,' Estella said, turning to Neha to make her

288

explanation. She spoke swiftly. 'We misjudged Keshav. I'm afraid we're neither of us the best judges of character. We thought Keshav was our friend and so we told him all about you and your connection with Sonya. But he turned out to be an opportunist and, when he realized that Sonya was not going to pave an easy path to England for him, he turned nasty. And now . . . now he's threatening to blackmail you. He claims he's doing it to get back at us but I would wager it's just money he's after.'

Neha sat back against her silk cushions. 'So that call I got was from him. You had nothing to do with it?' she asked Sonya.

'Of course I had nothing to do with it!' Sonya said hotly. 'What do you take me for? Sure, I was upset and came here to India looking for an explanation from you but your money means nothing to me. Let's get that clear.'

Neha sat in silence for another few seconds as all sorts of emotions coursed through her. Finally she said, 'Thank you for coming to warn me about Keshav. I shall have to think of the best way to deal with him.' Then she took a deep breath and, turning to look Sonya straight in the face, saying gently, 'I never gave you that explanation, did I? The one that you came to India for . . .'

At that moment, Ram Singh appeared at the swing doors that led to the dining room. 'Memsahib, chai,' he said, waving expansively in the direction of the dining room.

Neha nodded at him and smiled apologetically at the girls. 'It looks like he's serving high tea in the dining room. I'd asked for a simple tea service on a trolley but Ram Singh has a mind of his own and probably thinks you are weary travellers in need of sustenance and fattening up.'

Estella grinned. 'Well, if there's one thing I definitely

don't need it's fattening up! But high tea sounds great. Sonya and I have eaten nothing since breakfast today as we were worrying ourselves sick over how we would break this news to you.'

Neha felt tremendously touched. 'It's very sweet of you to have been worrying,' she said, smiling at Estella, 'and don't worry, we'll think of something. From what you're saying this is not your fault at all. Unfortunately in India there are a number of characters like Keshav, out for all they can get.' Then she got up to lead the way to the dining room, adding, 'In fact, I now feel so guilty for assuming that you were behind that phone call.'

'Do you mind if I ask how many times Keshav has called?' Estella asked, following Sonya and Neha out of the room.

'Just once. Yesterday. But I'm as certain as anything that he'll call again. He certainly sounded like he meant business,' Neha replied, entering the dining room. She waved them to an enormous table gleaming with polish and ringed by twelve chairs. On the table was a large spread: cucumber sandwiches and carrot cake and what looked like a semolina pudding. 'Come, sit. And help yourselves,' Neha said. 'In fact, if you're really hungry, I can ask Ram Singh to make something more substantial.'

'Oh no, please!' Estella said. She shot a look at Sonya and said. 'Why don't I help myself to something and clear off to the veranda. I think you need some space.'

Neha protested. 'You'll be much too uncomfortable on the veranda; it's the season of flies. But I could ask Ram Singh to take the tea trolley to the study? Lots of magazines and books there to keep you amused.'

Once Estella had been dispatched to the study with her tea, Neha sat down at the dining table, taking the chair directly across from Sonya's. She poured from the tea pot into two cups and, when Sonya nodded, added milk from a jug. Watching Sonya help herself to two cubes of sugar and, keeping her eyes on the teaspoon stirring the tea, Neha started to speak. It was amazing how tranquil she suddenly felt.

'Your friend said you were both poor judges of character,' she said softly before taking a deep breath . . . 'Well, you certainly can't be as bad as I was at your age.' Sonya was silent, looking questioningly at Neha and so she continued, trying to keep her voice as dispassionate as possible. 'I was eighteen when I got offered a place at Oxford. I'd worked all my life for that place because my father had told me when I was very small that I was going to join the Indian Foreign Service and Oxford was my best way in to that elite world. So, despite the fact that I was an only child and so young, they let me go when the Oxford offer came. It was my first time away from home and at first all quite exciting. But I must have got a bit lonely and was perhaps in search of a father figure of some sort. Despite a really nice boy called Simon pursuing me, I met this man . . .' Neha paused and took a breath. 'He was one of my tutors and I'm afraid I fell head over heels for him. Of course, I now recognize all the clichés: older man, well travelled, wordly wise, a great deal more smooth and sophisticated than me or any of the other men I'd ever met . . . you get the picture. Well, I ended up sleeping with him. It was entirely consensual, although friends later said that I simply hadn't recognized the cleverness with which he'd manipulated me. It was all so sudden and I was so naïve, I had not even considered contraception . . .' Neha paused again, her voice reducing to a near whisper. 'When I told him I was pregnant, he not only shunned me, he disappeared from the college. I hung on for a while, young and stupid enough to hope he would have a change of heart and come back for me. For us. But he didn't. I was seven months pregnant by the time college closed for the summer and a classmate and her mother took charge of me. They were so kind, taking me into their home and seeing me through those final few days of the pregnancy but, by September, I knew I did not have the heart – the courage – to go back to college. All I wanted was to be home in India, with my parents . . . to turn the hands of that clock back . . .' Neha looked down at her cup of tea, which was now cold with a brown skin forming on the surface. She paused, reminding herself that Sonya deserved honesty from her. 'It didn't take much for me to be persuaded to give you up, Sonya,' she finally said quietly. 'The social worker said there were long waiting lists of potential adopters. I imagined those couples desperate for a baby and how much more they would be able to give you than I would, a girl just turned nineteen with her life in a total shambles . . .' Neha stopped to take breath, painfully conscious of Sonya sitting as still as a statue across the table from her. Drawing her forefinger over the polished grain on the dining table surface, Neha continued, her voice low and trembling. 'I . . . I gave you up, convinced that both you and I would go on to have better lives without each other than we could together . . . Now that makes no sense at all but it did then . . . it did then but . . .' At this point, Neha finally started to cry, tears running freely down her face and onto the front of her sari. Disregarding them, she continued speaking, almost wanting to punish herself with the harshness of her own words. 'Then . . . then I did an even more cowardly thing . . . Seeing that no one in India knew

292

anything about my pregnancy, I decided I could keep it secret. Having weighed up all the options in the confused state I was in, it really felt like the best path to take at that point in time. I cut off all my ties with England and stopped writing to the people there – even those who had helped me – because I was terrified that something would leak out. Back in India, I told no one about you, or what I did to you: not my parents, not my best friend and, later, after I had got married, not even my husband . . .'

She trailed off, the silence that filled the room punctuated only by the persistent twittering of a bird outside and Neha's soft sniffles as she tried to control her tears, dabbing them dry on a serviette.

'Do you have other children?' Sonya asked after a long pause.

Neha shook her head and looked down. 'No. Maybe the gods decided I didn't deserve any after what I had done. Medically it's inexplicable but Sharat and I have never had children, no . . .' Her voice hung in the air as both women sat in silence again. Then, after another long pause, Neha looked up and into Sonya's eyes. 'I'm so very sorry,' she said, her voice trembling. 'Will you . . . will you ever be able to forgive me?'

In one swift movement, Sonya leaned out over the table and took Neha's hand in hers. 'Of course I do,' she said, her voice thick as she tried to swallow back her own tears. 'Actually, I don't think you realize how clearly I do understand what you went through then. Because, if you think about it, it's not that different from what I've just done. I thought I was falling for Keshav – enough to perhaps even sleep with him the next time we met. Luckily for me, he revealed himself before that but, if by some chance I had got pregnant by him, the last thing I'd want to do

293

is go through with it or even tell my poor parents. As it is, they were worrying themselves sick about the trouble I would get into here!'

'They know you were looking for me, though?' Neha asked.

'Yes, that they do.'

'And they don't mind?'

'They did at first. Mum especially was really anxious about the possible repercussions. The timing – with me leaving home for the first time to go to uni – wasn't great for her, I suppose.'

Neha nodded. Then she said, 'They must love you so much. And they must be so proud of you.'

'They're great,' Sonya said, wiping her nose with a tissue. 'And, when all is said and done, I think they'll be quite pleased that I met you and have an understanding of what happened when I was a baby.'

They were interrupted by Ram Singh coming in to clear away the tea cups, and Sonya withdrew her hand from Neha's, lest the cook wonder what was going on. But he seemed not to notice, his expression disappointed at the quantity of uneaten food. He began piling cups and saucers onto a tray but soon stopped clattering to cock his ear at the distant sound of a car coming down the drive. There was the slamming of doors followed by footsteps coming down the corridor and, suddenly, to Neha's astonishment and consternation, she saw Sharat walk in through the dining-room doors.

'Oh, sorry, I didn't realize you had company,' Sharat said, stopping at the sight of Sonya. He looked questioningly at Neha and she knew that, in one glance, he had taken in the sight of both their tear-stained faces.

Neha got up and took two swift steps to reach her

husband's side. She had to make a quick decision. In the midst of her panic, she suddenly felt a curious flood of relief at how easy it was, after all these years, to finally give way to honesty.

'Sharat, my darling,' she said softly, taking his arm. 'I want you to meet someone . . . it's a long story and a very old story that I should have told you before. I'm so very sorry now that I didn't. But this is Sonya, Sharat . . . there's no easy way to say this to you, my darling, but Sonya . . . Sonya is my daughter. From a time long before I met you.'

Chapter Thirty-Three

Whenever Sharat looked back at that moment, it felt as if he was living the confusion and torment of Neha's shocking revelation for the first time. The picture never left him: of Neha's tear-stained face beseeching him for understanding, of the young English girl getting up hastily from her chair and standing helplessly by, the mockery of a half-eaten celebratory high tea spread out on the table behind them, as though the sandwiches and halwa were trying to instil the most deplorable situation with an air of normality.

If Sharat were to be honest, his sudden reappearance at the house had been quite deliberate. He had left in the morning, having told Neha that he would be away in Mumbai for two or three days. But the plan all along was to return unexpectedly, concerned as he had become at Neha's strange behaviour and, perhaps more significantly, the sound of the American man's voice on her phone that day. Sharat had struggled with his conscience over such uncharacteristic guile on his part, but eventually decided that it would be better to try to find out for himself what was wrong, rather than to confront Neha and possibly end up having a row. That was the kind of unseemly behaviour into which they had never descended in their many years of marriage and Sharat had no intention of going down that path now.

He had walked into the house very nervous at what he would find, his imagination getting the better of him. But the last thing Sharat had expected was the revelation he had got. It was crazy – an illegitimate daughter from Neha's past! He still felt an odd light-headedness when he thought of the moment at which Neha had uttered the word 'daughter', as though he had consumed one too many whiskies and had moved mentally to an alternate world.

In the event, it was her – the English girl, Sonya (Sharat almost could not bear to think of her as Neha's daughter) – who had taken charge, insisting that she leave Neha and him to talk in private. Another young woman emerged from the study, the woman who had accompanied Sonya when she had first visited the house – he recognized them both instantly, of course – and the pair of them had exited the door without further ado.

Neha and Sharat had been left, facing each other in the dining room like unexpected adversaries, while Ram Singh silently cleared the food away behind them. Finally, Neha had spoken.

'Please will you let me explain?' she asked, her eyes now tearless but dark and filled with anxiety.

Sharat could only manage a wordless nod before walking out of the room and taking the stairs to their bedroom. That was the most private part of the house. As it is, Sharat wasn't very sure of how much Ram Singh had understood of the earlier conversation. Loyal a retainer as he was, it was the kind of gossip that would be irresistible to keep from passing on.

Upstairs, Neha had come out with it all. The whole sorry saga. She wept grievously off and on as she talked and

– perhaps for the first time since Sharat had met Neha – he did not reach out and offer to comfort her. He heard her out though, remaining silent and as impassive as possible, trying not to wince at some of her disclosures and the accompanying rambling explanations. Finally, when she finished telling her story and slumped into silence, leaning worn out and exhausted on the antique carved headboard of their bed, he had spoken.

'Do you know the identity of the blackmailer?' Sharat asked quietly. Not only did he want to deal with the most urgent issues first, but it was also somehow easier to focus on something practical, an aspect of this tangle that he could perhaps do something about.

Neha nodded. 'I know only his first name but Sonya has all the details.'

'And Sonya – your daughter –' Sharat trailed off, aware of how bitterly he had spoken that last word. Neha was looking at him questioningly and so he cleared his throat and continued, 'What happens now? Do you intend staying in touch with her?'

Neha was silent as though considering this question for the first time. 'I don't know . . . I don't think the choice would be mine to make . . .' she said finally. Sharat could not tell if she was seeking his permission or implying that the choice would be Sonya's. He also could not tell if there was regret in her tone or not.

He inverted the question. 'Have you any idea what she plans to do now that she has found you?' He knew he had not succeeded in keeping the resentment out of his voice.

Neha looked blank. 'No,' she replied, 'Sonya never said what her plans are. But she leaves Delhi in a day or two, I think.'

'Are you sure she is not secretly teaming up with the

blackmailer? It could all be a scheme to extract money from us . . .' Sharat said, searching Neha's face. He did not present the possibility that Sonya might be an imposter and not Neha's daughter at all. That would be ridiculous, given the physical resemblance between them.

Neha now looked him straight in the eye. 'I too considered the possibility of a ploy, Sharat. I even asked the two girls about that directly. But I'm as sure as I can be that they have nothing to do with this Keshav. Their distress at having trusted him was genuine, I could tell.'

Sharat got up and looked out of the window. 'The blackmailer needs to be dealt with first,' he said.

'What do you plan to do?' Neha asked nervously.

Sharat was silent for a long time before he spoke in a firm and loud voice. 'Well, the man is certainly not going to get a *paisa* from us. That's for sure.'

'But what if he starts talking as he threatens . . . you know, tells someone in the media . . .'

Sharat closed his eyes momentarily. The possibility did not bear thinking about. It would be big, this sort of news, and could completely ruin his hard-won prospects in politics. The Congress high command had made their dislike of adverse personal publicity quite clear. So far Neha and he had enjoyed a spotless reputation, and were generally liked by journalists for managing their money without being splashy. But how could one possibly expect newspapers and other publications not to fall upon a scoop like this with unmasked glee? It would be irresistible to a newspaper editor. Sharat could imagine even those whom he personally knew – friends like Iqbal Syed of the *Delhi Daily* – calling up with early warnings and commiserations, but insisting all the while that it would go against his journalistic principles to cover up the story on the basis of their friendship. Without a doubt, it was one of those stories that would run for weeks, given that it had all the right ingredients: photogenic subjects, moneyed lifestyles, glamorous homes – a scandalous secret – how could the media fail to love it?

'I will think of something,' Sharat said, before turning to leave the room. He was conscious of Neha staring at him, pleading with her eyes, but he did not look at her, stopping only to pick up the leather briefcase into which he had earlier packed his travel documents. He intended to get away for a while. How long for, Sharat did not know yet. He did not even have a very clear idea of where he was to go. However, a small suitcase packed with his clothes and toiletries was lying in his office cupboard and so he was free to fly straight away, and to any place that suited him. Right now, all that Sharat knew was that he could not bear the thought of being in the same room as his wife.

Neha sat very still on the bed as Sharat left the room, listening to the click of his heels running down the stairs away from her. A few minutes later, she heard the sound of the car starting up and rolling out of the drive and felt a deeper sense of loss than she had ever experienced before. Yes, this was even worse than the wrench of giving her baby away, because then she had been too young to understand the immensity of what she was losing. The metal gates clanged shut with a terrible air of finality. Perhaps this is what a bereavement was like, Neha thought, aware that she had probably lost Sharat's love and trust forever. She wanted to rush to the bathroom as waves of nausea overwhelmed her. Trying to quell the feeling, Neha curled up on the bed in a foetal position and stared sightlessly out of the window. Was evening falling, or had the entire world simply turned dark forever?

She knew she ought to feel some joy at having finally had the chance to explain herself to Sonya. And relieved at Sonya's graciousness to accept and understand that fateful decision she had made so long ago. But Neha's mind stubbornly refused to allow itself any redemption. She felt unworthy and undeserving, and all she could focus on at this point in time was the unbearable loss of Sharat's love.

Next to her, the phone rang; but to Neha the sound was a faraway clamour that had no bearing on her pain. The ring was insistent and, realizing that it was her mobile phone which no one else would pick up, Neha slowly sat up to answer it. The number was unfamiliar and, with sudden panic at the thought that the blackmailer might be calling again, Neha pressed her thumb on the green button and tentatively held the instrument to her ear.

'Hello?'

'Neha?'

'Yes . . .'

'Oh, hi, Neha! It's Arif here . . .'

'Arif?' For a few seconds, Neha could not process the information.

'Arif . . . the whacky old American from Ananda. C'mon, how many Arifs do you know, huh?'

'Arif . . .' Neha repeated, the cheeriness of the voice coming at her making her start to cry.

'Heyyy, have I caught you at a bad moment, Neha?' Arif's voice was filled with concern. 'I can hang up . . . call later?'

'No, no, wait . . . sorry, Arif. Yes, it is a bad moment. But I couldn't have asked for a better person to call me.

Please don't hang up,' Neha said, trying to compose herself. Arif waited and, in a few halting sentences, Neha updated him on the events of the past couple of days.

'Omigod!' Arif said. 'I did wonder what was going on with you. I'd tried calling you yesterday too and wondered why there was no reply.'

'You called yesterday?'

'Yes, but you cut me off. And, later, when you called back you didn't speak so I guessed it was your way of indicating that you were facing trouble over the reappearance of your daughter. I figured you would call me at a more convenient time but it's nearly time for my return to LA, so I thought I should try you once more.'

'Oh dear, that must have been your call I received while I was travelling back from a lunch with Sharat yesterday. Yes, I did cut off a call but only because I thought it might be that blackmailer guy. I did not call you back, though, Arif. I'm sure of that . . .' Neha trailed off, puzzled.

'You sure did, sunshine,' Arif replied. 'I've saved this number on my contacts list and your name was flashing at me sometime around four-thirty pm yesterday. It'll still be on the call register if you want to know the precise time. I answered it and was sure I could hear you breathing at the other end but then, just as quickly, you'd hung up. I thought it best not to call back in case it was a coded message of some sort!'

'Oh, Arif,' Neha said ruefully, starting to work it all out. Was it any wonder Sharat was so angry with her? He was obviously jumping to all sorts of conclusions – the expression on his face had been clearly disbelieving when she'd concocted a tale about crank calls to explain cutting off that call in the car. And, at some point, Sharat must have used the callback function on her phone to check on who had called her. It was so uncharacteristic, but could she blame him? She sighed. 'It looks like I'm getting very good at heaping problem upon problem, Arif,' she said with a small laugh. 'I think it must have been Sharat who called you. It certainly wasn't me. He'd seen me cutting off your call while we were in the car together and must have wanted to check who it was. It's not like him to do that kind of thing but I really couldn't hold it against him, given my strange behaviour. Listen, I'm so sorry I cut you off like that, but it was only because I thought you were the blackmailer calling again. And I couldn't speak in front of Sharat because I hadn't told him about any of this at that point . . . God, what an awful mess!'

'Sure is a mess, honey,' Arif replied. 'You've gotta do something to sort it out, Neha.'

'There isn't anything I can do. Not without making things worse than I already have,' Neha responded.

'Of course there must be something,' Arif insisted in his inimitable persuasive fashion. 'Would it help if I called him?'

'You? Speak to Sharat? Oh I don't know, Arif,' Neha said doubtfully. 'He doesn't know you at all. What would you say?'

'Well, have you mentioned having met me?'

'I did say I'd made a friend at Ananda . . . he may remember your name . . .'

'Good! That's all I need. I could call him, introduce myself and . . . well, tell him the truth essentially. Say that you unloaded your worries on to me when we met at Ananda. I'll make it a point to mention that I'm a very, very old man so that he won't be suspicious! As someone who is one step removed from the situation, I think I'd make a very good and totally objective intermediary. But could you bring yourself to trust me? I may have been a lawyer once but I've done plenty of mediation work in my time. It may just work . . .'

Neha considered Arif's kind offer for a minute and took the plunge. There was little to lose at this point. 'Yes, I'd appreciate your help very much, Arif,' she said, 'I'll give you Sharat's number.'

'Okay, but before that, tell me about your daughter too.'

'Oh, that's the saving grace in all this, Arif. My daughter. How strange it is to use that word, finally. "Daughter".' Neha gathered herself together to answer Arif's question. 'Well, Sonya was wonderful and showed such maturity when I told her my story. She was angry at first, when we first met, but perhaps her own experience with that Keshav boy helped her see how easily I could have been led into having her – and giving her up – when I was so young and so unprepared.'

'Do you think she'll stay in touch?' Arif asked.

Neha hesitated. 'I think probably not,' she said, explaining. 'She's about to embark on a busy phase in her life. I can't see that she needs to stay in touch with me and I'm certainly not going to force it.'

'You'd like to stay in touch with her though, wouldn't you?' Arif's query was spoken in a gentle voice.

Neha nodded, feeling the darkness in the room swirl and wrap itself around her as though it were there to stay. 'I have no hope,' she said, 'but, yes, Arif, I think I would like that very much,' she said simply.

Chapter Thirty-Four

Hours after she had left the Chaturvedi house in such a hurry, Sonya's ears were still ringing with the words Neha had used to her husband. 'Sonya is my daughter'. Words that Sonya had heard a million times before from her mum and dad back in Orpington but never with such a wealth of significance and meaning attached. It was ownership, it was belonging . . . pride, even.

And her own feelings? Sonya was astonished at how much she had needed to hear those words come from this distant person who was, by such a strange quirk of circumstances, her biological mother. It was puzzling, given that Mum and Dad could not have been nicer parents. But Sonya had learnt that even the love of the most adoring adoptive parents could not make up for the rejection of a real one.

She looked out of the window of the taxi that was taking her and Estella back to the Mahajan house. Delhi's citizens were going about their business, people in cars, on buses and motorcycles. It looked anarchic and the blare of horns rent the air. This really was a chaotic, messy old place, Sonya thought, but her experiences in this city had taught her a lot – and made her grow up a lot. She turned and smiled at Estella, grateful for the solidity of her presence.

'Penny for them?' Estella asked.

'I was just thinking, Stel, of how chuffed I am to have you here with me. Couldn't have asked for a nicer travelling companion. Truly.'

'Hmm, so you unceremoniously drag me away from supping a rather delish tea in a grand library. Just as I was not-so-delicately placing a morsel of fruit cake in my mouth too,' Estella said.

'Speed was of the essence, you understand.'

'That it sure was! Like a pair of bats out of hell, weren't we, scarpering out of there,' Estella agreed. After a pause she added, 'That Mr Chaturvedi, I can't help feeling sorry for him. He's been a mere pawn in this whole saga.'

'I was thinking exactly that. I don't doubt that the revelation of my existence will have a massive impact on their marriage. Do you think they'll split up over this?'

Sonya sounded troubled and so Estella put out a hand to comfort her. 'Don't worry, marriages can be really elastic, I've found.' Estella's voice turned sober, 'Remember that ghastly time my parents went through?'

Sonya nodded. She remembered a distraught Estella confiding in her when they were in seventh grade about her father finding out that her mother had been having an affair. The rows in the Wentworth home had been terrible that summer and Estella had been convinced that her parents were about to split up before somehow, miraculously, the crisis had simply blown over.

Estella took a deep breath and Sonya felt sorry that she had inadvertently reminded her friend of what was perhaps the worst time in her life. But Estella's expression was back to its normal cheery state now. 'I wager the Chaturvedis will ride over this,' she said. 'It's a big one, though, admittedly.'

'Do you think I should call Neha and ask if all is well? Not right now but say, tomorrow?' Sonya asked.

Estella thought for a moment before replying. 'It may be too soon. I'd say we give it a couple of days before calling, whatsay?'

Sonya nodded. 'You're right. Crikey, what *am* I going to do without you at Oxford?'

'What you'll probably do is have half the college, male and female, in love with you by the end of the first term so you can pick the finest specimen of carer to take over from where I leave off,' Estella responded airily. 'But what say you we stop off now at an ISD booth to call our folks back home? Twenty-four hours is about my mum's limit!'

'Twice my mum's!'

Estella tapped the cab driver on his shoulder. She knew the jargon now. 'ISD phone booth, *bhai*,' she said, like a practised Hindi speaker, and the driver nodded, beaming, before slowing down his vehicle to scan the shops they were passing

In a few minutes, both girls were standing in a minuscule phone booth set amidst a row of higgledy-piggledy shops, making calls to both their homes. Having conferred with Estella on how much to reveal to her parents about the visit to the Chaturvedi house, Sonya broached the subject to her father soon after the initial enquiries were done. There was no point beating about the bush and, fortunately, Laura was out doing the weekly shop.

'I met her again, Dad,' Sonya said, knowing it would be the subject topmost in Richard's mind too.

Richard briefly pretended not to have grasped whom she was referring to before swiftly correcting himself. 'Who . . .? Ah, you mean Neha Chaturvedi, I take it. Was it better this time, darling?'

'Yes, Dad, very much better. Cordial even.'

'Oh?'

'Well, she was a lot more receptive on this occasion and explained the circumstances that led to her giving me up.'

'Why the initial brushoff then?'

'She's never told her husband about me and was terrified of him finding out.'

'And now he knows?'

'Yes, he does.'

'And their children?'

'They don't have any, Dad.'

Richard was silent for a few seconds and Sonya imagined the troubled direction his thoughts would take. She spoke again, rushing to reassure him, 'I don't think they're desperate to become parents overnight, though. Certainly not to an eighteen-year-old penniless tourist in India. So no fears on that score!'

Richard fell in with Sonya's droll manner. 'So Mum and I are well and truly stuck with you and your penniless ways, I take it?' he laughed.

''fraid so!' Sonya giggled.

'And we wouldn't have it any other way,' he said firmly. 'So onwards and upwards. Agra tomorrow?'

'Is my itinerary etched on your heart then, World's Best Dad?' Sonya asked.

'No such luck. But it's in bold letters, on the sheet stuck on the fridge, under that metal plaque that says, "Bigger snacks means bigger slacks". Think you bought that magnet for Mum when she was on one of her extreme diets.'

'I know the one. We bought it at that car boot sale in Penge years ago. She keeps everything, bit like me, I guess . . . or is it me who's like her? Oh, I don't know! For now, would you just be your usual kindly self and explain all this to Mum when she gets back, please? You'd do it a lot better than I can . . .'

'Explain to her about extreme diets?'

'*No*! Oh don't be difficult, Dad.'

'Me? Difficult?' Richard echoed indignantly.

'Well, deliberately obtuse then. Dad, listen, I need you to explain to Mum about . . . y'know . . . about me meeting Neha and laying those ghosts to rest. It was something I needed to do but I really do want Mum to know that there's no one more special in the world to me than the two of you.'

Richard was silent and Sonya wondered for a moment if she had lost the line. When he spoke, his voice was gruff. 'I'm pretty sure she knows that already, darling,' he said, adding in his more characteristic manner, 'Just remember to provide us with an occasional reminder whenever you can, eh?'

Chapter Thirty-Five

Sharat walked into the elegant lobby of the Windsor Manor hotel in Bangalore. It had been years since he'd visited the city and the truth was that he had no work at all here, nor anyone to meet. But the first available flight from Delhi Airport had been an Air India one to Bangalore, and it suddenly seemed hugely advantageous to be in a place where hardly anyone would know or recognize him. At this point in time, all Sharat wanted was to crawl into a quiet corner and lick his not inconsiderable emotional wounds. It was bad enough to think that Neha had lied to him but it would seem she had been lying consistently, throughout the years of their marriage. How could that not make their whole relationship seem like a sham now?

Sharat followed a smartly-clad hotel employee down to the Towers section of the hotel where he was taken to what his pleasant young escort was describing as 'our very sought-after Lancelot Chambers'. He was only half-listening to the man's practised patter, but caught the phrase 'room that leads to a courtyard garden'. He liked the sound of that because, unusually, Sharat envisaged spending more time in this room than out of it. Normally he was in and out of the various plush hotel rooms that he frequented when travelling on business, and somewhere along the way they had all started looking the same to him.

He now looked around the spacious room he was being shown into and smiled as the hotel employee showed him the controls for the most enormous television set he had ever seen. Perhaps if everything between Neha and him had been fine, and she had been here, they would have watched a late-night movie together; but Sharat could hardly imagine himself watching a film by himself. He had, in fact, grown unused to doing most things by himself.

After the hotel employee had left, Sharat unlatched the French windows at the bottom of the room. They led to an enclosed garden complete with a white stone arbour and pretty park benches. The garden was empty and Sharat walked across to the western balustrade in order to watch the sun set beyond Bangalore's famed lush tree cover. It was a pretty sight but he recognized how everything would from now on be robbed of the total and unstinting pleasure he was used to experiencing.

Feeling his phone buzz in his pocket, Sharat pulled it out, hoping it would not be Neha. He really did need some quiet time to reassess his marriage and his life before he could deal with the supplications of people like Neha, or his parents for that matter. Sharat imagined the pain his parents would go through if he and Neha broke up. They were fond of her and, even if they wanted to stand by his decision, broken marriages did not belong anywhere in their orderly and conservative world.

Sharat's phone was flashing an unfamiliar number at him and he answered it with some trepidation. The voice that spoke to him was American and, in an instant, Sharat recognized it as being the same man he had got on Neha's phone yesterday.

'Yes?' he asked, his tone cautious.

'Is that Sharat, Neha's husband?'

'Yes,' Sharat repeated, trying to quell a strange feeling of dread that was rising within him, setting off a sour taste in his mouth.

'You don't know me, Mr Chaturvedi, and I must apologize for taking the liberty, but I've just had a conversation with Neha. I called her to ask if I could drop by and visit but found that the situation at your house is not good.'

'What's it to you? And who are you anyway?' Sharat asked harshly.

'It matters to me only on humanitarian grounds, sir, for I am a stranger to you and a near stranger to your wife. If I may explain . . . I met Neha at Ananda, and found her – like so many of the Indians I've met on these travels – to be kind and generous and dignified. But there was an air of sadness to her that I could not help being curious and concerned about. Neha finally came out with the story of her student days in Oxford. It was one she had told no one of until that point and I can only think that it was only because it was easier for her to reveal such painful details to a total stranger whom she was unlikely to ever meet again. Anyway, to cut a long story short, Neha was grateful for my support and had invited me around to meet you on my return to Delhi – I fly back to Los Angeles tomorrow – but, when I called her to arrange a time, she told me of how events had overtaken both of you. She said you had left the house in a most upset state of mind. It may be none of my business, sir, but – as perhaps the only other person who is even aware of these events – I would like to help if I can.'

'No one can help,' Sharat said shortly, suddenly afraid he might break down.

'Forgive my quibbling, sir, but I've worked in mediation for many years, being a very old man, and I feel quite confident of being able to assist in some humble way. Please.'

'What can you do to help, tell me?' Sharat asked after a pause.

'Not much, I grant, other than to remind you gently of how none of us can claim to have never made mistakes. In my experience, what sets one mistake apart from another is merely its consequences. I agree that, in Neha's case, these consequences are huge, and no doubt difficult for someone in your position to accept. But it was, after all, one mistake and one that was made when she was very young. It would be tragic to see two good lives ruined by it now, so many years down the line.'

Sharat was silent, trying to gulp down the horribly large lump that had formed in his throat. And, while he was still considering how to respond, the caller suddenly hung up. Sharat stood looking foolishly at the phone, wondering whether he had got cut off and whether he should call back. But Sharat did not even know the name of the caller and he guessed that the man had hung up as abruptly as he had because he'd said as much as he wanted to.

At least he now knew who the mysterious American on the phone had been. Sharat slipped the phone back into his pocket, feeling a little less miserable than before. He knew he ought to feel guilty at suspecting Neha of having an affair but, given that much bigger lies had been spun, he was not yet ready for sympathy. He sighed. Perhaps he should shower and change before going down to the hotel's bar for a quiet drink. He needed to think about how much to say to his friend, Ashok Mitra, who, as Inspector General of Delhi police, should be his first port of call in dealing with the blackmailer. It was best to be economical with his information and Ashok would be far too discreet to ask many questions.

Chapter Thirty-Six

As their taxi pulled into Fatehpur Sikri, Sonya and Estella jumped with fright when a whole variety of touts gathered around the car to thump on the bonnet and windows. In order to shake them off, the driver ignored the red light, narrowly missing a rickshaw in the process. Sonya looked out of her window at one boy who was pursuing the car with a few others, clearly desperate for her business. He looked no more than twelve and was weaving maniacally through the town's traffic as he tried to keep up with them. Sonya wondered if she should warn the driver of the possibility of one of their wheels going over the lad's foot but thought better of it. When they drew up outside the fort, Sonya almost did not want to get out of the safety of the locked car and eyed with trepidation the army of brown faces that were surrounding the vehicle again.

'This is crazy, we can't keep sitting here,' Estella said, reaching for the door handle. 'Ready? Shall we go for it?' she asked.

Sonya nodded and, as they got out, the driver emerged from his seat, yelling what sounded like Hindi's choicest abuse to send the touts scattering. Some of them ran off, laughing, but a few persisted.

'Five hundred rupee only, I will be guide,' one wheedled

while another jostled him, flicking a packet of postcards showing the sights of Agra and Fatehpur Sikri. 'Buy, madam, hundred rupees only, whole pack, only for you.'

'No guide, no postcards,' Estella said loudly, waving her guide book. 'We have book, see? No needing guides.'

'I thought we'd promised each other we wouldn't slip into pidgin English,' Sonya panted, trying to keep up with her friend who was striding in a determined fashion up a steep set of steps in an effort to lose the touts. Sonya looked over her shoulder as they climbed. Most of the men had fallen by the wayside, although one pair of boys remained in hot pursuit.

'Please, madam, take me as your guide, I know everything, I show you all the historic things,' the smaller one whined as he caught Sonya's eye.

'You can't know everything, you look about ten! I'll bet I know more Indian history than you do,' Sonya admonished.

'No, no, madam, you ask me any question, I will answer,' came the confident response. Then the boy added, more helpfully, 'You have to take shoes off over here. Inside is mosque.'

Sonya slipped off her sandals, hoping she would not return to find them missing. Following Estella, she stepped in through a massive archway to find a courtyard bustling with tourists and worshippers. They followed the crowd, who seemed to be gravitating to a small marble mosque situated at the centre of the courtyard, still tailed by the two boys bearing grubby satchels full of postcards and maps.

'You must cover head,' the smaller one advised, 'is like mosque. Salim Chishti's dargah. Salim Chishti was Sufi saint. Emperor Akbar prayed to him for a son and, when he got son, he name his son Salim and also build this dargah for Salim Chishti. Caalabrooney also came to pray for son.'

Sonya smiled, amused not just by the practised patter but also the breezy pronunciation of Carla Bruni's name. Estella, following directions from her well-thumbed copy of the *Lonely Planet*, was already fumbling around in her bag to come up with a pair of scarves, one of which she handed to Sonya before tying the other around her own head. Suitably clad, they stepped into the darkened interior of the mausoleum. An old man in Muslim garb was fanning a tombstone that was covered in flowers with a horsehair whisk, while another stood taking squares of glittering cloth off the queuing worshippers to place them on the tomb. The cloth squares all had tinsel borders and appeared to be some kind of offering. Sonya wished she had thought of bringing one along too. Instead she took a small piece of red thread that another man was handing out and, following the lead set by others in the mausoleum, she tied it alongside thousands of other little threads that were knotted onto a marble trellised wall.

She jumped as a sibilant whisper emerged from the vicinity of her elbow, '*Make wish!*' Turning, she saw that the ten-year-old guide had followed her indoors. Though tempted to tell him off for startling her, Sonya closed her eyes in order to concentrate. If it had worked for the Emperor Akbar, it was certainly worth a try. What should she ask for, she wondered, her mind going blank for a minute before she suddenly thought of it. 'Please make Keshav see sense and stop blackmailing us. Please don't let what I have done ruin anyone's life. Whoever you are, Mr Chishti.'

Opening her eyes again, she saw the urchin face looking

321

up at her. 'Make wish?' he asked. Sonya nodded. 'It will come true. Definitely,' he said with an air of utmost solemnity and faith. Sonya followed him around a narrow corridor and, together, they stepped out into the sunshine.

Estella, following her out, asked, 'Is he bothering you?' gesturing to the pair of boys who were hovering nearby.

'Naah, not really. He's cute, our pint-sized guide.'

'Don't!' Estella warned, laughing. 'My fingers are still smoking from our recent experience with Keshav. Be years before I start suffering from a bleeding heart again!'

An hour later, the girls were wandering around the Emperor's abandoned living quarters, enjoying the respite from the crowds in the neighbouring mosque complex.

'Phew, far nicer here,' Estella said, fanning her face with her scarf as she sat on a stone bench to pull out her book again. 'And I think we've managed to shake off Oliver and the Artful Dodger too.'

'Well, the rupee payment at the door will have put them off following us here,' Sonya said. 'But don't be surprised if you see them waiting right outside when we come out! I think we may have no choice but to pay them off handsomely, you know.'

Estella grinned. 'Such cheek,' she said, 'paying for the privilege of being left alone!' She returned to her guide book. 'Hey, did you know that the Emperor Akbar and his retinue only lived here for four years? This palace was specially commissioned and built so he could move here from Agra with his harem. And then, weirdly, it was abandoned just four years later when they all decamped back to Agra.'

'Really? Well, no wonder it's so pristine,' Sonya observed, looking around at the red sandstone complex of buildings that looked no more than a few years old.

'Ran out of water, apparently,' Estella continued reading. 'They got the whole place up and running before discovering that the local supply of water was brackish and undrinkable. Quite the modern-day ecological nightmare, eh? Like a B-grade disaster film.'

'I did notice that the tea we had back at the lodge tasted a bit funny, actually. Kinda salty. So there may well be truth in the theory.'

'Yikes, I'd have hoped they'd have had time to sort out the water supply since the sixteenth century. Else, I'm on that plane to Kerala pretty damned quick! Plenty of water there, going by the pics.'

'I guess the Mahajans will always take us back if we want to return to Delhi in a hurry,' Sonya said.

'True. She mentioned having no other bookings till next weekend, didn't she? But let's not panic just yet. The lodging house here did look a bit dicey but we don't have to stay. If we finish seeing what we need to, we could actually head off to Agra tonight, rather than wait till tomorrow.'

Sonya nodded in agreement. 'Be nice to get a bit of extra time in Agra, I reckon. Two days may not be enough to see all the sights, especially if you want to see the Taj by moonlight.'

'I sure do. I think I'd like to come back to India again someday but heaven knows when that'll be, and if Agra will figure in that. Okay, that's decided that. Let's get moving from here asap and try and blag our way into the Agra hotel one night early. We'll get exactly two and a half days that way before we get to Delhi Airport to catch our Cochin flight.'

Chapter Thirty-Seven

Back in Delhi, Keshav was sprawled on Gopal's mattress, sharing half a bottle of rum with his friend, when the phone rang. He pulled the jangling instrument out of his shirt pocket and saw an unfamiliar number. The caller identified himself as Assistant Constable Daulat Ram of the Sainik Farms police *chowki*. Keshav could not think what the man could want from him but it soon became evident as the policeman spoke in fluent, elegant Hindi, his tone high and his language peppered with a selection of the choicest abuse. He told Keshav in no mean terms of what was done to blackmailers when the police got their hands on them. Keshav started to sweat. The names Neha and Sharat Chaturvedi were never specifically mentioned, Daulat Ram saying only that Inspector General Ashok Mitra had called the station, concerned at reports of a young blackmailer operating in the Sainik Farms area. From the name and description, the culprit was clearly identified as Keshav Jha, son of the driver who was working at Number Twenty-Nine, the residence of one Mr Mahajan of Allied Advertisers.

Assistant Constable Daulat Ram finally paused in his tirade to ask Keshav if he intended going to the media as he had threatened. Keshav hesitated momentarily, opening his mouth to reply with some kind of explanation but, before he could speak, the constable informed him of what would be done to him if he did. The words 'lock-up' and 'laathi' and 'beating' were mentioned and repeated. Details of the kind of injuries offenders were often left with were described in detail and with immense relish. The constable appeared to be enjoying himself by this stage, his voice getting shriller and more aggressive. Suddenly, however, he drew his loud delivery to a swift end, hanging up as abruptly as he had begun.

Hands shaking from fear, Keshav looked at the blank screen of his phone, unable to believe what he had just heard. As this new development started to make sense, he flung the instrument down on the mattress almost as though it would burn him if he held onto it any longer. Beads of perspiration dotted his upper lip as he looked at his friend with fear darkening his eyes.

Gopal, who had not gathered much from the rather one-sided conversation, looked on in consternation. '*Kya hua? Kaun tha?*' he enquired of the caller's identity. But Keshav was suddenly too nauseated by fright to even speak.

Chapter Thirty-Eight

After checking in at Delhi Airport on their return from Agra, Sonya and Estella went upstairs to the food court. Sonya, scanning the names of the dishes on the colourful wall menus, marvelled at how quickly so many of them had become familiar to her. Thanks to the few meals she had eaten at the Mahajan table, she was now well familiar with everyday names like 'roti' and 'paapad'.

'Well, what do you fancy?' Estella asked, coming up behind her.

'It's nearly lunchtime . . . something a bit substantial, I guess. You do get used to full-blown lunches here in India and, we won't get given nosh for hours yet,' Sonya replied.

'Too right. Substantial always sounds good to me. But, y'know what, I think I'm a bit Indianed out as far as food goes. Feel like sinking my gnashers into something solid and comforting, like a foot-long Subway or something. Salami and jalapenos – yum yum! Although, d'you know what I could happily murder right now? A steak! Medium rare – ah, now you're talking!' Estella halted her momentary reverie to return to reality and the offerings at Delhi Airport's food court. 'Well you get what you want from here, hon, while I grab a table.'

Estella wandered off and Sonya went up to the Indian counter to order a masala dosa. Mrs Mahajan had made dosas for breakfast on their very first morning and Sonya had thought that the savoury pancakes stuffed with spicy potatoes were about the most delicious thing she had ever eaten. Unfortunately, they hadn't been made again, Mrs Mahajan obviously trying to vary her menus as much as possible. On their last morning, rather disappointingly, they had eaten eggs on toast!

After paying with her dwindling collection of torn and dirty rupee notes, Sonya collected a token before going to the table where Estella was standing guard over their bags and camera equipment. 'Mine will be served here apparently,' Sonya said. 'So, why don't you go off and get yours. Oh, and while you're at Subway, could I have a can of Diet Pepsi, please?'

She sat down while Estella disappeared in search of food and then took out her mobile phone. Neha's number had been saved in her contacts list and Sonya scrolled slowly down to her name. She looked at it for a few seconds before pressing the green button. After a few rings, she heard the soft, now familiar voice say, 'Hello'.

'Hi, it's Sonya.'

'Hello, Sonya. I recognized your number. I have it saved now.'

'Well, it wasn't working very well in Agra, for some reason. Perhaps it was only some sort of local sim card, I don't know. We bought it cheaply just after we got to Delhi.'

'You are back in Delhi now?'

'Yes, but only for another couple of hours. We took our cab straight to the airport, where we're now awaiting our flight to Kerala . . . we're there for four days and then it's back to London, via Dubai. I just called to say goodbye.'

There was a pause before Neha replied. 'I didn't realize you were going so soon'. Her voice was so quiet that Sonya was unable to detect the emotion with which she might have spoken.

'I couldn't remember if either Estella or I had mentioned our plans . . . we did leave your house rather hastily that day . . .'

'No, no, you hadn't mentioned it,' Neha replied. 'There wasn't the time, as you say . . . but I guessed you would visit Agra since it's so near Delhi.'

After another short awkward silence, Sonya asked, 'I wanted to know . . . there hasn't been anything more from Keshav, has there?'

Neha's reply was thankfully in the negative and Sonya heaved a silent sigh of relief when Neha added firmly, 'My husband is very sure we should not cave in to the demands of a blackmailer. I think he's dealing with it so don't worry about that.'

Sonya did not think it her place to ask how Neha's husband planned to deal with it, or what he could possibly do to stop Keshav from selling his story to the tabloids. Nor did she feel able to enquire whether he had come to terms with Neha's dramatic disclosure about having had a daughter before her marriage to him. Although Sonya had been the catalyst in causing the truth to emerge, the secrets in the Chaturvedi marriage were nothing to do with her.

Instead Sonya said, 'Well, thank goodness Keshav's gone silent. I really do hope he won't call and bother you any more.' After a moment's hesitation, she added, 'I feel I must apologize again for the part I played in that whole mess. But thank you for hearing us out that day . . . and thank you for understanding how much I needed to hear your explanation of what happened with me in the past.' Sonya was aware of how stiff she must sound. There was a great deal more she wanted to say then she thought the better of it. After all, she and Neha were, all said and done, still strangers.

'No, it's you I must thank, Sonya,' Neha replied. 'Not many youngsters your age would show the maturity you have done in accepting what I did. So . . . I thank you for that from the bottom of my heart . . .'

'Well, I guess it's goodbye from me, then,' Sonya said, her awkwardness exacerbated by Estella having returned to the table with a tray full of food and drink which she was trying to make room for with one hand.

'Goodbye, Sonya. And have a safe trip,' Neha said.

Sonya clicked off the phone and nodded as Estella cocked a sympathetic brow at her. 'Neha?' she asked. 'Wasn't too difficult, I hope?'

Sonya shook her head and avoided eye contact as she got up to put their bags and camera on the floor. 'No. It was okay. And Keshav hasn't called her again, thank God.'

'Good. I hope that's the last any of us hear from him!' Estella said with vehemence before turning her attention to her generously stuffed baguette. She peeled the paper off one end and took a bite with a satisfied 'Mmmm . . .'

Sonya looked around at the hundreds of people sitting around the food court, eating and drinking. There was the usual sprinkling of foreigners but most of them were prosperous-looking Indians. 'I feel totally mortified at how easily I was taken in by Keshav. Just can't seem to forget it,' Sonya said as her dosa was brought to the table.

'You taken in? We *both* were. You keep forgetting what an expert swindler he was, hon!' Estella's indignation spilt out even through a mouthful of bread.

Sonya hesitated. 'And yet – yet there's a part of me that wants to make excuses for him, you know, Stel –'

'You gotta be kidding!' Estella cried, halting her chewing to gaze horrified at Sonya.

'No, just think about it, Stel. It's all very well for us – y'know, rich Western kids with the world at their feet. Easiest thing in the world to judge Keshav and be angry at what he's done. But I'm not sure it's right to expect someone who's poor and desperate to be motivated by the exact same things as us. You know? I mean, you saw the desperation of those touts back in Agra, didn't you? No more than babies and already at it.'

Estella countered her theory. 'That makes it sound like we would expect all poor people living in third world countries to be criminal.'

'No, I'm not saying that at all. But, I don't know, it just seems *wrong* to judge someone who is desperately poor and lacking opportunities by the kind of airy-fairy moral standards we set for ourselves.'

Estella took another bite of her baguette, shaking her head. 'Criminal behaviour *is* criminal behaviour in my view. And blackmail's pretty damned criminal, you've gotta admit. Being rich or poor should have nothing to do with the ethics of it. And Keshav's had some pretty decent opportunities too. Nothing like those kids at Fatehpur Sikri. The Mahajans have educated him, don't forget.'

'Imagine, though, what it must be like growing up with the burden of that kind of gratitude. Never knowing whether you're overstepping the mark laid down by your benefactors . . .'

Estella did not argue any more but the expression on her face remained clearly unconvinced as she continued to put away her meal in typically hearty fashion. Sonya ladled a bit of coconut chutney onto her plate but she had lost her appetite for her now limp and soggy dosa. Nevertheless, she put a forkful of food into her mouth and chewed mechanically. Outside the window of the café she could see aircraft in various colours and sizes waiting to take off to their many different destinations. Beyond them, shimmering in a heat haze, lay Delhi's typical scrubby brown land. Sonya wondered whether she would ever come back. It hadn't exactly been a pleasurable trip but the city had sure knocked a lot of her corners off in the past few days. Perhaps it was true what all the hippies had said about India and self-discovery when they started flocking here in the sixties. Her own experiences had certainly taught her a few useful lessons, and Sonya guessed she ought to be grateful for them. It was no exaggeration to state that she felt years older than the girl who had first set out on this trip.

Chapter Thirty-Nine

Neha sat by herself in the breakfast room, her mobile phone still in her hand and Sonya's voice ringing goodbye in her ears. Her exact words had been 'Well, I guess it's goodbye from me, then'.

Would she ever hear from her again, Neha wondered, suddenly feeling as bereft as that nineteen-year-old back in Oxford who had given her baby away. Now, having found and lost Sonya again in the space of five days, and with Sharat's departure weighing down on her, Neha started to weep, great big silent tears coursing down her face as she gazed unseeingly out at her blooming garden. She was even heedless of Ram Singh who came in to clear her plate and coffee mug, turning her face away only when he peered at her in concern.

Unused to seeing his memsahib in anything but total control, the old cook disappeared into the kitchen and stayed out of the way for the rest of the morning. Gradually, the house fell silent, the only sound being the ticking of the antique clock on the stairs and the distant rumble of traffic from Prithviraj Road. After a long while, Neha finally got up to go in search of her reading glasses. They were by her bedside table, where she had left them last night. In her bedroom, only one side of the bed was rumpled, the creased linen giving away the sleepless night she'd spent. It felt like weeks since she had last slept well, her body curled around Sharat's under their quilt. Neha glanced at Sharat's unused pillow, feeling sick to note the missing indent left by his head after he had woken up in the morning. It had been an old joke between them about how deeply and dreamlessly he always slept, unlike her who tossed in a semi-troubled state all night.

Where was he? He hadn't called once since leaving the house over five days ago and Neha didn't have the heart to call him either. The thought of being rebuffed by her normally gentle and loving husband was just too unbearable.

Instead she scrolled down the list of names and stopped at Jasmeet's. Neha knew she had to speak to someone if she was not to go mad. It was too much, this careful control she had exerted over her life all these years, these mental shutters that had kept everyone at bay. When Jasmeet answered, Neha spoke just one line.

'Jasmeet, I need to talk to you – will you come over please?'

Jasmeet's response was typically generous. 'No problem. I have to come to Khan Market to pick up some chicken sausages this afternoon. So I'll be at yours at about four o'clock. Is that okay?'

When Jasmeet walked up the front stairs two hours later, Neha got up from the wicker chair on her veranda, where she had been waiting, to give her a hug.

Her friend held her at arm's length to examine her face. 'Look at you, *yaar*,' she said in consternation, 'you look like you haven't slept all night.'

'I haven't,' Neha confessed, trying to smile.

'God, *why*? What's wrong? I know you wouldn't call me out here unless it's important.'

'Sit,' Neha said, 'I'll get you some tea first. It's a long, long story, Jasmeet, and I think you need to be sitting down.'

Jasmeet settled herself, looking worried. Then her expression went through a whole gamut of emotions – shock, astonishment, anger, sorrow – as Neha recounted the story, going all the way back to her departure for Oxford, an event that Jasmeet remembered well, being part of the contingent of friends and cousins that had flocked to the airport to see Neha off. By the time Neha had finished telling her everything, twilight was falling over the garden and the birds were coming in to roost on the big neem trees near the house. Jasmeet had heard her out quietly, asking only the occasional question, and Neha felt no sense of being judged from the expression on her friend's face. She ended her account by telling Jasmeet about Sonya's short call from the airport this morning.

'Did you get the feeling she wanted to stay in touch with you?' Jasmeet asked.

'I don't see why she would want to. She has loving parents back in England and is about to start what is sure to be a very busy college life.'

'And Sharat? How upset do you think he really is with this?'

'Hard to say, Jasmeet . . . you know as well as I do that nothing normally upsets him. And, unlike Kul, he never, ever sulks. In fact, this is probably the first time I've known him to go completely incommunicado on me . . .'

Jasmeet heaved a huge sigh but remained in silent contemplation, looking out into the darkening garden as, in typical pragmatic fashion, she tried to think of a sensible and practical solution to offer her friend. But there appeared to be none and, finally, Neha broke the silence. 'Shall we go indoors?' she asked. 'We don't want to be chewed alive by the mosquitoes.'

The two women got up and, as they went into the drawing room, Jasmeet gently touched Neha's forearm. 'It was brave of you to tell me everything, Neha,' she said, adding, 'I won't break your trust, I promise.'

Neha shook her head sadly as she turned on a few lights. 'I'm sorry I didn't say anything to you earlier, Jasmeet. All these years. I should have known you well enough to trust you. It would have given me so much relief to be able to talk to someone.'

Jasmeet seated herself on a sofa before saying, 'You know, we keep secrets, fearing the day they may come out. But, in fact, the worse thing is when they never come out at all and people die with those secrets having burnt great big holes in their lives.'

Jasmeet's voice was suddenly bitter and so Neha looked at her in bewilderment. 'What do you mean by that?' she asked.

Jasmeet was silent for a few seconds before she spoke. 'Sometimes I have wondered if everyone has secrets. I have one too, that I think even you may be shocked by.' She paused and then carried on, trying to keep her face impassive. 'How do I say this . . . you see, I found out two years ago that Kul . . . yes, my husband whom you all like so much . . . had been having an affair with someone for over six years . . .'

'What?!'

Jasmeet nodded. 'When I found out and threatened to leave with the girls, he got very worried, begging me not

336

to go; and I finally agreed on the condition that he break off all ties with this woman.'

'Oh, Jasmeet! And has he?'

Jasmeet looked sad. 'I think he has, Neha. At least he says he has – but will I ever know for sure, I wonder? After all, if he managed to hide it from me for six years, then anything is possible.'

'And you kept it secret for the sake of the girls?'

'For their sake and because of the shame . . . Delhi's not such a big place, it sometimes seems. And I wanted to be able to go around doing my business with my head held high . . .'

'Poor Jasmeet. Always so jolly, so upbeat . . .' Neha trailed off, thinking of the anniversary lunch she had attended just last week where Jasmeet had, as always, been the life and soul of the party. She wasn't the only one who had put up careful facades, clearly.

Jasmeet turned to Neha at this point, leaning forward on the sofa to place a hand on her knee. 'One thing I did find out, though, Neha – if it brings you any consolation – when I first found out and told my mother and a couple of my *maasis* about what Kul had done, I found to my surprise that all of them – yes, every single one of them – had had some sort of similar experience. All those marriages that I thought were perfect when I was growing up, they had all suffered some trauma or the other at some point. Not necessarily affairs but problems of some sort. And *all* of them kept it secret. My mother told me, for one, that my father had spent the first few years of their marriage out drinking himself blind every night until he abruptly gave up – and I grew up thinking he had always been a teetotaller! My mother's older sister had suffered domestic violence, another auntie told me that her husband

337

had gone off for years to America where he had lived with a second family, but she had quietly taken him back when that came to an end. And no one ever found out. I don't know why we women do this to ourselves . . . but look at me talking about myself when you are going through this terrible thing right now. We need to think of a solution for your problem. First of all, we have to find out where Sharat is and get him back.'

'Dear Jasmeet, always so pragmatic,' Neha said. 'Don't worry, there's actually huge comfort in just sharing. Anyway, I don't think there's a solution to my problem right away. I know what *I* want but I have to wait to see what Sharat wants to do. And what Sonya decides to do. I am completely out of control – not a feeling I'm used to, as you know!' She tried to laugh but her voice caught in her throat.

'Are you prepared for Sharat to say he can't forgive you?' Jasmeet asked suddenly.

Neha contemplated the question before replying. 'I would be devastated but, in the end, I think I'd cope. Like you say, the shame would be terrible. Perhaps I'm too proud a person and Delhi society . . .' Neha paused and shuddered '. . . like vultures, waiting for you to fall so they can pick over your bones. But I would not carry on here. I'd go somewhere quiet and shut myself away, I think. Like Parmarth Ashram at Haridwar. I was there recently. But life in Delhi, without Sharat? Never.'

Jasmeet looked alarmed at Neha's dark tone and cut in, using her best no-nonsense voice. 'C'mon, Delhi is not as bad as that, Neha. There are good people and not-so-good people everywhere. You will find your friends if things go wrong. The rest you will have to learn to ignore. No, I'm certainly not letting you run away. Parmarth Ashram, my foot!'

Chapter Forty

A day after leaving Delhi, Sonya looked at the scene surrounding her with immense pleasure. Marari Beach, a few miles north of Cochin, was a terrific find, wild and unspoilt with its rolling grey sea and soft stretches of beige sand toasting in the sunshine. Warm breezes were blowing across the water and rustling the leaves on the palm trees behind her. A kiosk selling beer and tender coconut water was doing brisk business nearby and she watched a small girl pay for a pineapple lolly while her mother stood by watching. It wasn't a lolly like the ones Sonya had grown up buying from the ice-cream van, but a piece of fruit cut into a pretty serrated shape and stuck onto the end of a wooden stick. Sonya smiled as the little girl walked past, sucking on her pineapple stick with delight. She returned to surveying the sea and sank her toes into the sand, enjoying its texture, soft and dry like talcum powder. Then she threw her head back and heaved another huge sigh of pleasure. Delhi seemed so far away . . .

The resort into which Estella's Uncle Gianni had booked them provided basic accommodation, but its proximity to the beach more than made up for it. Sonya couldn't have asked for a more perfect antidote to both Delhi and Agra and the crazy events of the past week. And not a

339

tout around for miles! She smiled as Estella ran up behind her and wasted no time at all in stripping off a voluminous tee-shirt to reveal her generous curves in the tiniest of bright yellow bikinis.

'Corblimey, I was starting to think I'd never get the chance to get into my cozzie!' Estella said, bending down to loosen the Velcro on her beach sandals before kicking them off.

'Too right,' Sonya agreed. 'Well, we knew there'd be no beaches but it was bit of a shame that neither Delhi nor Agra had a swimming pool within hitting distance. Would have been too much to expect at the prices we'd paid, I guess.'

'Not that we'd have had the time in either place anyway,' Estella reminded.

Aware that Estella was about to jog down to the water's edge, which would put paid to all conversation for the rest of the morning, Sonya said, 'Hey, Stel, before you go – I feel I should apologize for the pretty shitty holiday so far. And say a big thank you for putting up with all my shenanigans in Delhi.'

Estella squinted in the sun. 'Hmmm . . . I could ask for money by way of recompense from you. But general trouperish behaviour is part of the service when you're best friends, I guess.'

Sonya pretended to kick Estella's backside with her bare foot, unsure of whether the reference to money was a deliberate and cheeky reminder of Keshav. That would be so typical! But Estella was already running down to the sea and Sonya watched her capering in, the water splashing around her ample bum before she gracefully dived in, head first. Sonya, who had always been much less of a water baby, pulled a beach towel out of her rucksack and spread it out on the sand. She also pulled out the hefty book she had found in the resort's library, along with a writing pad, before sinking down on the towel.

Mention of Keshav's name still made her start, although Estella seemed oblivious to this, chattering on about him at the drop of a hat. Sonya had not been able to fully assess her own feelings yet. She continued to be both ashamed at her naivety and vaguely hopeful that Keshav's behaviour had not been deliberately deceitful from start to finish. Surely – especially – the tenderness with which he had kissed her? It could not all have been made up.

Fortunately, the peace of this Kerala beach was causing all the tumultuous events that had taken place in Delhi to recede in Sonya's mind to a place that was far away and increasingly imbued with an air of unreality. She picked up the writing pad and looked out at the sea. This was the perfect place to write her postcards and letters. She had sent a postcard to Mum and Dad from Delhi airport, even though it had proven more difficult than she had imagined to choose the right one. The minuscule airport shop had millions of pictures of Delhi but they were all either of the Qutb Minar, or the Red Fort or Connaught Place, all of which reminded her rather starkly of the two sightseeing jaunts with Keshav. She could imagine Mum sticking it up on the fridge door forever-more and of her having to look at it and be reminded of Keshav every time she opened the fridge to get something out! Finally, Sonya had chosen a postcard that showed a handsome Mughal structure surrounded by stately bottle palms, and scrawled a couple of innocuous lines on the back.

Sonya lay back on the beach towel and covered her face with her book in order to blank out the sun. She wondered

341

whether she would ever be totally honest to her parents about the sequence of events that had taken place in Delhi; especially the more troubling bits about Keshav. It would only serve to distress them unduly. Certainly, that whole experience had helped her identify with Neha's predicament when she, as a teenager, had kept a pretty big secret from her parents too. Sonya still felt relief flood through her at the thought that she had somehow managed to stop short of actually having sex with Keshav and was now not stuck with an impossible decision as Neha once was. It was so easily done and poor Neha, escaping her sheltered Delhi life in far-off Oxford, must have been so easily led at that young age . . .

Sonya sat up and looked far out to the horizon where she could see the sails of what were probably fishing vessels. Was it true, then, about mothers and daughters and things that got passed down without warning or intention? How curious that when Neha had talked about Simon, the boy she should have fallen in love with, it was Tim's face that Sonya had seen in her head.

She looked down at the blank writing pad on her lap. She really ought to crack on with her letter to Tim, so she could post it as soon as she arrived in England. He would have already left for Durham by the time she arrived in Orpington and she did want to wish him luck in his new life. She had behaved abominably with him on that last meeting and now she felt deeply ashamed at having imagined she was somehow entitled to all that anger. Sonya had learnt a lot in these past few days, not least that no one had the right to blame anyone else for the circumstances of their own life.

She looked at the waves breaking gently nearby, foam mingling with sand and churning it up into a soft golden sludge. It was impossible to think that the Boxing Day Tsunami had landed with such force on these peaceful shores just six years ago, wreaking indescribable havoc. The concierge back at the resort had told them that Marari Beach had been particularly badly hit. But he had added cheerfully that everything that could have been restored was now back to normal. 'See now, completely peaceful,' he had said. 'No one will even know that such a thing ever happened here.'

However, Sonya knew – with her newfound wisdom – that this was never the case. When such dramatic events overtook places and people, some things were surely indubitably transformed forever.

Chapter Forty-One

Sharat spent over a week in Bangalore, going on long walks, exploring parts of the city he had never seen and, despite not being much of a reader, buying half the books in the hotel bookshop. Sitting in the courtyard garden attached to his room, or by the poolside, he read – at first with a kind of dogged persistence and then with increasing enjoyment – discovering a whole variety of writers whom he had never heard of before. Some books were hardback, some paperback in shiny lurid colours, and Sharat lost himself in each one of them, surprising himself by enjoying their offerings far more than he had ever anticipated. Where previously he had always considered fiction rather a waste of time, the valuable role it played came to him as he finished his eleventh book that week and closed it with a satisfied thump: it was these glimpses into other people's hearts and lives that allowed readers to know they were not alone. Made-up, fictional dilemmas and problems that provided readers with some kind of strange courage to face whatever *real* life threw at them. Why, a few of the books Sharat had read this past week had ended up changing some of his views completely. In his current state of mind, that felt to Sharat like a vital job indeed. Never again would he tease Neha of wasting time when he saw her engrossed in one of her novels . . .

He had not called her all week and, unsurprisingly, she had not called him either. That was not entirely unexpected; it was typical of Neha to wait to see what he would decide to do. And decide he must. Pleasant as the air in Bangalore was, and accustomed as he was growing to his room at the Windsor Manor, Sharat knew he could not stay forever. Besides, his parents were starting to ask awkward questions about the time he was spending away from Delhi. Having spent more hours introspecting than he had done in a long time, Sharat went one evening for his regular pre-dinner walk in Cubbon Park in order to firm up his decision. He stood watching a pair of children at play with a football, listening to their happy screams, his thoughts far off as he considered the consequences of what he was going to do. Having looked at it every way that he could, he finally knew what he wanted. He went back to the hotel, asked them to book him an air ticket, and then packed his sparse belongings in order to return home.

It was evening when Sharat reached the house and, as his car pulled into the drive, he saw Neha walking barefoot in the garden, as she sometimes did on the advice of her yoga teacher. He saw how she stopped and froze at the sight of him sitting in the back seat of his car and felt a renewed sadness that such a close relationship as theirs had become one of mutual fear and suspicion. Something had to be done to rescue it and Sharat knew that, at this point in time, matters were entirely in his hands. He got out of the car as it pulled up under the porch and walked purposefully in Neha's direction. He saw her face crumple at the expression on his and, without further hesitation, did what he had never done in front of the gardeners before. He took Neha in his arms and held her as though he would never let go.

It was a full two minutes later that he released her, suggesting that they walk up and down the lawn together. Neha nodded, with tears in her eyes, thankful that they would be able to talk without looking into each other's faces. Until she knew for certain that Sharat had fully forgiven her, it was going to be difficult to look him straight in the eye. But she reached out and took his hand in hers with the words, 'Thank you, Sharat, for coming back to me.'

'Of course I came back,' Sharat said. 'Where else would I go, Neha? You know how much you mean to me.' At Neha's silence, he continued. 'But, given how close we are, I don't think I will ever understand why you couldn't tell me about Sonya when we first met. I was hardly likely to hold against you a mistake you made when you were no more than a child, was I?'

'It was more than a mere "mistake", Sharat,' Neha replied gently. 'I gave a baby away. I had not even told my parents, so how could I bring myself to tell you? And, by the time I had learnt what a kind-hearted man you were, it was too late because I had never said anything at first. And later . . . later, my deed looked so much worse when we were denied children. Almost as though it it was a punishment I deserved and had brought onto you.'

'Come on!' Sharat exclaimed. 'Don't tell me you made some kind of karmic connection between those two things – that's nonsense!'

'Well, not if you're harbouring the kind of guilt I was,' Neha said wryly.

347

'Imagine carrying that pain around on your own all these years,' Sharat said, his voice deeply exasperated. He continued, 'Do you understand *that's* the hurtful bit, Neha? The fact that you thought I wouldn't understand.'

She lifted his hand to her face and kissed it. 'Of course, I'm sorry now that I made that assumption, Sharat. If I'd only had the courage to tell you earlier, I could have saved myself so much heartache. But the longer I left it, the more difficult it became to say. Now that it's all come out, of course, I wonder how I couldn't see that you would never blame me, or fail to understand . . .'

'Oh, I don't know about understand, because there I was thinking you might be having an affair,' Sharat laughed suddenly.

'An affair?'

'Well, it was your reaction to that call on your phone that day. Do you remember, coming back from Jasmeet's – you cut off a call without even saying hello. Which seemed like such a weird thing to do. And, because of your uncharacteristic behaviour, I did a silly thing too. I called back on that number and heard a man's voice. An American man's voice. So, by the time you told me about Sonya, let's just say I was as confused as hell!'

Neha looked up at Sharat and nodded. 'I thought that might be what happened. That caller was Arif, the gentleman I met in Ananda. Remember, I told you I'd invited him to come and have a meal with us when he passed through Delhi.'

'I'm sure you never said he was American! And, if you'd mentioned the name "Arif", I'd never have assumed he was American from that either.' Sharat's accusatory tone was joking and he grinned now as he added, 'Now, if he'd

348

been called "Todd" or "Hank", I think I'd have very easily made the connection, but not "Arif" for God's sake!'

They started to laugh and, having reached the canna patch at the bottom of the garden, started to walk back up the way they had come. The sounds of their laughter reached the gardener who was packing up his tools at the other end of the lawn, the sun having long set and the grass now getting quite damp with dew. The old gardener smiled because he often liked to go home and tell his wife – the mother of his four children – that the sahib and memsahib he worked for were among the happiest couples he knew, even though they had no children of their own.

Chapter Forty-Two

Sonya quickened her footsteps as she and Estella pushed their trolleys out of the baggage terminal at Heathrow Airport. The flight back from India had got delayed at Dubai and she was concerned that her father would have been waiting an extra hour. When she spotted Richard, standing near the metal barriers just beyond Customs, wearing an anxious expression on his face, Sonya left the trolley right in the middle of the passageway and ran towards him in delight.

'Daddy, darling Dad!' she cried, yelling with renewed glee as she saw her mother standing behind him. It was only when the first excited hugs had been exchanged that she was suddenly mindful of poor Estella trying to make her way towards them, now pushing two wayward trolleys. 'Oh, Stel, so sorry, I didn't mean to leave you standing there like that. Just got a bit distracted by the handsomest man in the world,' she said, giving Richard another hug.

'Typical!' Estella said, rolling her eyes upwards before parking the trolleys to one side in order to greet Sonya's parents properly.

'She hasn't treated you like that throughout the trip, I hope,' Richard Shaw grinned as he hugged Estella.

'Worse! Baggage handler, dogsbody, cook, chai wallah,

351

I've done it all on this holiday, I have. What one does in the name of friendship, eh?' Estella replied, bending over to kiss Laura Shaw's beaming face.

'C'mon then, let's get you both outta here. Car's that-away,' Richard said, making for the lifts that led to the multistorey car park.

In the car, Sonya and Estella chattered away, giving the Shaws all their news from India in a torrent of information but Sonya was aware that some of the more important subjects were being skirted around. There was time enough to tell her parents all about her meeting with Neha Chaturvedi when they got home and everyone had had the chance to catch their breath. She sat back while Estella narrated the story of their visit to an ancient synagogue in Cochin a day ago. Only half hearing her description of the sweet old Jewess they had met, Sonya looked out at the English countryside that was already turning to beautiful shades of rust and copper in an early autumn. It was lovely to be back, she thought, settling back with a small sigh. Mum and Dad, their cosy little house that always had a delicious smell of something baking wafting around it, her crazy gothic bedroom stuffed with bric-a-brac . . . much as she felt a sense of achievement to have taken on India and dealt so bravely with her past, this was home and this truly was where she belonged.

After dropping Estella off at her house and chatting briefly with the Wentworths, the Shaw family drove the two-mile distance to their home in companionable silence, listening to the one o'clock news on the car radio. It was only an hour later, after Sonya had showered and descended to the kitchen in her most comfortable pair of track-pants, that she finally took the chance to tell her parents all about Neha. She and Estella had discussed the Keshav business on the flight and decided that, while it would be necessary to tell their parents just enough to put them in the picture, the details were not required as they would only serve to distress them unduly.

Richard was pulling bottles of mustard and mayonnaise out of the cupboard while Laura sliced a giant sourdough cob on the bread board. Sonya took her usual place at the kitchen table and opened the subject in her customary direct fashion. 'Mum, Dad, I'm sorry I haven't touched upon my all-important news from Delhi yet. Not that Estella doesn't know everything but I thought you'd rather hear about my meeting with Neha Chaturvedi when it was just us.'

Richard nodded approvingly, as he carried an assortment of bottles to the table, 'Good thinking, darling,' he said. 'Much as I adore your Stel, some conversations do need privacy, don't they?'

'Dad said the second encounter was better,' Laura remarked. Her back was still turned so Sonya could not read her mother's facial expression but she felt reassured by how tranquil her voice sounded.

'Oh, very much better. I think she was in a state of shock the first time we met but she'd calmed down by the time I saw her next.'

Richard brought the pile of sliced bread to the table before sitting down next to Sonya. 'She hadn't told her husband about you at that point, you said?'

'Yes, definitely part of the reason she didn't want me popping up so unceremoniously,' Sonya replied, picking up a knife to start buttering the bread.

Laura was also seated at the table now. Her hands had been busy tearing up lettuce leaves and slicing up pickled gherkins but she stopped that to rest her gentle grey eyes on her daughter's face. Sonya could, thankfully, not discern on her mother's face any of the distress that had been so much in evidence before she had left for India.

'And your visit prompted her to tell him, I suppose,' Richard said. It was a question, rather than a statement, and so Sonya nodded.

'Yes, she was kinda forced to fess up everything to him but I gathered later that she was, in fact, quite relieved to have been given a chance to do so. She said later, when I called to say goodbye, that he was upset at first – understandably, I guess – but then accepted it in the end.'

'I can't imagine what it must be like carrying around a secret like that in a marriage,' Laura said, shaking her head. Sonya could not tell if the remark was a reproving one so did not respond.

Richard pulled the plate of buttered slices towards him and started filling them with mustard and cold cuts. 'Well, he must love her very much to forgive her so swiftly,' he remarked. Then, more gently, he asked, 'Did she explain why she gave you up?'

Sonya nodded and took a deep breath. 'She was an undergrad at Oxford, apparently having worked really hard to get there from India. Then she fell in love with her professor and – although she didn't quite blame him – I got the impression that he kinda took advantage of her. Having got pregnant, she hoped for a while that he would reciprocate her feelings and, by the time it became clear that there was no chance of that, it was too late for an abortion.'

'Nevertheless, once that decision was made, she could have kept you,' Laura said. 'Social workers don't take children away from their parents these days if they can help it. Instead they put in all kinds of support to encourage mums to keep their kids, which is why there's hardly any that come up for adoption. Not like it used to be when I was young.'

Laura was clearly still feeling a little judgemental but Sonya did not rush to Neha's defence. Instead, she said, 'I did ask her that but she explained that she was alone in England, with no family and no real friends. Her parents back in India would have been too conservative to accept an illegitimate child and so, when it was suggested to her that she could give her baby up to a childless couple, she did. The sad thing is that she later learnt that she couldn't have any children of her own.'

'She was very young, wasn't she? Eighteen? Nineteen?' Richard asked.

'Yeah, the same age I am now, imagine that,' Sonya said.

'Well, yes, that is very young. Most people that age don't know what's good for them, I suppose. She must have been so confused,' Laura conceded, 'and it's very sad to hear that she was never able to have any more children.' It was said a little grudgingly but Sonya was strangely touched to finally discern a touch of sympathy in Laura's voice.

The cuckoo clock in the kitchen broke the sudden silence and Sonya sat up to say in a no-nonsense way, 'Well, I had the explanation I needed so, in the end, we parted quite amicably.'

'Would she want to stay in touch, do you think?' Richard asked.

'We didn't discuss that, actually. And, when all is said and done, we occupy two totally separate worlds. But, if she does make contact again, I wouldn't particularly mind. Would you?' Sonya asked.

Richard looked at Laura and Sonya guessed that they

had already discussed that possibility between them when her mother replied, 'You know, darling, Dad and I would be perfectly contented for you to stay in touch with her if you want. After all, she's missed out on all these wonderful years we've had with you and, now that you're all grown up and leaving home, you should be free to make your friends in the world. Dad and I aren't ever going to stand in your way. We love you and trust you far too much for that.'

Sonya felt a lump form in her throat. How she loved these two marvellous people who had given her so much, and with so few expectations. And poor darling Mum had sure made a long, tortuous journey to get herself to this point from the emotional mess she had been in before Sonya's departure for India.

It was Richard who broke the silence this time, fearing a sudden deluge of female tears, Sonya knew. 'Oh, speaking of love,' he said, 'I've been meaning to say, princess – old Tim was on the phone all of yesterday, calling to ask whether you'd arrived. I wasn't sure how you'd left things before you went to India so I said something a little non-committal, I'm afraid.'

Sonya reached into her pocket for her phone. 'Thanks, Dad, typically thoughtful! Yes, Tim and I did go over a bump back there but he's such an old mate, I couldn't possibly leave for uni without saying goodbye properly, could I? Perhaps I'll give him a quick call to say I'm back. Stel and I could take him to the Shalimar tonight to regale him with all our stories from India over a curry. I know all their names now!'

'I thought you'd be up to there with Indian food, having only just come back!' Laura gestured at her neck and laughed. 'Those are your genes speaking, I suppose!'

'Genes or no genes, right now I'd kill for another one of your special mustard-mayo ham sarnies, Dad,' Sonya replied, holding her plate out.

'Ah, the one that employs my secret Shaw formula. Coming right up,' Richard replied.

Chapter Forty-Three

Sharat sat restlessly in the living room, listening to a Pandit Jasraj CD on his new Bose system, but keeping an eye on the antique glass clock to be sure he did not miss the next news bulletin.

The day had been a satisfying one, beginning with a hugely successful rally to launch 'Saamna', an organization he had recently formed to call for an end to local government corruption. At least three thousand people had attended – thanks in part to the huge advertisements that had been running in all the broadsheets these past few days – and nearly two thousand people had signed a joint petition which was later delivered to the Prime Minister's residence. Already CNN-IBN had covered the rally in their six o'clock bulletin and Sharat's contact over at NDTV had promised that they were running their package at seven, which included a one-on-one prerecorded interview with him.

Wondering where Neha was, Sharat picked up the intercom phone and clicked on the button marked 'Main Bedroom'. Neha's voice answered it within seconds. '*Haanji*, where are you?' Sharat asked. 'Aren't you coming down to see the NDTV piece?'

'Of course I'm coming. It's not time yet is it? Give me two minutes.'

'What are you doing?' Sharat persisted, always unhappy to be somewhere that lacked Neha's reassuring presence.

Aware of this, Neha laughed gently, '*Arrey baba*, I'll be with you in two minutes. I was just thinking of trying that new meditation technique Swami Dayanand showed me but right now is obviously not the best time!'

'That's exactly right. Come down, *na*. We'll watch it in the breakfast room. You can try all your meditation stuff later on.'

Sharat had already turned on the TV when Neha came into the breakfast room a few minutes later, settling himself on his usual wicker chair, remote control in hand. He shot a glance at her, observing the tiredness of her demeanour. It had certainly been a long day, and Neha had been firmly by his side as they handed out tea and refreshments at the rally, but, while the experience had led to a feeling of immense buoyancy in Sharat's spirits, it seemed to have had the opposite effect on Neha.

'You okay? Tired?' he asked, patting the seat next to him.

Neha settled herself on the sofa beside Sharat and put her head on his shoulder. 'I wonder, will you still be calling me to watch the TV news with you when you're a big politician and on the news every day?'

'Of course! Then you'll have to not just watch with me but also bring me endless cups of tea and press my aching legs. That's what good politicians' wives do, I am told.'

Neha smacked Sharat's thigh good-naturedly but they fell silent as the newscaster appeared on screen. The story of the anti-corruption rally was the third piece on the news, and they watched carefully as Sharat's face appeared in a close-up shot while he was interviewed.

'Very good,' Neha muttered as the interview drew to a

close. 'You sound like a really seasoned hand, Mr Sharat Chaturvedi!'

'I think I hesitate too much between sentences. Too much humming and hawing,' Sharat said, frowning.

'Nonsense,' Neha dismissed. 'You sound just fine. You don't want to be too smooth. People don't trust those silver-tongued politician types, I think.'

Sharat kissed her cheek. 'As usual, you're probably right, my dear,' he said. Then he cupped his hands on either side of Neha's face and gently ran the balls of his thumbs on the faint purple shadows under her eyes. 'What's this?' he asked, his voice gentle. 'Are you not sleeping properly?'

'I'm sleeping just fine,' Neha said, her expression suddenly defensive. Then she added, 'Maybe we've been attending too many events recently. Muniza's iftaar, Preeti's party, Pramod's book launch at the British Council. And, of course, all the preparations for yesterday's rally. A few quiet nights in will sort me out, don't worry.'

But Sharat continued to look concerned as Neha got up from the sofa and wandered around the room, turning on all the uplighters so that the room was suddenly filled with light. 'Will you give me an honest answer if I ask you something?' he queried suddenly.

Neha's back stiffened almost indiscernibly as she continued to face the Taiyyab mural that always looked stunning when the halogen lamps angled to highlight it were turned on. Sharat waited till she had turned round slowly to face him. 'Of course I will, Sharat,' she replied softly.

'Are you still grieving over Sonya?' he asked in his customary direct fashion.

Neha hesitated for a moment before answering. 'Why should I be grieving, Sharat? I mean, if anything, I should be happy to know that she is fine and in a happy place. Shouldn't I?'

Sharat felt she was asking him a question, rather than making a statement. 'I don't know, Neha. Should you? Maybe it's not as simple as that, you know. Maybe it was easier to cope when she was completely lost to you. But, now that that door has been opened slightly, you may feel you need to open it properly . . . let the light and air in to what was previously a very dark place for you . . .'

Neha remained silent and, because she was standing with the light behind her, Sharat could not read the expression on her face. After a pause, he said, 'I think you should go to England to meet her properly, Neha.'

Neha's reaction was surprisingly violent, her voice harsh as she said swiftly, 'No, sorry, that's a crazy idea, Sharat! I don't want to go to England. What would I do there anyway? I can't go chasing after her now! All these years later, and when she needs to concentrate on her new college life.' She calmed herself, her tone turning contrite as she added, 'It's sweet of you, Sharat. I know you mean well, but it won't work. We have to think of her too. She may not want to see me again.'

'How can you assume that? She might actually be wanting to see you too, Neha,' Sharat replied. 'I mean, it was all left half-finished, the way in which you met and then parted. She too may be in need of some kind of . . . what is that American psycho-babble thing they say . . . closure? Yes, she might be needing closure too. But she can hardly walk in here again, given what happened when she was here last. No, I think the ball is in your court. You need to write to her, and tell her how things got resolved over here, and then ask her if you can go and see her in England.'

'But . . . but her parents might mind, Sharat,' Neha said, now openly crying, tears coursing down her cheeks. 'Have you thought of that, Sharat? Her parents, who brought her up from the time she was a baby, they may not want me anywhere near her!'

'They let her come here to Delhi, didn't they? They must be more confident about her love than that, Neha. And surely they will understand that you aren't trying to usurp them in her affections after all these years? I mean, she's a grown adult now, for heaven's sake.' After a long pause, Sharat said, his voice gentle in the silence of the room, 'Go, Neha. Go to your daughter. Show her you care enough to do that. God knows, you both need that bit of assurance to move on. You will only need a few days in England. Go and sort this out, and then come straight home to me.'

Chapter Forty-Four

Hello, Neha,

Thanks very much for your email. It was very welcome on a leaden grey November morning.

I too had been wondering when and how to make contact with you again, so am very glad you wrote. As you can imagine, I'd been concerned about the state you were in when we last met – I'm referring, of course, to that sudden disclosure you had to make of my existence in front of your husband. Therefore, it was with great relief that I gather all is well there. I must say, it's really kind of your husband to insist that you make contact with me again. My deepest apologies once again for having been instrumental in putting both of you through all that. What an awful lot of stress it must have caused.

Thanks too for the update on Keshav. So glad he saw the error of his ways and did not make good his threat.

Yes, I will be going home for Christmas and am looking forward to my first proper break since joining college. However, I'm in Oxford until the middle of December and it would be terrific to see you here when you visit. No, Mum and Dad will not mind at all, please be assured of that. Of course, it took a while for Mum to understand why I needed to go to India and meet you but all that's sorted now.

Do let me know when you have a date and we can arrange a time and place. I'd better get back to my endless swotting now (Medieval Literature – gah!).

But, for now, it's very warm wishes from a freezing Oxford.

Sonya

Chapter Forty-Five

It was a dark English morning that threatened snow, and the journey on the ten-fifteen to Oxford was going to be a slow one. But Neha did not mind that at all. The man back at the ticket counter at Paddington had referred to this train as a 'trundler' and was clearly puzzled at Neha turning down the superfast that was due to leave only a few minutes earlier. She had agreed to meet Sonya at teatime, when her last class for the day was over, which meant that she had given herself almost a full day to get from London to Oxford! But there had been no other way to quell her restlessness and it seemed to Neha that there was little point in killing a few hours in her London hotel. She had already finished the odds and ends of shopping she had needed to do at Selfridge's: Rigby and Peller lingerie, her Crème De La Mer toiletries and a new pair of Church's shoes for Sharat.

And so she boarded the trundler, looking forward to seeing the English countryside properly, rather than in a blur from a superfast train window. Nineteen years since she had left the country in such a hurry! Taking a windowseat, Neha recalled how, off and on, Sharat had suggested holidays together in Britain and how she had always resisted, citing her fear of long-haul flights as the reason. Poor Sharat, he had always unquestioningly accepted so many of her lies . . .

Even the journey out of London was slow as they passed gleaming offices and grubby council blocks and row upon row of neat white townhouses like something out of a child's toy set. A little later came the suburban sprawl of west London, windswept and grey on this winter morning. Despite the unread *Daily Telegraph* rolled up in her handbag, Neha was distracted for the most part of her journey, her mind rattling alarmingly from past to present and, of course, to her imminent meeting with Sonya. As she lost herself in her thoughts Neha suddenly realized with a start that she was now in the heart of the English countryside and that the sun had finally broken out from behind the thick cloud cover. She looked out of the window as the train drew in at yet another station. 'Pangbourne' the board on the platform said, a name she did not remember from the past – but then she had hardly ever needed to be on a train from Oxford to London during her brief student life here.

The day outside now looked bright but cold. A pair of elderly women in long woollen coats boarded Neha's carriage, exclaiming in relief at having escaped the freezing platform as they took off their gloves and unwound colourful scarves that they stuffed into oversized carpet bags. They smiled briefly at Neha as they occupied the seats next to hers and, for a few minutes, she listened to their chatter before turning her attention to the scene outside the window again. The train was pulling slowly out of Pangbourne now and Neha gazed with pleasure at the quintessential English picture she was being treated to, almost like a caricature: red tiled roofs clustered around a small country church and sunlit rolling greens dotted with sheep. She was glad it wasn't raining, although snow had been forecast for later at night. For that reason, Sharat had wanted her to stay over at a B&B in Oxford when he had called this morning, but Neha insisted that it would be no trouble at all getting back to London.

'But it will be dark by four o'clock, Neha!'

'Oh, darling, as though the streets and stations won't be full of people trying to get back from work at night. I'll be fine, don't worry.'

Of course, Neha found herself unable to tell Sharat that she preferred not to stay any longer than absolutely necessary in Oxford, partially fearing raking up painful memories and also because she worried she would become a bother to Sonya. It was hard to explain why she felt that, by staying in Oxford overnight, a burden of expectation would be placed on Sonya that Neha did not want. It was good enough to know that she was going to meet her, and this time without having to skulk around, keeping it secret from Sharat.

The railway station at Oxford was bigger and busier than Neha remembered, people scurrying to catch trains and taxis. As she stepped off the forecourt, however, things started to look a little more familiar and Neha started to walk confidently in the direction of the city centre. She remembered that it was no more than a fifteen-minute walk and, seeing how much time she had at her disposal, she did not worry about the prospect of getting a little lost.

Over the little bridge spanning the Isis, past the bus station and a new Sainsburys, Neha found her footsteps leading to Wadham College. She had not planned this at all but, before she knew it, she was standing facing the familiar old building. With all kinds of feelings heaving inside her chest, Neha gazed at the sunlit quad, trying to recollect the emotion with which she had first laid eyes on this stirring sight. But it was gone. Try as she might, Neha could not revive any of the innocent excitement she had felt as an eighteen-year-old. This should have been unsurprising, after the passage of so many years, but Neha felt oddly disappointed and turned away to start walking around the quad.

'Hi, I'm Simon Atkinson. I'm looking for the college office . . .'

'I'm Neha from India, pleased to meet you.'

Neha could almost hear those young voices as she retraced their steps. Simon so warm and friendly. She, so formal, so stiff. Neha swallowed back the sudden bitter taste in her mouth.

Smart new sliding doors led to the college office and Neha stepped in, unable to stop herself now. A number of unfamiliar faces were sitting behind desks and computers and she approached the nearest of them, a young woman with red streaks in her hair and wearing metal studs in her nose and lower lip. She was nothing like the rather staid staff of her own time here as a student.

'Hi,' the girl said, looking up with a wide smile.

'Hi . . . I wonder whether you can help.' Neha hesitated and then started again. 'You see, I used to be a student here many years ago and I was wondering if you could help me find a faculty member whose contact details I appear to have lost.'

'I could certainly try,' the girl responded, adding, 'She may well still be teaching here. Change comes slowly to Oxford.'

'Not a she. He . . . the name is Henderson. Alastair Henderson. He used to teach us poetry.'

370

The girl's expression was blank at the mention of the name but she chewed her lip and screwed up her face, clearly keen to try and help. 'Doesn't ring a bell rightaway, I have to say. But gimme a minute, there's someone who might know. Who almost definitely *will* know, in fact!' She picked up the phone and jabbed at a few buttons before saying, 'Hey, Rita, you wouldn't happen to know of a tutor who worked here by any chance? Alastair Henderson. Poetry.' She waited as Neha heard a voice crackle down the line. The words were indistinguishable but the woman with the studs kept her eyes fixed on Neha's face while she nodded. As the voice continued to crackle for another few minutes, the girl before Neha rolled her eyes upwards in a friendly gesture of exasperation and formed her fingers into the shape of a quacking duck's bill. Finally she hung up and turned to Neha.

'Blimey, never thought I'd manage to turn her off, good old Rita! But you're in luck,' she said. 'I knew old Rita would have chapter and verse. Helps to have a few old gossips around, eh? Well, you may not be aware but Alastair Henderson went on from teaching here to fronting a BBC series on poetry. And, when that came to an end, he apparently returned here to Oxford. Fell on hard times, according to Rita – flagging poetry career, broken marriage, hit the bottle big time, that kind of thing. He eventually ended up living off the goodwill of a couple of his old students who hired permanent digs for him at a pub called Head of the River. Do you know it? Anyway, that's where he lives now, eking a living out of writing occasionally for the *Poetry Review*, you know, articles and reviews, that sort of thing. Clever chap, according to Rita. 'Cleverer than was good for him,' to use her exact expression. But I don't need to tell you all that, I guess. He must have left a lasting impression on you, seeing that you're in search of him so many years down the line. It sure sounds like he'd be grateful for the company of an old student too. Do you know where the Head is?'

Neha shook her head, overwhelmed by the sudden barrage of information. The girl drew a pad towards her and proceeded to draw a map with an assured hand. Neha watched dumbly as pen-pictures emerged: roads and bridges and a squiggly pond, only half-listening to the accompanying commentary: 'If you turn left soon as you cross the river and walk down the steps, you'll find it right there, bang on the river. Tudor-style building.' As she finished, the girl tore the page out of her pad and gave it to Neha with a broad smile. 'It's sweet, you know, when students come back here in search of their teachers. Makes me feel all warm and glowy. And determined to go in search of my crew back at the FE college I went to in Leicester. Except I never do, as it's invariably straight down to the pub with my mates! Well, happy hunting and have a lovely time with the old boy, won't you? Sounds like he might appreciate a lunchtime drink!'

Neha mumbled her thanks and fled the office, her head reeling with confusion. She took stock once she was back in the main quad again. Alastair, back here in Oxford! Fallen on hard times . . . broken marriage, fractured life . . . it ought to be music to her ears, the notion that some kind of of divine justice had been done. Instead, the information was making her feel strangely sick. Neha pulled the collar of her coat up around her ears, trying to warm her suddenly cold bones. In order to save herself from her tortured thoughts, she walked swiftly back onto the street and dived into a tearoom, blinking in confusion at the sudden warmth and the brightly lit counters filled with scones and flapjacks and luridly coloured cupcakes. She followed a girl in uniform to a small table next to the window and sank into a metal chair with relief.

Having ordered a soup and toasted sandwich for lunch, Neha leaned her cheek against the freezing window pane next to her, trying to cool her suddenly flushed face. Outside, the day was darkening quite suddenly and Neha remembered the forecast for snow. Feeling something rustle between her fingers, she looked down and realized she was still clutching the piece of paper containing Alastair's address. Neha placed it on the table and, using her palms, straightened out the crumples to study the roads and arrows that pointed to a small oblong next to which was scrawled 'Head of the River' . . . How hard she had searched for Alastair while pregnant with Sonya . . . and how something like this might have changed her life – and Sonya's. Neha pressed a tear back as she suddenly felt the stabbing pain of that time.

Lunch arrived and she worked her way through it, hardly able to taste a thing. Then, putting the knife and fork together, she sat back, wiping her mouth with a paper serviette while the waitress approached to clear her plate. 'Thank you,' Neha said and, just before the girl whisked everything away on her tray, she rolled her serviette and the directions she had been given into a tight little ball and chucked them among the debris of her meal. Neha was suddenly very grateful that she had never divulged any of Alastair's details on Sonya's birth papers, nor mentioned his name when Sonya had come to Delhi. Sonya, for her part, had not seemed interested in learning more about her biological father either and Neha wondered if it was in disgust at his behaviour towards her. And thank goodness he knew nothing at all of Sonya's existence right here in Oxford. Neha shuddered as she thought of how his presence could have so easily marred the golden life Sonya would hopefully go on to have.

Neha spent the rest of the afternoon wandering around the Ashmolean, the museum that Sonya had said was not far from her college, trying to stay warm and dry while waiting for her watch to tell her that it was time to head to Balliol.

When it was at last four o'clock, Neha stepped out into the half-light of that winter afternoon. A few stray snowflakes were drifting in the yellow orbs cast by the streetlights. It was bitterly cold and most people had their heads down as they hurried down St Giles on foot and on bicycles. But Neha walked with deliberate calm in the direction of Balliol, now impervious to everything else but the knowledge that she was going to enjoy a little time in the company of the lovely and beautiful girl she could finally think of as her daughter.

Read on for reading group questions . . .

Reading Group Questions

1. Is it possible to sympathize with Neha's decision to give up her baby?
2. And what of the moral dilemma she faces later when Sonya reappears in her life as an adult?
3. How do readers' feelings for Neha develop over the course of the book?
4. Does Neha's wealth alienate her from the reader? As Estella points out to Sonya, would Neha's decisions have seemed more forgivable had she not been so wealthy?
5. What do you think really motivates Sonya to go in search of her birth mother?
6. Do you empathize with this decision?
7. Consider Neha and Sonya's characters. Do they have more in common than either are willing to first acknowledge?
8. Sharat is one of the more straightforwardly sympathetic characters in the book; does this affect his credibility?
9. Is it possible to understand Keshav's motivation in the blackmail plot? Explore Sonya's remarks about morality playing out differently in the light of a person's financial circumstances.

10. Do Richard and Laura's initial resistance to Sonya wanting to find her birth mother feel like a natural response?